Also by *Margaret Lane*

Fiction

FAITH, HOPE, NO CHARITY
AT LAST THE ISLAND
WALK INTO MY PARLOUR
WHERE HELEN LIES
A CROWN OF CONVOLVULUS
(short stories)
A NIGHT AT SEA
A SMELL OF BURNING

Biography

THE BRONTË STORY
THE TALE OF BEATRIX POTTER
EDGAR WALLACE: THE BIOGRAPHY
OF A PHENOMENON
(Introduction by Graham Greene)

Africa

A CALABASH OF DIAMONDS
LIFE WITH IONIDES

Essays

PURELY FOR PLEASURE

The Day of the Feast

THE DAY

Margaret Lane

OF THE FEAST

Alfred A. Knopf · New York / 1968

c.1

Library of Congress Catalog Card Number: 68–12674

THIS IS A BORZOI BOOK,
PUBLISHED BY ALFRED A. KNOPF, INC.

FIRST AMERICAN EDITION

BL

DEC 3 '68

The Day of the Feast

★ I ★

"I know I'm asking you something rather difficult."

"That's not what's worrying me."

"On the other hand it needn't necessarily be unpleasant?"

"No. No, certainly. Quite the reverse."

"And you aren't a stranger, Miles. You do *know* Colin. I fancy he used rather to admire you."

"I only saw him once. He couldn't have been more than thirteen. You moved into that bungalow at Headington, I remember, during my last term."

"Well, he hasn't changed," said Mrs. Thewless, sighing, "not in appearance, that is. Except that he's improved. I wish I could say the same for his behaviour." She got up and moved to a small writing-desk in a corner of the room, opened a drawer and with the precision of habit extracted a coloured snapshot. "This was last summer." She put it in Miles's hand and leaned above him. "More than a year ago, but he hasn't changed. I think these colour prints are marvellous, don't you? You can see how brown he is."

Miles studied the photograph in silence. It showed a tall youth in bathing-trunks standing with legs apart on a harbour wall in sunlight. His hair was fair and his face distinctly charming. His skin was that rather improbable golden-brown which comes from bad colour-processing, sky and sea were postcard-blue and between his legs the masts of yachts could be seen, as though he bestrode the harbour, a young Colossus. Miles dwelt for a moment on the long straddling legs, so confidently balanced, and handed back the snapshot.

"He's certainly a good-looking boy. I wouldn't worry too much about him if I were you. Hasn't he written?"

"Once. A postcard!" Mrs. Thewless made a face and went back to the desk. This time he was offered a picture of a kneeling camel wearing a headdress of woollen tassels of bright colours. Its eye was thickly fringed and its expression cynical. "Read it," said Mrs. Thewless, "it's not private."

Miles turned the postcard over and concentrated on the barely decipherable writing. "Have fetched up here and think I may stay. Have made good friends and am thinking of investing in biz. Money to be made if one knows how—climate wonderful. Am looking around, don't worry. Colin."

"You see what I mean, Miles. No address. Very disquieting, don't you think? And who are these friends, I should like to know? Crooks, every one of them, who've smelt out the fact that he's got five thousand pounds."

"He won't have it on him, at least. What about the travel allowance?"

"Aha, I see you think I'm being alarmist. Let me tell you that I went to see the bank manager on Friday and he told me Colin had transferred the whole lot to Gibraltar."

"Can he get it out of there?"

"You may be sure there are ways and means."

She sat down on the sofa opposite and they stared at one another. Observing her faded hair, her once-pretty face now wrecked and slackened by time and presented to his view with touching candour, without benefit of make-up, Miles felt a pang of sympathy. He had known her, really, more or less all his life, for she had been a friend of his mother's, and as they gazed at one another his awareness of her anxiety for Colin shifted sharply, like the changing of a photographic plate, and became his mother's concern for himself when he was a little boy, a long time ago it seemed, at the beginning of his lameness. For a moment he tasted the old relief, the cessation of any need for further struggle, then brought himself back with an effort and looked about him.

He had never been in this house before. The Thewlesses seemed to move every two or three years, following fluctuations of fortune with which he was no longer familiar since his mother's death. They were always more or less in the same part of London, an area of which the heart and capital was Earl's Court, and they lived by various ingenuities which helped to augment Major Thewless's army pension. For a time they had advised on window-boxes and town gardens. The major had been very good at this, being keen on the practical side and having that kind of spellbinding personality which always convinced the timid that he knew best. But he did not always know best, not by any means, and as nursery plants grew outrageously dearer and dearer and his long-suffering mini-van wore out, the fancy back gardens and the window-boxes were abandoned. Then there was a very small antique shop, economical to run because the premises were scheduled for demolition and the major cleaned all the brass, in which he specialized, and himself carried out the furniture repairs. But furniture, even Edwardian horrors which Mrs. Thewless said would have disgraced a boarding-house, was becoming increasingly difficult to find, while the dealers and their hangers-on saw to it that he never had a chance at anything worth having. He was sharp enough to see that this could even be turned to some advantage; that by enamelling old flat-irons pink and presenting them as book-ends, by painting discarded casseroles and frying-pans with Union Jacks and roses and treating them as ornaments, by stripping and waxing those destitute pieces of furniture, desiccated cane-bottomed chairs and spindly wash-stands which used to be seen only in attic bedrooms in the days of housemaids, he might have created a small centre of advanced taste to which the fashionable young would have flocked in their search for a talking-point for their bed-sitters. He was capable of the necessary skills, more or less, being a man who believed in nothing that he had not made or at least improved with his own hands, and this gave him great energy of application, which is usually half the battle. But he was a serious man, and the cultivation of rubbish morally disgusted him. He could no longer trust himself to speak of the outrageous objects that he saw from time to time in junk-shop windows. So the furniture business was a loss, and the Thewlesses turned to paying guests to eke out their income. This was harder work than anything they had yet done, for the right kind of guests were hard to come by, and when the house was full (their capacity was six) there was no end to the meals and shopping and housework and general maintenance. The work, Mrs. Thewless had explained to Miles when she was showing him round, divided up well enough; she did the cooking and housework, with occasional help from a daily when they could afford it, he did the shopping and the washing-up, answered the door and telephone, mended fuses, kept in touch with agencies and the small ad. columns, received and dealt with complaints, looked after general maintenance and discipline (this last was quite often necessary, since the guests they preferred were young and apt to be students) and presided at interviews with applicants and parents, on whom he made a strong impression. The only relief in the day was at the beginning of the afternoon, there being no lunch and preparations for the early dinner not yet begun. Mrs. Thewless had this hour to herself in their private sitting-room; the major normally employed it in sawing and hammering. Miles guessed he was in the house though he had not seen him; the sound of tacks being smartly knocked into wood on some lower level had provided a staccato accompaniment to their conversation.

"If you really think somebody should go out," said Miles at length, smiling at Mrs. Thewless because she looked so forlorn and he felt fond of her, "oughtn't it to be some member of the family? I mean, why should Colin take any notice of me?"

"Ah, that's just the point. He mustn't know that I've sent you. That would be quite fatal. You must just come across him by accident and use your influence. Any member of the family would be worse than useless, you must realize that?" She felt in both sleeves for a handkerchief, found none, and tentatively touched her nose with the back of her hand. "Besides, who could we send? There isn't anybody. You're literally the only person I could think of." She gazed at him with mournful protuberant eyes and he became aware of a stiffening of the throat, the old nervous yet pleasurable awareness of some sort of challenge. He leaned back in his chair, letting the faint sensation run right through him.

"What does the major think of the idea?"

"Oh, good heavens, we naturally haven't discussed it. You must never breathe a word. He hasn't the least sympathy with Colin any more, not a scrap of patience. Well, I understand it in a way. You know what a worker he is, he's never idle for a second. He simply can't understand Colin's not wanting to do anything just yet, he thinks it's vicious. And when Colin came into this money so unexpectedly—well! his father was more annoyed than pleased:

it seemed to justify everything he'd been arguing against."
She gave a little sad laugh. "And then, for Colin to go off
like that and send the money to Gibraltar, and all we get is
a postcard saying he's thinking of investing it! You can
imagine what his father thinks of *that*."

She felt about under the cushions of the sofa and located her handkerchief. From below, as though Hamlet's
father's ghost were stirring, came muffled thuds at dramatic
and ominous intervals.

"Not, of course, that it's the money we care about—it
would have been nice if he'd offered us *something*, a hundred pounds, perhaps, for a dish-washer—but apart from
the whole thing being hurtful it's so *insane*, his going
abroad like that, to a country he doesn't know, where he
hasn't anyone to advise him, taking all that money, the only
capital he's ever likely to possess . . ."

She blew her nose despairingly and looked at Miles
with a tender, envious gaze. Miles had a regular job, he was
settled and steady. She wasn't quite sure what it was, something to do with publishing or libraries, not very lucrative
probably (she had noticed the lining of his duffle-coat) but
he had stuck it out for several years and was now thirty. She
had seen him once in the Earl's Court Road arm-in-arm
with a girl and supposed he would soon marry. He was
quite good-looking in a quiet way and his dark hair, glossy
as a cap of sealskin, had attractive glints in it. But he was
not tall, and one had to be careful not to notice his lameness. Whereas Colin . . . she dwelt for a moment on the
image of her tall son, so well made, so (she could not help
considering) handsome, replete with all the qualities one
could desire, except common sense perhaps, and those
prosaic virtues that Miles possessed and which were now
unfashionable.

"Have you any idea," said Miles, "why he picked on
Morocco?"

"I haven't a clue; we've none of us ever been there. I think he has a friend there or something. There were one or two letters."

"It may be a love affair, of course. Does he go about with girls?" Mrs. Thewless caught his eye for a moment and looked away.

"Oh, of course he knows lots of girls, but he doesn't bring his friends home much, that's one of the troubles. We're always so busy with the house and the lodgers, there's nothing for them to do here really. They go about to bars and discothèques—I think that's what they call them. It doesn't do nowadays to pry, you know, and ask questions."

"I suppose not, but a clue would be useful. What are his men friends like? Boys of his own age? Older?"

Again Mrs. Thewless's glance seemed to flicker and evade him. She knew quite well, Miles thought, what he was getting at, but was reluctant to seem to take the point too readily.

"Oh, well. All ages, I suppose. It's so difficult to tell. It seems to be a point with young people to look peculiar. I don't know which are the odder, the men or the girls." Miles saw that she was unwilling to be more explicit.

"The trouble is, if I go, supposing I can get leave from my job, it's more than likely I won't succeed in finding him. And if I find him it may still be a complete failure. And however careful I am it's bound to be expensive."

"I've thought of all that. I've got this two hundred pounds, that's all I can manage. If it doesn't work I shan't blame you, but at least we'll have tried. I can't just let him disappear and get into some frightful mess without trying to stop it. He hasn't a grain of sense, Miles, he's a perfect ninny about anything practical."

"But surely there's some preliminary enquiry you can make, before spending all this money? After all, he's a minor. Have you tried the Foreign Office?"

"Oh yes, I had a long telephone conversation with somebody the other afternoon. They weren't very encouraging. They said they *could* make a routine enquiry through consular channels, but it wasn't a consul's business to search for people, and if he happened to know where Colin was, he would leave it to Colin whether or not he passed on the information. After all, as far as they're concerned, he's just a young man of nineteen who's probably spending a perfectly harmless holiday."

"That may be true, after all."

"My dear Miles, I've gone over all the conceivable possibilities, and that isn't one of them."

Miles sighed. "I wish we didn't have to keep it a secret from the major."

"I know, but what's the alternative? We ask his advice, and he'll tell us to leave it alone. He's in that state of mind when he simply won't discuss it. If *after* that I say I'm going ahead, there'll be a row. I can't face it, Miles. You don't know what my life's like any more. Like walking a perpetual tight-rope." Her eyes filled with tears and this time she made no attempt to check them. They welled up, trembled for a moment on her lower lids and spilled over into the creases under her eyes. "After all," she added shakily, groping for her handkerchief, "the money's my own, it's nothing to do with this house or anything like that. I've a perfect right to use it in an emergency."

"Of course," said Miles. "Can you give me a day or two to think it over? I shall have to ask for leave. It may be difficult." He got up and stood in front of the electric fire, making a formal pretence of warming his hands. It was getting dark, though not yet four o'clock; a yellowish dusk crept in through the closed windows.

"Of course, dear Miles." Mrs. Thewless had eagerly risen. "Naturally if you can't get away there's no more to be said, is there? But you know how grateful I shall be if you can manage anything. Even a week might be enough, if you were lucky. Or perhaps a fortnight? Are you very busy at your job at this time of year?"

"We're always busy." He took her hand, and after the faintest hesitation kissed her. Her skin felt unexpectedly dry and soft, and he realized that it was years since he had given up this once familiar, almost filial intimacy. "I'll see what I can do. The thing that bothers me is that if I go it may be an expensive failure. It's only too likely you'll be wasting your money."

"Don't think of it like that, Miles. Think what it means to me if you'll only try."

They were still gazing at one another in the dusk when the door opened and Major Thewless snapped on all the lights. He looked at them briefly and turned them off again, moving his hand over the switches until he found one that illuminated a reading-lamp beside the sofa, a small, economical light. He grunted at Miles as he crossed the room and sharply pulled the cord to draw the curtains.

"Wants oiling," he said, when the screech of metal runners had subsided. "Don't either of you want tea? There's a pot in the kitchen."

"I can't stay any longer, I'm afraid," said Miles. "I only dropped in for a moment on my way somewhere else."

The major regarded him unsmilingly, almost with a look of suspicion. He was strangely dressed, wearing over his flannel shirt a sort of tabard or jerkin which had certainly never been made by female hands. It had a pouched apron, bulging with something heavy, and a looped band had been stitched across the breast to accommodate tools. "You look like conspirators," he said, fitting a screw-driver into its appropriate slot, where it hung like a fountain pen. "What have you two been up to? That is, if one may ask."

"We've been having a chat about old times," said Mrs. Thewless, gently propelling Miles towards the open door. She followed him downstairs and gave him his coat.

"Don't go without looking at the improvements," said the major, turning off the landing light and switching on a fluorescent strip to illuminate the hall. He turned briskly to the lower stairs, his tools clinking. "It's rather an ingenious idea, though I say it myself. Won't take you a minute." He preceded Miles to the basement, his bald head gleaming lividly in the mauve light, and through into a small room at the back which was furnished with sofa and chairs but which had obviously started life as a kitchen or scullery. Where there had once been a window a half-glazed door was in process of being hung; it was evidently at this that the major had been hammering. The door was ajar, admitting an almost visible front of cold air. Outside, in a yard like the bottom of a well, stood a group of dustbins.

"You see the idea," said the major, taking the door by the handle and moving it to and fro, as though this were an entirely new principle. "Only a window before, no use to anybody. Going to be a playroom, television and all that. Now they can open the door and go out into the garden."

Miles looked out at the dustbins and the little yard, which was square and flagged, with no visible means of egress beyond an adjacent door which led back into the house. The garden, he guessed, was higher, at street level.

"How will they get into the garden?" He looked about for an extending ladder, a fire-escape or some other military ingenuity.

"They won't. You've missed the whole point. I shall make a garden here. Patio, rather. Urns with ivy, ferns and creepers in pots, that kind of thing. I've got a couple of chairs and a table waiting to be painted. Somewhere to sit out with a drink and enjoy the air." He beckoned Miles after him with an authoritative movement and they stepped into the yard. There was no sound to suggest that Mrs. Thewless had followed but it seemed to Miles they were both aware of the possibility that she was listening.

"Did you just drop in by chance," said the major, moving the door with his foot so that it almost closed, "or did Bertha telephone you?" He fixed his light-coloured eyes on Miles and the tobacco-stained fringe of his moustaches lifted slightly.

"She kindly rang me up yesterday, and I had some rather special books to deliver in the neighbourhood."

Major Thewless continued to stare at him, but whether with suspicion or not it was impossible to guess.

"I'd like to see some specimens of what you do there, sometime. All done by hand still, is it? No machines?"

"No machines, unless you count the presses."

"Of course I don't count the presses, they're hand-operated, aren't they? I suppose they print the end-papers?"

"Well, naturally, yes."

"Interesting," said the major, feeling about in the depths of his apron pocket. "I've sometimes wondered . . . repairs and so forth, nothing fancy. Of course one would have to see it done, and have the proper tools."

"The presses are pricey," said Miles, "but there are quite a few good amateurs in the business. You'd probably be good at it." The flagstones were filmed with damp and his feet were cold.

"So it wasn't anything to do with that son of hers?" said the major, holding his eye steadily. "She didn't get you here on purpose?"

"How do you mean?" Miles opened his eyes wide to express surprise. "Mrs. Thewless told me Colin had gone away for a while, I'm not sure where. I somehow got the feeling you didn't approve."

"Approve?" The corners of the major's mouth turned

down and his moustache lifted in disgust. "I don't give a damn what the stupid sod does. He can rot for all I care. I hope he does. You know what women are like, his mother's a fool. Crying into the cooking and lying awake at night thinking up damn-fool schemes. I'm sick to bloody death of the whole thing and I won't have it encouraged. I trust I make myself clear."

"I wasn't, I'm afraid, able to offer any encouraging suggestions," said Miles, buttoning his coat and turning with an air of finality to the door. "I have problems of my own, believe me. And now I really must get back to the bindery. I shall have to run for it."

Thewless followed him upstairs, breathing audibly.

"You don't do much running, do you, with that leg? Still giving you trouble?"

"Occasionally."

"I've got a bullet in the left knee. Gave me hell for years, but it's settled down. Only thing is, I can't kneel on it. Nuisance sometimes, of course, but you get used to it."

Mrs. Thewless was still standing where they had left her. She and Miles exchanged non-committal glances, both too wary of the major to do more.

"Lovely to see you," said Miles. "I'll ring up some time, when I'm coming this way again," and escaped down the steps and away at a jerky pace, disappearing as quickly as he could among the derelict-seeming cars which had long ago invaded and now permanently held and occupied the square.

He kept this up until he had turned a corner, then relaxed into his normal walk, which was careful and leisurely. It was absurd to hurry, but there was an uncomfortable feeling that the major was likely to be visited with an afterthought and to come striding after him with fresh injunctions. Nothing of the sort occurred, however, and he turned into the Earl's Court Road and hailed a taxi. This was a bit of luck, in spite of the extravagance, for if he were to catch old Dowding he would have to be back at the works before five o'clock. He was still not clear in his mind as to what he would say. If Dowding gave him leave of absence, which was doubtful, when it came to the point would he have the courage to go? As he sat in the moving taxi and asked himself this question the business of Colin Thewless faded from his mind. Instead he tried to imagine what effect his going off on such a wild-goose chase might have on Lucy, and on the outrageous situation which had totally unhinged his life for the past three days. As to whether she meant what she said, or were merely teasing, he was no longer sure. For some reason, after less than a year, she was tired of the arrangement. It was possible that she had some other man in mind; it would be a sort of painful comfort if she had, since that at least would explain everything. Anything, almost, would be less wounding than the suspicion that she was going, quite simply, because she was getting bored, because she fancied a change, because she felt about him rather as she did about the various jobs she'd flitted through, always with enthusiasm at first and then impatient, during their ten months together. Would it give her a jolt if she heard he was going to Morocco? He tried to see her in tears, but this was difficult. Quite easily, on the other hand, he could imagine her saying, "Morocco? How super! Lucky you," in that light-toned childish voice that matched her movements, all the time going on composedly with what she was doing. In a way it would solve the problem if he were to pack up and leave. It would take his mind off his own depression and resentment, if only for a fortnight. But the flat would be empty and desolate; it would be hateful to come back to.

An idea struck him, jerking him suddenly upright in the taxi. If Lucy and he could embark on this thing together! If he could offer a prospect so thrilling that it would tempt her! She would pack in her job with relief and they would leave the cold and grime of winter behind them, as one was always exhorted to do in the travel advertisements. But even as he saw the brilliance of the scheme he saw also its depressingly obvious and inevitable weakness. Mrs. Thewless's two hundred pounds could not, most emphatically must not, be spread to include Lucy. He had nothing in reserve himself and admitted a prudish fear of borrowing money. Even if old Dowding could be persuaded to fork out he was unlikely to lend much more than, say, twenty pounds. He sank back into the corner of the taxi, biting his nails. But by the time they had turned out of New Oxford Street and were threading the complex one-way maze of his destination his spirits had lifted again with irrational hope. He went up the three flights of stairs at speed and arrived breathless.

★   ★   ★

Mr. Dowding's office was locked; he had already gone. Bratby, the senior partner, was away on holiday, so there was nothing to be done in that quarter. Miles hesitated, staring at the massive press, polished and handsome as a baroque tomb, which stood between the closed office and the entrance to the workroom. He had passed that press every working day for more than five years, always with a sense of pleasure in its dignity, but now it had the ugly look of a giant thumb-screw, pressing on heavy plates to extinguish hope.

He turned and went through the open door of the first workroom, where the women were still stitching at their frames among stacks of paper, and hung his coat on a nail already burdened with mufflers and leather jackets. The place at this hour was always warm, however cold it might be outside, and there was a pleasant smell of glue, hot iron, and leather. On one of the littered tables someone had opened a roll of Nigerian goatskins, varying in colour from orange to reddish chestnut, and the warmth had brought out their mysteriously animal odour. He ran his hand lightly over them as he passed, feeling the rough, dry underside and the polished surface, but without looking at them. He touched, too, as he passed them the stacks of stripped-down volumes, already sewn and encased in naked boards, laid like stones of a wall separating the finishing benches from the rest of the workroom. Beyond them he could see the top of Purkess's head, still intent on his work though the others were packing up with a good deal of clatter. He neither looked up nor spoke when Miles stood beside him.

"Dowding's gone early, I see," said Miles, watching the faultless advance of the lining wheel as Purkess's experienced hand pressed steadily on it. "I came back in a taxi on purpose, I wanted to catch him."

The old man as a rule was not much of a talker; he had been in the firm for fifty years—fifty-four if you counted the years of his apprenticeship—and in exchanges with the younger men was apt to leave a weighty pause between question and answer. This time, however, he replied immediately, though without lifting his eyes from the ragged furrow of gold-leaf on the binding.

"*Mister* Dowding left at a quarter to five, to attend a meeting. He did ask if you were back yet. I had to say no."

"Well, he knew where I'd gone," said Miles. "It just took longer to get back than I expected." He leaned against the high bench, watching the unhurried progress of the work. Purkess had laid down his tool on the crowded rack above the gas-burner, and with a sponge like a lump of putty, so impregnated with gold as to have become slimy, wiped over the ridges and smudged lettering of the spine, so that all immediately became clear and sharp and Miles could see the title. *Adventures of Thomas Pellow in Morocco*, he read, and felt a faint shock of pleasure.

"Let's have a look at that, Reg," he said, putting out his hand, but Purkess went on with his sponging in silence and went over the binding with a cloth before he gave it to him. It was a stout, rather heavy volume, though not large; here and there the pages opened of their own accord at a folded canvas-backed map or faded engraving. The paper and type, however, were late nineteenth century, and there seemed to be a fairly lengthy introduction. "The Moors," he read, opening the book at random, "no longer enslave the whites, and in most parts of Western Morocco the Christian can travel without any danger of being held to ransom, or even of receiving worse treatment than a little rudeness from a boor or a little polite insolence from a Bashaw. Not a year passes without Fez, Mequinez, Morocco and Wazan in the interior being visited by Europeans without the slightest mishap befalling them."

Miles laughed delightedly. "Funny you should be doing that today. Someone's just been trying to persuade me to go to Morocco." He turned to the title-page for the date; the book had been published in London in 1890.

"So that's why you were late," said Purkess, taking the book from him and tenderly fitting it into a cardboard case. He removed his apron, turned off the gas-burner and began to clear up. There was a subdued commotion at the far end of the workroom where the apprentices were putting on their helmets and leather jackets and the swing door banged to and fro as one or other of them clattered down the stairs. Purkess was always the last to leave, after methodically arranging his own corner and making a tour of inspection round the finishing benches to make sure no one had left a burner on or forgotten to return a tool to its proper place. Some of the stamps had been in use for two hundred years and were as delicate and elaborate as the settings of Renaissance jewels. He glanced over the stack of lockers where they nested, each in its slot according to type and date, before taking any further notice of Miles.

"So when are you leaving us, then?" he said at length.

"That's what I don't know. Would I get leave of absence, d'you think? Say for a fortnight?"

Purkess regarded him over his gold-rimmed half-lenses, thrusting his arms into the pull-over that he always wore under his rain-coat for the journey home. He lived at some unimaginable distance, at Esher or Woking, and twice a day made the pilgrimage without complaint, as though it were part of the rhythm of human existence. Yet Miles could see, from his sceptical expression before it was eclipsed in the struggle with the grey jersey, that the few hours' flight to Morocco was something he would consider too outlandish, too altogether extravagant to be considered.

"You could take it as your holiday, I suppose," he said with a faint smile, accepting the whole thing as a joke, "if Mr. Dowding was willing. Who's to stop you, anyway? Leaving's all the go nowadays. Walk out of a job and walk in again whenever you feel like it. Passes my comprehension."

"We're short-handed as usual, that'll be the difficulty."

"Always are. Makes no difference. When I first come to work here we were double the number. We're never going to catch up with the backlog, not this side of Judgement." Reg Purkess had been bred to the trade, and in spite of a sourness over some of its latter-day aspects regarded it reverently. In his youth he had learned the craft under the great Cockerell himself, and the idea that anyone should wish to leave it, for whatever reason, was a blasphemy. He locked up his desk and waited at the outer door while Miles put on his coat.

"What d'you want to go for at this time of year, any-how?" he demanded as they went down the stairs. "Bathing and sun-bathing and all that sort of caper, is it? Very hard on the chest, I should say, in the middle of winter."

"It's not for a holiday. More in the nature of an emer-gency, to do something for a friend." They reached the street to find it gleaming with rain and blocked from end to end with throbbing traffic. Purkess adjusted his scarf and carefully buttoned the wrists of his leather gloves.

"Well, please yourself, boy. Anyway, there's no prob-lem as far as you're concerned, not at your level. I don't see 'em replacing you in a hurry. Talk to Mr. Dowding in the morning, I should. Only thing, I'll be surprised if he lets you loose before those Yale Baskervilles are finished. How-ever, it's none of my business. See you tomorrow." He was gone before Miles could answer, crossing the jammed street without looking to right or left, his shoulders hunched, his hands in his rain-coat pockets.

★ ★ ★

Miles set off in the opposite direction, turning up his coat collar as he walked. The rain was not cold; it drifted in fine drizzle, collecting in dew on his eyebrows and occasionally running a trickle down forehead or cheek. He found that the brief exchange with Purkess, pointless though it was, had brought him appreciably nearer to a decision. How this had happened he was not sure; the Moroccan book had struck him as an omen, but he was unwilling to admit that this could have much influence. He was not like Lucy, seri-ous about her horoscope in the newspaper and impressed by anyone who claimed to read character from the hand or who told fortunes. It was not the small coincidence, he decided, that had moved him, but Purkess himself; the daily journey to Esher or Woking, the leather gloves, the pull-over under the rain-coat, the air of inflexible habit dic-

tating each movement—each of these fragmentary impres-
sions, like stones pressed one by one in the bed of a mosaic,
had gradually evolved a sombre and discouraging picture.
He did not wish to examine it, nor to ask what possible
bearing it could have on his own problem. He only knew
that this image, which before had inspired some fondness
and even respect, now suddenly, as he glanced at it, dismayed him. Was it from the Purkess in him, some atmosphere that he and Purkess shared, that Lucy was preparing to escape in her random fashion?

After perhaps twenty minutes' walking he turned into
his narrow street, a chasm of warehouses and back en-
trances of new offices with a few tall, narrow houses surviv-
ing between. The light was on in the basement and the
curtains not yet drawn. As he came down the steps he
could hear music and saw that the room was in more than
its usual confusion. He opened the door with a latch-key
and stumbled over Lucy.

"Oh hello," she said, glancing sideways for a moment
before going on with her rummaging in the bottom of a tall
cupboard, "d'you want tea or anything? I've got a kettle
on."

Miles said nothing but hung up his coat and went
through to the kitchen, passing the open door of the bedroom, where a heap of clothes announced that she was
packing. The kettle was boiling noisily and the kitchen,
which was small, was full of steam. Lucy followed as he
turned down the gas and opened the streaming window.

"I can't find my long boots," she said plaintively,
putting her head on one side. "Have you seen them, by any
chance?" Her manner was coaxing, conciliatory; it occurred
to him that she had perhaps not expected him so soon.
There was a transistor radio, teapot, milk bottle and single
cup on the draining-board, which did not look like preparations for a joint homecoming.

"I haven't seen them, I'm afraid. Are you going out?"

He avoided looking at her and switched off the radio.

"Of course. I told you, darling. Don't let's be difficult." She reached a second cup from a hook and stood twisting her fringe in her fingers while he made the tea.

"I'd be difficult if I knew how," said Miles, "but I'm still not clear what all this upheaval is about."

"Oh darling, *don't* let's go through all that again. I told you, remember? Elli and Van are having a thing tonight, I thought I'd do my packing quickly and get it over with. Then there won't be a frightful rush; I'll be able to help them."

"I see. You're going there tonight, straight away, with all your stuff?" He poured himself a cup of tea and looked her in the eye for the first time, with hostility.

"Well, yes." There was a tiny pause. "You could come along too, if you wanted. There'll be masses of food, they're making a huge effort."

"You think it would cheer me up? The food, I mean. How very thoughtful."

She gave a tinkling laugh and turned away to sit on the kitchen table, where she perched clasping her cup in both hands and looking at him over the rim of it, her legs swinging.

"I'm not going to have a row with you, sweetie pie, so you may as well give up. And I think it's frightfully unfair to try and make me have one, because there's nothing wrong, I'm not quarrelling with you or anything, like I told you. It's just sort of come about, like a law of nature."

"You haven't given me a single convincing reason."

"Oh God." She cast up her eyes and swung her legs protestingly. "What am I supposed to do? Go to the Town Hall and get a permit or something? I've *told* you, I *haven't* a reason. We've just got to that *stage*, that's all. It's silly to go on and on, as though I were doing something sort of criminal."

Miles frowned at her.

"Do stop swinging your legs like that, it's too irritating."

She became at once unnaturally still, and her childish legs, their youthful plumpness stressed by the geometrical pattern of her stockings, hung down like little pythons from the table. She was wearing blunt-toed shoes with ankle-straps and her skirt was as short as a small child's—everything, Miles reflected with a faint pang, insisting on youth, on childishness, on the utter inconceivability of growing up. Yet Lucy was twenty-four, as he well knew, and it was time she began to take life seriously. Or himself for that matter, he painfully reflected. She had treated their living together as a kind of game, as something one might as well do because it didn't matter. Or worse, because everyone shacked up with somebody sooner or later and nobody made a fuss because it was temporary. What she was proposing to do now was equally frivolous—to move into a crowded flat with these other girls, where they could run in and out of each other's rooms squealing all day long and keep up the kind of racket he detested. He continued to frown at her.

"Have a mixed biscuit," said Lucy, reaching behind her for the packet and holding it towards him with the beginnings of a smile, as though he were a cross child. He shook his head. She shrugged her shoulders and chose one carefully herself, watching him as she ate it with a playfully contrite but also alert expression. One smile from him, he knew, and she would be all over him, like a dog in disgrace that has been eagerly waiting for the moment of being forgiven. Against his will and his better judgement he smiled.

"Oh darling, *that's* better!" cried Lucy, setting down her cup and sliding off the edge of the table to embrace him. He hurriedly put his own tea on the draining-board and allowed himself to be kissed, taking care to remain unbending and unresponsive. Lucy seemed not to notice this, but held him by the ears and kissed him on both cheeks and then on the mouth, looking enquiringly into his face between kisses, as though for evidence that there was now the most perfect amity between them. Her breath was sweet from the biscuit.

"There, there," she said at last, stroking his hair, "now we can be perfectly comfortable and talk sensibly. I can't bear it when you're cold and disapproving; it doesn't feel normal." She turned with an air of relief to the sink and poured herself a fresh cup.

"But I *am* cold and disapproving," said Miles. "What do you expect me to be, when you're walking out on me? What have I done? Why are you doing it? It's just childish to waltz off like this, without any reason or explanation. Hasn't our being together meant *anything* to you? You always pretended it did."

"Of course," said Lucy, her eye wandering to the door, as it often did when a look or word suggested that love was in question. "D'you mind if I get on with my packing? We can talk in there."

Miles followed her unwillingly into the bedroom and made a point of not sitting down when she cleared a place for him. He leaned against the chest of drawers, his hands in his pockets.

"You've never once told me what was wrong," he accused her. "Is there something about me you don't like, after all this time? Haven't you been happy?"

He could not quite bring himself to say, with an edge of sarcasm, "I was under the impression you liked me making love to you," because he was suddenly not quite sure that this was true. It had been so enchanting only a few months ago, like a secret game of which they invented the rules to please themselves, wanting nothing better than to hurry home and go on where they had left off, secure against the world in their basement fastness. But as the love-play had grown more absorbing, or as Miles thought it had, so Lucy had begun to withdraw from the shared ritual. She seemed to detach herself more and more from what was going on, as though it had reached a stage where it could look after itself, and she could give her wandering attention to something important. Once or twice she had infuriated him by breaking the voluptuous silence with a random remark, making it clear that she had been thinking of something else for most of the time. When she discovered how totally this wrecked him, leaving him touchy and silent, she had been more careful; but the suspicion that she often consciously checked herself made him alert and anxious and spoiled everything. From this point she had developed a habit of offering him caresses as though they were sweets, as bribes or perhaps rewards for good behaviour. She would coax and pet him with love if he were out of humour, but if all was well between them there was usually some reason why love-making was inconvenient or out of the question. She would spend hours in bed at night varnishing her nails, and when the operation was completed took exaggerated care to protect them from the least damage. Or she would be absorbed in one of the women's magazines which were her chief reading, and when his hand approached her would hastily turn a page, and sigh resignedly. He had come to the defensive conclusion that she was immature, that all that was wanted was tenderness and patience, as one read in those articles by doctors who usually signed themselves "Family Physician." But of course that wasn't the whole answer. She was twenty-four, would be twenty-five in August, and had never pretended that this was her first affair. That being so, it was impossible not to suppose that she found some fatal lack in him as a lover, and this, though she denied it with hugs and

kisses when he brought himself to question her, under-
standably did nothing to lessen his mistrust. What was he
to think but that her dwindling responses were no more
than friendly indulgence and good manners? And now, of
all things, she was going off to this communal sanctuary
of her kind, this *garconnière* of kindred spirits where she
would recover the virginal image that best suited her before flitting off in some unforeseen direction.

"Of course I've been happy," she said reproachfully,
feeling to the back of a drawer to make sure she had missed
nothing. "Haven't *you?*" She returned to the bed and
stuffed a tin of talcum into her suitcase. "It's been as cosy
as can be. I wouldn't have missed it for anything." She
smiled with her head on one side as though to encourage
him, but the concentrated air with which she immediately
went on searching for odds and ends suggested that she
had no intention of pursuing the subject. Before he could
speak again she put her hand to her brow with a comically
stylized gesture of remembering something.

"God, I forgot. Your father rang up half an hour ago. I
forgot to tell you. One of the boys has got chicken-pox, he
said not to come for the present if you were thinking of
it."

"I wasn't," said Miles. "And anyway term doesn't start
for another fortnight, there aren't any boys there." He was
at a loss to imagine why she had invented this diversion.

"Oh yes, there are. Two of them have come back early,
I forget why. He said not to worry, he and Matron were
coping."

Miles sighed, visualizing with painful clarity the
draughty Victorian house which he had not visited for
months, where his father still struggled with a day prepara-
tory school, with a large neglected garden and a handful of
boarders. He ought to have gone at Christmas, but he had
not. It was only an hour's journey by bus, and the fact that

he had invented excuses made him feel guilty. It was not that he lacked sympathy with his father, but since his mother's death they had grown gradually apart. His father had retreated totally into the absorbing problems of his life as a small headmaster, with no time or interest for what went on outside. Besides, there was Mrs. Mills, now known as Matron, who had come in years ago during his mother's illness and had taken over completely when she died. She ran the domestic side of the school and Mr. Asshe into the bargain, and thanked nobody for what she construed as interference. Miles's behaviour to his father was closely scrutinized; in spite of her welcoming speeches she always managed to suggest some private suspicion. And the friends who visited at Richmond were all her friends; she had drawn a close little enclave round him, frequented by chosen neighbours and a few parents. Clearly she had found herself a job for life; for his father's life at least, and he could hardly blame her. But the effort of trying to communicate on the old footing, as in the pre-Mills days, had become increasingly wearisome and discouraging. He found himself always exasperated on the journey home, weighed down by the old ache of guilt and depression.

"I'll ring him later," he said, not wishing to be diverted from his present discontent with Lucy's behaviour. He could not, however, help adding, "Wasn't he surprised to find you here, with me out?" The fiction that there was not an engagement exactly, but an understanding between them, and that Lucy lived nearby, had always been consistently maintained, though Miles suspected that Mrs. Mills knew better.

"No, no. I said I'd just dropped in and was waiting for you. I said I was cooking something, we were going to the cinema."

"Sounded quite a pleasant evening, in fact." Miles moved to the window and stared out at the grimy wall of the basement area. The light from the bedroom illuminated its face in cheerless detail, the coal-house door, the railings, the battered dustbin. God, what an outlook, he thought. Not even Major Thewless could have done anything with it.

"We could do a cinema tomorrow evening," said Lucy encouragingly, either missing or ignoring the sarcasm. "And tonight there's this thing at Van's; you can come if you like, honestly. They'd love it."

"Thanks a lot. Do you really imagine I feel like going to a party?" She was busy closing the largest suitcase, having trouble with the lock.

"Well, why not? I don't see what you're going to gain by moping around." She finally snapped the lock and stood up, putting back her hair from her face with both hands. "And anyway I don't see why we're going through this Last Act performance. What difference does it make, sweetie, to be quite honest? We'll see each other almost as much, and I'll come here as often as you like. It'll be better that way, I promise. It will, honestly." She looked at him with a slowly softening expression, smiling with her eyes and turning her head sideways in a pantomine of invitation that he found outrageous. In another moment, he thought, she'll be lugging the suitcases off the bed and pulling me down with her just to make me do what she wants, and stop being angry.

"You may be right," he said coldly, "but I'm afraid we won't be able to put it to the test. I'm going away in a day or two, as it happens. To Morocco."

"You're not!" She looked genuinely startled, but not, he thought, displeased. "Where to, exactly? And why, for heaven's sake?"

"I can't say why, at the moment. It's confidential. I could tell you about it if you thought of coming with me." He tried to look serious and important as he said this, but the words struck him as futile even as he uttered them; he was no longer clear what he wanted her response to be.

"Wouldn't that be a lark, though!" she said, the interest visibly fading from her face. "I can't, obviously. Van's getting me an interview next week, for a marvellous job." She looked at him reflectively before pulling the big suitcase off the bed and cramming some odds and ends into the corners of another. "Who's paying for this jaunt, if one may ask? Not you, I trust."

"No."

"A newspaper?"

"Nothing so plushy. It's purely a private affair, on very little money."

"Then how could I possibly come with you?" she cried, on a triumphant note. "Heavens, look at the time! Darling, be an angel and call me a taxi, will you? I swore I'd be there by seven."

He moved without answering to the telephone and dialled a number. From that point there was nothing more to be said. Only at the last, when she had flung on her coat and scarf and the taxi was at the door, she clasped him tightly in her arms and kissed him hard.

"*Do* come over later," she said, "then I'll know you're not brooding. It's not to be a sentimental old slop-cat. Promise?"

"We'll see."

"I'll ring you the minute I get there. You're not to brood."

"I won't brood."

And then she was gone, and he was back in the strewn bedroom, staring with black dismay at its disorder. Apart from displeasure at the room's untidiness he felt nothing. It was as if the slamming of the taxi door had solved all problems and left him curiously empty. He picked up a piece of newspaper from the floor and stood crumpling and squeezing it in his hand, then carried it into the kitchen and aimed it at the bin. It bounced off the edge and rolled under the sink and out of sight, but by this time he had lost interest in it. He went to a cupboard and poured himself some whisky, taking elaborate care with his movements as though he were listening for something, some interior voice which would tell him what to do. There was some imminent act, he knew, waiting to be performed, and when he knew what it was he could do it quickly. His mind was empty, even of anxiety; he might have been just awakening from sleep. He had expected to be angry and desolate, yet here he was, listening to the silence and warming himself with whisky. "The Moors," said a voice inside him, very faint and small as though heard from a great distance, "no longer enslave the whites . . . the Christian can travel without any danger of being held to ransom."

"Colin Thewless," he said aloud, startling himself with the sound of his own voice. He swallowed the last of the whiskey and went quickly to the living-room, took some sheets of paper from a drawer and sat down at the desk.

"Dear Mr. Dowding," he wrote at once, forming the letters smoothly in his cursive hand, "An old friend of my parents has asked me to undertake an immediate trip abroad for family reasons. The journey will be paid for and I do not expect to be away for more than a fortnight. I am sorry to cause you any inconvenience and I will advise you as soon as I know the date of my return. I was unfortunately late getting back to the bindery this afternoon and missed seeing you . . ."

The letter was quickly written, re-read, folded. When he had addressed the envelope he felt in his pocket for coppers, snatched his coat from the hook, and as the telephone began to ring set off in the rainy darkness for the post office.

★ 2 ★

As soon as the ship was well into the Straits the swell began, and the Spanish passengers staggered to the rail. The great cloud hanging over Gibraltar was left behind and green water hissed along the sides of the ship in full sunlight, but from where Miles sat in his corner, knees pressed against his suitcase, the view was obscured by their backs and it was difficult to ignore the distressful noises. He had travelled too little to know whether or not he was a good sailor; he hoped and believed he was, but was unwilling to put himself to the test by moving away in search of a better place. Those hardy passengers, most of them men, who passed him on their rounds of the deck did so with occasional lurches and little involuntary excursions in a sideways direction; with his unsteady gait he felt he could hardly trust himself to follow them. So he sat where he was, trying not to watch too closely when the couple on the rail before him took it in turns to groan and lean further over, clutching each other's rain-coats in their extremity.

They were a rather touching pair, he decided, quite young, both evidently much reduced by the ship's motion. They took it in turns to be very ill indeed and to comfort one another, the girl dropping her head on the man's shoulder while he stroked her hair and then putting a steadying arm around him and clasping his forehead when he reached his own crisis. Miles wondered how they could bear to face the crossing at all if it made them as ill as this. The plunging of the ship, the hiss of the water, the bright sun and buffeting wind were beginning to exhilarate him so long as he sat quite still and closed his eyes occasionally, but all round the deck and clinging to the rail were these Spanish unfortunates, solitary men with brief-cases, bulky funereal women, even whole families, so that he could only suppose that it was a national characteristic.

Sitting beside him, beautifully still and not even talking to one another, was a Moroccan family. Miles watched them whenever he could without seeming to do so; they appeared to be wholly self-possessed and tranquil. The man was dressed in a European suit and hat but wore sandals and an open shirt; he smoked continuously, from time to time thoughtfully scratching his cheeks and jaws, which needed shaving. The women were almost completely covered by their grey *djellábas*, irresistibly interesting to Miles since they were the first veiled Muslim women he had seen. The older one, bulky as a soft sack in her enveloping garment, had tied her veil—to Miles's disappointed eye more like a crumpled handkerchief—across her nose and knotted it at the back of her head, over the hood of the *djellába*. From time to time, as though for greater comfort, she pulled it down and hooked it under her nose, where it looked like nothing so much as a crude gag. The younger woman on the other hand displayed a certain elegance; when she crossed her knees a pointed patent-leather toe appeared at the hem of her garment; she had a brand-new patent-leather handbag and wore several rings. Her veil was more becomingly arranged, concealing the whole

of her face below the eyes, the ends disappearing neatly
under the hood. But the colour, Miles considered, was disagreeable—surely it ought to have been white? It was a
brilliant raspberry pink scalloped with black, and the effect
was hideous. Even her stealthily dark glances, occasionally
and as though by accident turned in his direction, seemed
neutralized and defeated by this garishness. Catching her
eye for perhaps the fifth time Miles became suddenly embarrassed and looked away.

At the man's feet, between a loaded basket and the end
of his own suitcase, lay a bunch of fowls. He looked at
them curiously, wondering how long they had travelled in
this condition. There were five of them, tied together by
the legs and lying with breast or head against the deck.
The middle three were supported by the others and more
or less upright, but the outer pair, beaks gaping and eyes
closed, lay sideways with wings outstretched and feathers
in disarray, occasionally struggling for a less unnatural
position. In one of these sudden movements, with an indig-
nant squawk, the nearest bird spread a wing across his foot,
so that he felt the warmth of its body and a strained trem-
bling. He stooped unobtrusively and folded the wing back
under the ruffled body to lie more easily, but the movement
was evidently construed as one of annoyance, for the man
came suddenly to life and with his foot hooked the bunch
of hens out of Miles's way. This produced an outburst of
polite merriment, gold teeth flashing and a scuffling shifting of luggage. The women in particular were delighted,
their eyes shining joyously and their veils stirring over their
mouths with silent laughter. "It's all right," said Miles,
"they're not in my way," but the birds were kicked further
under the bench while they all continued to smile and nod
at him, as though the incident marked the beginnings of a
happy friendship. Feeling that some gesture was required

of him Miles offered the man a cigarette and when this had been accepted and they had shared a match, made a feint of having his attention caught elsewhere, in panic at the imminent difficulties of conversation.

With relief he at once found something to engage him. A fair-haired small young man, whom he had noticed before on account of the bulky case slung over his shoulder, was crouched on the deck a couple of yards away, unobtrusively intent on a tape-recorder. Miles stared in surprise: the leather-covered lid was open, the spools were moving smoothly on their spindles. There was nothing to record that Miles could see or hear, only the rhythmic hiss of the sea and the almost amorous groans of the couple embraced at the rail, but the young man undoubtedly held some sort of microphone and crouched with the stillness of technical concentration. Was he recording those agonized retchings at the rail? It appeared that he was: as Miles looked from the couple to the revolving spools and back again the young man caught his eye and charmingly smiled, and a moment later switched off the recorder. He closed the case, lifted the thing by its strap and sat down beside him.

"Seems kind of mean to record them," he said in a confidential undertone, "but I can't resist it." The voice was American, very soft and pleasant. "You don't have a cigarette, by any chance?"

Miles offered the last in his packet.

"Hey, I don't want to take your last."

"Go on, I've plenty more." The stranger produced a lighter. "I couldn't make out at first what you were recording. They're certainly vocal."

"God, isn't it amazing? I guess it relieves them some or they wouldn't do it. Makes me sick to my stomach to hear them, and then I thought, hell, why not put it on tape? You never know, the strangest things come in handy."

"I can't think how, in this instance."

"Well, neither can I, now that you say it. Maybe you're right. That's the worst of these damn things, you never can hear a noise without wanting to tape it."

"Are you doing this professionally?" said Miles, beginning to be interested.

"Kind of. I'm engaged right now on a project, though this isn't part of it. It gets in the blood, I guess. You hear a sound and you just can't bear to miss it."

"It must be interesting. What kind of a project are you on?"

"I'm on a research grant right now. Moroccan leisure patterns. This is a wonderful country for cultural study. We're only just scratching the surface."

Miles was not quite sure whether he had said "leisure" or "leather," and looked at him enquiringly. Moroccan leather was something he knew about, but it might not have been that at all.

"You visiting here for long?" asked the young man presently, glancing at Miles's luggage. "My name's Sam Hardback, by the way. I guess you're British, aren't you?"

"You guess right. Asshe is my name, Miles Asshe. I'm only going to be here for a short while, I think. I don't know the place at all. Could you give me a bit of advice as to where I should stay?"

"Sure. Plenty of hotels, all prices and conditions, from plumbing to bugs. How much d'you want to spend?"

"As little as possible. I can't afford much."

"You know anybody here?"

"Not yet. I may have a friend out here somewhere, but I don't know where he is. I'm hoping to find him."

"You could stay over at my place for a day or two if you want to," said Hardback tentatively, looking him in the eye with a calm, benevolent, do-unto-others expression. "It's not exactly ritzy, but it's clean. Might amuse you, in fact, if this is a first trip. The house is a joke; I oughtn't to call it that, it's a furnished staircase. But you're entirely welcome."

"Thank you," said Miles, "I'd be glad to do that. It'd give me a breathing space for looking around." He considered Hardback's delicate profile with attention. It was a clear-cut face, the brow smooth and tranquil under the crew-cut hair, eyebrows firm, the nose a little pointed. It was a face without much expression, suggesting reserve; a Puritan face, Miles thought, the mask of a person capable of strong prejudices. But it was a good face, for all that; it inspired confidence.

"That all your baggage?" said Hardback, touching the suitcase with his foot. "No sleeping-bag?"

"No sleeping-bag, I'm afraid. I'm not much of a traveller."

"You're kidding. Everyone keeps on the move nowadays."

"Well, I don't. I've never been this far from home before."

"You must be unique. The sleeping-bag isn't that important, though; I've got plenty of blankets."

"Have you been here long yourself?"

"Fifteen months plus. It's a whole way of life, you know? Seems like a week."

"You've had time to make friends."

"Sure. It's fantastic. Everybody knows everybody in this place." And as though to illustrate this statement he raised a hand and said "Hi" to a tall man with a mop of dark hair who had turned his back to the wind to light a cigar and was now moving on again. The man nodded absently, without speaking, and continued along the deck. Miles was not sure whether Hardback had been recognized or not.

The ship was no longer rolling; they were slipping through smooth water in the arms of a bay, past the tumbled cement blocks of an outer mole on which derricks and cranes presently appeared and here and there a few solitary figures. There was a sudden purposeful commotion among the passengers, and moving with them further along the deck Miles saw for the first time a steep bastion of rock, honeycombed and creviced in every part with terraces of stone and concrete, rising without design or plan and almost without colour to the summit. There was an absence even of shadow, for the sun was high, bleaching all but the palest shades out of the town's complexities, leaving only the colour of bone. On the left hand, following the line of the bay, rose the angular pallid blocks of the new town. Miles found himself vaguely disappointed, though he could not have said what it was he had expected. Something more exotic, he supposed, based on the faded engravings of Purkess's book, or some other childish supposition. He always expected new places to be stranger than they were, whereas now the world was becoming uniform all over: he had often heard it said. The gangplank, the stolid crowd, the customs shed, the fierce competition for porters, the hooting taxis, these things could have belonged to anywhere in the world. Nevertheless it was confusing; he was glad not to have arrived in it alone.

★   ★   ★

In the taxi he smiled gratefully at Hardback and asked him, "Is it far?"

"Very near. Just over there, in fact." He pointed upwards. "We could walk it in twenty minutes, but you have to go way around if you go by road."

They passed through the harbour gates and almost at once were climbing a steep hill, following a narrow street between high walls. At each turn they came upon groups of people reluctant to scatter, who moved aside nonchalantly only at the last moment; the driver made no concessions of any sort and kept his thumb on the horn. Soon they were among shops and market stalls and the crowd was denser. Hand-barrows, donkeys, crates, baskets of mint and vegetables were edged out of danger by a hair's breadth, and more than once there were fierce or derisory thumps on the body of the taxi. Twice, when they seemed on the point of disaster, Miles closed his eyes. They had passed through a crowded archway and were now hooting their way through a press of bodies, past a café where passers-by pushed among tables on the pavement, grazing the trays of sweet-meat-sellers on a corner where boys clustered like swarming bees, and at last, after an ear-splitting *sostenuto* on the horn and a crash of gears, ground up a long ramp towards a massive front of wall and a forbidding archway.

"Nerve-racking driving," said Miles, putting out a hand to steady himself; at the last swerve he had been thrown against Hardback's shoulder.

"Sure. It's a game they all play. The driver loses face if he slows down and pedestrians lose face if they appear to admit the existence of an automobile. Why the streets aren't strewn with dead I can't tell you." He smiled calmly. "Wait till the end of Ramadan. That's really something."

They had now plunged into a tunnel between high walls where groups of boys were running about and screaming. Most of them flattened themselves at the side as the taxi shot downhill, but once or twice a boy darted out in front of them, offering himself like a toreador to the bull and avoiding disaster by a last-minute swerve and contortion of the body. Miles involuntarily closed his eyes again, opening them a moment later to find the cab bumping over the cobbles of an open space where a crowd of tourists was clustered under a palm-tree. Someone hidden in the crowd was beating a drum, but the sun was momentarily dazzling and he could distinguish nothing. The taxi ran sharply

downhill into a corner of the square and they were in
shadow again, moving more cautiously down a narrow
street between overhanging houses. It did not look like a
street intended for motor traffic, but they soon emerged
into a small irregular open space and the car stopped.

"*Nous y sommes,*" said Hardback, and got out into a
knot of children. One would have said that they had never
seen a car before, such was their reaction; more came running from steps and doorways, opened Miles's door, laid
hands on the wings and bonnet and struggled among themselves for possession of the luggage. Hardback ignored
them, pausing only as he paid the driver to push aside a
boy's head which was thrust between his chest and the
money in his hand. "Give your bag to the biggest," he
called to Miles, shouldering the tape-recorder, "he'll get it
anyway, and it saves a battle."

They set off down an alley at the corner of the square,
boys pattering beside them. The cobbles gave way to a
short flight of steps which Miles negotiated carefully,
avoiding scraps of peel and vegetable refuse. After several
turning they came into a narrow *cul-de-sac* and stopped.

"You hurt your foot or something?"

"No, I'm a little lame. It doesn't bother me."

"Too bad. It's easy to stumble on these stones, I've
done it lots of times." He unlocked a shabby green door in
an otherwise blank wall covered with chalk scrawlings and
the two boys carrying the baggage stepped inside. There
was only just room for them to stand there, for the door
opened directly on a flight of stairs, walled and faced with
tiles, leading steeply upwards.

"O.K.," said Hardback, and paid the boys, propelling
them gently backwards with his free hand. He seemed to
be on excellent terms with them. "Not a bad bunch of kids,"
he said as he closed the door, "but enough's enough. I don't
have them go upstairs if I can help it."

The staircase was uncommonly steep, and at the top there seemed to be only one small room with nothing in it but a wooden chair and some luggage.

"You want to leave your bag in here, Miles, or go right on up?"

"Whatever you say. Do I sleep in here?"

"Not unless you want. It gets better higher up." They climbed another flight and came out into a large airy room which at first glance seemed to be filled with sunlight, but the brightness, Miles discovered, was golden light reflected from whitewashed walls; the windows were small and looked out on a dazzling sky. It was an austere place, giving an impression of deliberate and disciplined emptiness, though the arrangement suggested an equally deliberate comfort. Two divans, covered with bright rugs and cushions, were set in a corner of the wall, and in an alcove partly screened by curtains there was a glimpse of a brass bedstead of obsolete pattern, covered with books and papers. The room contained nothing else but a low table.

"Well, there it is." Hardback set down his bag and pushed the tape-recorder under the table. "You can have either one of the divans, or you can have the bed. They're all pretty much the same, hard-wise, but the bed rattles."

"Whichever's the least inconvenient," said Miles politely. "Where do you sleep normally?" He eyed the double bedstead with some misgiving. Hardback lifted his eyes to the ceiling and pointed upwards. "Don't tell me there's another storey?"

"There certainly is. When you've got your breath I'll show you. It's worth the climb."

There was a curtain in the corner of the room which Miles had not noticed before, and behind it a wooden stair which was little more than a ladder, with a rope as well as a handrail. Hardback went up lightly as a grasshopper and Miles followed more cautiously. The room at the top was much smaller than the one below and seemed to be used chiefly as a kitchen, though there was a table covered with recording equipment and a low bed in it. Hardback unlocked a door leading out to a flat roof, and as he did so someone near at hand began hammering. "Sam Hardback, his refuge," he said, and stepped out into a dazzle of sunlight.

Miles came out on the roof beside him and drew a deep breath. They were higher even than he had imagined, looking over a silken sea to an empty horizon. Moving to the parapet he saw below a descending jumble of other roofs and terraces, complicated by washing lines, television aerials, hen coops, broken crates and other débris, and below that again, inconceivably far off, a stretch of beach where tiny figures moved among rocks and seaweed. It was a dazzling expanse, too complex to be taken in so quickly. He leaned on the breast-high wall, feeling his heart beat. He was mysteriously aware of a sense of elation and lightness, as though without effort he could have risen over the parapet and floated on a current of air over the sea itself, down to the strip of beach with its rocky fringes. The drone of the sea was faintly audible and the hammering kept up a noisy continuous rhythm.

"Fantastic, isn't it?" said Sam, leaning on his elbows beside him. "The orchestration, I mean. It's so damn complicated. Stop listening to the hammering for a minute and you'll get the rest of it." He strummed lightly with his fingers on the wall, as though trying to elucidate a tune, and Miles listened. There were voices at varying distances, and a muffled thumping beat too metallic for a drum, as well as a confused shrill far-away echo which might have been either swallows or children screaming.

He had located the hammering by now; on a roof some way below a man in a scarlet cap was methodically knocking nails into a wooden framework. As his eyes wandered he became aware that what he had taken for empty roof-scape was by no means unpopulated. He and Sam were being watched from a parapet a little higher than their own; there was certainly a row of heads, though they ducked out of sight when he turned and all that remained was a childish arm stretched out across the parapet, as though proud of its pretty shape and shining bracelet. And down below a woman in a white garment was feeding pigeons, and others were huddled companionably in corners where the sun was already turning the whitewash rosy. The hum of the town rose in waves below and around them, and all the time the man below kept up his relentless hammering.

"It's a curious thing," said Sam, gesturing with outspread hand at the scene in general, "the dominance of the rhythmic pattern—you beginning to get it? Drums, well, that's a pretty big subject in itself; very basic. I'll play you some tapes later. But the thing is, these rhythms go right *through;* they're built right into these people. Take that hammering, now." They both looked down on the man intent on his carpentry. "First thing a Moroccan does when he gets home, up to a certain age that is, he starts in hammering. He'll keep it up after dark, what's more, though in Ramadan of course they stop when the gun's fired. First one rhythm, then another. It's fantastic. And at the same time," he held up an admonitory finger, "somewhere in the house his wife'll be going like hell with the pestle and mortar. Another rhythm." Miles's ears were invaded once more by the steady metallic pounding somewhere beneath them. "Are you getting the drums as well? That'll be the kids. First thing a kid does, soon as he can walk, is bang on a can or box with a stone or something, and pretty soon they give him a drum of his own, and then he's on to it seriously." There were indeed, now that his ears were beginning to distinguish them, soft thuddings and tappings going on in every direction, like the signals of mice in the tailor of Gloucester's kitchen, and a louder, more insistent drum was sounding nearer, banging a monotonous message at street level.

"Come over here," said Sam, moving to the opposite corner and leaning over. "This is a pretty crude one, but it's all related. You'll see them in a minute." That they could at one moment be apparently poised above the sea, and the next, from only a few yards away, gazing down into the narrow canyon of a street, Miles found astonishing. He accepted the change of view in silence, looking down past the open shutters of the house opposite, where a couple of women were hanging out of the window, into one of the alleys through which, he supposed, he and Hardback had just come. It was thronged with children, who as he watched drew closer to the wall to make room for a group of men in turbans and *djellábas*, one of them beating a drum and two or three others mournfully blowing into some kind of wind instrument. They stopped at a door and the leader of the group set up a fierce authoritative chant. There were rhythmic breaks in the recitation, and at each pause the followers answered their leader, as though crying "Amen!" The performance went on for several minutes and the street became congested, since nobody could pass. When at length they moved, drumming and blowing as before, the children went too and the racket diminished with distance until it ceased on a high note at the next standstill.

"What on earth was that?" said Miles, hanging over the wall as far as possible. He had identified the street now; the shallow steps he remembered were just visible.

"God knows; I keep meaning to find out. Some kind of religious brotherhood, I guess; the place is lousy with them. Some of them dance—it's fantastic—but this lot just drum and pray and collect money. Not a very interesting beat; I've got miles of it on tape. I kind of hate to miss anything; it'll weave in somehow."

Miles continued to gaze in a sort of trance. Where on earth in this teeming hive was Colin Thewless? The futility of his mission forcibly struck him. Mrs. Thewless and her anxieties were miles away, and if Colin were truly here, hidden and determined to remain so in this ant-hill, what possible hope could he have of ever finding him? He ought, he knew, to start worrying, but instead he continued to lean on the wall in a bemused state, unaccountably happy. To observe the comings and goings in that narrow chasm, himself unseen, had the magic of a dreamlike glimpse into another world. Every movement below possessed an indecipherable significance: a tray of loaves balanced on a boy's head and apparently moving by itself, a cat delicately scavenging in a corner, a woman enveloped in white, moving with majestic slowness, all seemed to be part of a pattern of cryptic meaning. And when at last the street was empty, and the shutters of the window opposite were closed, a smell of cooking reached him from below and sharply reminded him that he was hungry.

"D'you want to eat now?" said Sam at his elbow, as though divining his thought.

"Good idea. Whenever you're ready." He could not quite identify the smell, but it made his mouth water.

"The gun'll go off in a minute," said Sam, still lounging on the wall, and almost as he spoke, marking a growing chill and fading of the light, a cannon boomed, making the house tremble and sending up a clatter of startled pigeons.

"Good God, what's that?"

"The gun. It's sunset. They all go home and eat now. Funny, isn't it? All that mob in the street a minute ago, and now it's empty."

It was not quite empty, as Miles saw. A light-coloured figure was moving up the alley, going very slowly. The

light was fading now, but there was still enough to distinguish a fair-haired girl in sandals and pale bluejeans, carrying a child. She stopped at the foot of the stairs and shifted
the baby, which seemed to be asleep, on to her other
shoulder, and leaned for a moment against the wall, as
though to get her breath for the ascent. Miles and Sam
regarded her in silence. As she stood there, putting back
her hair with one hand and with the other holding the
child against her shoulder, the street-lights suddenly came
on, weak naked bulbs suspended from overhead wires, and
she turned and lifted her face with a startled expression.
She was staring blindly upwards in their direction, as
though she saw them, though against the overhead lighting
this was improbable. She stayed like that for a moment,
perfectly still, unexpected and incongruous apparition. And
then she moved, shifting the child again to her left hip, and
Miles watched her long legs vanishing up the steps, out of
the circle of lamplight and out of sight.

"Who's that?" he said quickly, as soon as she had gone.
They had both drawn back from the parapet and he looked
into Sam's face, feeling a little foolish at the question and
yet, because of Sam's air of omniscience, expecting him to
know.

"I forget," said Sam indifferently. "There's a lot of
those around. The Moroccan government cleared them out
two-three years ago, but they're seeping back."

"What d'you mean? A lot of what?"

"What used to be called beatniks," said Sam primly,
with a slight grimace. "They hang out with these bearded
messiahs and live like bugs in a wall. Some of them've been
here quite a time, they've even bred. You get the same
thing all over, don't you? Torremolinos is terrible."

"That girl didn't look like a beatnik," objected Miles,
who knew little about the species beyond what he had read
in the newspapers. The girl had vaguely reminded him of

Lucy, who whatever her faults could never be called that. Not that there was much resemblance really, except in colouring; Lucy was much too timid to go alone in such a place, and the idea of her having a baby was unimaginable.

"Well, maybe she isn't," said Sam on second thoughts. "I've seen her before, now that I think of it. I don't know her name, she lives around here some place. Sure, I know who she is. She goes about with that tall guy we saw on the boat. Remember?"

"The one you spoke to?"

"Right. He's English, I think; name's Quattrell. Someone was telling me the other day he was working on a film treatment; something to do with Morocco. Say, there's an idea in that. You know what? Maybe he could use some of my tapes for authentic background." He rubbed his hands as though the idea pleased him. "I'll look him up some time, but let's go and eat anyway, and then I'll show you the town."

They went in through the low doorway and while Miles washed his hands at the sink and went below to unpack Sam opened a tin of ham and prepared a tray. This, out of deference to Miles, he brought down the ladder and set out with a bottle of wine on the low table. All his movements were quiet and deft, with the decisiveness of a person who knows and loves what he is doing. Besides the ham, which he had cut in symmetrical slices, there was a flat loaf of bread, some butter, a plate of tomatoes. They ate for a while in silence, not very conveniently because it was difficult not to drop crumbs among the cushions, but they were both too hungry for this to bother them. After the second glass of wine, which seemed fairly strong in spite of its pinkish colour, Miles decided he ought to ask about Colin Thewless.

"Can't help you, I'm afraid," said Sam, when he had

listened to the cautious account with which Miles thought it prudent to broach the subject. "Shouldn't be difficult, though. There's a vast English colony out here and the grapevine's pretty efficient. Boy of nineteen, you say, on his own? Doesn't sound like the mountain. More like some cheap hotel in the *medina*, if he doesn't know anybody."

"I'm not so sure about that. Why should he have picked on this place if he didn't know anyone? And he's not hard up. His mother told me he was thinking of going into business."

"He is? Well, that changes the picture. Good-looking, too, huh?"

"I suppose he is, in a rather conventional way. I last saw him when he was at school; he's shot up since then."

Sam looked at him for a moment speculatively, but said nothing. He burped gently, said "Pardon *me*," brushed the crumbs from his jersey and stood up. "I'll give a buzz to a boy on the mountain who knows everybody. If he can't give us a line we'll try something else." He took a jacket from an open closet (none of the cupboards, Miles noticed, had any doors, which was a little odd) and nodded at Miles's coat on the brass bedrail. "Better put that on, it gets cold at sundown." Miles obediently picked it up and they went downstairs.

It was not yet dark in the street, but the place was deserted. A cold breeze stirred at the corners, lifting little eddies of straw and scraps of paper. The few small shops they had passed on their way down were shuttered and locked; the hanging light bulbs swung erratically in the wind, casting shadows which made the street seem even more desolate. But this was only a momentary impression. As soon as they had turned out of the *cul-de-sac* and mounted the steps there were lights in windows and from doors that stood partly ajar; crocks full of burning charcoal flickered on doorsteps and there were sounds of voices and smells of food everywhere. Everyone, as Sam said, had vanished indoors; even the children had disappeared, though to judge from the noise in some of the houses they were not much less in evidence for being invisible. Presently they turned into a wider street, where there were signs of life. A little girl staggered past them with a pail of water and lifted it, grunting, over a high doorstep, where it was snatched from her hand by somebody within. Some of the shops here—cupboard-like booths, each barricaded with a counter—were still open, but in each the shopkeeper was crouched inside over a bowl of food, apparently neither doing nor inviting business. Sam walked steadily ahead, and presently they came to a *bacál* which was better lit and evidently more prosperous than the others. "I'll phone from here," he said, coming to a sudden stop, and slapped his outstretched hands on the wooden counter.

Inside the place was comparatively spacious, though crowded with a jumble of goods to the high ceiling. On a sack of flour in a corner sat an old man, handsome and bearded, supping a bowl of buttermilk without for an instant ceasing to keep watch on his fortress of groceries. He rose at once with a benign air, and he and Sam shook hands and exchanged greetings. Miles had a moment of panic on hearing their Spanish, but when he was introduced and had shaken hands he found himself addressed in excellent French, and collected his wits sufficiently to mumble something. An obsolete-looking telephone was unhooked from the wall and the shopkeeper dialled and handed Sam the receiver. He held it to his ear and waited, and in this brief interval two or three small children stealthily insinuated themselves between his legs and Miles's, clinging to the edge of the counter and watching with rapt faces, as though expecting a djinn to be conjured out of the telephone.

"Ozzie? Hello there," cried Sam suddenly, from force of habit covering his other ear with his free hand though the street was quiet enough, "I want some information from you—are you set to listen?" Ozzie apparently was, and Miles listened too, though with a touch of appprehension. He had a freakish impression that Colin himself was in that unseen room where the unknown Ozzie listened at the telephone, and that he would not be pleased to hear that Miles was there, and would be anxiously signalling. Ozzie, however, seemed to have plenty to say, and when Sam finally handed back the instrument and paid for the call his face had a smug, a childishly pleased expression.

"That was a good hunch. Ozzie thinks he may know where your friend's staying, though he didn't know the name. But Morley Crosier's going round with a young English boy, he thinks it's probably him because Morley's pushing some scheme about a tourist camp."

"A camp?" They had started to walk again, keeping abreast since only a few people had emerged from the houses and this was possible.

"Yeah—you know, thatched huts on a beach some place, tourists imported by contract at so much a dozen. Didn't you say your friend had money, and was looking for an investment?"

"He may be, I think. But how will we know if it's him?"

"We'll pick up Morley in the morning. He's always in the same café around twelve o'clock. If he doesn't know your friend he'll soon find him out. He knows everything."

"And he wouldn't be in the café now, you think? Should we go and look?"

"At this hour? In January? Have a heart! No, Morley loves his comfort and gives it lots of thought. He'll be sitting by a good log fire right now, with a book on his knee and the lamp just so, looking forward to his dinner. If that's where your friend is, you needn't worry. He'll be comfortable."

"What sort of a man is he?" said Miles, rather grudgingly fitting Colin into this picture. If it turned out as Sam predicted he might be difficult to dislodge.

"A bit of an original, I'd say. Has some pretty weird ideas. Collects things, and all that. Only time I was up at his place he showed me a quite fantastic collection of *objets futiles*. At least that was what he called them. Nineteenth-century mostly, I guess; very fragile. Kills me to see him handling them, it's so incongruous. And then he'll get bitten with some other idea, like this stupid camping. If only people would leave this country *alone*," said Sam with sudden passion. "Soon there'll be nothing authentic left, the way it's going."

"What d'you mean by authentic?" said Miles, hurrying to keep up. They had turned into a street which descended steeply by a series of steps to what was evidently a more frequented and lively quarter. Here there were several cafés and food-shops open, and a sound of musical instruments. Sam paused at an open doorway and looked in.

"I'll buy you a glass of tea," he said, "the band's good here," and confidently led the way to an empty table. The place was extremely bare and shabby and brightly lit. There were some wrecked-looking tables and chairs, but beyond these nothing whatever had been provided for human comfort.

"*This* is authentic," said Sam, glancing with approval at the groups of men and boys who sat silent at a few tables, some of them hunched over bread and soup, others with glasses of tea and some with nothing. On a rough platform at the far end two or three men squatted with musical instruments, for the moment staring apathetically in front of them and as silent as the customers. "At least,"

Sam corrected himself as he sat down, "these chairs and tables are an innovation, but that's not important. The place fulfils its purpose perfectly. If a European got hold of it a lot of time and money would be wasted on inessentials. What do we go into a café for, any of us? Food, drink, company, music. They're all here; there's nothing to distract us, we can concentrate on them."

"I could concentrate just as well if the walls were clean."

"O.K., maybe you could, but the emphasis would be different. We're interlopers here, it's our role to *accept*. What *we* want isn't what *they* want, remember. And as far as I'm concerned the things they want, by and large, are more important. They're still in the main stream of traditional life. What God wills, *is*. The whole philosophy of life is based on acceptance." He twisted round in his chair to look for the waiter, who was watching them without interest from a distance. He came slowly across in answer to Sam's signal and departed again in silence. Miles watched a fly scraping its wings among grains of sugar on the table and said nothing. It was curious, coming from the maidenly cleanliness of Sam's place, to find him enthusiastic about this one, but it might seem uncivil to argue and so he said nothing.

"That's what burns me up about people like Morley Crosier and their damn fool schemes. They come here to escape into the past. O.K., so do we all. Then why don't they leave it alone, that's what I want to know? Why must they contaminate it? The pattern of life here has a definite rhythm; it's very slow and subtle, it's crazy to try and change it. Wait till we get back home and I'll play you some tapes. You'll see what I mean then."

"I'd like to hear them," said Miles, trying to resist the impression that Sam was talking nonsense. He had been puzzled for the last few seconds by sounds of music, a whisper of tune that seemed to come from nowhere, since the musicians on their platform were still idle. Now, as the waiter wiped the table and set down the glasses he suddenly located it: a youth at the next table, crouched with dreamy intentness over his soup-bowl, was listening to a small transistor in the folds of his *djellába*. He lifted it out, made some small adjustment to the dial and tenderly replaced it. When the musicians began to drum and play he dropped his head still lower, determined not to miss a note of his private music.

"Perhaps they want to be contaminated," said Miles, secretly amused. "Perhaps they don't want to stay in the past, any more than we do." He was not sure that Sam had heard him; the band was noisy. He was sipping his tea with a critical air, no longer attending to Miles but wholly absorbed in the musicians and their strange instruments.

"Fantastic," he said at length, when they ceased abruptly. "That drummer's too good for this dump; he's quite something. I'll try and get him up to my place tomorrow and maybe record him."

"We're going to see this man Crosier tomorrow, you said?"

"Sure, we'll do that as well. We can do that any time." He had clearly lost interest in Miles's problems, and presently got up from the table, excused himself, and wandered to the back of the café in search of culture.

* 3 *

Morley Crosier was found next day without difficulty. Around noon, Sam said, he would be sitting at his usual table in his favourite café, and there he was, not in his accustomed corner under the awning but inside. Although the sun was warm there was a cold wind; most of the pavement tables were deserted.

"Hi, Morley," called Sam, threading his way between empty chairs, "are you expecting company, or can we join you?" Miles came to a stop behind him, a little out of breath. The walk to the European town had been a long one; the last few streets had been crowded and mostly up-hill.

"I am alone, as you see," said Crosier grandly, "waiting for whatever company God sends." He pointed to vacant chairs. "Sit down, sit down." Miles shook the freckled hand extended to him and was surprised by the vehemence of its grasp. The man was pale and heavy and his flesh sagged. He was at least well into his sixties; grey, rather bald, with strands of hair combed sideways over his scalp and a voice with an undercurrent of wheeze to it, like a muted accompaniment.

"I'm not at my best this morning, I fear," he told them, turning from one to the other. His eyes were not quite a pair, and looked at the world with two distinct expressions. One was benign and pale, a watery blue; the other darker and almost alarmingly alert, as though it did duty for both and missed nothing.

"Miles here is looking for someone he knows. Colin something. What was it—Thewless? I rang Ozzie last night and he thought you might have a line. English boy, not long been over here." Sam broke off while Crosier beckoned the waiter and ordered coffee.

"Well, Ozzie was perfectly right," said Crosier, when the man in tarboosh and crumpled jacket had gone. "If it's Colin Thewless you want I can tell you precisely. He's been staying in my garden cottage these last two days, and at this exact moment," he lifted a slow arm and consulted his wrist-watch, "he's out on the Old Mountain, talking to Ozzie."

"Well, what d'you know?" cried Sam in surprise. "How come? Ozzie didn't even know his name last night when I spoke to him."

Crosier looked from one to the other with a knowing smile and rocked a little in his chair, as though this amused him.

"Quite right," he said, "quite right. He's only being careful. Young Colin doesn't want it noised abroad, that's all. He's recently absconded, I believe, from a tiresome situation at home. Impossible parents. Ozzie would be discreet until he knew who it was who was doing the enquiring."

Sam said, "Oh, I see," and looked doubtfully at Miles. "Didn't you say you knew his family?"

"I've known his mother a long time. She's not impossible at all. As a matter of fact it was she who told me he was here, or might be. I told her I'd picked on this place for a holiday, and didn't know anybody. She meant it kindly."

Miles had a wary feeling that if he were not careful at this point his chance of success with Colin would be gone for ever. He glanced at Sam as the waiter set down the cups. Sam had been helpful so far, but to say more in front of Crosier might be risky.

"So everything is satisfactory, then," said Crosier comfortably, unwrapping a cube of sugar and dipping a corner of it in his coffee. "Young people are very defensive nowadays, I find. They feel in honour bound to conduct a continuous campaign against the experienced generation." He popped the sugar in his mouth and sucked it slowly. "In most cases, I'm bound to say, I think they're right. One needs a little warfare occasionally to relieve the tedium. It's good for the system; increases the flow of adrenalin."

He coughed as he swallowed the sugar, making his eyes water.

"Asthma," he explained, laying a hand on the upper part of his waistcoat. "I dare say I did the same at his age. No doubt he exaggerates in order to make himself interesting."

He continued to wheeze spasmodically, his pale eye full of tears; but the other, Miles thought, was sizing him up quite sharply.

"I expect that's it," he agreed with a smile, determined not to appear to know too much. "I just thought it would be nice to see him if he was around."

"If you're free to have lunch with me," said Crosier, "you can see him tomorrow. Both of you, of course," he added, turning to Sam. "I've got a little project I want to discuss; I'd be glad of your opinion. I've been trying to get hold of Robert Quattrell for the last few days, but it seems he's away. He's an energetic type, wouldn't you agree? He might be useful. But that horrible hotel where he stays said he'd gone to Gibraltar. They may be right; they're not usually. They specialize in misinformation. If he were here I'd have seen him somewhere or other. Everyone goes past this point at least once a day." He shifted in his seat for a better view of the window.

"He's back, he's here," said Sam. "I saw him yesterday, on the boat. I'd quite like to see him myself, come to that. Why don't we try the hotel again?"

"I did, not an hour ago. If he's back, as you say, he's evidently not staying there. I can't say I blame him; had you noticed that sinister smell of disinfectant? No, my dear, the best way of picking up anyone is to sit here." He unwrapped another cube of sugar and watched while the coffee crept into it from one corner.

"Hell, I can do better than that," said Sam, suddenly animated. "That girl we saw, Miles—remember? She goes around with him all the time, she'll know where he is. I know pretty well where she lives, it's not far from my place. Why don't we go there right now, and settle the question?"

"How far is it?" asked Crosier doubtfully. "This isn't one of my energetic days, I fear. I couldn't face a door-to-door search in your sordid area."

"You won't have to. We can take a cab practically all the way. If you like you can stop by at my place while we two reconnoitre. It's too easy."

Everyone approved of this suggestion, including Miles, who was pleased with the idea of seeing the girl again. Remembering that moment in the street, under the misleading light, he had only a vague impression of what she looked like. Something or other about her had struck him as memorable; he felt a stir of curiosity.

When they had drunk their coffee Sam went out for a cab and in no time at all they were threading through the crowds and buses of the Grand Socco and taking the long way round which led to the Kasbah. The taxi was small and Crosier had not been got into it without difficulty. Now there was hardly room to breathe, and his wheezing rose and fell against Miles's ribs like the sighing of a turtle. He was not prepared to sit in silence, however, and turned his benign eye in Miles's direction.

"This young friend of yours, now," he began, his phrases punctuated by the struggle for breath, "whom I've been so rash as to instal in my gardener's cottage. He seems a nice enough boy. Would you say he was steady?"

"Steady in what way?"

"Well, he seems to have a little money that he wants to invest. Have you any idea of the amount? Would you say he's sensible?"

"I don't know very much about it. He came into a little legacy, I believe, from an uncle or aunt. You probably know more than I do."

"Well, only in the vaguest terms. I shall rely on your advice. These parents, for instance; would I be wrong if I thought they sounded a little troublesome? Would they have any control over what he does? I mean, of course, with regard to the use of the property?"

"I haven't the least idea," said Miles, determined not to be pumped by this dubious stranger. "You'll have to ask Colin himself. I haven't seen him for a long time."

"This is rather a cherished little project of mine," Crosier went on amicably, ignoring the rebuff. "I've been offered—or at least I *may* be offered—the concession of a nice little plot of land a few miles down the coast. You know Robert Quattrell, perhaps? He has a cottage not far from there, so his advice would be useful. Being young, you probably know more about holiday camps than I do. But it would be a speculation, after all. One has to be careful."

Miles could think of no reply to this, so he said "Of course," and nodded, watching the walls of the Kasbah fly past as the taxi plunged into the tunnel.

"In this charming town that I inhabit," Crosier pursued, "there are far too many expatriates with too little money. I, as you may have guessed, am one of them, and much too timid to think of doing business with the others. On the other hand, there are surprising opportunities of making money if one has something substantial to start with. As in the process of fermentation, a good starter is essential. This offer of a camping site is a case in point. The scheme collapses unless one can buy the freehold. Building the huts and so on can be a piecemeal business. But one has to have a starter."

They jolted to a standstill in the little square where Miles and Sam had arrived the day before, and from there, having provided a spectacle for the children by extracting Crosier with difficulty from the cab, set off at a slow pace in a new direction. Crosier, with a word of apology, took Miles's arm; in spite of the asthma he intended to go on talking.

"So long as it isn't uphill, and we don't hurry, I can manage adequately," he said, and indeed he gave the impression that he could talk in any circumstances. Sam stopped to ask for directions once or twice, and eventually, guided by little boys who displayed a competitive eagerness to point the way, they passed under an archway into a narrow courtyard.

"*Pesetas, pesetas,*" chanted the little boys. Sam began feeling in his pockets but Crosier checked him, uttering a sharp "tt-tt" and wagging a finger.

"Knock first, dear boy. It may be the wrong place."

Sam knocked, using the iron ring out of reach of the children, and the children knocked more vigorously, using fists and knuckles. The door opened at once, but only an inch, and when Sam had spoken it was quickly closed again.

"What did I tell you?" said Crosier. "Wrong house, inevitably. Blast them."

But "No, no," said Sam, "it's all right, I think she's coming," and distributed some coins among the children.

The door opened a second time and the girl of the previous night appeared in the doorway; she looked startled. She was dressed as before in sweater and jeans, but had evidently taken some trouble with her appearance. Her hair was carefully brushed and tied up with a ribbon, as though she were expecting company.

"Oh, hello," said Sam, "we're looking for Mr. Quattrell. My name's Sam Hardback, and this is Mr. Crosier and Miles Asshe. I'm sorry I don't know yours."

"He isn't here," said the girl, holding the door doubtfully. "I don't know when he'll be back. He's gone to the bank."

"Then perhaps, my dear young lady," said Crosier, wheezing, "you would allow us to wait inside? We're all friends of his, and if he's only gone to the bank he'll be back presently."

"Well . . . I expect you can," she said unwillingly, and glanced over her shoulder. "Just wait a minute, please."

She all but closed the door and disappeared. There was a sound of women's voices and muffled scuffling. When she returned she seemed to be out of breath, but more composed. "Come in, please," she said, opening the door wide and holding back the folds of a cotton curtain.

They passed into a smallish room which was rather dark, and apart from the girl and themselves conspicuously empty. The curtains of two other doorways were faintly stirring, as though more than one person had recently left in a hurry. There was no furniture of any kind in the main part, which had whitewashed walls and a floor of patterned tiles, but at the further end, under a shallow arch, there

was a spacious alcove, and this had a low divan running
round the wall, backed with some garish material and furnished with cushions. As his eyes became used to the dim
light (there were only two small windows, both above eye
level) Miles saw that the floor was glistening with water.

"I'm afraid it's rather wet," said the girl, following his
glance, "it's just been washed. But do sit down, you'll be
all right over here." She led them to the alcove and stood
politely aside while they filed in. Behind one of the curtains
somebody moved a bucket, and there was smothered gig-
gling.

"We ought to have removed our shoes, of course," said
Crosier, settling back heavily against the cushions. The girl
herself was barefoot; her feet left narrow prints on the
damp tiles. Miles wondered how old she was. Eighteen,
perhaps? She was tall and a litle too thin by his own standards, which were inclined to be old-fashioned; he found
himself covertly watching for that deliberate turn of the
head which had charmed him the night before, but when
there was no need to move she remained still—in itself an
unusual accomplishment. There was an air of physical
repose about her, whatever she might be thinking, as
though she had learned to be quiet, and were used to waiting.

"That's quite all right," she said, still standing and
watching them politely, without smiling. "Would you like
some coffee or something? I don't now how long he'll
be."

"No, no, my dear, quite unnecessary." Crosier was
laboriously feeling about in his pockets. "But would it distress your hidden friends if I were to smoke? Only these
disgusting asthma cigarettes, I'm sorry to say. They smell
like a garden bonfire, but they help my breathing."

The girl glanced over her shoulder at the hanging curtain, behind which it was evident that several people were

cautiously moving and listening. There was a plaintive murmur of a child's voice, which was hushed at once.

"Of course. I'll get you an ashtray." She disappeared swiftly behind the curtain and a small dark head looked out and was forcibly withdrawn. When she returned she was carrying a low table and a saucer; the disturbance of the curtain briefly revealed a space little larger than a cupboard in which several women and a small child were sitting.

"Aren't you going to sit down with us?" said Sam, when she had carefully placed the table and saucer before them. "You haven't told us your name."

"No, I haven't. It's Tavy Williams." She obediently sat down in the angle of the divan, her hands folded in her lap and her long legs crossed at the ankle. She looked from one to the other without expression, as though assuming that they, not she, would do the talking.

"You live here, huh?" said Sam at length, making a polite effort to ease the silence.

"Part of the time I do. Not always."

"And the little boy? He's yours, isn't he? Can't we see him?"

"Yes, he lives here most of the time. He won't come out, I'm afraid. He's rather shy."

"No wonder," said Crosier. "We're an intimidating invasion. We fill the house to bursting and terrify the family." He knocked the ash from his cigarette into the saucer, his eyes wandering to the curtain. The pale eye was benevolent and mildly bored, the dark one sharp with curiosity.

"Oh, *they're* not afraid of you," said Tavy, with the beginnings of a smile. "I expect they're dying to come out and be introduced."

"What are we waiting for, then?" He threw up his hands. "Do ask them to come out of hiding and join the party."

She got up at once and moved soundlessly across the floor, catching Miles's eye as she did so. It was a quick look, veiled yet speculative: he was the only one of the three who had not yet spoken. She thrust her head through the curtains and murmured something: the signal, evidently, for which the party concealed behind it had been waiting. They came out at once in a body, embarrassed but pleased, eager to see and be seen, delightedly smiling.

They were, as one could tell at a glance, three genera-tions of the same family. One of the women was handsome, with fine eyes and delicate cheek-bones, her face a little too hollow for healthy beauty, her skin too pale. She was clearly not dressed for company, having a nondescript scarf tied over her hair and a faded cardigan fastened across her gown with a safety-pin, but her manner and carriage both had a certain grandeur. She touched her breast with her fingers and shook hands.

"This is Zohra," said Tavy, laying a hand familiarly on her arm. "It's her house, you know, I'm only a lodger. And these two are her mother and daughter."

The old lady made an incomprehensible little speech; she had lost most of her front teeth. The daughter said, "Bonjour, monsieur," three times, bowing so low over their hands that Miles for a moment thought she was going to kiss them. The palms of her hands, like her mother's, were stained with henna.

"Well, well," said Crosier affably, though with a touch of impatience, "after all that we can sit down again, I sup-pose. They all speak French, do they? Now we shall have to conduct one of those interminable conversations." He subsided with a groan among the hard cushions, his face gone suddenly slack and peevish with boredom.

"Aminah does, a little," said Tavy, "and Zohra knows quite a bit of Spanish. But they won't sit down and talk, if you don't mind. They don't expect it."

"We still haven't seen your little boy," said Miles after a pause, speaking for the first time. "What have you done with him?"

"He's here." She stooped to the old woman's skirts where the child was hiding and hoisted him up to her shoulder. He was very small and solemn, and except for the blue eyes almost Moroccan-looking. He gave Crosier a long incredulous stare, and then, as though the sight were too much for his presence of mind, turned and hid his face in his mother's hair-ribbon.

There was a sound of footsteps in the street and a brisk knock. Tavy loosened the child's hands from her neck and gave him hurriedly to Zohra.

"What's going on here?" said a man's voice as the door-curtain blew inward. "You there, Tavy?" He came in against the light, stooping a little under the curtain and making the room appear even smaller than it was. He seemed taken aback at the sight of so many people, but when the women shrank out of his way and he saw Crosier he burst out laughing.

"Why, you old reprobate, it's you! I thought for a minute I'd broken up a family party." He put an arm round Tavy and pinched her shoulder. He was very much taller than she was and his arm was heavy; she detached herself at once with an obstinate look, as though reproving this demonstration before strangers. He seemed not to notice this, but advanced into the archway, propping himself on an elbow against the wall and looking down with an air of amusement at the three of them. He had heavy, rather craggy features, marked with strong lines and hollows which in repose might suggest harshness, or perhaps melancholy; but his smile revealed a row of irregular teeth which were oddly attractive, the canines noticeably longer and sharper than the others, so that at moments he had the engaging look of a dog laughing.

"My dear fellow, we came along to have a talk with you." Crosier glanced with meaning at the group of women. "Shall we have it here, or move to some public place where there's a smaller audience?"

"No, no. Stay here. I've only just come in." Quattrell detached himself from the wall and glanced at Tavy. "Tell them to make some coffee, or tea or something. You might have thought of that."

"I did. They don't want any."

"Well, tell them to make some now. I could do with it." He sat down at the end of the divan, his elbows on his knees, opening a pack of cigarettes. Tavy did not move, and Zohra and the others continued to stand behind her, Aminah holding the child and all of them gently smiling, as though the men in the alcove were a pleasing spectacle.

"I won't do that, I think," said Tavy in a clear voice. "It isn't fair. I'll do it myself if you like. Tea or coffee?"

"Oh God, I forgot," said Quattrell, glancing up under his eyebrows with a look of annoyance. "Get rid of them anyway, will you? And make us some coffee." He turned back to Crosier and the others with a cheerful grimace. "It's Ramadan still, of course; I'd forgotten about it. I've been out of it for a week, thank God, doing a few things in Paris."

"It's such a *bore*, my dear," said Crosier, "and gets worse as it goes on. It always seems much more than a month to me. I positively hate it."

Tavy moved unwillingly, then hesitated.

"Joe can stay, though, can't he? I was going to start packing."

"No, no. Get rid of the lot. Tell them to take him for a walk." He gave her a sharp glance and she turned away immediately, retreating with Zohra and the others behind the curtain. It stirred and bulged with their movements and there was a sound of whispering. The women were evidently putting on their outer garments.

"I'll tell you what it is I want your advice about," said Crosier, taking out a gold lighter and holding it for Quattrell. "And by the way, what a charming girl that is! She remembered, you see," he turned to Miles, "that it wouldn't be right to ask those mysterious ladies to make the coffee. Not a bite to eat, not a drop to drink, from sunrise to sunset! I believe, when cleaning one's teeth, one mustn't swallow so much as a drop of water. While as to the *other* pleasures"—he broke off to wheeze and cough, coming out of the slight spasm with a roguish expression—"nothing, positively nothing, not even a kiss! And here we were, forgetting it all, saved by the presence of mind of that dear young lady."

"Well, she lives with it," said Quattrell impatiently, "so naturally she's aware of it."

"Does she keep the rules herself, I wonder?"

"I suppose so, when she's here. It's not so difficult, you know. A little discipline and fasting never hurt anybody."

"Hey, listen to him!" cried Sam. "You ever try it? Racketing about all night and anyways getting up at three or four in the morning for the last meal. And *then* a day's work on top, without food or drink. Must be murder."

"It isn't obligatory to racket," said Quattrell, inhaling smoke. "Sensible people go to bed early if they've got to get up to eat at the end of the night. And they can sleep again after five o'clock if they want to. I know Tavy does, except that Joe gets her up again pretty early."

"It must be difficult with small children," said Miles, trying to piece these fragments together and failing to make a comprehensible picture.

"Well, naturally children don't keep Ramadan. I wish they did, it might subdue them a little. As it is, they stay up to all hours of the night, making one hell of a din." He glanced up as Tavy approached, carrying a brass tray laden with glasses of black coffee and a bowl of sugar. Zohra and her companions, each now dressed and veiled for the street, sidled out behind her and moved to the door. Nobody took any notice of them except Tavy, who followed Joe with her eyes. As soon as the door was shut she took a cushion from the divan and sat on the floor at a little distance, her back against the wall.

"Now that we're *at last* on our own," said Crosier, wrapping a handkerchief round his glass of coffee, "I can ask your advice, perhaps, about a little piece of property in which I'm interested. You know the area, I think; it's not far from your beach house," and went on to describe to Quattrell his notion of buying a strip of land and establishing a small camping site. He had, it seemed, one or two friends in high places; purchase was not easy for foreigners, but this strip of ground was agriculturally useless and he had been given to understand there would be no objection. Building could start when the rains were over and with luck the thing would be ready to open in June. "Twenty-five huts to start with, and an administrative bungalow. One doesn't want to throw money about, one must husband one's capital." The following summer, if all went well, they would enlarge. The Pasha of the district was quite keen, and there had been an encouraging response from the Ministry of Tourism. What he needed to know at this juncture was Quattrell's opinion of the site itself, from the point of view of amenity. The bathing, for instance; could it reasonably, without stretching the point too far, be recommended? Was the distance from the town too great for transport and labour? What could Quattrell tell him about the nearby villages—were they a likely source of supply, or a thieving nuisance? "All in all, my dear fellow, I shall rely very much on your opinion at this early stage. I don't want to make an ass of myself. I would prefer to make money."

"Quite," said Quattrell. "Have you made up your mind where it's coming from? Who's providing it?" His eye had a glint of amusement as he said this, as though he would be surprised to hear that Crosier had any.

"Well, naturally it's all in the discussion stage. What *I* can put in, of course, is hardly worth considering. But the opportunity's there. I am open to offers."

"Ah," said Quattrell, inhaling a mouthful of smoke, his eyes still smiling. "No good appealing to me, I'm afraid. I live on air, as you know."

"My dear man, I am *not* asking you for money. On the contrary, if the project develops I might be *offering* you some." His pale eye looked reproachful, a little offended. "This young friend of Miles's wants to come in as a partner. Only a few thousands, I dare say, but enough to start on." (Miles thought, So the old man knows something. Has Colin told him how much?) "And at this very minute," Crosier continued, "he's gone up to see Mollie Brockhurst about it; she's *quite* a possibility. Plenty of money, no family, no one to leave it to. I have a strong feeling she'll be interested."

"If she's got no family and a lot of money, why should she want to make more?" Sam asked innocently, and buried his nose in his glass when Crosier frowned at him.

"Well, if that's so, it's rather different," said Quattrell, the amusement dying out of his face. He was now attentive. "All I can say is, since you ask, that I wouldn't have chosen that strip of beach myself. There's a lot of fog in summer, you know; comes in from the Atlantic. And what about the wind from the other direction; have you thought of that? There's not a blade of shelter. Point two: the bathing's dangerous, there's an abominable undertow. And I don't know if it's any better there than at my place, but a lot of my friends won't go there because of the mosquitoes."

Everyone except Quattrell and Crosier burst out laughing.

"Sounds just perfect," said Sam. He exchanged a glance of merriment with Tavy.

"Listen to me," said Crosier patiently, his pale eye sharing the joke but not the dark one, "your objections are frivolous, and can be disposed of immediately. One: there may be a little sea-mist occasionally, but nobody in their right mind would describe it as fog. Two: this is a windy country, everybody knows that. But there are more windless than windy days in summer, and anyway what are the huts for? A well-built hut with a strong thatch—wouldn't you call that shelter? Three: as to the bathing, my dear fellow, people must use common sense. Most of the bathing is tricky; it's no worse on that stretch of beach than anywhere else. Besides, the kind of customers one'll get never come twice anyway. There's a new lot every time, shipped in by the travel agencies. And as to this talk of mosquitoes, my dear, *your* place is on the edge of a marsh, at the mouth of a river, whereas *my* piece of beach is a mile away and as dry as the Sahara. You aren't going to tell me mosquitoes can survive where there's nothing but sea water."

"What will the tourists do when they want a drink?" asked Sam, with a deadpan face.

"They'll buy orangeade and Coca-Cola at the bar. Wine too." He looked at Sam severely. "Schemes of this kind rely very largely on the bar profits. Water for the showers can be supplied by lorry in the first year. We shall instal tanks. After that, if all goes well, we shall bore for water. The water table's quite high all over the area."

Tavy said, "But what about the children? Won't they want baths?" She caught Miles's eye and looked swiftly away. Her own eyes were brimming with suppressed laughter.

"People who've been in and out of the sea all day don't

want a lot of fresh water," said Crosier, brushing the subject aside with an impatient hand. "It would be ridiculous."
He turned back to Quattrell as the only person capable of
serious discussion.

"There's another thing too, of course, before one goes
an inch further. One's got to have someone with a head on
their shoulders, to run the place. That's one of the things I
wanted to ask you about." He tilted his head on one side
with a coaxing smile. "If you had any ideas, for instance,"
he said. "I shall need a manager."

Quattrell shook his head. "A year ago I'd have jumped
at it. Just now my hands are full. I'm in the middle of this
novel that I hope'll be made into a film. I've just been over
to London to see my agent."

"My dear fellow!" Crosier laid a deprecating hand on
his arm and shook it playfully. "It wasn't *you* I was thinking of. Good gracious! If you think of joining me at all it
must be at top level." He beamed and wheezed, and had a
little coughing fit to cover the fact that his idea of sounding
out Quattrell for manager had been a failure.

"Do you know some people called Burridge?" he asked
presently, bringing out his second-best proposal for Quattrell's inspection.

"I don't think so."

"I want you to have a look at them and tell me what
you think. Nice types, both of them. They ran one of those
bathing and beach bars a couple of summers ago, so
they've had experience. In short," said Crosier, looking
round at them all with the air of a man who has been carefully leading up to a pleasant surprise, "they're coming to
lunch with me tomorrow. Ozzie will be there as well, and
my young friend Colin Thewless. I want you to come and
inspect the Burridges, and give me your impression."

From somewhere appallingly close at hand, from the
very air above the house it seemed, a mechanical wail went

up like a cry of pain, and then broke into booming words, rising and falling, distorted and dehumanized by the brazen tones of a loud-speaker. It was the hour of prayer. At the first pause other, more distant mosques took up the cry, and for an intolerable interval even Crosier himself found conversation impossible. He covered his ears with both hands.

In the ringing silence that followed Tavy spoke.

"We're going to the cottage tomorrow. We won't be here."

"We'll put it off," Quattrell said. "One day's as good as another." They exchanged a long look, and she saw that his mind was made up, and said nothing further. She dropped her eyes and examined her nails with a discontented expression.

"Good. So that's settled, then," said Crosier, heaving against the cushions and casting about for some means of getting up. Sam got to his feet and pulled him to a standing position.

"Thank you for the coffee," said Miles, finding himself beside Tavy as she opened the door. For a moment she looked as though she were about to speak, staring him full in the eye with a strange expression; but shook her head instead and made no reply.

Outside in the courtyard Zohra and her mother and daughter were waiting with the child, watching from a discreet distance so as not to seem impatient. They did not approach their door until Crosier had made his stately exit and followed Sam and Miles through the low archway.

★ **4** ★

CROSIER moved slowly round the dining-table, making minute adjustments. The table, as always, had been perfectly laid, but nine was an awkward number and he was having trouble with the decorations. For special occasions he liked to enliven the setting with little objects chosen from his collection, and was now in two minds as to whether or not he had hit on the appropriate theme. Lace-paper valentines would have been nice for the time of year, but they were fragile; whatever he used would have to survive handling. Some of his best items, excellent as talking points, were quite unsuitable for display on a crowded table—comic postcards of people in bathing-machines, for instance, or handbills of Last Dying Words of criminals about to be hanged; people passed them around too freely and sometimes damaged them. Then there were the Victorian hair-tidies, some of them quite ravishingly pretty; but the association, when one was eating, was undesirable. He had finally settled for a transport motif, since anything to do with travel could be relevant to the subject of camping, and had set out a number of tiny toys, penny objects sold in the streets a hundred years ago, with their modern

plastic equivalents from Hong Kong. Cabs, trains, motor-
cars, tractors, rickshaws were dotted the length of the table
like dried beetles, some of them stuck with paper flowers
for gaiety, others surrounded by groups of lead soldiers. It
had taken a long time to arrange, for the soldiers were early
ones and inclined to be unsteady. He moved round the
table with a reading-glass, setting up a fallen hussar, pausing to examine the paint on a worn drummer, his lips
silently working in concentration. Alawi, already neat and
handsome in his white jacket, was passing in and out between dining-room and kitchen. Crosier was too deeply
absorbed to be aware of him, but when Colin strolled in
from the other room he stood back and regarded the table
with dissatisfaction.

"The effect's rather bitty, don't you think? Too late to
change it now, unfortunately."

"I like it," said Colin, leaning over to pick up a cart as
light as a butterfly, made of matchwood and coloured
paper. "It's very original."

"Well, of course. Rather too *busy*, that's the only trouble. And would you mind, dear boy, not touching anything? Everything's arranged in relation to everything else;
I'd just got it to my liking."

Colin replaced the toy and put his hands in his pockets.

"I don't see how you can prevent them being moved
about. Everybody'll pick them up as soon as they see
them."

"That's not the point. Of course the effect will be
spoiled as soon as we sit down. The important thing is to
make an initial impression. That, after all, is in keeping
with the nature of ephemera."

Colin smiled politely and moved to the window. It was
a clear, bright, windy day with the tall bamboos in the
garden all in motion; stimulating weather when seen

through panes of glass but tiresome to be out in. The house, as always, was marvellously warm; central heating all over and a fire in both rooms, flickering in warm reflection from the dark furniture. When one thought of the chilly grime of Earl's Court it was most comforting.

"Ozzie will love it," said Colin, meaning to please. "He's always mad about your taste. He'll be sick with envy."

"That's as it should be, but it's more important to make an impression on Mrs. Brockhurst. The money's hers, not his. Not that I underrate Ozzie, mind. He has influence."

"By the time your scheme comes to anything," said Colin, watching him, "the money may be Ozzie's after all. It's not impossible."

Crosier came to a sudden stop, one eye attentive.

"What does that mean? She isn't going to die, is she? Is she leaving everything to Ozzie?"

"Good lord, no; she's indestructible. She *ought* to leave everything to Ozzie, after all he's done. But how often do people do that, in your experience? The sensible thing would be for Ozzie to marry her."

Crosier looked stupefied for a moment, breathing heavily, both hands on the back of a chair.

"Are you mad? The idea's obscene. The woman's a wreck, and old enough to be his mother."

"Well, why not?" said Colin mildly, smiling a little at the effect he had made but taking care not to let it go too far. "I don't think she's more than forty-five and Ozzie must be thirty. He's been secretary-nanny for years, a hell of a job. Why shouldn't he get something out of it?"

Crosier continued to gaze at him, screwing up his good eye in a shrewd effort to interpret Colin's expression.

"Is this something you've made up, or has Ozzie said anything?"

"Oh, nothing specific. It was just an impression. He

worries about the future, that's all. She's quite well off, with no one to leave it to. It seems a waste."

"If it's just your impression," said Crosier, looking relieved and at the same time faintly contemptuous, "we needn't worry, need we? If she cares to invest some money she'll have something to live for, and if it takes her mind off her ailments Ozzie should be grateful. If the topic comes up again you'd better discourage it."

"Ozzie doesn't discourage so easily," Colin was beginning, but at this point Alawi sped through the room on his way to the front door and there was a sound of car doors slamming and raised voices. Crosier hid his reading-glass under a napkin and went into the hall.

Sam and Miles had arrived at the same moment as Ozzie and Mrs. Brockhurst, and everyone was acclaiming and introducing.

"Heavenly," Ozzie was saying, pressing Miles's hand, "heavenly to be in this divine warm house on a day like this, and to find we all know one another after all, and are old friends." He had not met Miles before, and they both knew that he had not, but this fact had no effect on his enthusiasm.

They proceeded to the drawing-room, Mrs. Brockhurst cautiously testing the rugs at each step with her ivory-handled stick, and assembled to stand in the radius of the fire while Alawi served drinks.

"What charm, what beauty," she said feelingly to Miles, sketching a little movement with her sherry glass to indicate the room, the scrap screens, the needlework pictures and velvet-buttoned sofas, "how did you collect all this? So difficult to find, I imagine, in this barren land?"

"It isn't my house," he told her, "it's Morley Crosier's. I've never been here before. I arrived in the other car, the same time as you."

"You haven't?" She looked at him doubtfully, grey eyes opening wide and searching his face. She was delicately made up and her features were still pretty, framed in silvery-blue hair. "What a clever man he must be. How very wonderful."

"Wait till you see what else he's got," said Ozzie, appearing at her shoulder. He straightened the glass in her hand and glanced quickly at the carpet. "He's got hundreds of things that other people always lose or throw away, and all so *pretty*. I like the paper bags best, I almost think, with all that improbable printing, but he only brings those out on special occasions."

"What is it that Oswald almost thinks? Have I missed something?" Crosier joined their group, bringing beaming benevolence to bear on the conversation.

"Oswald almost thinks," said Ozzie, smiling up at him, "that Morley is a clever fellow and has agents everywhere. Where does he get those delicious objects, for instance?" He pointed to a row of optical toys on the chimneypiece, kaleidoscopes, miniature telescopes, knicknacks even more complicated and unidentifiable.

"Well, my dear, since you ask, I've had them a great many years, since before I left England. You don't find things like that over here. Everything of antiquity or interest was shipped out of this country years ago, when the French left."

"But you're always adding things!" cried Ozzie, raising his eyebrows almost to the level of his fringe, "every time I come there's something new! That's what's so mysterious."

"Not mysterious at all, my dear. I have, as you guessed, a good many contacts, all of a humble description. I have an aged cousin in Bath who picks things up, and one or two dealers who know what I like and keep their eyes open. Some of the most delicious *objets* come nowadays from Hong Kong, and cost sixpence. You remember that extraordinarily plain Chinese student who was here last year, washing up for the Burridges? He's gone back home now, and supplies me regularly."

"Monsieur et Madame Bourrij," whispered Alawi in his ear, and the group fell apart.

Crosier, it appeared, was the only person who knew them. He introduced them all around, laying special emphasis on the rank of major for Mrs. Brockhurst's benefit. Burridge was, indeed, almost painfully distinguished-looking, tall and straight, with grey hair and well-clipped moustaches, and to crown all, a smart black patch held in place by a silk elastic over his left eye. His nose was darker in colour than the rest of his face, and this too was appropriate to the general effect, by its downward droop leading one's eye to the striped tie and pepper-and-salt jacket, far from new but perfectly presentable, which he wore with a throw-away air of reserve and confidence. The most scrupulous researcher into the traditional image of the military man would have found not a single detail to add or reject.

Mrs. Burridge was small and thin, with expressive eyebrows. She might have been good-looking once, but her appearance and manner suggested that she had long ago given that up in favour of vivacity. She was immensely pleased to see everyone and had a great deal to say, enlivening every pause with a fresh question. Her darting glance made Miles uncomfortable; he was relieved when Robert Quattrell arrived, apologizing for his lateness, and he found himself placed at table between Quattrell and Colin. Mrs. Burridge fell at once, with sprightly cries, on the table decorations, and the *objets* were passed from hand to hand and examined, and Crosier patiently ex-

plained them to Mrs. Brockhurst. The arrangement, as he
had predicted, was soon spoiled, but it had served its purpose; if there had been a little constraint at first it had now
vanished.

Up to this point Colin had given Miles no sign of recognition, but as he unfolded his napkin he sociably turned
and smiled.

"I remember you now," he said, "it's been bothering
me. You came out to Headington once, didn't you, that
very cold summer?"

"I did. I don't think I'd have known you either, except
that I saw your mother some time ago, and she showed me
a snapshot."

"Really?" Colin's smile remained unchanged, but there
was a marked pause. At length he said, "When would that
be, I wonder? Recently?"

"About a week ago, before I left. She told me you were
out here somewhere. I was to look out for you."

"I see." He turned his back on Miles and helped himself from the dish being held at his elbow. When the soufflé
had passed to Miles and gone further up the table he ate
for a moment in silence and then said, "How was she?"

"She seemed well enough," said Miles, "if a bit de-
pressed. They both have a lot to do. I wonder how they
manage." It came to him with dismay how unprepared he
was for his secret mission. By now he ought to have worked
out some sort of plan, and he had thought of nothing. He
had supposed that when the moment came he would play it
by ear, but something in Colin's manner disconcerted him.
He was oddly self-possessed, more circumspect and grown-
up than he had expected.

"They needn't take on so much," said Colin, busy with
his food. "It's ridiculous, you know; that awful house, and
all those ravenous lodgers."

"Well, I imagine they have to do something. Most people do."

"Perhaps, but not that. My father's just crazy with energy, it's pathological. Do you know that one day when she was out he actually knocked a great hole in the wall and moved my mother's bedroom door to a different position? Why can't he retire like other people, and live quietly? There are lots of oldies here who manage on a pension." He filled his mouth and scraped the plate with his fork, as though disposing of the subject.

"I dare say it's easier here than in England. Things are expensive."

"Why stay in England, then? He's not obliged to. They could settle down somewhere warm and cheap, and stop fussing." He reached for a *croissant* and set about buttering it vigorously. "I'm sorry if I seem unsympathetic, but I'm just about sick of the subject. He wastes more money than he makes, and it's always the same. He shouldn't have taken on a thing like that; he's got no head for business."

There was a pause while the plates were changed, and Miles wondered whether he dared go a little further. Quattrell, on his other side, was in the midst of a lively argument with Crosier and Mrs. Burridge.

"How long are you going to stay out here?" he said at length. "I gathered from our host that you're interested in his scheme. Or are you just here for a holiday?"

"I *hope* I'm not just here for a holiday," said Colin. "If I can find something decent to do I'd rather stay. I'd rather do *any* job, almost, than go back to London, and Morley's being awfully helpful. He's a surprisingly sensitive and imaginative person. As much as an older person can, he understands the situation."

"I'm not sure I know what the situation is."

"Oh, well. You know my parents, but you can't have any conception what it's like at home. My father's impossible. I really hate him, you know. Funny, isn't it, how one can say that out loud nowadays? My mother was shocked to death the first time I said it, yet she knows jolly well it's true. It seems to her, well, unmentionable, like talking about constipation in the middle of lunch."

"You don't feel that way about your mother, though?" said Miles. "She's very different."

"No, not at all. I'm very fond of her. But that doesn't alter things, does it? She's completely under his thumb and always will be. She's stuck with him, poor dear, but I am *not*. I'd rather scrub floors or be a waiter than go back to the sort of life they think O.K. Luckily I'm fairly all right as far as money goes. I'm in the happy position of being able to pick and choose."

"I see. And what do you pick and choose, when it comes to the point? Or haven't you decided?"

"Well, not absolutely," said Colin, leaning back against Miles's shoulder while he helped himself to a dish piled with pieces of chicken in creamy sauce, strewn with almonds, strips of lemon and black olives. "All I want, really, is to be able to wake up in the morning and say to myself, What shall I do today? I don't mean just bumming around, I mean making my own decisions. I should like to feel I can change the whole course of my life if I want to, without reference to anybody. I've got plenty of time to do it in, you know. I'm only nineteen."

"And you think you'll be able to make your own decisions if you go in with Crosier's scheme? Supposing it doesn't work out like that? He may think differently."

"Then I should make a decision to take my money out again," said Colin, smiling. "It's as easy as that."

"And in that case you'd go home, and think again?"

"Not necessarily. There are plenty of good opportunities here, if one knows the runs. That's where Morley's so good; he's always made a fuss of the Moroccans. He doesn't trust them a yard, of course, but he knows some quite high-up people. They aren't the problem, as I see it; it's the others." He lowered his voice and brought his head casually closer. "What about our friend on your right, for instance? D'you know anything about him?"

"Nothing at all. I met him yesterday for the first time. Your friend Crosier knows him fairly well, I imagine."

"I don't think he does, you know. He's met him once or twice and is rather impressed. He's obviously a bit of a go-getter, and he talks big; but I've never heard of anything he's written and he's never had a film produced. It makes one wonder where he gets his money."

Miles glanced uneasily in Quattrell's direction; he appeared to be teasing Crosier, who was taking it amiably. Mrs. Burridge and Mrs. Brockhurst were both laughing.

"He spoke yesterday as if he hadn't any," said Miles quietly. "So perhaps he hasn't."

"Well, I don't know. He stays in a bed-and-breakfast hotel most of the time, it's true, but it can't be cheap; none of them are. And then he's just been to Paris and London, and he keeps that girl. She's rather attractive, by the way. Have you seen her? We ought to have asked her to lunch. I suppose Morley never thought of it."

Quattrell turned round abruptly to Miles, fixing him with a mock-questioning look from under heavy eyebrows. "I suppose it's too much to hope," he said, "that you're a catering expert?"

"Much too much," said Miles. "I'm a book-binder."

"I don't see where we're going to work you in, then. Perhaps as a riding instructor? The latest idea is to have ponies for riding on the sands. But of course Rex Burridge will have to take care of that. He looks the part perfectly."

"I can't be fitted in anywhere," said Miles, "because I'm only here for a fortnight. More's the pity." He looked into Quattrell's face with curiosity, surprised to find himself thinking that it would be very much easier to like this man than not. He didn't exactly inspire confidence, but he had atmosphere. Admitting this, Miles made a half-hearted effort to adjust his ideas. He had been prepared to dislike him extremely on account of Tavy.

The plates were changed once more and a delicious pudding made of spiced oranges and whipped cream was offered to everyone except Crosier, who had a slice of melon. Mrs. Burridge gave a little shriek of protest.

"Not again!" she cried, "I can't bear it." Failing to catch Crosier's eye she turned to Sam. "The self-control," she said, "it's really too much. All through this delicious meal he's had something different. What must his cook think? It's quite heart-breaking."

"I guess he's used to Morley's fads," said Sam. "He gives up everything in turn, but it doesn't last. Right now I believe he's in favour of protein and has something against carbohydrates. He worries about his weight, but a while back he was converted to a system which prescribed cream with everything."

Crosier was deep in talk with Mollie Brockhurst. Mrs. Burridge paused, fork in mid-air, and with an expression of mild astonishment considered his outline.

"But if he does that sort of thing," she returned to Sam, placing a blob of orange and cream in her mouth, "how can he expect to lose weight? A loss of a couple of stone would hardly make any difference."

"I guess he's not all that ambitious. He doesn't expect to lose weight any more, he just clings to the idea of maintaining the *status quo*."

"But the *status quo*," said Mrs. Burridge in a low voice, "in his case is hardly—or am I wrong?—a thing one would wish to maintain? I'm considering, of course, his health. There comes a point where it's no longer relevant to regard appearance."

"Well, if you know of any fancy diets," said Sam, "or can think of something he can give up without really noticing, he'll be your friend for life."

"No, really?" Mrs. Burridge gave a little laugh, meeting Sam's eye with a flash of understanding. Something in what he said had made an impression, for she looked back at Morley reflectively and for a while said nothing. Presently, however, taking advantage of a burst of laughter she said in a low tone, speaking almost from the side of her mouth, "What can you tell me about our *amigo* opposite?"

"Rob Quattrell?" Sam glanced across the table and judged that it was safe; Quattrell was explaining something to Mollie Brockhurst. "Not much, so far. He's a newspaper man of sorts, isn't he? Or was. And he's writing a novel that he hopes will get made into a film. Moroccan background and all that. I want to talk to him about it some time."

"Yes, yes, but as a person?" She screwed up her eyes in a manner suggesting shrewdness. "He's got personality, I grant you, and obviously gets on with people when he chooses. But why has he settled in this country? What does anyone know about him?"

"Why have any of us settled here?" said Sam. "The answer is, I guess, for very good reasons." He was becoming bored with the conversation and tried to catch Miles's eye.

"Well, of course." Mrs. Burridge brought him back at once with one of her little laughs. "We've all come here for excellent reasons—climate, servants, nice country, no income tax and so forth—but I've sometimes noticed—or am I wrong?—that we're apt to impute odd motives to other people. Unreasonable, isn't it? One ought to take people at their face value until one knows better. Personally," she dropped her voice again to its confidential level, "personally I find our friend not unattractive."

Mr. Burridge, on Sam's right, was making dignified conversation with Ozzie. He had, he said, as Ozzie probably knew, run a little place on the beach for a couple of summers. But things had been against them; it had not been a success.

"What sort of things?" Ozzie asked, opening his eyes wide and letting them dwell innocently on the eye-patch.

"Well, the wind, for one thing. You remember how it blew and blew last year? Six weeks at a stretch, if you don't mind. And then the season was over."

"Oh dear. How awful for you."

"And then there was trouble with the waiters. One of them stabbed the other in the second week, and it was never the same after that."

"I suppose not. Oh dear, poor Major Burridge! Whatever did you do?"

"I sorted it out, naturally, but it was a bit tedious. And just for the record, you know, I'm not a major."

"Good heavens," said Ozzie, starting back, "have I made a *faux pas*? I *thought* Morley said major, but he probably said colonel and I wasn't paying attention. How awful of me!"

"Not at all," said Burridge stiffly. "I've never been near the army, as a matter of fact."

Ozzie stared again and clasped his hands.

"Oh, too extraordinary! I never saw anyone look less civilian. I suppose one thinks of the war when one sees the eye-patch?"

"I know," said Burridge, touching it gently with his finger, as though he owed it much. "But I lost my eye several years ago, soon after I retired, you know, and we came out here."

"Don't tell me!" cried Ozzie, shaking his head and covering his eyes with both hands. Presently he peeped through his fingers. "Was it one of the waiters?"

"As a matter of fact, no. I got a stone in the eye from a scrofulous boy who was trying the door of my car. I saw him off, you know, and he ran up the hill. And just when I wasn't expecting it, unlocking the door, there was this shower of stones. It took me by surprise, and the worst of it was—well, you can imagine. And then I couldn't identify him."

Ozzie shuddered and passed the coffee sugar. "Don't tell me he wasn't caught?"

"Oh, they sent a boy to jail all right, but I'm pretty sure it was the wrong one. I went to the parade, naturally, but they all looked alike to me." He touched his moustache reflectively with the back of a finger. "Not that it makes much difference, in the long run. The one they jailed would be just as bad, and the one that did it's in jail by now, most probably. They're in and out all the time. Not a shred of discipline."

"Well, you must miss that. After the army, I mean. It must all seem so very different."

"I never had anything to do with the army," said Burridge, with a touch of asperity. "I told you that just now."

"Oh dear," said Ozzie, "whatever is the matter with me? Do you suppose Morley's put something in the drink? I'm not usually *quite* so stupid, and I did remember about your being retired, so I thought it must be the . . . What did you say you retired from?"

"I didn't say," said Burridge, looking at Ozzie rather sharply out of his right eye. "Insurance chiefly, if it interests you."

"Insurance? Oh, how fascinating," said Ozzie, and signalled desperately with his eyes to Colin across the table. I can't stand another minute of this, the signal said, and

Colin caught it and looked meaningly at Crosier, who nodded and pushed back his chair. Alawi opened the doors and they all moved at Mollie Brockhurst's pace into the drawing-room.

★   ★   ★

A certain amount of business, it now appeared, had been discussed during the meal, although Miles, Ozzie and Colin had been rather out of it. Crosier had made headway, if one could judge by the fact that he was addressing everyone except Mollie Brockhurst by their first names; Quattrell had become Rob, and Mr. and Mrs. Burridge Rex and Dora. All three seemed to be definitely in the scheme now, or at least gathering with marked interest on the edge of it. Rex Burridge had provisionally been offered the job of manager—depending on a good many things, of course; and had said in a steady voice, betraying no eagerness, that in principle he was perfectly willing to consider it. Nothing was definite, naturally, Crosier explained. He would have to see people first; might even have to go to Rabat and do a little wire-pulling; and Burridge said, "Fair enough" and "Not to worry," displaying the utmost good form in showing no curiosity about the salary.

Quattrell's contribution had been more prosaic. It was all very well, he said, to set up a camping, but a thing of that sort couldn't be expected to function in a vacuum. It had got to be filled, and kept full; and that meant setting aside a slice for the travel-agents. It was best to work through one and let him split it with the others; somebody tough, for preference, if you didn't want trouble.

"Who do you suggest?" said Crosier. "Monty Maxwell?"

"He's the obvious one. The most efficient, anyway,

· 8 5 ·

though that's not saying much. Bearing in mind that if you *don't* have him he can very easily see to it that there aren't any customers."

"He's rather a nice guy, anyway," said Sam dreamily.

"Precisely. He'll be perfectly tolerable to work with, and that's important. And with Maxi-Tours behind him he could be useful. I suggest we have a conference as soon as possible."

So it was settled that Quattrell and Crosier would go and see Maxwell next day, and in the meantime would draw up a list of questions to ask him. Nothing was said about the Burridges staying for this, so after one or two pauses and glances Dora Burridge said that alas, they must really go.

"But I thought you were going to the country tomorrow," Miles said to Quattrell, when they were all on their feet and Ozzie was hunting for Mrs. Brockhurst's walking-stick. It occurred to him that if Quattrell put off his trip, as he evidently intended, there might be a further occasion of seeing Tavy.

"I can put it off for a day or two," said Quattrell. "One day's as good as another; it's only thirty kilometres." He jingled the money in his pockets, apparently thinking. "If you're going anywhere near the house," he added, "would you mind telling Tavy? There's no telephone, and she'll be packing up to leave this afternoon."

"Certainly I will. I practically pass her street. What exactly shall I tell her?"

"Wait," said Quattrell, "I'll scribble a note. There's no point in your getting involved in an argument." He turned away to Crosier's writing-table.

What argument, Miles asked himself, could there possibly be? Either one went to the country or one didn't, and Tavy's long silences the day before suggested that, whatever else she mightn't be, she was at least docile.

He put the note in his pocket with a feeling of pleasure. The Burridges had already packed into their aged Volkswagen—"the V.W.," Burridge had called it, replying, when Ozzie politely asked if it were a good car, "I think one can say the best car, full stop"—and Ozzie was tenderly arranging Mollie Brockhurst in the big Mercedes.

"You came in a taxi, didn't you?" Ozzie said to Sam. "I'll give you a lift into town."

Sam and Miles got into the back of the car and covered their knees with a lemon-coloured mohair rug. The shelf at the back was full of attractive oddments—a pair of binoculars, a head-cushion, a scattering of paperback books, tins of imported cigarettes. It was apparent that Ozzie and Mrs. Brockhurst did themselves well. Gazing at the backs of their heads and vaguely speculating, Miles perceived something that had not been entirely clear to him until this moment: he didn't want Sam along when he went to see Tavy. He had been pleasing himself with a fantasy of sitting alone with her, sipping mint tea or coffee perhaps, leaning at ease among cushions in that cell-like room. There was no place at all for Sam in this quiet picture: just as, he realized with satisfaction, this was neither the time nor the place for remembering Lucy. The recollection of that littered bedroom, where he had watched her pack, filled him with astonishment—how long ago had it been? It was even an effort to remember the room in detail, and this, he decided, was surely for the simple reason that he didn't want to. What he wished to dwell on was a bare and whitewashed interior, narrow, conventual, admitting a minimum of light, where he would lean against hard cushions with a glass in his hand while Tavy, with the utmost candour, would tell him everything. What place could there possibly be for Sam in this austere scene? And as though his thoughts had passed through the silver-rinsed hair and reached a still-sensitive area inside her skull, setting up a faint vibration, Mrs. Brockhurst turned suddenly round and gazed at Sam.

"I wish I could hear some of your tapes some time? The ones you play to Ozzie."

"Sure, any time. Which ones d'you mean?"

"Music, wasn't it? Or drumming? Something immensely complicated, Ozzie said, that those strange men play when they do that extraordinary dancing."

"Say, I've got something better than that," said Sam, hunching forward to lean with his elbows on the back of the seat, his face almost touching her hair. "Why'n't you come up to my place now, and I'll play you some pieces I'm fitting together? I'm making a fantastic counterpoint of chanting and prayer rhythms." Sam was quite carried away by this suggestion, which promised, since Mollie seemed strangely pleased and Ozzie was amenable, to go far to redeem an otherwise wasted day. He had not recorded a thing all morning, not so much as a splendid quarrel on the next roof, or the *you-you-you-you* screaming of women at a wedding in his own street. Trapped for the whole of luncheon between the Burridges he had not, to tell the truth, enjoyed himself much. Now what was left of the afternoon would be seriously employed, for this Englishwoman, though weird, was not without intelligence, and Ozzie could always be relied on for inside gossip. Sam hardly noticed, at the square, when Miles shook hands with Mollie, making his excuses, and went off at his odd gait in the opposite direction.

Early that morning Zohra's uncle, who lived just beyond the outskirts of the town, almost in the country, had
sent his youngest son to the Rue de l'Ecurie with a present
of a kid. Though healthy and long in the leg it was childishly thin, but there would be time to fatten it before the
end of Ramadan and the gift had been received with appropriate pleasure. It was, in fact, a rather handsome
present, for the feast which marked the end of the fasting
was in no way comparable to the Aid el Kebir which came
later, when every family, even if it crippled them, would
buy a sheep at the very least and sometimes two, so that
their roof should run with blood like the rest at the hour of
slaughter. For the Aid last year, almost at the last minute,
the uncle had sent a brown sheep as large as any in their
neighbourhood, and Zohra's relief had been so great that
she had wept. Weeks before the feast the prices of sheep
and goats always rose steeply, and by the final day they
had reached such a level that even a mediocre animal was
out of the question. Zohra and her mother had stayed indoors all day to conceal their shame. And then, sudden and
magical as a happening in Holy Writ, a man with a sheep

on his shoulders had knocked at the door, and had set it down on the tiles and untied its legs, delivering the message and blessing of Hadj Abd-el-Aziz, which was the name of the uncle. He was a religious man of the old stamp, who in his younger days had made his pilgrimage, as the "Hadj" implied, and was sensitive to the standing and reputation of the least of his relations, even Zohra, who was well below the poverty line, had no son or other male relative and had been both widowed and divorced. It had been an evening of great excitement, in which Tavy shared. A message had been sent to one of the neighbouring butchers, since without a man in the house there was no one to do the ritual throat-slitting and flaying, and as time was short they had not tried to get the sheep up to the little walled and whitewashed space which was all that the house boasted by way of a roof. Instead they had tethered it to an iron ring which hung from the door without apparent purpose, unless it were this, and the sheep, which was a dusty cinnamon colour and had a heavy fleece, had stood there patiently, dropping its pellets of dung on the tiles and accepting as a matter of course the teasing of Tavy's baby and the occasional jovial buffets of visiting neighbours. Next morning, a fairly long time after the gun fired, the butcher had reached their street and done his work, cutting the animal's throat outside the door and roping it up by the hind legs to a ladder he had brought with him, wedged securely in an angle of the outside wall. The whole thing was done with skill and despatch, the skin taken off entire, like a heavy garment, leaving the creature naked as a pearl, the entrails dropped in the street and swept into a corner, liver and tripes received by Zohra in a basin, hoofs and horns wrenched off and thrown aside, the carcase decapitated and carried indoors, where it hung in a cool corner from a wedged cross-beam.

Tavy was the only one who had taken no part in the

ceremony. Although this was the third Feast of the Ram that she had been through, sharing in the general excitement, she was still not proof against hysteria if she actually saw the sacrifice, the head twisted upwards by the horns, the stumbling legs, the gush of blood and emptying of the bowels. She had learned to be fairly stoical about cocks and hens, since if one were not, life in that teeming quarter would be intolerable. They lived on most of the neighbouring roofs and sometimes on Zohra's own, and a throat-cutting was something one was liable to encounter in the street at any time, since even a child could do it. But the deaths of sheep and goats were harder to bear, occurring at such close quarters and leaving so strong an aftermath behind them. Sagging heaps of entrails would lie in the alley until night, when the scavengers arrived with cart and spades. And by early evening the knife-grinders' braziers would have crowds of children round them, and a succession of flayed heads, the eyes still dark and lustrous, would be held out over the flames on a thick poker, the iron thrust straight into the mouth between peeled lips. There was something devilish and frightening about these night scenes, and she avoided them as far as possible, though when the time for eating came she enjoyed it as much as anybody. Liver on the first day, hot, pungent and delicious, the tripes and offals on the second, swimming in a sea of oil, and on the third the tender meat itself, a loin or shoulder cooked in the great *tajine* on a mound of *cous-cous*, dripping with oil and spices, with saffron, almonds, raisins and fat olives.

The smaller feast to celebrate the end of the fast was nothing like so sumptuous as the Aid el Kebir, and much less expensive: most families made do with a *tajine* of fowls, with cakes fried in oil, a *pastilla* if there were still a woman in the family capable of cooking one, and, of course, *cous-cous*. The significant thing was the breaking of the fast, the being able to eat in the daytime instead of only between the hours of sunset and sunrise; the kind of food was not of great importance. But Zohra's uncle, piously observant of the meaning of the feast and performing the ritual charity for the poor of his family, liked to think of his sister and niece having a little meat to comfort them after their long privation. They were not the sort—nor could they afford to be—to sit up eating and drinking through the nights of Ramadan with visiting and music, like their more prosperous neighbours. So the kid, a thin one—Zohra and her mother being, after all, at the bottom of the Hadj's list—had arrived when there was still a fortnight left for fattening, and Zohra and her daughter had set out at once for the Socco, where on the outskirts of the market, on the pavement of the Rue San Francisco facing the Muslim cemetery, there were always a few Berber women with bundles of fodder, shrivelled-faced peasants of the poorer sort who had walked into town from the hills during the night, bent under a load of the only crop at their disposal, sweet grass and clover.

The kid meanwhile was tethered on the doorstep, where Joe, entirely absorbed and entranced by this new playmate, was offering it scraps of bean-pods salvaged from the meagre refuse of the day's *harira*. This comforting soup, which normallly they all ate in the early evening after the firing of the gun, had been made in the morning and set aside on a shelf in that curtained corner which Tavy, without much justification, thought of as the kitchen. It was the place where the *tajine* and a few pots and pans, the coffee-pot and the primus stove, were mostly to be found, if they were not in use on the main floor of the room or even on the roof; but there was nothing else to suggest a kitchen—no table, no chair, no cupboard of any sort. What there was, was on the floor, ranged neatly against the wall, and when you considered that there were five people in the house it was not much.

Tavy and Joe lived out of a suitcase; there was really nowhere else to keep anything. Where Zohra and her mother and daughter concealed their possessions was a mystery; it had taken Tavy a long time to realize that by European standards they possessed practically nothing. Khaimo, the mother, had the clothes she stood up in; the enveloping white *haik* which she wore out of doors hung, when she was not occupying it, on a nail. Zohra and Aminah each had their cotton gowns and an everyday *djellába*, and in a painted chest on the upper storey a new *djellába* each, a pair or two of high-heeled shoes and a *kaftan* for festive occasions. And that, apart from a Western-style rayon frock which Aminah wore in her emancipated moods, was all. Even in a house as small as theirs (and it was impossible to imagine anything much smaller) there was no problem of storage.

Tavy kept her suitcase on the upper storey, at the top of the ladder-stairway leading directly to the roof. The room itself—or stairhead, it was scarcely more—was too small to sleep in, but was useful for keeping the big galvanized vessel in which Zohra did the washing, together with a few spare pieces of matting and the various crocks and pots used for cooking over charcoal, which was done in the open. The suitcase was too big to take up and down the ladder single-handed, and Tavy used it as a wardrobe, stuffing her personal belongings into a knapsack whenever Quattrell decided to take her to his sea-house, or to Meknes or Fez, or to any of the other places, for change of air or because he could no longer work in his hotel bedroom, that he liked to visit at short notice for a week or fortnight. She was now packing Joe's odds and ends, with a change of clothing, in the bottom of a rush basket of the kind she had learned to speak of as a *koffah*. She was at the top of the ladder when the knocker sounded, and assuming it to be Quattrell she wondered, since the door was open, why on this occasion he had bothered to knock at all. He could surely see there was nobody there but Joe?

"Coming!" she called, beginning to descend the ladder, pulling the basket after her. Nobody appeared or replied, and when she drew back the curtain it was not Quattrell at all but one of the young men who had come with Morley Crosier the day before.

"Oh, hello," she said, the look of eagerness fading out of her face. "Rob's not here. He's not back yet."

"I know. I've brought you a note. I saw him at lunch."

She looked at him sharply at this and held out her hand. "Has something gone wrong, then? Come in if you want to. I'm in the middle of packing."

Miles stepped over Joe and came into the shadowy interior. It was exactly as he had imagined it, cool and clean and orderly, with only Tavy there. The cushions on the low divan were arranged for company and the curtain stirred a little in the doorway, causing a rhythmical variation of light. The only thing that was wrong was Tavy's silence.

"Oh *no!*" she said at last, pushing a lock of hair up from her face and reading the message again, as though it were possible to have misunderstood. "Oh *no*, not again!" —letting the hand with the letter in it drop despairingly. He wondered with embarrassment if she were going to cry. It appeared she was: her eyes were already brimming with furious tears. They stared at one another in silence, and then Tavy turned to the alcove and angrily sat down, her elbows propped on her knees, her face hidden. After a while she felt in the sleeve of her shirt for a handkerchief.

"Is there anything I can do?" Miles asked her, sitting cautiously down on the cushions beside her and hoping that Zohra and Aminah would not come home. Joe was happily occupied on the doorstep and the voices of children in the street had receded for the moment to a point where it could almost be said that they were quiet.

"Oh no, there isn't anything," said Tavy hopelessly, wiping the tears away with the back of her hand. "I'm sorry to make such a scene, but it's always the same. At least, quite often. I absolutely *hate* him at times." She spoke without constraint, as though Miles were someone of her own age whom she had known for a long time.

"Really? Why?" Miles was delighted by this sudden atmosphere of candour. "Aren't you happy, then?"

"Oh, I don't know. Most of the time, I suppose. But he can be so *abominable* . . ." She stared past Miles's attentive face, remembering old affronts. "I'm told to be ready at a certain time, I pack up and get Joe's things and make all the arrangements, and at the last minute it doesn't happen because he's decided to go out to dinner or sleep at the hotel or something. He's just bone selfish."

"I think he and Morley Crosier are meeting some travel-agent tomorrow morning."

Tavy shrugged her shoulders. "It doesn't matter what it is, he doesn't give a God-damn. You haven't got a car, have you?" she added irrelevantly. "At least I don't have to take Joe down to Panya's if we're not going."

"I haven't got a car, no. Do you need one?"

"Not really, now. When we go to the cottage Rob can't work with Joe around, so I take him down to Panya's —Madame Lemaire's, that is—and she and her housekeeper look after him."

"Why don't you leave him here, with your Arab friends? They all seemed so nice."

"They are. Zohra, anyway. She'd look after him all right on her own, but her mother's hopeless. She gives him sweets and greasy things to eat, and carries him off to show to the other old women, and takes him to the *hammam* with her, and things like that. He's always out of sorts when I get home."

Joe's voice rose suddenly in conversation on the other side of the curtain, carrying on some private discussion with the goat. Tavy listened for a moment, making sure from the murmuring tone that all was well. The house felt very peaceful.

"Where are all the others?" said Miles at length, hoping that they were still at a great distance. He looked curiously about him. "I can't make out at all where you all sleep. Or are there some more rooms?"

"There's a little place upstairs, but it's too small for anything. Zohra and Aminah and I sleep down here, and Joe has a mat and cushions on the floor, or comes in with me. There's a sort of overflow across the way, in the street you turn out of, next to the *bacál*. Khaimo or Aminah sleep there quite often. It's not as big as this, just a staircase leading up to a room." Miles took this in with some difficulty.

"And behind the curtain?"

"It's all the same. Just pots and pans and the water-pail. The curtain's for tidiness."

"How did you come to live here, in the first place?"

"In the ordinary way, I suppose," said Tavy, looking surprised. "I've been here since before Joe was born. Rob's away a lot, and we have to live somewhere. Some people mightn't like it but I do—quite; and it's frightfully cheap. Rob knows I'm perfectly safe, and it's not uncomfortable. We can't be together all the time, so I might as well be with Zohra."

"I see," said Miles; but he didn't. It seemed to him extraordinary that if Quattrell were living with this girl, he should do so in this eccentrically half-and-half manner. He could think of a dozen questions to ask, but all of them

seemed too personal and inquisitive. "You speak Arabic, do
you?" he said at length, retreating from the difficulty, "or
do you talk to Zohra in Spanish?"

"I know some odds and ends of Arabic, but I don't try
much. What's the use? I pick up the odd word here and
there, that's all. Zohra's Spanish isn't much better than
mine, so we just about manage. Aminah's French is passa-
ble—she's been to school. But then I've forgotten mine, so
that's not much use. And old Khaimo's so stupid, I just
point and push."

"What an extraordinary life," said Miles, his eyes on
her face. The desire to know more about her was over-
powering. Where had she come from, in the first place?
Her accent, to which he had listened deliberately, told him
nothing; one of those classless voices, with barely perceptible eccentricities of its own; in some of her tones he detected an echo of Quattrell.

"I dare say everyone's life is, if you knew it," said
Tavy, with the flicker of a smile. "Here, especially. What
about yours, for instance? What are you doing here?" Her
eyes dwelt on him curiously for the first time. She no longer
felt angry and disappointed, but strangely at ease. She
could not remember when she had talked with such famili-
arity to anyone.

"Oh, I'm just here for a holiday. I go back in a fortnight."

"I expect you'll stay longer than that. I came out for a
holiday—when was it, three years ago? And here I still am;
isn't it fantastic? I tell you what, I'll look in the cards for
you some time. Would you like that? I've got a tarot pack
and an ordinary one; you can have whichever."

"First one and then the other, perhaps?" said Miles,
smiling, delighted with this method of spending the next
hour. He had been given the tarot treatment before, Lucy
being an addict of fortune-telling, and knew how a session

of prediction could lead to confidences.

"It's too late today. I wonder why Zohra's not back? It must be nearly time for *harira*. And I must go down to Panya's before she closes, so she won't be expecting Joe. Did you say you had a car or not? I can't remember."

"No, but we can take a taxi, surely? Or would telephoning do?" He was reluctant to leave the intimacy of this peaceful place, but even as he spoke there were voices beyond the curtain and a sound of kissing, so that it was evident that Zohra and her daughter had come home. Zohra came in at once with Joe in her arms while Aminah stayed to strew clover for the tethered kid. In Zohra's arms, with his dark head pressed against the hood of her *djellába*, Joe more than ever looked mysteriously Moroccan.

"We can walk, it isn't far," said Tavy. She kissed Joe and followed Miles into the street.

★   ★   ★

There were not many people about; most of the *bacáls* were shut and the smaller children clustered together on doorsteps, waiting for the first gun. There was a certain amount of coming and going at the pump, where a man was gutting fish on the wet stones and some bigger girls were chattering among their pails. As always, it sounded as though a peculiarly bitter quarrel were in progress, but this was not so: they enjoyed the sound of their voices and shouted at one another at close quarters. Tavy skirted the splashing water and turned into a narrow passage between the houses.

"We'll go the short way," she said, "but this loop's because I want to show you something." The passage ended in steps with an iron handrail, and below this, to the right, another obscure channel. The walls themselves, flaking with dirty whitewash, had been scrawled all over the lower part by children. In one place there was a little hollow between the stones, where someone had placed a crust and a lighted candle. "Look," said Tavy, pausing, "they believe there's a holy man buried somewhere in the wall. My uncle used to say it was part of the ramparts."

Miles looked at the candle burning in the hollow, and at the fragment of bread, and found himself touched by some inexplicable influence, as though the things had power. Absurd, of course, but there was something primitive and arresting in their simplicity. The hole in the wall had some of the authority of a shrine.

"Do children put these things here?"

"I don't think so. It's the old women. Khaimo comes down with a candle-end now and then. I think it protects her from something." She stood for a moment, staring at the flame. "But that isn't what I wanted to show you." They moved on. "Here it is," said Tavy, "this was my uncle's house. This was where I came to stay, three years ago. Nobody lives here now."

They had come to the end of the gully, still blank except for this peeling and battered door. It had been painted green at some time, but the paint had cracked and flaked and the colour faded. It was armoured all over with iron studs and there was a smaller, cut-out door within the larger one, with its own lock. The knocker was a ring of iron, formidably heavy, suggesting echoes and ramifications within.

"What an ominous-looking door," said Miles. "Who does it belong to now? What happened to your uncle?" He lifted the ring of the knocker, feeling its weight.

"Oh, he died. He was my great-uncle actually. I hardly knew him; he wasn't a real relation. It was my great-aunt I came out to stay with; she was his sister-in-law. Not that I expect you to be able to unravel all that." She gave him a tentative smile, as though trying to judge how much he might care to know. "I wish I could show you inside, but it's all locked up. You don't want to buy a house, do you, while you're out here? My aunt wants to sell it."

They were retracing their steps down the passage when the gun went off. Other detonations followed as they passed into a tunnel with a beamed ceiling, where the houses on either side met overhead. Here the doors of the houses were mostly ajar, but nothing could be seen; always a curtain had been hung for privacy, and only the smells of bread and soup, or an occasional crock of charcoal flickering on a doorstep, were evidence that the family was within. There was a concentrated hush at this time, the hour of breaking the day's fast, which was quite unlike the quiet of any other time of day. In effect they had the Medina to themselves.

★　　★　　★

Now that she had shown Miles the green door Tavy became silent. She was absorbed in the story she would have preferred to tell him, turning it this way and that in an attempt to arrange the parts coherently and at the same time to appear in it to advantage. This was not altogether easy. It was not a pretty story, and she was not at all sure how far it would be safe to tell it. Yet she felt very much at ease with Miles, which in itself was strange, for she had spent the last three years more or less in hiding, and in all that time had never been alone with any man except, inevitably, Quattrell. This seclusion was not the result of deliberate policy on his part; it had just happened. In the beginning they had gone to the south for several months, keeping out of everyone's way, and so much had happened since that her recollection of their wanderings had become hazy. She could remember the insufferable heat, the flies, the unspeakable hotels, and those periods of relief when they retreated to the mountains and found even humbler beds in *fonduks* and villages, where at least the water was drinkable and there was cool air. Quattrell was chary of the mountains because the car was old; he was afraid of being caught with engine trouble in inaccessible places, where within an hour every inhabitant, including the police, would be aware of his predicament. So they moved about in random fashion, keeping to the good roads, which took them over stretches of stony desert glittering like metal, through gorges of rose-red rock and dried-up rivers, and sometimes even out to the Atlantic coast, where there were always reviving breezes and fewer flies. And then, as the weeks passed and Tavy had her sixteenth birthday, it had begun to feel safe, and they worked their way back to the north again, to the point where they had started. Their reappearance caused little or no remark. Tavy was first relieved and then astonished. It was at this point that she began to realize how completely she had burned her boats by going off with Quattrell.

How could this story, if she told it, be presented so that she appeared in an admirable light? She disliked the notion that Miles might disapprove. The only way, she supposed, was to make it more romantic than it had actually been; though perhaps she could leave the facts to speak for themselves, since she must in the beginning have been madly in love with Rob. And yet, when she looked back on that early time, it was clear that she had been nothing of the sort. She had even faintly disliked him in a childish way, had been annoyed that his voice and presence, his height and laugh and battered countenance were so impossible to ignore. She had been acutely aware of him from the beginning, that was all. And afterwards, when he had done that terrifying and unimaginable thing to her, there had been nothing romantic about their flight together. She had been stunned and frightened, and at the

same time, in a way she still found it difficult to understand, triumphant. No one had ever taken much notice of
her before, and there is a certain potent flattery in being
abducted.

After that, for a while, it had been rather splendid, a
sort of prolonged holiday, when for the first time she had
felt grown-up and important, had bought herself clothes
from the French shops in Fez and disguised herself with
sun-glasses. Quattrell was a conspicuous figure wherever
they went and she found it exciting to be seen with him. He
was, besides, a far from disagreeable companion; gloomy-
tempered at first, even resentful, as if running away with
her had been the last thing he had meant to do and he
regretted it; but this had worn off quickly enough in the
pleasure of love-making, which, since it was totally new to
Tavy and she had a charming body, was enough to make
him delightedly in love with her. Not seriously, of course,
or with much tenderness, but certainly up to a point, and
the role of lover showed him at his best.

This halcyon period lasted for several months, during
which Tavy learned a lot, both about herself and Quattrell.
She discovered that the fact that he frightened her was part
of his attraction, and that when they were not in bed together he either ignored her completely, or was teasingly
indulgent. She was often at a loss how to meet his incalculable moods, and frequently wept and sulked at the
wrong moment. But on the whole the months of wandering
had been a success; the difficult time had come afterwards,
when he left her in Zohra's house and she knew that she
was pregnant.

This was the point, she thought, as she and Miles
turned into a passage so narrow that they could no longer
walk abreast, this was the point at which the story would
be difficult to manipulate. She wished, without quite knowing why, to justify herself; to appear independent and up-to-

date in deciding to stay where she was and have Quattrell's
child; although in fact she had been extremely frightened,
incapable of making a decision of any kind. "It's tremendously *chic* today to have bastard offspring," Quattrell had
teased her, when Zohra's brews had produced not the least
effect. But she had not felt *chic;* she had felt trapped and
helpless; and since Quattrell for one reason or another had
been away a good deal, the only person who had comforted
her was Zohra. The idea that she might at this stage have
communicated with her aunt, or even with her so-called
father, had never once crossed her mind; they belonged to
the indifferent world that she had forsaken. Later, when
Joe was three months old, she had made herself write a
letter to Phoebe Townsend—really no more her great-aunt
than her father was her father—but chiefly in order to
emphasise the point that no rescue, no scheme or salvage of
any sort was necessary. She was still only seventeen and
not particularly sensible. Her whole life up to this point
had been a long and meaningless exercise in not belonging;
not to the real parents whom she had never known, nor to
the adoptive father who had so soon lost interest in her, nor
even to Miss Townsend, who had sent for her to Morocco
out of kindness, and found her a very difficult creature to
be kind to. She had belonged to none of these, and now (so
she privately argued), now at least she had this baby, and
belonged to Quattrell. It was not perfect, certainly, but it
was the best she had known. It could be made to seem
quite desirable as a situation.

"You're very silent," said Miles, pausing at the top of a
flight of steps and laying his hand on the parapet. They had
come to the end of the narrow passage and were looking
down on the port with its complex of walls, sheds, railway
lines and buildings. The light was fading rapidly, but the
walls still reflected a rosy glow.

"I was thinking of what you said," Tavy answered,

"when you asked me how I came to be living with Zohra. It started a train of thought, and I was following it."

"Was I very inquisitive? You've probably forgotten by now how strange it seems. I couldn't help wanting to know."

She gave him a doubtful look, half serious, half smiling. "I'll tell you the whole story, perhaps; or some of it. But not now. Now I'd better tell you about Panya, as we're going to see her. She's tremendously old, but really she's my best friend." She gave the words "best friend" an unconscious emphasis, as though she were still a schoolgirl and a best friend a person whose status, when so described, would be understood immediately. Miles recognized the emphasis and was touched by it. It made her seem even younger than she was; as if, in spite of Quattrell and the child, her crossing of the grown-up frontier were incomplete. Some of her movements, too, had a childish awkwardness: she was thrusting her arms into the sleeves of her jacket as she spoke and groping for the top buttons. The air, now the sun was gone, was becoming cold. He felt a sudden tenderness.

★　★　★

They went down the steps and set off on the endless pavement of the waterfront. Here there were people moving about as usual and a certain amount of traffic; the cafés had a few early customers and there was a crowd of country women—huge hats, gaiters and bunched-up clothing making each one indistinguishable from the rest—waiting at the bus-stop. They were now across the boundary and into the European town, and the solemn atmosphere of the hour had wholly evaporated. Bars, restaurants and souvenir shops were open, young men in sports shirts and tight trousers lounged confidently in doorways, calling or whistling at passers-by to attract custom. "I hate this part of the town," said Tavy, and indeed it was an area which seemed to have missed every natural and unnatural opportunity, cut off from the sea by railway line and station and scarcely at all improved by municipal palm-trees rattling metallically in the wind and municipal flower-beds derelict and empty. She turned up a steep side-street and soon they were under the neon lights of the boulevard, threading their way through the drift of the evening *paseo*.

"Panya was marvellous to me when Joe was born," she said, taking up the thread when they had left the boulevard and crowded pavements behind. "She's Russian; her real name's Proskovy, but she likes to be called Panya, it's less formal. She used to be a doctor here, but she gave it up years ago. She looked after Zohra in the hospital when Aminah was born; that's how she knew who to go to. I always think she saved my life, but she says she only saved Joe's." She laid a guiding hand on Miles's arm as they turned the next corner, and here, as they passed the open door of a *pâtisserie*, a woman came out with great suddenness and all but fell on him.

"*Pardon—je m'excuse,*" she said breathlessly, clutching her cardboard cake-box and then adding, "Oh, good heavens, it's you! How perfectly extraordinary!" Miles, regaining his balance, recognized Mrs. Burridge.

"I do hope I haven't hurt you?" she cried, looking rapidly from Miles to Tavy and back again. "I'm always in such a rush—such a bad habit!" She laughed and looked more attentively at Tavy. "But perhaps you can tell me the result of this afternoon's meeting? So thrilling, all of it! I haven't met Mrs. Quattrell before, but of course"—glancing at Miles and back again to Tavy—"I know who you are, and I'm longing to know what you think of the scheme, and all about it."

"I know very little about it," said Tavy in an indifferent voice, making herself as tall as possible. "You're Mrs. Burridge, no? I'm Octavia Williams. I've only just heard of the scheme and I don't know about any meeting."

"Oh dear! How stupid of me!" Dora Burridge was all apology, but there was something about her expression that suggested pleasure. Her eyes quite markedly lit up at Tavy's name; she regarded her with interest.

"I didn't realize you didn't know one another," said Miles, "I'm so sorry." But Mrs. Burridge continued to pay him no attention.

"Well, my dear, I hope we shall be seeing a lot of you from now on. I've heard all about you from . . . well now, who could it have been? He said such nice things about you, I wish I could remember." She smiled at Tavy encouragingly, her head on one side. "I dare say it was that nice Mr. Quattrell after all. He was so amusing at luncheon! I do so hope the scheme comes to something! Then we shall all be working happily together in the summer."

"Well . . ." said Tavy, shifting her feet and glancing unhappily at Miles.

"Are you just hurrying off somewhere, you two young people?" asked Mrs. Burridge, struck by an idea. "It's rather the hour for a martini, isn't it? Or rather," she corrected herself, remembering the expense, "a cup of coffee at Pilo's, or a glass of tea? We could have such a nice talk, and I could ask your advice, you know, about so many things."

But Tavy had slipped her arm through Miles's. Sweet of you," she said, "but we're late for something already and in a hurry. Let's do it another day," and smiled her polite smile and drew him away with her.

"I gather you're not very keen on Mrs. B.," said Miles, when they were out of earshot.

"I've never met her before, but I'd say she's the type of person I hate on sight."

"Why, I wonder? She was perfectly agreeable at lunch."

"Oh yes, I dare say. Trying to ferret things out of you, I shouldn't wonder. That's the feeling she gives me."

And sure enough, when they reached the corner of the street and looked briefly back, there was Mrs. Burridge standing exactly where they had left her, clasping her box of cakes with a gloved hand, staring thoughtfully after them.

★ 6 ★

A⊤ ⊤ʜᴇ ʙᴀᴄᴋ of a shop in the Rue Poincaré, screened by
a rack of Moroccan-style evening jackets and other dubious
garments, Madame Lemaire was engaged in composing a
difficult letter. It would have been better, she reflected
calmly, to close the shop earlier than usual and retire upstairs, where she could concentrate in the comfort of her
own sitting-room, but she had not had a customer all day
and acknowledged a superstitious feeling against doing
anything so precipitate. If she closed the shop now, at a
quarter to six, a rich American would arrive almost immediately, wanting expensive costume jewellery, or a *kaftan*
for his wife, or one of those near-antique objects displayed
in the window, which it would be such a pleasure to sell
him. She was not wholly dependent on the shop for her
living; it could be considered more in the light of a congenial occupation, something to provide a little extra and
occupy the long leisures of her widowhood; but she took it
seriously for all that, and only wished she could enlarge her
stock as fast as her *clientèle*. People would buy anything
nowadays, but it offended her taste to offer them absolute
rubbish. The chief trouble was that practically everything

genuine had disappeared. Only five years ago, on a leisurely tour to the south in her old-fashioned Peugeot, she
could buy silver earrings and fibulas and bracelets, rough in
workmanship and undoubtedly authentic, some of them
fairly new and others, perhaps, as much as fifty years old,
which in the Moroccan market counted as antiquity. And
there would be other things, too, of a trivial and endearing
charm—looking-glasses from the walls of vanished harems,
or painted marriage-chests with handsome locks, or pieces
of that fine geometrical embroidery with which young girls
once calmed their thoughts in the months before marriage.
But now all that had long ago disappeared, and rubbish
and reproductions flooded the bazaars. She did the best she
could, employing a Spanish jeweller to gild the odd pieces
of debased silver that one could still find, and a Spanish
seamstress to make up brocades and silks into house-coats
and evening jackets of a Moroccan flavour; but it was not a
stock that she could genuinely respect, and she sighed for
the lost world that had once existed, when she had first
come to live in this country with her husband in the days of
the French Protectorate.

She lifted her eyes from the desk whenever a shadow
paused for a moment at the window, and then, when the
shadow passed, returned to her letter. She must, she told
herself, rearrange the whole of the window tomorrow
morning. It had not drawn a single customer today. It
lacked interest. But this evening she must keep her mind on
the task before her; she must try and give sound advice to
Constance Quattrell.

"I ran into that extraordinary husband of mine in Paris
recently," Constance had written from New York, "and
gathered that he was now writing and living in Morocco.
Isn't that just too strange? From what he told me I think he
must often be quite near you. We caught sight of each other
in the Ritz bar and talked for only a short while unfortu-

nately, as we were both with other people. I got the impression he was going through a thin time, and *also* the feeling that he hoped I'd suggest a reunion—this would be the third! I let him have some money to go to London, as he wanted to see his agent, and I thought, well, something might come of this, so maybe it's the moment to help. But I didn't give him the flicker of an excuse for thinking I can do more. My mind's made up, Panya. I need your advice. I shall really go ahead with the divorce this time, and I don't intend to be talked out of it. I've held my hand these last two years because I didn't really know where he was or what was going on, but seeing him in Paris brought me to my senses. I'm going to London on the eighth, will you write to me there? The flat's shut up, I'll be staying at the Connaught. The thing I want to know is this—what is Rob's position financially, and what are his prospects, if any? I don't want to kick him if he's down—at least, not all that hard. If he's really up against it, I'd be willing to make a small settlement. On the other hand, if he's doing reasonably well I shall let it alone. He's done pretty well out of me in the past, I just don't want to end it on a mean note. Can you, with all your contacts, find out about this? Why does he have to stay in Morocco anyway? Is there really a film project brewing, or is there some other reason? He has to keep clear of Spain, I know, but that's an old story. The thing I most want to know about is the financial position. And you're such an angel of goodness, you'll forgive me asking."

Panya re-read the letter for perhaps the fifth time, frowning slightly. It would be impossible, she told herself, to answer Constance's query without mentioning Tavy, since Tavy was her only link with this man Quattrell, indeed her only source of knowledge. Or, if she found it possible, it would be dishonest, and therefore, from Constance's point of view, unhelpful. It was important that

Constance should know about Tavy and the child, just as it
was important that Tavy's future should be taken into account. If Robert Quattrell were free he might conceivably
marry her, and although that might not be all happiness it
was a thousand times to be preferred to her present situation. Panya was too old to be able to believe that an incon-
grous union of this sort could be successful. Quattrell must
be forty-five at least, and Tavy, when she had first gone off
with him, was not quite sixteen. But she had shown a surprising resolution in staying where she was after the child
was born; so strong a resistance, in fact, to Panya's reasonable pleadings that she sometimes wondered if Tavy secretly doubted the possibility of rescue. She was an
adopted child, it had emerged; she had never known who
were her real parents. And the childless Mrs. Williams for
whose sake she had been adopted had disappeared when
Tavy was about fourteen, supposedly with a man, and
Tavy had never been told what had become of her. Panya
had only the vaguest ideas about Eric Williams, Tavy's
adoptive father; she had the impression that they took a
less than conventional interest in one another. He lived in
one of the eastern counties of England and had some kind
of business; that was all she knew, for Tavy rarely spoke of
him. This curious indifference was evidently mutual, for he
seemed to have set no investigation on foot when Tavy
disappeared; had made no enquiry through the consul, had
not even written a letter. The search for Tavy—and there
had been a search of a sort, after a little while—had been
made entirely by his aunt, Miss Phoebe Townsend, who
had been keeping house for her brother-in-law, in the very
house from which Tavy had run away. She did not begin
the search immediately because the child's disappearance,
on that day of all disastrous days, at first seemed by com-
parison unimportant. Lytton, her brother-in-law, had collapsed with a coronary, and in the anguish of getting him

first to hospital and then on a plane for England, the naughty non-appearance of Tavy (for this was what it seemed) was something that other people must take care of. The other people, and one especially, had done their part. A few days after Lytton's death in London Miss Townsend had had a letter saying that Tavy had not returned on the day of departure; had not returned at all; and that by a curious coincidence Robert Quattrell was not to be found either, and what were they to do? The Moroccan police had been informed, and were totally uninterested. If the man had taken the girl that was quite normal, no? They took a cynical view of the *mœurs* and morals of foreigners. Nor had the British Consulate been particularly encouraging. By the time that Miss Townsend communicated with them Tavy was already sixteen and in any case had vanished without trace; it was no part of their function, the appropriate department said, to make an officious search for missing persons. At that time Tavy and Quattrell were far away to the south, wandering about in the pre-Sahara, seeking the shade of palm-trees or Kasbah walls by day, clasping each other against the desert cold at night in dark and comfortless rooms where cockroaches rustled.

In the end it was Panya herself who made Tavy write home, or at least to Miss Phoebe Townsend in her Gloucestershire village. She refused point-blank to write to her so-called father, but now that the baby was born and she had gone through so much, Panya felt it right to insist on some family *rapprochement*. She had seen Quattrell once or twice by then, and had found him genial but not, so her instinct told her, reassuring. Tavy must have an escape route in case of accidents, and accordingly a letter was sent to this lady whom, for want of a better term, she referred to as her aunt. Panya saw the letter before it was posted and found it far from satisfactory, even though in some obscure and unpractical area of her mind it increased her respect

for Tavy. The letter made no appeal; it distinctly repudi-
ated the idea that she might need rescuing. She was sorry,
she said, for the worry she must have caused. She had no
idea that Uncle Lytton would be taken ill that evening, or
she would never have gone. She had never planned or expected to go away with Mr. Quattrell (she called him that
throughout), but now that she had, assured her aunt that
she was perfectly happy, and had a dear little baby, a boy,
whom she hoped to be able to show to her one day. She
gave no hint of the circumstances of her seduction, still less
of the nightmare of her lying-in. She expected to be married before long, she said, but would not be returning to
England for some time. She concluded by giving as her
address a post-office box number.

In the course of a week or so Miss Townsend replied,
and this letter, too, Panya saw, and on the whole approved.
It did not recriminate; it scarcely grieved; it was brief, ad-
mirably impersonal and to the point. Evidently this Miss
Townsend had been through some gruelling experiences in
the last few months, and was too stunned by Lytton's death
and the loss of her home to be able to work up much feeling of outrage over Tavy's defection. She wished with all
her heart, she said, that it had never happened, but now
that it had, she wanted Tavy to know that as long as her
health lasted (she was over sixty) there would always be a
home in her cottage for Tavy and the baby. She was sorry
to say that Tavy's father was still angry; she did not recom-
mend an appeal to that quarter, even if it became necessary. She would prefer Tavy to get in touch with herself,
and she would see what could be done.

Reading her letter, Panya conceived a certain liking
for Miss Townsend. Her means were evidently small, and
there was nothing to suggest that she had been able to feel
particularly fond of Tavy. Nevertheless she had made her
.offer, and her tone made it clear that she could be relied

upon. Panya made Tavy write again, thanking her aunt, and promising that she would always tell her if she were in any difficulty. Since then there had been one further exchange of letters, polite and uncommunicative on both sides, and then no more. Tavy had flung herself with anxious passion into her new life, and received no further news of the weather in Gloucestershire.

Panya roused herself from her reverie and dipped her pen in the ink. It was one of those strange chances of life, which she reviewed with less and less surprise as she grew older, that the American woman whom she had met in Paris and had assumed to be a *divorcée* or perhaps a widow, should prove to be the wife of the man with whom Tavy was in hiding. The connection was not apparent for a considerable time, for Constance had reverted to the name of her first husband, long since mislaid, and it was only six months ago, during one of Panya's visits to her French relations, that she had discovered that there was a second unsatisfactory husband to be accounted for, and that his name was Quattrell. And now there was this letter to be answered, and advice given. She frowned with concentration and wrote the date with care at the top of the paper.

"My dear friend," she wrote, and paused, her mind's eye dwelling attentively on the image of Constance; so confident, so dashingly dressed, so attractive in a plain style, her features only slightly coarsened by a too long taking for granted of the necessity of alcohol. There she was, as clearly present to Panya as if she stood in the shop, bringing her unmistakable atmosphere into the narrow space between the garments and the writing-desk, smiling her dazzling smile and waiting for an answer. And Panya was still not sure what she ought to tell her.

★   ★   ★

"You have asked me," she wrote swiftly, determined to hesitate no longer, "for some advice which I find it not easy to give. I have seen this husband of yours sometimes during the last two years, but I am not able to say anything about his financial position. What I *can* tell you (and I think, *ma chère*, that you should know) is that he has been living during this time with a young English girl, and they have a child together. I was summoned to assist in the emergency when the baby was born—this is how I know her. Whether he will marry her if you divorce I cannot judge. *C'est un homme peu scrupuleux, n'est ce pas?* But if he does, it will be better for the girl, because she seems to have no connections and I am afraid for her. It will be easy for you to have evidence if you wish it. He keeps her with a Berber family while he lives and works elsewhere, but he has also a small house in the next province, and they are often there together. Also they have done trips by car many times. She has told me this—there would be no difficulty of proof. From time to time I have the child while they are away together; my *bonne-à-tout-faire* looks after him. I am even expecting her today for this reason, and will try to discover what is the money situation. But if I do not succeed, dear friend, what then? I think this girl knows little of his affairs."

A shadow paused at the window and Panya looked up. It was time to switch on the lights; she was islanded in the circle of her desk-lamp, the rest of the shop being dark. Two people were peering in by the orange glare of the street-lighting, and she saw from the silhouette that one of them was Tavy. She was arm-in-arm with a man who was definitely not Quattrell; much less tall, not quite so tall in fact as Tavy herself, neat and compact in build, a youthful outline. Panya switched on the lights and they opened the door and came in among the brocades and lamps and jewellery where she could see them clearly. She advanced smiling with outstretched hands, startled by a thought which had so far not entered into her calculations. Who was this sober-looking young man with the nice face, whose arm Tavy was so surprisingly holding? She had never before seen her with any man but Quattrell: was it possible that something new was afoot, of which she had been told nothing?

"My darling child!" She kissed Tavy resoundingly on both cheeks and extended a hand to the stranger. "I thought it was Joe you were bringing to me, and you arrive with a young man?"

"I know," said Tavy, starting to unbutton her jacket, "we're not going, at least not today. So Joe's at home, and this is Miles. I've forgotten his other name."

"Asshe," said Miles, taking Panya's smooth plump hand and liking the feel of it. There was something extraordinarily real about her appearance which immediately appealed to him: it was a face and figure without artifice, and in the total absence of beauty still wholly charming. Panya was, and had been for many years, entirely shapeless, clothed from the neck down in amorphous black. Her grey hair was combed strenuously away from her face and its ends skewered into a little black chenille net about the size of a tea-cake. She wore a plain pearl in the lobe of each ear and a string of pearls round her neck, while among the indistinguishable folds of dress, blouse or cardigan a fine gold chain or two occasionally appeared, an essential part of her effect but apparently purposeless. Nothing could have been dowdier, unless it were the black lace-up shoes which she wore on every indoor and outdoor occasion, but in spite of this her appearance had a positive distinction. She must, Miles guessed, have been nearer seventy than sixty; the contours of her face were slack and at the corners of her upper lip there was a hint of a moustache. But the eyes were not quenched, they were alive with intelligence,

and the generous way in which she showed her large, irregular, excellent teeth when she smiled suggested a readi-
ness for all human contacts and a desire to meet them
benevolently whenever possible.

"Miles brought me the bad news," said Tavy, seeing
from their faces that they liked the look of one another and
feeling relieved on this account, since Panya's opinion was
important, "so I thought I'd better come and tell you, and
Miles walked down with me." Her eyes wandered with interest round the shop, looking to see what was new. The
elderly-seeming brocades had no appeal, but there was a
tray of amber necklaces and oddments of jewellery. She
picked out a small gold object and examined it.

"So you are not going away after all, then," said Panya,
"is that it?"

"Tomorrow perhaps. Maybe the day after. He didn't
say when."

"I see. So you will let me know." There was a feeling of
something unspoken in the air between them and Panya
noted with disappointment that the young man showed no
sign of going away. He had turned to a little mahogany
bookcase on a side-table and with a careful finger was
drawing out one of the books. Scores of accounts of Morocco, travellers' tales, partial or inaccurate histories, de-
scriptions of manners and customs of the Moors, had been
published since the latter half of the eighteenth century,
and Panya's only intellectual amusement was to preserve
and add to her husband's old collection. The best books,
the permanent collection, were upstairs, but duplicates and
related oddments, mostly French, had proved to be a
profitable sideline once they were repaired or bound,
and made to look desirable. Many a resident or visiting
Morocco-fancier had carried away from Panya's at a steep
price some modest item originally bought in Paris for next
to nothing.

"I haven't seen one of these in gold before," said Tavy, holding the fibula against her shirt and stooping to look at herself in a clouded mirror.

"Nor I. They are always in that bad silver, but I have them gilded. They are quite pretty as brooches."

Tavy held it against her hair, then on the breast of her shirt again, and returned it without comment to the tray. It did not occur to her to ask the price; such things were not for her. Panya noted the absence of struggle and drew conclusions from it.

"Where do you have these bound?" Miles asked from the bookcase, holding up a small volume. "I see they're all done by hand."

"There is a man in Fez who does that work for me. I take a few to him each time I go."

"Quite nicely done, aren't they? The lettering's a bit rough, but that doesn't detract from the effect. Where does he get the end-papers?"

"I have no idea. They are appalling, I agree. The people here have no feeling for paper, it is quite absent from their mentality."

"I could send you some from London," said Miles, looking at Panya with a growing feeling of respect. "I'm in the trade, I could send you some real beauties." He put the book back in the shelf and drew out another.

"Look at them all," said Panya, "and give me your opinion. They are not worth much, but put together in the bookcase they look pretty." She turned to Tavy, resolved to make an opportunity of speaking to her alone. "And if you don't mind being the shopkeeper for a few minutes, Tavy and I will go upstairs and make some coffee. You can call me if a *cliente* arrives, but I am afraid it is not very likely. And if no one does, I will shut up the shop early and we can be comfortable."

She laid her hand on Tavy's arm and they went to-

gether through the curtain concealing the corner used as a
fitting-room, and also the door to the stairs leading up to
the flat. It was a very small sitting-room above the shop,
crowded with books and miscellaneous objects collected in
desultory fashion throughout a lifetime, all arranged for
the convenience of one still alert but now mainly sedentary
person. There was one soft and comfortable armchair with
a little shawl thrown over the back of it, a table beside it
covered with a fringed cloth, on which were a scattering of
books and papers and Panya's spectacles, everything arranged close at hand under a hideous brass lamp. On the
other side, easily within reach, was a bookcase filled with
books in all stages of newness and shabbiness, paperbacks
and fine bindings all mixed up together, French, English
and Russian.

Tavy loved this room, and when she was not made
nervous by the presence of Joe (who was not of an age to
be let loose in a room full of small objects) liked staring at
the photographs and pictures and fingering the ornaments,
asking Panya incredulous questions about her early life,
which was as strange to Tavy as existence on another
planet, since it was all about a country town in Russia
before the Revolution. No one else that she had ever known
had such a room. The house in Ipswich, the home of her
adoption, contained few books and fewer objects of interest. The chief thing she remembered when she thought of
it, which was not often, was its excessive cleanliness.
Everything was fanatically, inimically clean, so that one
was always in fault for having stepped on, disarranged, or
finger-marked something. The polished linoleums were
traps for unwary prints from rubber gym-shoes, the kitchen
floor in particular had always just been washed and must
never be walked on. It was cold, too, because the windows
were always open, and the curtains—some washing material in a peculiarly cold and comfortless shade of mauve—

sucked restlessly in and out when the door was opened. In Panya's room there was no excess of fresh air. Closed windows kept out the cold in winter and the heat in summer; the most she would do was to manipulate little ventilators as the seasons changed. And on cold evenings, such as this one, an iron stove of Gothic pattern snored and gurgled in the fireplace, rattling its doors when the hateful Levanter assaulted the narrow chimney, but always yielding a grateful and life-giving warmth.

It was to this room, to a made-up bed on the red sofa in the window, that Tavy was first brought after Joe was born. She did not remember the actual birth very clearly, it had been too painfully confused; but the return to life had been in Panya's sitting-room, and she had nearly two weeks in which to learn its detail. Panya, on the other hand, remembered everything, and sometimes gave startling answers to simple questions. It was a horribly windy night, she would say, if pressed for the story. She was reading comfortably by the fire when Zohra arrived, incoherent and evidently frightened. It appeared that somebody, a *roumi*, a Christian woman, had given birth to a child in Zohra's house, and that the child was dead. It was the will of God, Zohra explained, and the mother was growing rapidly weaker since neither she nor Khaimo nor any of their female neighbours could stop the bleeding. It was *nakes*, Zohra went on, a premature child, but nicely made; the father of it was away somewhere; nobody knew where to find him.

It was a long time since anyone had called on Panya in a professional capacity. She had retired from practice years ago, and would be the first to protest that she was completely out of touch with modern medicine. But there was an element of alarm and secrecy in this appeal; it was to her that Zohra had come, and not to the hospital; and knowing how time could be wasted by dealing with an

emergency through the proper channels, Panya had put on
her coat and telephoned for a taxi.

And there, as she had often told her since, there on the
floor in Zohra's house, with only a strip of matting between
her and the cold tiles, lay Tavy, with a knot of women
crowding round her by candlelight, offering her bitter infu-
sions and staunching her with rags. "Where is the child?"
Panya had asked them in French and then in dumb-show,
but they only clucked and shook their heads, and said, in
Spanish and Arabic, that the child was *mayiht*, still-born,
and that it was certainly the will of Allah and also, since it
was a boy, a pity. Panya was too busy at first to pursue this
further, attending to Tavy with all the professional briskness at her command, and it was not until she went behind
the kitchen curtain for clean water that she saw the little
object in a shallow dish, naked and bloody as a skinned
leveret, in the flickering light looking oddly as though it
breathed. And she was not mistaken, it did; or at least
began to do so when picked up by the heels, and it went on
breathing and pulsing with weird determination and even
eventually wailed, opening a little O-shaped mouth in its
creased face and uttering cries that sent the women into an
ecstasy of terror. They knew, they had seen with their own
eyes, that it had been born dead.

This was the strangest thing of all, that once he was
plucked out of the dish and given a second chance, Joe
never looked back, but acted as though he were desperate
to make up for lost time, ignoring his prematurity as a
thing of no account, noisily sucking for days before Tavy
had milk and latching on to any proffered nipple as though
it were a thing he had been doing all his life. He recovered
from the shock of birth more rapidly than she did, but
Tavy was young and healthy and a fortnight of Panya's
nursing was all she needed. Propped up among pillows on
the hard sofa she was seized by an astonished curiosity

about this creature that she had produced and which slept in a basket under Concepción's kitchen-table. She was afraid to touch him at first and dismayed by his appearance, but in less than a week, when to other eyes he was no less ugly than before, a metamorphosis occurred, and she became prouder of Joe than she had ever been of anything. She could hardly wait for Quattrell to come back from Rabat, or wherever it was that he had disappeared to, to show him this glorious achievement, which had hair and nails and waved its quavering limbs as it lay in her lap, undeterred by having arrived two months before anyone expected it. And Quattrell finally came, while Tavy was still in the Rue Poincaré, and this was the first occasion on which Panya saw him. She had been not favourably impressed exactly, but well enough; he was certainly tender with Tavy and did his best to conceal his lack of enthusiasm for Joe. Panya judged that he was old enough to value Tavy's freshness and immaturity, and that he might possibly be trusted. This talk of despising marriage, which Tavy had insistently expounded during her convalescence, she took as a state of mind which would change with time. And later, when she learned from a casual remark that Quattrell was married, she interpreted Tavy's arbitrary attitude as self-defence in an unmanageable situation. Whether or not marriage with Quattrell would give Tavy much security Panya was doubtful; but to continue as she was, either with him or alone, seemed to her an even less promising alternative. The important thing was to discover the truth about Tavy's feelings, if that were possible, and any financial details that might be relevant.

"Well, what has this man of yours put off the trip for?" she began, shepherding Tavy into the kitchen and setting about preparations for making coffee. Concepción had left a tray prepared for one: Panya added cups and almond biscuits.

"There's a scheme on foot," said Tavy, wandering to the dresser shelves and looking one by one in the kitchen canisters. "You know Morley Crosier, I expect? It's his idea. He's going to start a camping on one of the beaches some- where near our cottage, and he wants Rob to go in with him somehow or other. They had a lunch to talk about it today, and they're seeing a travel-agent or something to- morrow."

"I see. And Mr. Quattrell will put money into it. Is that the idea?"

"Oh no," said Tavy candidly, helping herself to raisins, "he's very hard up at present, that's why he's interested. He's to give advice, and organize, and think out the public- ity. I'm almost sure that's it. You know, in return for a share of the profits."

"But is he really so hard up, dear child? What about this novel or film you say he is writing—won't that suffer? I'm not at all fond of these schemes; they fail one after another. And if he is so hard up as you say, how does he manage to go to Paris and London? Such trips are expen- sive, you know, on one's own money."

"Oh, he borrowed some in Paris to go and see his agent in London. He met someone he used to know on some newspaper. It'll be worth it, you see, if he gets a contract. He has it all worked out."

"And in the meantime you and Joe are kept sadly short. I shall be glad if things go well, and you can have a little more."

"Joe and I don't need much," said Tavy, moving fur- ther along the shelf and taking down a glass jar. "Do you mind if I have one or two of these walnuts? I adore them, the sight of them makes me hungry."

"Help yourself, dear child. Does Zohra not feed you properly, during Ramadan?"

"Oh, goodness, yes. I get what I want for Joe and we

have a tremendous meal at night. As a matter of fact I quite often keep the fast myself, in the day. Zohra says one loses power if one doesn't."

"And what does she mean by that?"

"Oh, you know, they have lots of ideas, but some of them are quite sound. I never take any notice of Khaimo's nonsense. She's always carrying on about the Evil Eye, or saying I mustn't cut Joe's hair on a Wednesday, or some such thing."

"I would be happier, I think," said Panya, concentrating on the coffee-pot, which was beginning to murmur, "if you had somewhere else to live. I think you have been with our friend Zohra long enough."

"Why? Where else would I go?" The question had obviously startled her; she was at once on the defensive.

"You and Mr. Quattrell could have a little flat together, for less than it costs him to live in the hotel. You would lead a more normal life."

"What do you mean by normal?" Tavy turned her back on Panya and began fiddling with the coffee-mill. "We've got the cottage. I think it would be very boring to live like other people. One might as well go home at once and live in Ipswich."

"Would that be such a very bad thing?" Panya asked, busy with the coffee-pot.

"Thanks, I'd rather die."

"But supposing he were free, and you could marry, that would put a different complexion on it, no?"

"No, it wouldn't. Darling Panya, that's such old stuff. It doesn't mean a thing to me, honestly. I don't even know what you're talking about."

"Then I will talk about something else," said Panya, picking up the tray and carrying it into the sitting-room. "Supposing, one of these days, he goes off to Paris or London and doesn't return. Have you thought about that?"

"But he always does return. It's an understood thing."

"But I am asking you to think of the possibility. Such things can happen. What would you and Joe do then? Would you go on living with Zohra, and be like Aminah? Or would you write to the old aunt, and go back to England?" They faced one another across the coffee-tray, Panya smiling, Tavy with her sudden obstinate look, the hostile face she put on when she was frightened.

"If it happened," she said in an offended voice, "I'd make him come back, that's all."

"My dear, you are talking like a child."

"Not at all. I have more power over him than you think."

Panya laughed, not at all unkindly.

"My Tavy, one does not talk of power. You are not an Arab woman, believing nonsense." She began to pour out the coffee and handed the first cup to Tavy, still smiling at her.

"What did you mean about Aminah?" Tavy asked after a short silence, frowning at her nails.

"I know about Aminah," said Panya gently. "Her mother told me. She goes with the police." Tavy continued to examine her nails. There was an uncomfortable pause.

"What absolute rubbish! Zohra will say any nonsense when she's angry. Look, aren't you going to shut up the shop and give Miles some coffee?"

"Of course. Will you go down and bolt the door, and ask him to come up?" Tavy scrambled to her feet with a look of relief and went over to the door. As she opened it Panya added, "That is rather a nice young man, I think."

"Is he? I don't know anything about him." Her voice was cold with displeasure, as though she suspected Panya's motive, and was disconcerted by it.

★   ★   ★

Later, though, when they had said good-bye to Panya
and were walking towards the boulevard, she said without
preamble, "Let's go back along the beach," and they went
down one of the steep streets between big hotels and
crossed the railway line and the sand-swept enclosure of
one of the shuttered beach-bars, and suddenly their feet
were ploughing through soft sand.

"I love it here at night," she said, "but I never can
come alone." She noticed Miles's heavy going and said at
once, "What's the matter, have you hurt yourself?"

"I'm a bit lame. I'll be all right on the hard sand."

She looked at him in surprise, never having imagined
that there was anything permanent the matter. There was
still enough light to see by, although the lights along the
front were far away. The wind had dropped, as it often did
in the evening, and in this abrupt calm the surge and sigh
of the sea was suddenly near. They walked across endless
beach towards the line of breakers, and came upon
hard sand at last, moist and resilient to the foot. Tavy took
Miles's hand.

"I love running on this," she said, "but if you can't . . ."

"I'm not much good at running, I'm afraid. You run if
you want to."

"Oh, I wouldn't alone. The beach is a bad place at
night. I'd rather stay with you."

"In what way, bad?" It looked almost totally deserted;
there was a man with a dog some distance off and some
boys intent on something in the shadow of a wall. Otherwise the beach was empty.

"Oh, this and that," she said. "They won't worry us if
we're together."

When they had passed the railway station and could

go no further they turned once more into the soft sand, which here was full of litter and building rubble. There was a flight of steps in the sea-wall below the level of the road, and Miles stopped in the shadow of it and took something from his pocket.

"I really bought this for you," he said, putting it in her hand. She opened the tissue paper and saw the gilt fibula.

"But you said it was a present for someone?" She looked at him in astonishment, genuinely at a loss.

"I know, but it was you I was thinking of. I thought it would suit you."

"Goodness, do you mean it?" She held it above the shadow and turned it this way and that in the light of the street-lamp. "I *love* it. I've always wanted one. But can you really . . . ? I mean, I looked at the price. It was thirty dirhams."

"Of course I mean it. That's very cheap, and it struck me as rather attractive when you were looking at it."

"It's lovely," she said, and opened the front of her jacket to pin it to her shirt. "I simply love it, but how shall I account for it?"

"Do you have to?"

"Well, sort of. I wouldn't have bought it for myself."

"Can't you say we saw it at Madame Lemaire's, and I gave it to you? It isn't worth anything. It might almost have come out of a cracker."

"I don't think I'd better say that." She looked down at the brooch once more, then buttoned her jacket. "Would you think it very odd if I said Panya gave it me? It would sound more likely."

"I don't mind what you say. Does she give you things like that?"

"No, never. I don't think it would occur to her. But I can say it did."

"And your friend Mr. Quattrell wouldn't mind that."

"No, he wouldn't mind that."

"Say whatever you like, then," said Miles. "It's not important."

They went up the steps together hand in hand and at the top Tavy said, "Thank you, Miles, a lot," and looked at him gratefully. But all the way home after that, under the street-lights, though she talked from time to time and was almost gay, they walked separately.

★ 7 ★

Pᴿᴏɢʀᴇss had evidently been made with Monty Maxwell. Maxi-Tours at Mini-Prices, said Colin on the telephone, was his new theme-song; he'd jumped at the whole
idea like a dog at a rabbit. Maxwell was already writing off
to brother travel-agents who dealt specifically in Germans.
He envisaged the thing, Colin said, in Teutonic terms.
West Germany was loaded with money and the krauts, if
not good spenders, were at least docile.

It was nine o'clock the following morning and Miles,
driven by guilt, had walked to the *bacál* after breakfast and
nerved himself to telephone Colin at Morley Crosier's. The
operation was less difficult than he had feared, in fact it
was not difficult at all; he wrote down the number on a
piece of sugar-paper and the shopkeeper did the rest. When
someone answered he spoke gravely in Arabic, then handed
the instrument to Miles across the counter. At this a couple
of boys came and leaned against him, one on either side,
thrusting their coins across and staring into the shop. They
were not interested in Miles, but in cigarettes, which could
be bought singly; his standing there seemed to have stimu-
lated them to the point of making their purchases at this

identical moment, shoving silently for a place. They pushed
quite hard, without looking at him, and Miles leaned against
the counter and stood his ground. This seemed to give no
offence, as though pushing and counter-pushing were a
normal part of business, like paying for what one bought.

All this time there was nothing to be heard from the
telephone but crackling, and Miles's heart sank. He had
wakened in the night with a feeling of foreboding to find
that the person who came instantly to mind was not Tavy,
with whose elusive and perplexing image he had fallen
asleep, but Mrs. Thewless, clutching a shawl round her
shoulders and looking anxious. As well she might, Miles
told himself despondently. Not only had he made no
progress with Colin at lunch, but for the rest of the day he
had never given him a thought. During the late evening,
which he spent alone while Sam went out with his tape-
recorder, he had thought almost exclusively about Tavy,
Quattrell and Panya; and also, as being now mysteriously
involved with them in some way, about himself. He had
not remembered to think about Colin at all, or to make
plans for the best method of approach, or what indeed he
would eventually say when he next saw him. He had not
even written to Mrs. Thewless, as he could easily have
done, to tell her that he had seen Colin, and would do so
again. He had eaten his solitary meal and gone to bed with
a succession of visions merging and flowing in his head.
Tavy serenely alone in Zohra's house, with a goat on the
doorstep. Panya's upstairs room and Tavy's hair falling forward and screening her face from the lamp. The dark
beach and the wet sand, and Tavy's hand firmly but imper-
sonally clasped in his. This was not what he had come out
for, spending Mrs. Thewless's money. He would ring Colin
up at the earliest possible moment and invent some plausi-
ble reason or excuse for seeing him.

And Colin, unexpectedly and immediately, saved him

the trouble. Crosier and Quattrell and he were going out that very morning to inspect the site. Ozzie was driving the Burridges in Mrs. Brockhurst's car, and Sam and Miles might just as well go in Crosier's. "We're taking lunch," he said, "to eat at Quattrell's place. Come too, why don't you? It might be rather amusing."

"I'd like to do that," said Miles, "if I can prise Sam off his tapes. Where shall we meet?"

"Meet you in the Kasbah square at eleven o'clock. No need to bring anything with you, unless perhaps the odd bottle. We've got enough food for everybody."

Miles paid for the call and bought two bottles of wine. As an afterthought he added a tin of tunny-fish and a pack of cigarettes, but could see nothing else on the shelves that would be a useful contribution to Sam's supplies. They had had a financial talk at breakfast, and it was now settled that Miles should pay nothing for his accommodation but might buy the food for both of them as long as he stayed. This already made him feel at home, and the prospect of the day's outing lifted his spirits. He would concentrate on establishing a friendly relation with Colin. He had purposely not even asked whether Tavy would be going.

★   ★   ★

The cars sped out of town and along the new road parallel to the coast. Colin drove Crosier's saloon, with Morley beside him; Miles and Sam, separated by a picnic-basket and a carton of bottles, occupied the back seat. Mollie Brockhurst, driven by Ozzie, was giving the Burridges a lift; the Volkswagen was said to be having an overhaul, but in fact they never missed an opportunity of saving petrol. Quattrell was in his large old Citroën, bringing up the rear at first but presently passing the others in a burst of speed for no particular reason, apparently, but high spirits. Miles saw with satisfaction that Tavy was with him, and accepted this joyfully as a bonus for not having asked if she would be there. As the old car roared past on a straight stretch she turned and waved, and he thought he caught a gleam of gold at the neck of her sweater, but was not sure. It gave him pleasure to think of her wearing the brooch and Quattrell not having the least suspicion that he had paid for it.

Tavy gazed ahead through the windscreen, her hands in her lap. Now that they had passed the other cars the road was as empty as the countryside; nothing moved except ranks of massed and ragged clouds trailing their shadows over the dead landscape. These came from the direction of the Rif and were travelling westward over the Atlantic, chequering the road with brief sunlight and long ominous stretches of shadow as they sailed across; there seemed to be no end to them. Tavy hunted for her sunglasses and put them on, making the sunless patches even darker. She took no pleasure in the landscape at this season, it was too complete a negation of everything she loved. The green which had returned to the parched verges with the winter rains was still sparse and meagre; great herds of goats were cropping it beside the road and soon it would be gone; it had been a droughty season. Zohra had tales of crops failing and sorcerers consulted because of the lack of rain, and surveying the bleached thorns and skeleton thistles silvering the colourless earth as far as one could see, it was possible to believe that in those naked plains and hills nothing would ever grow again. But in another two months the miracle would occur, long after the rigours of Ramadan had been forgotten and the feast that followed it, long after the Aid el Kebir and the Feast of Ashor, when the children went mad with trumpets and drums and explosive caps and plastic noise-makers of every description, and in self-defence one got out by hook or crook into the country.

Then it would be like a world new-born, unrelated to this one. Tides of colour would flow from the foothills to the edges of the road, the plains would be flooded with mari-golds, lakes of bugloss would spill over and flood the ditches, there would be pink convolvulus scrambling across the verges and arum lilies crowding the mud of streams. Tavy had never got over the occasion when, picnicking with Quattrell during their first spring, she had found the grass sprinkled with arums no bigger than her thumb, a sombre green in colour, striped with black. Under this pro-tective hue they were almost invisible, but once she had found one she saw them around her in thousands, stiffly and brilliantly populating the short grass. And there had been another day when they had taken the old road through the hills, and running down at last to the alluvial plain, which had lain cracked and dead all winter, a khaki waste, had found it smothered to the horizon in white flow-ers, not a blade of grass to be seen, nothing but this snowy weed in which the cattle waded to their knees, as though in paradise. "O were I in the wildest waste," Quattrell had chanted at the wheel, "Sae black and bare, sae black and bare, The desert were a paradise, If thou wert there, if thou wert there." But it was the spring miracle, not Tavy's pres-ence, which had made the difference. There was always a hint of mockery in his snatches of poetry.

★   ★   ★

The car slowed abruptly, searching for a track through the scrub-thorn and palmetto. There seemed to be no land-mark of any kind in the flat stretch between the road and the sea; only far ahead, where the coastline wavered slightly, there was a bastion of rock and broken fortifica-tions, and behind this, veiled in mist or spray, the white and mud-coloured honeycomb of a small town. On the left of the road, where for a quarter of a mile there had been sharp stones sticking out of the dry earth, the ground fell away to a shallow valley where one or two corrugated iron roofs could be seen and a cluster of rounded shapes that might have been thatch. The roofs were a scattered hamlet and the quarter-mile of stones its burying-ground. They were nearly there. Further on there was an almost invisible track to the right. Quattrell signalled vigorously with his arm and turned into it.

It did not seem to lead anywhere in particular, unless eventually to the beach; it wound through gravel and scrub in a haphazard fashion and petered out behind sand-dunes in a patch of stiff palmetto and dead grass. Beyond the dunes was an endless stretch of sand and beyond that the sea. The sea was a long way off; presumably the tide was out. There was a distant roar of breakers and a haze of spray, but it was too far off to make much of an impression.

"This is it, isn't it?" said Quattrell, standing beside Crosier's car as he was levered out. The third car bumped to a standstill and the Burridges emerged. There was a slamming of doors and everyone's hair and clothing started blowing in the wind. Mrs. Brockhurst decided to stay in the closed Mercedes.

"This is it, indeed," said Crosier, "the very place." He looked about him, inhaling deeply and labouring to convey the impression that he liked what he saw. "This area was cultivated once, as you can see. Hence the cart-road or track, and a couple of acres at least have been drained and levelled. But it didn't answer, I suppose; agriculturally it's quite worthless, fortunately. I have a strong feeling, judging by those patches of rushes, that there's water quite near the surface. It shouldn't be expensive to bore, when we reach that stage."

They stood about him in aimless groups, looking at the dunes and the sky, turning their backs to the wind.

"But the sea," said Mrs. Burridge in a doubtful voice, "there isn't a view of the sea. One can't even see the beach."

"You've missed the whole point," said Crosier, giving her a corrective look. "This dune, or sand-bank, is one of the prime advantages. It affords complete protection from the sea breeze. You will know how important that is, from your own experience. There could be quite a wind from the sea, and we wouldn't feel it."

"It's coming from the mountains today," said Burridge, screwing up his one eye and studying the clouds, which were certainly sailing across in a seaward direction.

"Well, naturally at this time of year it can be variable. Today there will be perfect shelter on the other side, and the huts will be built to face that direction, obviously. (Incidentally I think it's time we stopped calling them huts: chalets would be a better image.) And we shall build a wall extending from the administrative block, and the canteen and bar will be inside that, fully protected. Our main problem won't be the wind, my dear, but creating shade. We shall build a permanent sort of pergola thing, with concrete uprights, and roof it over in the summer with bamboo matting."

The Burridges took this in gravely, nodding agreement. They had had plenty of experience with bamboo matting and knew to a nicety how it could transform a naked pavement into a haven of shade, and equally, in an unlucky season (they were both remembering last summer) how the canopy could shudder and clap and break loose from its moorings, until nothing was left in September but fragments rotting in corners and splinters of cane sticking up from the dirty beach.

"Let's go and look at the sea, then, " said Ozzie, hugging himself and hopping from foot to foot. He looked at Colin, but Colin was rather pointedly in attendance on Crosier and ignored his signal. Ozzie caught Tavy by the hand and they skipped off together and were caught at once in the soft sand as they set foot on the dune, shrieking and pulling one another up through the blade-sharp grasses. They floundered and struggled to the top, stood on the crest for a moment hand in hand, then swooped down the further slope and disappeared.

"How far from here is Mr. Quattrell's house?" Mrs. Burridge asked Crosier. She was glad to be rid of these irresponsible elements and to return to the matter in hand.

"About a quarter of a mile," said Quattrell, to whom she had not addressed the question. "You can see it from the top there. It lies rather lower than this, in marshy ground."

"Too far to be used as an office," she persisted, "or not?"

"It depends by whom," said Quattrell guardedly, his face creasing in a smile.

"Well, by you of course, when you're doing your directing and overseeing." Her smile matched his, displaying an even greater range of teeth. "When we had the beach-bar, Rex used to do a lot of his office work at the flat, didn't you, Rex? And that was a good quarter of an hour away. He used to like the walk."

"I don't see myself doing much office work," said Quattrell, turning up his collar against the wind to light a cigarette. "I rather imagined that would be your responsibility. I don't go to the cottage very often anyway. It's shut up mostly."

"Well then," said Mrs. Burridge triumphantly, "wouldn't it be a splendid thing to use it as an office *temporarily*? I mean, we shall need an H.Q. and a refuge while they're building the admin. block. Wouldn't that be just the answer?"

"No," said Quattrell coolly, exhaling a mouthful of smoke. "It's not mine anyway. I rent it from an absentee

American and there's no question of sub-letting. I use it
when I feel like it, and that's the way I want it. The office
will have to be built."

"I dare say you're right," said Mrs. Burridge, nodding.
"One can't mix business and pleasure. It never works." She
gave Quattrell one of her liveliest smiles and glanced at her
husband, but so discreetly that one could hardly have detected the signal passing between them.

"Now then," said Crosier briskly, "strong lads wanted.
I must get to the top of this sand-bank and study the view."
Colin and Sam each took him by an arm and Miles pushed
from behind, so that with a minimum of back-sliding he
achieved the summit and stood with his wisps of hair blowing from back to front and his trousers flapping. Sam and
Colin slid down to the beach and began strolling about in
circles, stooping to pick up pebbles and throwing them to a
great distance at nothing in particular. Tavy and Ozzie
were already far away, two epicene figures dwindling at
the edge of the sea in the direction of the cottage.

Miles surveyed the beach and found it disappointing.
It was not wholly featureless, but almost so. It stretched
away indefinitely to the north, the only break in its uni-
formity being a shallow outcrop of rock temporarily uncovered until the tide turned, on which a couple of boys were
fishing with rod and line. There was no other sign of life,
apart from Tavy and Ozzie in the distance, and it came to
him that the camping scheme, with its concrete buildings
and thatched huts and sun-umbrellas, was as forlorn an
experiment in this landscape as if it were planned for one of
the craters of the moon. It was easier, far, to imagine the
camp in ruins than in a flourishing condition. It was the
sterile and unpopulous look of the place that was so forbidding: it had been empty, surely, since the beginning of
the world, and Crosier's schemes were not likely to change
its nature. The grey cube of Quattrell's cottage, easily seen

from the dune on the near side of a small estuary, fitted as perfectly into the picture as a bluff of rock; it had probably been there for years, remains of a peasant holding which had scratched a precarious living from the sand and the river. Where the fishing boys had come from he could not imagine.

Crosier was deep in calculations of development. He stared down at Sam and Colin larking about on the sand and pinched his lip reflectively. The voices of the others rose from behind the dune, and turning in their direction Miles was astonished to see three boys, two of them in ragged jeans and sweaters, one in a *djellába*, who had appeared from nowhere; the eldest, who was perhaps fourteen, was talking quite volubly to Quattrell. Evidently they must have come from that settlement in the valley, more than a mile away; the speed with which they had sighted strangers and covered the distance was, considering everything, disconcerting. One saw at once what a godsend the camping and the tourists would be to all such enterprising characters in search of an interest in life and a chance of profit.

Quattrell and the Burridges moved to the foot of the dune, two of the boys sidling round them. The third, the hood of his *djellába* flapping, ran back on an inspiration to Mollie's car, and Miles saw her look of alarm as she wound up the window. The boy pressed his face to the glass, and when Mollie tried nervously to ignore him continued to stare through the windscreen, hitching himself up to lean on the bonnet of the car in a more comfortable position.

Quattrell stopped in the soft sand and gave the boys some money. They looked at the coins in their open palms, counted them, and moved reluctantly away, but only for a few yards. They joined the third boy at Mollie's car and sat down beside it. Mrs. Burridge stopped indignantly halfway up the slope.

"I must say, Mr. Quattrell, I think you make rather a mistake, giving those boys anything."

"Why so?" He offered her a helping hand. "It was what they wanted."

"Exactly so. Now we shall never get rid of them. You notice, I hope, that they still haven't gone away."

"I told them to guard the car. They're used to doing that."

"But what about poor Mrs. Brockhurst? Hadn't some-one better go back to her?"

"She's all right," said Quattrell. Finding his hand ignored he ploughed on to the top of the slope, the Burridges following laboriously.

"Dora's right, you know," said Burridge, breathing heavily as he reached the summit. "Doesn't do to encourage them. Next time we come they'll be back with their scrofulous friends."

"Well, what d'you expect?" Quattrell looked faintly exasperated.

"Just that—don't *you*? There's a village not a mile off, if you happened to notice. Sort of thing that sets a damn bad precedent. We've had experience of it."

"They've had experience, too," said Quattrell, "that's why they came."

Mrs. Burridge stood by Crosier and looked up and down the beach. It was clear from her face that the tiny incident rankled.

"What did they say to you?" she asked suspiciously, unable to leave it alone. It was an added irritation that Quattrell had a smattering of Arabic. "Did they know why we were here?"

Quattrell looked her in the eye with a gleam of malice.

"They said they were in need of money. They said that business was bad in the winter, when there were no tourists. They said they hoped we would come again, and bring our friends."

"Well, how ridiculous! What business can they possibly have, little brats like that?"

"They explained," said Quattrell, watching the expression of her face, "that in summer they do very well. They get five, ten dirhams a time. They have their regular customers."

"For what, for heaven's sake?"

"For going into the bushes and being buggered, I understand. So far they have done business only with male tourists, being still young. Forgive me if I seem indelicate."

Mrs. Burridge met his eye for a long moment and her neck turned a deeper colour. Her husband, his moustache quivering, looked away. Miles had the impression that he was not altogether unamused by his wife's discomfiture.

"Well, all I can say *is*," said Mrs. Burridge, recovering her poise with spirit, "that if that's the situation it will have to be coped with. We shall have to take a firm line from the very beginning. Isn't that so, Mr. Crosier?" She moved away from Quattrell as though to dissociate herself.

"Why, my dear, that's really a minor problem," said Crosier, coming out of his reverie. He had been visualizing the camping site as he hoped and intended it to be by the beginning of the summer. In this vision the tide was in and the sea very much nearer. The sand would be swept in the early morning, a channel would be cut through the dune between camp and beach, and on the beach itself there would be couples lying about under sun-umbrellas, all young and elegant, all slender, all vaguely epicene, a variant of the typical beach-scene in a travel advertisement. This prospect gave him no pleasure, but he made an effort of imagination and dwelt on it resolutely. The only point of the thing was to make money, and the only way to make money was to transform an empty and inoffensive site into something from which his soul recoiled with loathing. His tastes turned wholly to the past, rejecting the modern world. He liked to see the beach precisely as empty as it was, and if he were to people it at all would prefer a cavalcade of Moorish horsemen, turbaned and wrapped in white with pennants flying, after the manner of Delacroix. In default of which, sighing, he returned to his visionary plans. It was all too opportune to be missed; one must not be squeamish. Colin's five thousand, well deployed, would get the whole thing going.

"Of course there will be problems with troublesome boys, as you must have found with your beach-bar. The thing is to appoint the biggest and strongest to keep the others down. The better ones can be employed in all sorts of ways. Guarding the car park, preventing other boys from pestering motorists. Sweeping the sand in the early morning and picking up rubbish. Running errands, fetching in riding ponies from the farms when we reach that stage. The way to render them harmless is to keep them busy."

"You sound as though you're prepared for quite a task-force," said Quattrell, treading his cigarette-end into the sand and shading his eyes to look for Tavy and Ozzie, who were nearly at the cottage.

"Well, my dear, wherever you go, even if it were the fringes of the Sahara, there would always be a village within a walkable radius and within ten minutes of setting foot in the place you would be surrounded by boys. It is a fact of nature, like the tse-tse fly in other parts of Africa. A nuisance in many respects, but in others"—his pale eye sought Burridge's single one and seemed to question it—"in others, one is bound to admit, there are compensations. The great thing, my dear Mrs. Burridge, is not to get rattled. Our friend Quattrell will decide on policy and the Major there will implement it. It's a very simple question when you know how to handle it."

"My policy at the moment," said Quattrell, "is to go and open a bottle. We've looked at the beach, we've examined the site, we've observed the rushes on behalf of the water-diviner, we've considered the problem of employing the local twelve-year-olds in any manner but the one to which they're accustomed, and I vote we pack it in. Tavy will have opened the cottage by now, so let's get there with the lunch."

He slithered down the steep sand-bank and strolled across to Mollie Brockhurst's car. The three boys were sitting quietly enough, and Mollie herself had recovered sufficiently to open the window about two inches. She had put on her horn-rimmed spectacles and with her nail-file was cutting the pages of a French paperback as the best means of calming her nerves until Ozzie's return.

"Ozzie's gone ahead to the cottage," he told her, stooping to the open crack at the top of the window. "Rex Burridge can drive you, it's only a quarter of a mile," and moved quickly away to the Citroën before she could protest or make difficulties.

When the cars moved off one after the other, bumping over the rough track, the boys ran alongside cheering, and stood waving on the edge of the road as long as they were in sight. Such an enthralling interlude and windfall was an unheard-of gift of God in the middle of winter. They sat about on the stony verge for a while, waiting for something else to happen, and then, as nothing did, picked themselves up and set off in the direction of the cottage.

★   ★   ★

Tavy and Ozzie kept along the edge of the wet sand, following the reach of the tide, until they came into full view of the sea-house in a fold of the dunes, squatting within its barrier of prickly-pear. Quattrell had replaced the old thatch two years ago, and the corrugated roof, bleached white as salt, gave the place a spuriously new and disciplined look. Stout wooden shutters had been fixed to all the windows and the door had an iron bar and heavy padlock. Tavy produced a key and tried it this way and that.

"My, my, you're certainly fortified," said Ozzie, watching the experiment with interest.

"We have to be. It was broken into eleven times until we put up this bar, and the windows were continually broken until we had shutters."

"And of course everything was stolen."

"Well, no, there wasn't much to lose. It wasn't until we'd made it thief-tight that we left our things in it."

The padlock, stiff with sand and salt, opened at last and they went into the dark interior. The place smelt damp, but not excessively so: Quattrell had evolved a system by which each window, inside the shutters, was left slightly open, propped on a stout nail. The windows had to be fully opened before the shutters could be unbolted: in this way a small but constant draught was maintained and the enterprise of the local boys frustrated.

"You've made it much nicer," said Ozzie, when they had taken down the shutters. "How clever of you; a home from home, as they say. The first time I came it had a quite *abandoned* look. In a disappointing sense, I mean. It just looked miserable."

"Well, it isn't very comfortable now," said Tavy, looking at the hard divan and ramshackle cane chairs, "but it's better than it was. It's so dreadfully damp, everything moulders away. There might be some kerosene left, however; we could light the stove."

With the portable oil-stove lit and doors and windows

open it became quite cheerful. The clouds were fewer now; there were long intervals of sun and brilliant sky. Tavy found a rag and swept the sand and grit from the table, then went through into the second room which served as a kitchen. Here there were plates and glasses on a shelf, knives and forks and bottle-openers in the table drawer. She held the glasses one by one to the light and wiped them on the rag.

"Bother, bother," said Ozzie suddenly, "I ought to go back for the car. Mollie will be stranded."

"Why should she be? There are five men there to drive her."

"Well, but she gets so fussed, poor sweet. She'll be in a panic."

"Nonsense. If you go back along the beach you'll miss them on the road."

"Too true. Oh dear, she'll be so plaintive."

Tavy gave him a glass and reached down a gin bottle from the cupboard.

"Thanks, dear, I never touch it. Only wine. I have to be a tiny bit careful."

"Well, there won't be any wine until the others come. Surely she won't mind if Colin or someone drives her?"

Ozzie drew a chair to the table and sat in it, propping his chin on his fist.

"You never can tell, you see. She's very unstable. There was this frightful thing happened to her, you probably know about it. Her husband was drowned when their yacht went down, and she was the only one picked up afterwards by a freighter."

"I vaguely remember something," said Tavy. "She came to a party once at my uncle's house. I remember thinking she was rather peculiar."

"Well, peculiar, dear, isn't really the word. It was the *shock*. I couldn't get over a thing like that, could *you*? The way it took her was, she thought it was her fault. Of course it couldn't have been really, but she used to keep on so, I sometimes find myself wondering." He began drawing patterns on the table with the tip of a finger. "So it makes her rather tricky to live with, but she's *much* better than she was. She loves going about to parties *now*, but she didn't once. We sometimes didn't go out for months together. So *that's* something of a consolation."

Tavy looked at him curiously and began wiping the knives and forks.

"You've been with her a long time, haven't you?"

"My dear, it's not much more than four years, but it feels like life. I don't mean to say that in a nasty way, I'm devoted to her really. But how could I ever leave?" He looked up at Tavy appealingly, his eyes very blue and wide. "Sometimes I think we ought to get married, and then it would be more *stable*. But then again, it's not for me to suggest."

"But she's so much older than you," said Tavy, to whom this was a very strange idea. She turned away to conceal a smile at the thought of Ozzie married.

"That wouldn't make any difference," he said seriously. "It would be a *marriage blanc*, of course; that would be understood. Not like yours, dear, I know—if you ever contemplate it."

"I don't," said Tavy, going back to the cupboard. "That's not on the programme at all."

"Ah well, it seems rather a pity. Rob's married, isn't he?"

"He is. He has a wife somewhere or other. She's not bad-looking, I believe, and has lots of money." Tavy sounded rather proud of this, as though by implication it enhanced her position.

"Goodness, aren't you afraid of him going back to her?"

"I would be, terrified; only she won't have him."

"Well, that's all right then," said Ozzie cosily, following her with his eyes as she moved about the kitchen. "I knew someone who knew him once. Well, of course you knew them too. The Askew-Martins."

"I knew Anthea when I was young," said Tavy, to whom three years and a bit was almost a lifetime. She opened the table drawer and pulled out a plastic cloth. "I was rather fond of her, but him I don't really remember. They came once or twice to my uncle's that first summer." She began spreading the cloth on the table, pressing out the folds with her hands. Ozzie lifted his elbows while she did this and then replaced them.

"I don't think they got on very well, did they? Gerald and Rob, I mean. I think something had happened once that made them dislike one another. Or was it that Rob was a bit sweet on Anthea? Yes, that was probably the reason, now I come to think of it."

"Well, he was," said Tavy. "Even I could see that. But after we went off together he soon forgot about it. We went down to the south for a time, and when we came back they'd gone."

"I *see*," said Ozzie, with just enough emphasis to suggest that this threw some welcome light on an old problem. After a pause he said, "Is he *kind* to you, dear, and all that?"

"Of course he is! In what way?" Tavy laughed, looking more astonished than offended.

"You mustn't mind *me*, dear; I'm notoriously inquisitive. I just wouldn't like to think that he treated you stingily, that's all. Or that divine baby either, that I'm so jealous of."

"Goodness, *no*," said Tavy emphatically. "He's ever so generous really, only we have to be rather careful at present, until he gets an advance or a contract or something." She cast about in her mind for a convincing example. "For instance, he lets me have my eyebrows and eyelashes tinted at that expensive hairdresser's, the French one. They charge quite a lot, and nobody could say it was essential."

Ozzie looked at her with increased interest. His own eyelashes, like his hair, were dark by nature.

"No, are they dyed, really? How riveting! I always thought them one of your best features."

"They're not bad, but the trouble is, they're practically straw-coloured. I don't tell people I have them darkened, if you don't mind. I just mentioned it as an example."

"Tell me," said Ozzie presently, watching absorbedly as she set clean plates, glasses and knives and forks on the plastic cloth in preparation for the picnic, "why is it Rob won't go into Spain, or Spanish territory? Mollie asked him a few weeks back to drive with us to Ceuta when she wanted something, and he laughed and said he might get pinched if he crossed the border. He's not old enough to have been in the Civil War; I wonder what he meant?"

"I'm not very clear about that either. It was something that happened before I knew him, when he was in Egypt. I think he carried a package for somebody or something when he was flying to Barcelona, and there was something in it, I forget what, and the police got on to it. He makes a joke of it now, but I expect it was rather frightening at the time. Jumping bail, and all that. He says he's only once been in Spain since then, and that was only in transit, at Madrid airport. He'd think it was asking for trouble, going with you two to Ceuta."

A car door slammed behind the cottage and Ozzie sprang to his feet.

"Oh *good*, they're here. I'm ravenous—how about you?"

"I've been hungry for hours. The food ought to be

good, too, oughtn't it, coming from Mr. Crosier's?"

"Oh *yes*, dear, *really* nice; one of the reliable sources. And he'll have made a special effort, too, to impress Mollie. Let's go and hurry them in."

They went round the house to the cactus hedge and sandy stretch behind it, where the three cars were jockeying for position. The Burridges were together in the front of Mollie's Mercedes; Mollie herself had taken refuge with Quattrell. The three young men were still with Crosier, Colin easing him out of the driver's seat and Miles and Sam busy with bottles and hampers. Ozzie went at once to Mollie, hands outstretched, and Tavy stood at the corner of the house on a step of rock, shirt-sleeves rolled up, one raised arm shading her eyes from the sun, while the whole procession trooped round and in at the door. Then, regretting Joe more than ever now that the afternoon promised to be fine, she jumped on and off the smooth rock once or twice, humming to herself, before following the others round to the front of the cottage.

The three ragged boys, leaping across crevices and ditches on a short cut from the road, arrived on the scene therefore at a most favourable moment. They made a quick reconnaissance of the cars, discovering that although all doors were locked Mollie's and Quattrell's had windows slightly open. The Citroën contained nothing worth having, and they gave it scarcely a glance. The Mercedes, on the other hand, which could be opened by the smallest inserting an arm through the top of the window, yielded a haul which more than repaid them for their trouble: a mohair rug, an unopened tin of imported cigarettes, Ozzie's suède jacket and pigskin driving-gloves and a fascinating pair of Japanese binoculars.

★ 8 ★

Towards the end of the meal, which was eaten both indoors and out according to taste, Colin sat down by Miles, who had found himself a place in the soft sand, supported by a tussock of grass. The sun was now almost hot, and here in the lee of the cottage they were out of the wind. Tavy, assisted by Sam, was going round collecting dirty plates and pouring out coffee, and Ozzie was following them with fresh plates and knives and a basket of oranges. These oranges were exceptionally fine and large; from Marrakesh, Crosier said, from the garden of his esteemed friend the Caid. Whether this were true, or whether Alawi had bought them in the market only that morning, was unimportant; they had evidently ripened in the south and were still on their green stalks among glossy leaves; a handful of waxy blossoms had been scattered over them.

Miles held up his mug to Tavy and they exchanged smiles. Balancing on long legs over him as she tilted the thermos he saw her for a moment against the light as a symbolic figure, a sculptured and archetypal goddess dispensing plenty. And then, as she shifted slightly and turned to Colin, the familiar features reasserted themselves—the threadbare jeans, the sketchy outline, the childish concentration of expression—making such a grandiose image inappropriate. Yet there was something poetic and arresting about her appearance, due probably to nothing more than her being clad in that faded washed-out blue which was her best colour. As she straightened herself before moving on and with one hand flung back the hair lying over her shoulder, he caught sight of the gold ornament pinned to her shirt. It lay close to the open neck, like a secret sign. As he looked at it her hair once more fell over it like a curtain.

"Ve-ry attractive," said Colin, before she was quite out of hearing. "Every time I see that girl she strikes me as more of a smasher."

"She *is* rather pretty," said Miles indifferently, recoiling from the idea of discussing her with anyone, let alone with Colin. He was still not sure to which camp, sexually speaking, Colin belonged. His association with Crosier suggested one thing, but it might after all be what it purported to be—a straightforward business connection. Colin's appearance, good without being striking, gave nothing away; in any case Miles had long ago abandoned the illusion that he could spot a homosexual simply by looking at him. Some of the young nowadays deliberately adopted a camp manner, or elements of it, for the sake of perverse smartness or simply for a laugh; while staid bachelors, who looked and behaved as normally as Purkess at the bindery, turned out to be married in the sight of God, and to another man. Colin had once before made a point of admiring Tavy, and while Ozzie was helping her distribute food had gone to sit next to Mollie Brockhurst on the divan; he had talked to her closely for quite a time, with apparent earnestness. It would be helpful to know on which side of the line he counted himself, if only to throw some light on his choice of territory, but it was not essential. The important thing was to arrive at some view of his intentions, to influence them if possible, and send a report of the situation to Mrs. Thewless.

"Well, are you satisfied with the site?" he began by asking. "Does it come up to your expectations?"

Colin was intent on his orange, scoring the peel in sections with a pocket-knife and opening out the skin in points like clumsy petals.

"I don't quite know about my expectations," he said, not looking up, "but they'd have to be pretty low for this to come up to them. However, it seems it's difficult to get land, especially for foreigners, and this bit's available. Morley seems to think it's all right; I suppose he'd know. And he's seen the Pasha and the Commissaire de Police, and they're both keen on it."

"What would they have to do with it?"

"Well, not much really, except that it's in their administrative area, and what they say goes. If they didn't like the idea it wouldn't happen. But since they're mad keen on development and tourism they may not help, but at least they're not likely to hinder." He broke apart large segments of his orange and put one in his mouth. Juice spurted between his lips and ran over his chin. "Blast," he said, dabbing with a silk handkerchief at the front of his shirt. The oil from the peel on his plate smelt astonishingly strong, overpowering the honey-sweet smell of the orange flowers.

"So you've quite decided," said Miles, "to go into this scheme, then. May I borrow your knife a minute?"

Colin passed it over, sticky with juice.

"Oh, I decided that some time time ago. I'm committed already. The clearing of the site's going to start in a couple of days, and someone's got to pay the workmen. I got five hundred quid over from Gibraltar this week, though that's between ourselves, if you don't mind. I'm hoping we can count on Mollie Brockhurst for the next five hundred."

It evidently gave Colin pleasure to talk in this large way about such a sum, but in fact he was a little worried. It had begun to dawn on him that no one else was producing any money at all. Crosier had never promised anything; he had been quite frank about that from the beginning; but there had always been a strong assumption that other people would be glad to invest in the scheme when it was once started. Now, however, it seemed that the only serious possibility was Mrs. Brockhurst, and though Crosier had discussed the scheme in her presence and was making a great fuss of her, Colin was sure there had been no definite proposal. A tremor of misgiving, faint but uneasy, had begun to disturb him. It had not manifested itself until, by a devious but apparently trusted method, he had conveyed five hundred pounds to Crosier's account, and now he was beginning to wonder if this had been wise. The work, Morley said, could begin immediately, but they must have funds. Workmen must be paid and there were building materials to be ordered. Every item of expenditure as it occurred would be submitted to Colin, but this was unlikely to be much comfort. No one, Crosier explained, could expect to see any return until the scheme made a profit, and this was reasonable enough; but the fact remained that with the money he had already spent Colin's capital had dwindled to a sum appreciably nearer to four than five thousand pounds. He still assured himself that he was free to withdraw his money whenever he chose, but in point of fact, was he? Part of it no doubt was already earmarked for contractors, and it might well be the end of the summer before he saw it again. Meanwhile there was the question of salaries. Quattrell being in an advisory capacity could afford, presumably, to wait; but other people might be in a less fortunate position; there was a marked air of expectancy about the Burridges. What Colin found himself most unusually longing for at this moment was advice. Or, if disinterested advice (as seemed likely) was not available, he would feel better if Mrs. Brockhurst were sharing the burden. He had made up his mind to approach her, and the second stage of uneasiness had set in when he met her transparent astonishment at the proposition. "It's certainly an interesting idea," she admitted, looking slightly startled, "but I shall have to ask Ozzie." And at this, for instinctive reasons, Colin's heart sank. Ozzie was as friendly as possible, but he had an eye to the main chance. He already had worries of his own, as Colin knew; why should he welcome a cuckoo into the nest?

"Has Mrs. Brockhurst shown interest, then?" Miles asked. He remembered Colin's earnest talk on the divan, and guessed that this had been the gist of the conversation.

"Oh lord yes, she's interested. She thinks it's a marvellous idea. But she's very much under Ozzie's thumb, and whether he'll like it or not's another question."

Miles peeled his orange in silence and divided the sections. When he had eaten one or two he said, "I hope you haven't been precipitate. Five hundred pounds is a lot of money." He was thinking of Mrs. Thewless's two hundred, with a nasty feeling that it was good money thrown after bad. "If I were you I'd sit tight on the rest until you get advice. Where is it, still in Gibraltar? You could have it transferred back to London, and then at least it would be safe."

"What do you mean, safe? And what would I do meanwhile, without any money?" Colin looked aggrieved, as though this mild suggestion had offended him.

"What about going back to London yourself, and thinking it over? I don't know anything about these schemes, but I'd be wary if it was my money."

"Well, it isn't," said Colin shortly, "and what you don't seem to understand is, that if I pull out now, there's five hundred quid down the drain. If I stay in, and the thing develops as it should, I shall make a profit. Labour's as cheap as dirt, you know. Five hundred goes a long way."

"I just wish you had some good advice, that's all. Any lawyer would be able to work out a few safeguards. Why don't you come back to London with me, and we'll find somebody?" In spite of his opinionated manner Colin, it seemed, was in exactly the mood of a boy determined to be both mean and reckless with his own pocket-money.

"I can find a lawyer here if I want one, but actually I don't. Morley's very shrewd; he's great friends with this *cadi* in Rabat. He can find out anything he wants about Moroccan law without arseing about with some futile London solicitor."

This was evidently an unprofitable line to follow, and it seemed pointless to ask if he trusted Morley, since he so obviously did. Miles decided to risk a nearer touch.

"Well, there's one person who'd be pleased to see you back for a bit, and that's your mother. I didn't think she looked awfully well when I saw her recently."

"Why? What's the matter with her?"

"She misses you," said Miles, "and also she worries. I think it would mean a lot if you came home and talked things over. You could meet on neutral ground if you don't want to see your father. My place, if you like. You'd have time to sort things out, and see them in proportion."

Colin hesitated. He had no intention of going home to be scolded, but the idea of cheering his mother had something to it. The thought of her anxious, even ailing, was uncomfortable. Still, how much better to return in six months' time, with a vastly increased capital! He would be in a position to stand no nonsense then, not even from his father. Besides, even with this uneasy feeling in the pit of his stomach, life with Crosier was more amusing than Earl's Court. Soon the weather would get warm and the winds drop—everybody said so; and he and Morley would have the camp to organize, which would be both interesting and profitable.

"No, my dear," he said at last, unconsciously falling into Morley's way of speaking, "I'm really too busy at present to think of such a thing. Later, maybe; when everything's going smoothly I might think of it. I don't want to upset Morley." "Upsetting Morley" was a more convenient way of saying that if he withdrew his money he would lose the only asset which made him interesting. Morley was an old man; youth and looks alone could no longer hold him. He did not put it to himself like this, being not unskilled in the art of mincing motives. It did occur to him for a moment that his mother might have got at Miles, but he dismissed the idea as irrelevant. She would hardly have had the gumption for such a manoeuvre, and if she had, it would not be himself she was fussing about, but the money.

"There's one thing certain," he said finally to Miles. "Nobody's to get a penny out of it until we show a profit. I mean, nobody's thinking of salaries, or anything like that. I suppose Rex and Dora will get their meals when the thing's started, but it won't be more. And I'm sure Rob Quattrell doesn't expect to get anything out of it."

"I only hope you're right," said Miles. He was suddenly so deeply irritated by Colin's stupidity that he could think of nothing more to say. He got up, knocking the sand from his clothes, and carried his mug and platter back to the house.

★   ★   ★

The older members of the party were now all gathered in the one room, smoking and finishing their wine. When he had first come into possession of the sea-house Quattrell had divided it up so that one room was always free for working and sleeping; it was also, with the two divans, a comfortable place for drinking and discussion. He and Crosier were now going into details for Mollie Brockhurst's benefit, describing the finished scheme in all its glory, so that already in imagination the area was dotted with bee-hives of reed thatch, with whitewashed walls and outbuild-ings and light-hearted campers strolling between the cha-lets and the bar. They would even be planting trees that autumn, Crosier said. They grew so fast in this climate that it was ridiculous not to—one had only to look at the miles of eucalyptus planted by the forestry department. "And then," he said, "eventually we shall have our own wood for burning, and there will be camp-fires and community sing-ing in the evenings." The Burridges exchanged a derisive glance, but said nothing. When the kitchen and store-rooms were discussed they made suggestions, following ev-erything that was said with close attention.

Sam and Ozzie had gone back to the beach and Tavy was in the kitchen. She was scraping the refuse from the plates into a cardboard box, which the tide would presently take care of. Since it was Crosier's picnic there was no point in washing the containers, which were Alawi's affair. The plates and glasses could be washed in river-water.

Miles brought his plate to the table and tipped the orange-peel into the box. It was the second bonus of the day to find her alone.

"A good picnic," he said. "That way of doing chicken was delicious."

"I know, wasn't it? And the oranges were super. I've saved two for Joe." She picked up a plastic bucket. "Now all I need is some water, and then we're finished."

He took the bucket from her hand. "Is there a tank, or what? Where do I go?"

"Oh, that's awfully sweet of you. You go down there, to the river." She pointed from the window. "It's not far. Look out as you go, though—the bank's steep." She spoke solicitously, as though he might hurt himself, and he concluded with chagrin that she had remembered his lameness.

But when he came to it it was not difficult at all. The bank was steep, but hard with wind-packed sand. Even the lower part, slimy with mud and weed, had drained with the outgoing tide and was still firm. He filled the bucket and brought it up without mishap. On the marshy stretch along the river, between the cottage and the road, he caught sight of three smallish figures wandering away. They were probably the same boys who had begged from Quattrell, but at that distance one couldn't be sure. They were walking slowly, heads bent, as though examining something. By the time he reached the house they were out of sight.

Tavy put the tumblers in the bucket of water and washed them with a rag. There was nothing to dry them on, so she stood them on the shelf as they were, to drain at leisure. The plates she did one by one, handing them to Miles.

"Just put them away like that. They'll be dry by the next time we come."

"Do you come often?"

"Not so very. It depends. Sometimes we stay for a week if Rob feels like working, but mostly we come for a night or two. It's really better that way, because of Joe."

"You don't ever bring him with you?" Miles was distributing plates on the lower shelf.

"No, I told you. I always have to leave him with Zohra. It's ridiculous really." She was holding a dripping plate in either hand, waiting for him to take them. Their fingers met as he did so, but Tavy seemed not to notice. Her hands were slippery and cold.

"I'm glad to see you're wearing the little brooch. It looks just right."

"I know. It's a success, isn't it? And nobody's even commented on it."

Miles looked up to see Quattrell watching them from the doorway.

"Commented on what?" Quattrell asked, grinning impartially at them both.

"Why, on the brooch that Panya gave me," said Tavy at once. "I was wondering when you were going to notice it."

He glanced at Miles and for a moment did not reply. It was a curiously attentive look, as though he were consciously observing him for the first time.

"I saw it last night," he said, "when you came home with what's-his-name."

"With Miles," said Tavy, correcting him.

"That's right, with Miles." He continued to watch them from the doorway: it was obvious that he was making Tavy uncomfortable.

"So Panya's giving presents out of stock," he said, moving into the kitchen. "I wonder what else she's got?"

"She's got lots of things," said Tavy, "but she's not giving them away. I just happened to like this pin, and so she gave it to me."

He drew her to him by the shoulder and lifted the brooch between thumb and finger to examine it.

"What is it—gold? Or has she had it plated?" He glanced at the underside and let her go again.

"Oh, it's not gold," said Tavy, picking up the last of the plates. "She fakes them up like that. They're not worth anything."

"I bet she charges a pretty price, though," said Quattrell, smiling at Miles. "How much did you pay for it?"

"I *told* you," said Tavy, wringing out her rag. "I don't know the price at all, because Panya gave it me." She began a perfunctory wiping of the table. "They're only a few dirhams anyway; she said so."

Miles picked up the bucket of water and moved towards the door. He did not like Quattrell's tone, and saw that he had put himself in a ridiculous position. He was perfectly willing to admit to the brooch, but Tavy's denials made this impossible. He was almost sure that Quattrell had overheard their conversation, and had decided to humiliate him.

"Help him, baby," said Quattrell as Miles reached the door. "The floor there's very uneven"—thus confirming Miles's suspicions, for what was the point of the remark if not to stress his lameness?

"I can manage, thanks." He went out with a firm step, stumbled atrociously in full view of the window and swore under his breath. He threw the water violently over the grass, narrowly missing Sam and Ozzie as they came rushing round the corner.

"Those boys!" cried Ozzie indignantly, bursting in at the door, "they've forced the window of the car and stolen everything!"

There was an immediate outcry from the other room. Mrs. Burridge jumped to her feet.

"Which car?" she cried, and then, "my God, my handbag!"

"It's here," said Burridge, behind her, "you brought it with you."

"Oh, thank goodness, but what about my gloves? I'm sure I left them on the rug."

"Well, the rug's gone," said Ozzie distractedly, "and *my* gloves, if you don't mind, and my hideously expensive new suède jacket and Mollie's binoculars." He went in hurriedly to Mollie and took her hand. "Darling, I'm *frightfully* sorry, it's *too* awful, but we must have left the window open a crack, and they've taken everything."

"Who have?" said Mollie, lifting a scared face.

"Those scrofulous boys," said Burridge, and added, "typical!" His wife had rushed out of the house to confirm the damage.

"Well, never mind," said Mollie soothingly, now that she understood. "I expect they were all insured, and there's nothing valuable." She could see from his woebegone face that Ozzie was upset, and this distressed her more than the loss of binoculars.

Everyone now went round to the back of the house and the other cars were examined and found intact. Colin, arriving late on the scene, tried all the handles of Crosier's with a smug expression. He was the only one, apparently, who had locked up properly; Morley's brief-case was still on the back seat.

"Well, that was unfortunate," said Crosier, when Ozzie had unlocked the Mercedes and Mollie had immediately got in, as though anxious to be gone. Mrs. Burridge too had climbed in eagerly, and was smiling from the back seat, having found her gloves. "But I know the Commissaire de Police," he said, stooping at Mollie's window, his hand on the car roof, "and I shall telephone him the moment I get home. Don't worry, my dear Mrs. Brockhurst. We may recover the things tomorrow. I shall report progress."

"What a hope," said Burridge, turning up his one eye, but he was careful to say it as Ozzie pressed the self-starter. Ozzie then reversed at speed and went off with a spurt of sand, callously bouncing the Burridges over the ridges.

★   ★   ★

When Crosier's car had finally gone Quattrell went back to the house. Tavy was punching cushions and emptying the large sea-shells they used as ashtrays. There was a half-finished bottle of wine still on the table.

"Let's stay," he said, picking up the bottle by the neck and looking about him for a glass. "Let's not go back till tomorrow."

Tavy did not reply. She finished straightening the room and closed the window. Quattrell came back from the kitchen, a glass in either hand.

"Alone at last," he said. "I thought they'd never go, didn't you? Have a drink."

"I don't want any."

"I can't drink alone," said Quattrell, "or if I do I'll be drunk by bedtime. We've got two more bottles."

"Take them back with you to the hotel, then. You know I don't like it."

"But I'm not going back to the hotel. I'm staying here."

"You can't be serious." She faced him for the first time.

"I certainly am. What's the matter with you? You made an ugly enough scene about not coming yesterday."

Tavy gave him a hostile look and carried her unused glass back to the kitchen.

"There isn't any food," she called, in a peremptory voice. "*Or* blankets. You know that perfectly well." She came back as far as the doorway, keeping a safe distance. "You should have thought of it before, if that's what you wanted."

Quattrell sat down on the divan and poured himself another drink.

"Come on, baby," he said, "let's not be difficult."

"I'm not being difficult, it's you. There's nothing to eat and nothing to do. We didn't bring anything with us."

"Don't tell me you're hungry after that blow-out? There's plenty to drink, anyway. And if you can't think of anything to do, I can." He patted the divan beside him. "Come on, my pretty one."

Tavy picked up her jacket from the chair and turned off the oil-stove.

"Look, Rob, be sensible. It's going to be cold very soon, and we didn't bring blankets and everything's damp."

"Well, it won't be the first time without them, will it? And there's a rug in the boot." He continued to look at her indulgently, setting down his glass on the floor to search for his cigarettes.

"And it's not only that; there's Joe. I told Zohra I'd be back by five definitely; you heard me tell her."

"What difference does that make? What's got into you all of a sudden? Have you got a secret date with your funny boy-friend?"

"Of course I haven't. I don't even know who you mean."

"I mean the one with the odd leg, who bought you the brooch."

Tavy's face stiffened. She looked at him with distaste.

"I think you're hateful, if you want to know. Nothing would induce me to go to bed with you after that. You know perfectly well he's not a boy-friend, and that Panya gave it me."

Quattrell said nothing to this, only raised one eyebrow. He smoked and continued to watch her with an alert expression. Tavy knew that look of old. In this mood he would tease her as long as it amused him, but there was no doubt about the outcome. Excitement was always sparked off by their hostilities, and the moment was very near when it would come to a struggle.

"Look," she said, changing her tactics, "if we go back

now I can see Joe, and we'll be in time for *harira*. And after that I can get my things and go back with you to the hotel. Wouldn't you rather have it that way? I could stay all night. It'd be ever so much more comfortable."

He looked at her quizzically through the cigarette smoke, weighing the pros and cons. The hard divan without blankets was certainly comfortless, but his desire was rising and it would be quick satisfaction. And afterwards —well, of course he had no intention of staying the night; any fool would know that. It was quite touching to see how transparently her mind worked, offering him little bribes to get back to Joe.

"I'll have both," he said, throwing away his cigarette at random and holding out a hand. A change had come over his expression; it was both sensual and heavy. She knew that look well enough; when his face was engrossed like that it was futile to argue. She came unwillingly closer, fingering the buttons of her jacket.

"But if I do," she insisted, "we won't stay the night here, will we? Is that a promise?"

"Shut the door now, baby. Better lock it."

She did as she was told.

"Rob, did you hear what I said? Honestly, I mean it."

He was lying at length among the cushions, his eyes closed, fumbling at his trousers with one hand.

"Come on, baby. Stop talking."

She came slowly to the edge of the divan and rested one knee on it. He opened his eyes and focused her.

"Well, take those things off, sweetheart. What's the matter with you?" He ran his hand over her thigh, feeling for the zip.

"Nothing," said Tavy in a flat voice, and again did as she was told. She took off her clothes slowly and lay beside him.

★   ★   ★

By the time they reached the town it was nearly five o'clock. Quattrell drove along the waterfront to the western end, the dockside quarter in which his old-fashioned hotel was now marooned; it had seen better days before neon-lighting and concrete had begun to appear and proliferate along the bay. Now the restaurant was closed and its clients subsisted modestly on bed and breakfast. This on the whole was an advantage, since it spared them the hotel's food more than once a day. Breakfast at least was harmless: flabby Spanish bread without a trace of flavour, a smear of jam and butter, bitter coffee. This everyone took in his own room, or in summer on a balcony. Quattrell's room was high up, looking over the port. Tavy had several times spent a night with him there; once or twice booking a small back room, more often sharing his larger one in secret. It was the only real hotel she had slept in since she was a child, and frowsy as it was it gave her a special feeling. She loved at night, if there were a cruise liner in, to see the glittering skeleton ship pricked out in lights, and to wake to the putter of tunny-boats in the morning.

Quattrell squeezed the car into a side-street and they set off uphill through the Medina. The streets were already surprisingly quiet, everyone alert for the gun and business at a standstill. The apprentice boys who normally stood outside the tailors' shops, holding their skein of thread, had been sent home; some of the tailors had already put up their shutters. Those that had not sat cross-legged and pre-occupied among bales of cloth, waiting for the covered bowl to be brought by a younger member of the family.

"You must be fed up with Ramadan," said Quattrell, holding Tavy's elbow as they came up the last flight of steps. "Everyone gets so bad-tempered."

"They do, but it doesn't affect us much. We don't sit up all night, like a lot of families. Khaimo likes to go to bed about nine, but I don't think Zohra sleeps so well during Ramadan. She's getting dreadfully thin."

"I'm beginning to feel thin myself. Will they have enough?"

"Oh, I expect so. They'll think it a great honour." She gave him a sidelong smile. "It makes me laugh, I must say, to think of you breaking your fast when you haven't fasted. Have you ever?"

"Not if I could help it. Mortifying the flesh has never been my speciality."

The gun fired as they turned into the courtyard; the street was already deserted. Tavy drew aside the door-curtain and went in.

Khaimo, wearing a discarded sweater of Quattrell's over her cotton gown, was sitting cross-legged on the floor, stirring a pan of soup over a primus-stove. Her head and neck were swathed in a towel and she was wearing a pair of thick socks. She gave a little cry of dismay on seeing him; she was not dressed for company.

Zohra looked out from the kitchen curtain and emerged drying her hands. Her gown was pinned up to her hips, displaying a voluminous pair of cotton bloomers patterned with sunflowers. Her bare feet, henna-stained, were thrust into broken plastic sandals, but despite this she looked elegant and even romantic, a princess fallen on evil times in an eastern tale. She was, as Tavy had said, quite painfully thin; her face was sallow, with hollows under the cheekbones. From under the gauzy head-scarf the thick hair hung down like a soft bell-rope.

Tavy and she embraced, kissing both cheeks.

"*Donde está el niño?*"

"*Arriba, con Aminah.*"

"*He traido al señor para que coma con nosotros.*"

"Honra a nuestra casa." Zohra smiled at Quattrell and
gave him her hand.

*"El habla también el arabe. Ten cuidado con lo que
dices."*

"He does not speak as we do." Zohra's eyes lit up with
merriment. She gave Tavy a pat on the arm and gently
withdrew.

"Sit down and be comfortable," said Tavy, pointing to
the alcove, "while I go and get the tiny one." She bounded
up the stair to the first floor. There was no one on the small
landing, but she could hear voices.

Aminah had been washing clothes and was pegging
them to the line. Her feet were bare and her gown pinned
up like her mother's; her hair was smoothed to a cone with
henna mud. (She would sleep like that, turbaned in a
towel, and wash it in the morning, the long dark wavy truss
emerging a little redder than before.) Joe and the little
goat were playing in a corner, the kid with a ribbon round
its neck and a small harness-bell. Joe, since the air was
cold, had been put into his *djellába.*

Tavy ran and snatched him up in her arms, burying
her nose in his soft cheek and breathing in the mysterious
baby fragrance. He kissed her effusively and put his arms
round her neck, but almost at once arched himself vigorously backwards, pointing towards the little goat, which
was munching clover.

"Jid," he said urgently, *"jidián . . ."* and struggled so
much that she put him down again. He had only lately
begun to talk, and his vocabulary, such as it was, was
rather mixed. *"Sullah!"* he told her, holding up a handful of
greenstuff, and then, to demonstrate, held it to the goat's
muzzle. It accepted the offering with delicacy, drawing in
the stalks with a rotating movement of the tongue and toss-
ing its head upwards, so that the budding horns brushed
against Joe's *djellába* and the harness-bell tinkled. Watch-

ing the two of them, the lamb-like creature and the absorbed child, Tavy felt a pang of love so great that she
dropped on her knees between them and put an arm round
each, drawing them to her and kissing the top of Joe's head.
Her passion was all for him, but the kid had some share in
it, for it was knowledge of the coming slaughter which had
caused the spasm. The kid was doomed, and in some inexplicable way it was identified with Joe. She had been away
from him all day, and was full of remorse. Soon he would
be running the streets with the boys of the Medina, and she
had wasted this precious day. She hid her face in his hair
and hugged him fiercely.

Aminah, who was used to the sight of these embraces
and considered Tavy, if anything, an undemonstrative
mother, laughed her approval and called out something
cheerful. Tavy did not reply. Presently she released Joe and
got to her feet, rubbing her forehead and eyes with the
back of her hand.

"*El señor está abajo,*" she said, pointing to the door of
the stair.

Aminah gave a little scream and snatched a cloth from
the line, hurriedly covering her head. She gathered up the
kid and a handful of grass and they prepared to go below.
It was clear that without the goat Joe would have been
immovable.

Zohra and Khaimo had smartened themselves and
Aminah disappeared quickly behind the curtain. Quattrell
was ensconced in a corner of the alcove, buttressed with
cushions, his feet on a square of matting. They had evidently done their best to make him comfortable.

"I thought you were never coming," he grumbled,
catching Tavy by the hand. He extended a finger to Joe and
got no response. The goat had been tethered by the door
and Joe's attention was not to be wooed away. Reluctantly
Tavy let him go and sat down beside Quattrell.

The low table was set before them, covered with its plastic cloth, and they were offered buttermilk.

"*Bismillah*," said Zohra, when she had filled their glasses.

"I can't drink this stuff," said Quattrell in a low voice, and set his down.

"You'll drink it and like it, my love. Don't hurt their feelings."

They sipped in silence, smiling and nodding at Zohra. As soon as the buttermilk was finished the glasses were removed and Khaimo and Aminah brought spoons and steaming bowls. Quattrell pressed Tavy's hand against his thigh, but she pulled it away and balanced her bowl on her knee. Zohra sat sedately near but the other two squatted on the floor at a little distance. On the few occasions when the uncle had taken *harira* with them they had performed all sorts of small services for his comfort, had combed his beard and brought him a bowl and ewer, sprinkling his hands and clothing with orange-flower water. But with Quattrell they were shy, anxious not to seem too ignorant of Western manners. They smiled at him from the shadow and sucked up their broth with loud appreciation.

"How long does this go on for?" said Quattrell gloomily, when they had finished their soup.

"It's not polite to hurry. There's tea to come."

He sighed. "Will it kill them if I smoke?"

"Of course not. They want you to enjoy yourself."

"In that case they can skip tea, and go for a long walk."

"Don't," said Tavy, and gave him her hand to hold. She felt too peaceful to cope with his ill-humour.

The tea, as always, took an interminable time. The mint was bruised and stuffed into the silver pot, the sugar broken and added with the boiling water, all in a leisurely manner and with an air of ceremony. While it was brewing cakes were brought, dry almond-flavoured biscuits and rosette-shaped coils of pastry fried in oil, smelling of spice and honey. Joe broke away from the goat at last and leaned against Tavy's knee, staring blankly at Quattrell while she fed him.

"Let's go," said Quattrell, holding out a flake of pastry to Joe and throwing it back on the plate when he wouldn't take it. "We've been here long enough."

"Later," she said. "Please be good. I want to play with Joe and put him to bed."

"Zohra can do that, baby. Let's go to the hotel."

"What's the matter with you, for God's sake? It isn't six o'clock."

"You know damn well what's the matter." He took her hand again in a warm grasp, separating the fingers and pressing them against his thigh. The hand remained unresponsive. "Tell them to go for a walk, then, and take Joe with them." Tavy still said nothing. Zohra got up from her cushion and poured more tea. Khaimo and Aminah were smiling and murmuring together, as though the evening were going well. None of them seemed to be bored, or to find the atmosphere oppressive.

"Lallah Zohra," said Quattrell presently, laying his hand on Zohra's. Giving her a coaxing smile, he spoke carefully in Arabic. "Take your mother and daughter and the child, and leave us for an hour."

Zohra seemed not at all surprised. Her face even quickened with interest; she looked almost roguish.

"*Ouaha*," she said, and got up at once from her cushion.

"What did you say to her?" Tavy demanded, justifiably suspicious.

"I asked her to take Joe and the rest of them and go for walk."

"You didn't! You can't! Whatever will they think?"

"They'll think what they've thought many times before. It isn't the first occasion."

"But I'm *coming* with you to the hotel," cried Tavy,
suddenly near to tears. "And this is their time for being at
home, you clot. What on earth's come over you?"

Quattrell put her hand to his lips and kissed it.

The three women by this time were behind the curtain, putting on their outer garments. Veiled to the eyes
and with the hoods of their *djellábas* neatly pinned, Zohra
and Aminah took Joe by the hand and moved gently to the
door. Khaimo, voluminously muffled in her *haik*, came
bundling after them. Zohra gave Tavy a parting glance; a
triumphant look, as though to say, "You see, my doubting
friend—what did I tell you?"

"*Sahha*," she said knowingly to Quattrell, and closed
the door.

"There you are," he said, turning Tavy's face towards
him and shaking it playfully by the chin, "they frankly envy
you, you cold little fish. What have you got against me, if I
may ask? Still thinking of what's-his-name?"

"Oh, drop dead."

"Anything to please you, baby, but not yet." He held
her tightly against him and fell back against the cushions,
so that she looked down fiercely from above, one elbow on
his chest. "Cold, cold, my girl," he teased, "but we shall
change all that."

"That's just where you're wrong," said Tavy, "it's you
that'll be changed." She even, as she said it, smiled, as
though at some secret jest.

⋆ 9 ⋆

SEVERAL days went by before Miles could bring himself
to write to Mrs. Thewless. The state of mind in which he
found himself was extraordinary—almost a paralysis of the
will; he had not only made no progress with Colin, he had
lost interest in making any, so that frustration was complicated by guilt. He told himself repeatedly that he must
make a fresh effort, must try to have a talk with Crosier or
something of that sort; but as soon as he made a resolution
he abandoned it. Crosier was always with Colin these days,
he was impossible to catch alone. And if he did see him,
why should Crosier be expected to encourage him? It was
all so hopeless, as Miles saw it, that without an effort of will
it was impossible to keep his mind on it. But he also knew
that the real trouble was that his thoughts were busy elsewhere, with Quattrell and Tavy.

This, too, was a sufficiently hopeless situation, and he
knew it; but each time he returned to it an obstinate sensation of anger stirred inside him, encouraging a growing
resentment against Quattrell. At first he had put this down
to Quattrell's behaviour at the picnic. Quattrell had chosen
to see him as an adversary, and for Tavy's benefit, in a few

words, had demolished him. But he was not by any means demolished, rather the reverse; and the effect of the incident had been to make him see that in other circumstances nothing would have pleased him better than to be saluted as a rival.

At this point, whenever he reached it, he fell into a daydream. He and Tavy were on the ship, heading for Gibraltar, happy because Quattrell and everything to do with him had been left behind. Everything, that is to say, except Joe, for Joe was naturally with them—where else did he belong? And the ship would presently dissolve into the Conway Street flat—cleaned up and vastly improved since Lucy's day—because that was where they must live as soon as they were married. In this fantasy he laid great stress on the point that he would be looking after Tavy— that she would have a home of her own, where she and Joe would be safe. The thought of this moved him strangely; his protective instinct was aroused and in the last few days he had soothed himself with this mirage more often than was sensible.

Each time he came out of the dream it was with a sense of shock, for in the centre of any rational view of Tavy's situation there was always Quattrell; and the thought of Quattrell brought with it the even more distasteful idea of his making love to her—or for that matter leaving her alone for days in Zohra's house, which was almost as bad. There was nothing, in fact, that Quattrell could or could not do for which Miles was not prepared to hate him, and the obsessive circling of his thoughts round this one subject made it quite impossible to fix his mind on Colin.

He had come to the point, however, where he could no longer put off writing to Mrs. Thewless, and this morning had bought paper and airmail envelopes and gone further down the street to a Spanish café where the coffee was good and where he hoped that Tavy would join him later in the morning. Quattrell had left for Rabat two days ago, with Crosier and Colin, for a private conference with some official whose good will, Crosier hinted, would be worth having; schemes had a way of collapsing if one failed to plant seeds of interest in the right quarter. This Miles had learned from Colin when he telephoned the house on the morning of their departure. His first thought had been, not that Colin would be out of reach, but that Tavy was accessible. He had wandered down to the Rue de l'Ecurie as soon as he guessed them to be at a safe distance.

But only Aminah was at home, entertaining a policeman to coffee in her mother's absence. She did not invite him in, being as much embarrassed by the smell of coffee as by the policeman's presence, since Zohra was stricter about Ramadan than about some other matters. Her mother and Tavy, Aminah told him, had gone to Larache; they had gone by bus and would not be back before evening. He had scribbled a note, asking her to meet him for coffee the next morning, and had gone away disconsolate. Evidently she was taking advantage of Quattrell's absence to give herself the rare treat of an outing with Zohra. She had left the *niño* behind, Aminah called after him; he had gone not long since to the women's *hammam* with Khaimo.

In spite of this disappointment it cheered him to think that he was probably responsible for making the outing possible. Two days ago Tavy had turned up suddenly at Sam's with Joe in her arms, and while Sam went upstairs for Coca-Cola asked Miles in a whisper if he could possibly lend her some money. He thought at first it was a serious sum she wanted, her manner was so apologetic; but it turned out to be only fifty dirhams—say three pound ten—and this presented no problem.

"I can't tell you what it's for," she said in a low voice, stuffing the notes in her hip-pocket, "because it's secret.

You won't say anything to anybody, will you? Not even
Panya?" She gave him an anxious smile. "It's meant for a
surprise."

"I won't say a word. I'm good at keeping secrets."

"Oh, good. So am I. One has to be at times." She
glanced round to make sure that Joe had not wandered into
any difficulty and turned back to Miles with a look of grati-
tude. "It's frightfully kind of you, I must say. I'll pay you
back as soon as possible, but it might be a week."

"It doesn't matter when. Any time will do."

When Sam came back they drank their Cokes side by
side, very conscious of one another and of the slight but
distinctly pleasant advance in intimacy.

Choosing a table in the sun Miles ordered coffee and
unwrapped his writing-paper. The position was strategic;
he was screened from the wind and could see both sides of
the street. The Burridges, sitting snugly inside, observed
his arrival and silently nudged one another. They were
absorbed in their own conversation and made no comment.
Anyone they knew, even remotely, was worth watching.

"You will be wondering what I've been doing all this
time," Miles wrote slowly, in his best Italic hand. "A whole
week has gone and I seem to have accomplished nothing.
I've seen Colin, more than once, and had long talks with
him, but I'm afraid without success. Returning home—
anyway at present—is something he just won't consider. He
is well and happy, and has made friends. He is staying with
a man called Morley Crosier, who is obviously interested in
Colin's money for a promotion scheme; whether he's interested in him from any other point of view I'm inclined to
doubt. He is an oldish man who has lived here a good many
years. It's possible they both see it as a sort of father-son
relationship."

Miles paused, unwilling to worry Mrs. Thewless un-
duly. He wondered whether he had not already said too

much. Colin's sexual tendencies seemed to him totally unimportant, but the Thewlesses might think differently. His
own guess was that Colin, though stupid, was a cool calcu-
lator, prepared to play any rôle for his own advantage. This
was not a thing one could put in a letter to Colin's mother,
and the longer he thought about it the more difficult it was
to find anything to tell her.

★   ★   ★

"I tried to find out the extent of it," said Rex Burridge,
following the line of thought which had occupied them
through several cigarettes and cups of coffee, "but he either
doesn't know, or pretends not to. Difficult to tell."

"The boy's very cagey too," said Dora. "I said to him
the other day, when we were out at the site, 'It must be
marvellous, at your age, coming into ten thousand pounds!'
—and all he said was, 'I imagine it must be.'"

"H'm. Didn't say anything else?"

"Not a word. I said, 'Well, *you* ought to know,' and
gave him a jolly look; but he wasn't having any. I had the
feeling at the time that I'd hit the nail smack on the head.
Morley's too shrewd to embark on all this for much less."

"It won't be a penny too much," her husband agreed.
"Construction alone will absorb more than they reckon for.
Not the labour so much, but the materials. When every bolt
and screw's got to be imported it runs into a pretty useful
sum."

"We shall *have* to have a refrigerator," said Dora, "to
say nothing of a deep-freeze. And you know what *they*
cost—the earth! Bad enough at home, but with eighty per
cent duty! I suppose they just want people to live with dirt
and flies."

"Oh, we shall get that all right, don't worry. Money
will be spent on equipping the place—in the beginning,

anyway. Once it starts working it won't matter so much; the same people never come twice—why should they? There's always a fresh supply."

They sat in silence for a while, eating lumps of sugar and smoking. Miles, Dora Burridge observed, was rather stuck with his letter. He was sucking the end of his Biro and staring at the street. Silly waste of time, she thought, watching him without sympathy. Why not scribble a few postcards and have done with it?

"What *I* should like to know," she began again, "is this. We're supposed to be opening in May, on a small scale or whatever. We get our petrol and meals up to that point, and then move in. But how long after that do we wait until we go on salary? We might have to work all summer before it shows a profit."

"That's not the point, Mousie. I don't think you need worry about that. A., we can let the flat for the summer; we shall be living rent-free. B., we can get all our meals on the establishment. C., we charge out petrol, and there's a mileage rate for the car. You do the ordering, I keep the books. Salaries won't really matter the first season. The thing is to get well entrenched, on the ground floor. If we can't have things the way we want them after that it'll be our own fault."

Dora nodded, automatically glancing at Miles and across the street, in case she missed anything.

"The boy's no problem," she said. "He only wants flattering. But Crosier's a shrewd old sod, you can smell that a mile off. Have you come to any conclusions about his real income? He always puts on an act about being poor, but then look at his house! It's the sort of protesting rich people go in for, to make one sick with envy."

"I don't think it's that, Mousie. He's got enough to be comfortable as a bachelor, but there's not much margin. He's counting on Thewless's cash, and his own influence.

That's *his* contribution; we wouldn't get anywhere without it. He knows just who to suck up to, and who isn't likely to be offended by a discreet present. Quite, quite invaluable."

Dora Burridge thought this over and on the whole approved.

"The one point he seems to have slipped up on," she said, "is this Quattrell person. I simply can't see the point of bringing him into it. *We're* going to do all the work, and *he'll* get the pickings. That's about the size of it."

Burridge did not contradict her. They had been over the same ground before and would return to it again, like dogs persuaded that someone has buried something.

"Morley's impressed with him, I can see that. He's got plenty of brains and energy; doesn't miss a trick. He worked with a publicity outfit once, I believe; supposed to have ideas. What I don't like's the idea of his hanging around and interfering, poking his nose into everything. He isn't in this for his health, if you want my opinion."

"Oh, the day will come when we have to get rid of him," said Dora Burridge decisively, snapping open her powerful handbag and rummaging for cigarettes. "Soon, too. He's far too pleased with himself, for one thing. I was quite prepared to like him at first—perfectly open-minded —but it's no use. I know the type; it's not one I happen to care for."

Burridge flicked his lighter and held it steady for her. "I wonder if a talk with Morley . . ." he began tentatively, then shook his head. "No good without ammunition. Morley's got faith in the feller, for some reason."

They stared in front of them silently, revolving possibilities.

"Why can't he go to Spain?" said Dora suddenly, turning to her husband. She was sitting, as she was always careful to do, on his right side, so that she could keep in touch with the eye and its infinitesimal changes of expression. "Do you remember that conversation with Ozzie, when he was talking about going to Ceuta? He *definitely* said Quattrell couldn't go because it was a Spanish frontier. What could he have meant by that, do you suppose? I made a mental note at the time, I remember. You know how one has a sort of instinct a thing may be useful."

"H'm," said Burridge, and touched his moustache with a finger. "Could be anything, I suppose. Sounds as though he might have been in trouble with the authorities."

Dora thought this over with care, but could find nothing to take hold of. Never had a lack of data seemed more provoking.

"The police . . ." she said, and fell into a further silence. Presently she stirred the dregs of sugar in her cup and swallowed them. "I wonder . . . could that mean . . . d'you think it's at all likely he's been in prison?"

"I wouldn't think so, frankly. Still, one never knows. I wonder if there's any way of finding out, from the police at this end? Morley knows that Commissaire, Abd-el-What's-It, but he's not very high up, unfortunately. One would need to know someone at ministerial level."

At the thought of the Spanish prison Dora brightened. "It would be perfect," she said, "because *if* it could be proved, and a discreet word slipped to the police through Morley's friend, next time he goes to Paris or anywhere they might decide not to readmit him."

"True. But since he *is* in this country it wouldn't work. And now that he's in Morley's scheme I have a feeling he'll stick pretty close. No more trips to Paris or London—he might miss something. Anyway, I've a shrewd idea this book he's supposed to be working at has gone sour on him. The other day, talking to Morley, he said, 'The damn thing's at a standstill. I must give it a rest,' and I thought, dear me, how convenient—and so soon after telling us how much too busy he was, etcetera. I thought, aha, he sees quicker returns to be got out of Morley's plan."

"Listen," said Dora, who had not been listening at all to what her husband was saying. "Lots of people go to Gibraltar for a day's shopping. Why shouldn't we go one day—*and* Quattrell—to buy this and that in the way of general equipment? Then, don't you see," she warmed to the idea, "if he were met on the ship by the police, or at the airport for that matter, he wouldn't be allowed in. He'd have to go back to Gibraltar and stay there! It would solve *everything!*" She was so carried away by imagination that her colour rose and her eye recovered its sparkle.

"Now then, Mousie!" Burridge smiled indulgently and patted her knee. "You've defined the objective, but haven't plotted the course. They'd need a reason, you know. A word dropped in the right place might well do it, but there'd have to be a reason. The police don't operate in a vacuum."

"But if he's been in prison?" she cried, then checked herself, looked round and lowered her voice. "Isn't that enough to make him undesirable, as an alien? They don't want jailbirds here, I shouldn't have thought. They've got enough already."

"But we don't *know* that he has, Mousie. That was only a shot in the dark. Nobody's going to be interested without facts to go on."

"The facts are there all right, you mark my word. They've only got to be uncovered. Besides, look at the rumours people believe in this place without a shred of evidence!"

"True, but the police don't act on them. They have to have chapter and verse."

"Then we must prove them," she said stoutly, crushing out her cigarette. "Why should Ozzie have said it if it wasn't true? It was Quattrell who told him."

Burridge considered this without enthusiasm.

"Ozzie says a lot of things I wouldn't care to depend on."

"But he's not malicious, Rex. He wouldn't invent it."

"Possibly not. But would Master Q. have said it, if it had been anything important? He was probably smuggling something and got caught by the customs. Could happen to any of us."

"Smuggling from where? On which frontier?"

"From Ceuta, say. You know how hot they are."

"But in that case it wouldn't be the Spanish police, would it? It would be the Moroccans. No, no, Rex; that's not it at all. It was something quite different, and serious. Of that I feel positive."

"You could have a little talk with Ozzie, I suppose," said Burridge doubtfully. "But I should be careful how you do it."

"Well, naturally. When am I not?" She thought for a moment. "I'm not sure it wouldn't be better to try Mollie Brockhurst."

"That would be a bad mistake. She's dotty if you like, but beginning to show interest, Morley says. We don't want to scare her."

"True, that's a point. I hadn't thought of that."

"The thing is, not to rush it. Just keep it at the back of your mind and something'll come of it."

"Don't worry, I'll think of something. Funny how one's mind goes blank just when one's concentrating. It'll come to us quite suddenly, you know, when we're least expecting it."

★   ★   ★

Panya had had several customers that morning and was a little flustered. Not tourists—it was too early in the year for that—but two or three resident ladies who had separately dropped in and turned over her entire stock before drifting off to the ritual of morning coffee. One of them had even ordered a brocade coat and another had asked her to set aside a piece of jewellery. There was a party pending, and they were looking for something out of the ordinary to wear. When the last of them had gone every article in the shop was out of place. Panya began methodically to restore order, returning garments to their hangers and jewellery to the glass shelves of the display-case. If Tavy came while the place was in chaos, or if there were more customers, it would be difficult to keep the issues clear and to talk seriously.

Tavy was fairly punctual, opening the shop-door quietly while Panya was rearranging trinkets in the window. With such a miscellaneous stock these things were particularly vulnerable; an arrangement that had taken an hour could be destroyed in an instant.

"I got your note," said Tavy, returning Panya's kiss. "Rob's gone to Rabat, so there was no problem."

"It was good of you to come so soon, dear child. It is important I talk to you. Do you want some tea or coffee, something to eat? Getting up early, as you do, makes a long morning."

"Since Zohra can't see," said Tavy, tempted, "I'd love something. Everyone fasting makes me much hungrier than usual. I don't think I'd notice it so much if I was alone."

Panya patted her arm and called up the stairs to Concepción.

"Now, child, let us sit in the private corner and hope there are no customers." She gave Tavy a low stool and sank heavily at her desk. "I want you to listen without interruption because there is much to say. When I have told you the situation we can discuss."

Tavy clasped her knees and gazed obediently at Panya. For once she was not wearing jeans but a plain grey skirt and jacket which Panya's seamstress had made her the previous year. It was meanly cut and had an institutional air, which her faded and freshly washed shirt did nothing to modify. Panya's intentions had been good, but the seamstress had been trained on *kaftans*, which are conveniently shapeless. Tavy looked rather like the head girl of some decent orphanage, but she so rarely wore conventional clothing that she saw nothing wrong with it.

"This Rob of yours," said Panya, fingering her gold chains as though, in spite of her serene air, she was a little nervous, "he is married, as we know. You have known that a long time, yes?"

Tavy nodded, her eyes widening slightly with apprehension.

"I have never told you this before, but for some time I have known his wife. She has gone back to an earlier name and at first I had no idea about it. I discovered it only last year, when I met her at the house of a mutual friend in Paris."

"You didn't tell me," said Tavy, her eyes on Panya's face.

"Well, no, my dear, obviously. What purpose would it have served? I know your situation and do not like it, but while there was a wife in the background there was no sense in worrying you. In my experience, in a relation of this kind, it is happiest to know as little as possible about the third person."

"I never think about her," Tavy said. "And Rob never mentions her."

"That is good, because now she has decided to divorce him, and when once he is free you need never think of her again."

Tavy sat perfectly still, and Panya could deduce nothing from her expression. She had dropped her eyes and was gazing at her clasped hands.

"You have always told me," Panya went on, "that you do not wish to marry. If the chance comes you must give up this foolish idea. If not for your own sake, then for little Joe."

"I don't mind either way," said Tavy, not raising her eyes. "It's not important."

"Decide on its importance when I have finished telling you. I have had a letter from Mrs. Quattrell, or Mrs. Graves as she is now calling herself, and yesterday she telephoned from London. She has seen the *avocat* already about the divorce, and he is sending somebody. It is a matter of evidence."

Tavy's eyes were on Panya's face once more. She had become more than usually pale.

"But this has happened before," she said, "before I knew him. She started a divorce twice, and then changed her mind. Why should it be any different this time?"

"It is different this time," said Panya, "because of you and Joe. She is sick of her situation, and she is also rather a nice woman. She had decided to divorce before she knew of your existence. Now that she knows, there will be no going back."

"How did she know about me? Did you tell her?"

"I thought it best for your sake that she should know. I am being frank with you, dear child, because I want you to be sensible. He is not the most perfect man in the world, but there must be no silly nonsense about not marrying him."

"Don't worry," said Tavy, with the ghost of a smile. Her colour had begun to come back and the muscles round her mouth relaxed. "At least, not on my account. I always took that line about getting married because I knew there was no chance. So many people think it's stupid anyway. But I expect you saw through me when I said that; I always thought you did."

The door behind them was pushed open by Concepción with a tray. She was a meagre grey-haired Spanish
woman who had been with Panya since the early days of
her marriage. She had married herself quite recently, very
late in life, and now lived two streets away with her Spanish husband, who was employed in a dairy. It was a profitable arrangement all round, for she brought Panya good
cow's milk, to say nothing of cream and yoghurt when
there was any to spare. She looked keenly at Tavy as she
set down a plate of sponge-cakes.

"*La señorita tiene la cara palida. Este tiempo es muy
molesto.*"

"I'm all right, thank you." Tavy smiled at her.

"*Donde está el precioso niño? No lo habras perdido?*"

"*Está bien, y no está perdido.*"

"*Y esta, la pobre,*" glancing sternly at Panya, "*quando
se va a casar?* When is she going to be married?"

"*Pronto, muy pronto,*" said Panya, in the tone of one
who considers the question impertinent. She busied herself
with the coffee.

"*Bueno, gracias a Dios! Los hombres han de responder
de muchas cosas.*" She nodded with sibylline emphasis on
her way to the door.

"Are you surprised by what I tell you?" Panya asked,
when Concepción had gone.

"Yes . . . no." Tavy took a bite of sponge-cake. "I had a
feeling something good was going to happen."

"What made you think that?"

"Zohra told my fortune the other day, and the cinders
fell several times in the same way, all pointing to a marriage."

"My dear child! And you supposed it was your
own?"

"Well, I know you think it's silly, but so many things

come true. They know lots of things we don't. I can't explain it."

"Ah, so. And you felt that this was a good thing, if it came off?"

Tavy hesitated. "It can't be a bad thing," she said cautiously, "can it? Do you think it might change Rob's attitude to Joe and me? Mightn't it be much safer?"

"I would think so, yes. It would be better in every way, more *convenable*. You would have a home together."

"I don't think Rob would care for that. He likes the present arrangement."

"But, my dear, when one is married one cannot be so eccentric."

"He doesn't mind being eccentric or anything like that; he's that kind of man. To live ordinary people's life he'd have to change."

"You will have to change him, then."

"Yes," said Tavy, and gave Panya a curious look, wondering if more were implied than she intended. But Panya was peacefully drinking her coffee, quite self-contained. Tavy helped herself to sugar and for a while neither of them said anything.

"Now I must explain to you," said Panya presently, "something that is going to happen. As I said, a man is flying out from London about this evidence. He is due to arrive this evening and I think will come to see me tomorrow morning. It is Rob he wants to see, but you tell me he is gone to Rabat. So I will advise him to come to you first, and you will be very helpful."

"Helpful, how? What will I have to do?"

"You must tell him everything, dear child, and answer his questions. He will ask you if you sleep with Rob, and if the child is his—things of that sort. You must tell him everything, truthfully."

"I'd rather see Rob first. He mightn't like it."

"No, no, it will be all right. And the man cannot waste time, you know; private detectives are expensive."

"Detective?" said Tavy sharply. "Look, Panya, I don't think I'd better . . ."

"No, no, they are not detectives, they are called something else. Enquiry-agent, I think it is, only Constance said detective. He will come to see you tomorrow, and you must help him. I think you would be wise to stay in the house all day."

"I can do that, but I'm not sure . . ."

"My dear, it is quite simple. If you want your Rob to be a free man, so that he can marry you, you will answer the questions with truth. If not, you will tell lies. Do you understand?"

"I shall tell Zohra," said Tavy, clasping and unclasping her hands. "She must stay with me whatever happens, when he comes. I wish I could remember the Spanish for detective."

"Tell her he is an *abogado*, that will do. Or better still, an *oficial de policía*. That will give her confidence, no? —she is used to Aminah's friends."

★   ★   ★

Threading her way through the crowded market Tavy tried to interpret what she had been told. She always paid serious attention to Zohra's predictions, but this one (or part of it) seemed to be coming true with uncanny speed. If the detective arrived as Panya said, it was a blessing that Rob would be still in Rabat; she could not imagine him tolerating such a person. On the other hand, the second part of Zohra's forecast might take time. The forces at work were invisible and not to be hurried.

She went up the steps between fruit and vegetable

stalls, looking for the flower-sellers. This was not the *socco* she was used to but the grander market in the European town, where foreign residents did their shopping. She still had a little money left from Larache and wanted to mark the occasion with a bunch of flowers. These would be for Zohra, who had willingly given help and arranged everything. Tavy bought some wild narcissus, sweet-scented papery offspring of the winter rains, and sniffed them as she strolled uphill in the direction of the café.

The idea of marriage was so strange that she could hardly imagine it. It was a contingency that had never arisen, for Rob had told her from the start that it was impossible. His wife, he said, would never divorce him; she had refused in the most implacable manner; she was that kind of woman. It made no difference, in fact, and couldn't matter less. These old ideas were finished and nobody bothered with them.

All this she had accepted as true, and in the world she lived in there seemed to be no special safety in being married. Zohra had been divorced because she had no son and her husband had decided he wanted a younger woman. Marriage was a contract between families, involving gifts and sums of money; nobody made too much fuss if the return of the *sadak*, the bride-price, were agreed on and the contract broken. European marriages, she knew, were totally different, but even so there was nothing to make them binding. Quattrell had left his wife and Constance her first husband. What Tavy wanted was to make certain that, marriage or no marriage, he would never leave her. Each time he went away she sickened with anxiety. What she needed was not some legal process but a power that would put it beyond question that he would come back to her. Power, *poder* . . . that had been Zohra's word. "*En todas partes existen poderes invisibles.*" There were powers everywhere, whatever some people might say. Was it too much to believe they were working already?

As to the marriage itself Tavy was very ignorant. She had been to more than one wedding in the last two years and her memories were all of magnificence and exhaustion. She knew it would not be like that, for these were the festivities of Zohra's relations, who had indulgently accepted her as a guest. The receptions had always been in summer, in a house and courtyard crowded to suffocation, lasting with noise and music far into the night. She had sat for hours between Zohra and Aminah in a crowd of women, marvelling at the glittering *kaftans* and gauzy finery, her head ringing with noise and the ear-splitting *you-you-you* of female rejoicing, until it had seemed to her that almost nothing could be worth the endurance of such an ordeal. And at last, like a gold-encrusted effigy, her face powdered and painted beyond recognition, the bride appeared, preceded by little girls with lighted candles, trailing their muslin finery in slow procession. If it were a girl she knew by sight she had become another creature, rigid, expressionless, performing her traditional role with sleep-walking calm, carried through the uproarious ritual in a trance of tension. Afterwards, when tea and cakes had been offered and wedding gifts received, those guests who were not intimates were expected to depart, and Zohra, a humble member, took Tavy home. By this time the bride would be in the nuptial chamber and the bridegroom and his friends (a noisy procession of taxis nowadays) hammering at the outer door. The drivers sounded their horns continuously, rending the night with klaxons.

Zohra was always reluctant to leave, no matter how late, for a wedding was the most rapturous entertainment she could conceive of—a night of sumptuousness and rejoicing for which families cheerfully ruined themselves—and all the way home would relate the glories and dramas of many occasions. Tavy did not much like these stories, for they always came to the point where the bride's linen was exhibited in triumph, and this in turn led to the great joke of a fowl's having to be sacrificed in secret, and the blood sprinkled. Such a ruse was undoubtedly funny and she would force a smile. But her own experience had been too frightening to be reminded of, and she disliked any disturbance of the tender layers of untruth with which she covered it.

★ IO ★

"THERE's that girl," said Dora Burridge, checking herself in the act of getting up. She had her gloves and bag in her hand, gathering herself to leave, but at the sight of Tavy at Miles's table she paused. This was the second time she had seen them together and it was not, she was almost certain, a chance encounter. Miles had been there for a good hour when the girl walked straight up to the table and sat down with him.

Burridge had paid for their coffee and was pocketing the change, but at this he sat back and his eye swivelled to the window. The pair were evidently pleased to see one another; there was a bunch of flowers on the table.

"What d'you make of *that?*" said Dora, keeping her voice low. "I saw them together a week ago, not a hundred yards from here."

"I don't make anything of it, that I know of. They were both at that picnic, weren't they?"

"Yes, but that was to be expected. She came out with Quattrell and young what's-his-name with Crosier. Quattrell's gone to Rabat, remember, with Morley. Those two are on their own." She said this as though the circumstance were significant, but in fact she was rather at a loss to know how to interpret it. If the girl were having a flirt behind Quattrell's back it was an interesting thought, but hardly relevant or useful. At the same time she had a feeling that Tavy's presence here was a clue to something, if she could only put her finger on it.

"Come on, Mousie," said Burridge, getting restless, "I want to buy a paper."

"Just a minute. I was trying to remember . . ." She withdrew her gaze from the window and consulted his unshaded eye, but it told her nothing. "Wasn't there a scandal about that girl, some years ago? I don't mean their not being married and having a child—that's what one would expect. There was something else, I'm positive."

"I don't think so. She was very young, and it was all rather unsavoury, but I don't think there was any more to it than that. Nothing to get hold of," said Burridge, who had followed his wife's line of thought perfectly.

"Well, I'm not so sure. Age of consent, and all that sort of thing. Mightn't it come under the heading of moral turpitude?"

Burridge smiled. "Here? Don't make me laugh. Why should anyone care? There are all sorts of grubby teenagers living in cracks and under stones—as you've often noticed. Some of them even have scrofulous babies in dirty prams. I often see them in the evening, when they come up for air."

"She doesn't look a bit like those. She's a different kind of animal." Tavy, indeed, was looking surprisingly conventional this morning, drinking a *citron pressé* through a straw and listening attentively to Miles.

"Well, I dare say Quattrell's cleaned her up a bit," said Burridge, "for which I don't blame him. It's an acquired taste, liking to be seen around with the unwashed."

"So you don't think much of it? The moral turpitude, I mean."

"Good heavens, no. You're losing your sense of proportion. It's got to be something much better than that, or we'll make ourselves ridiculous."

On her way out of the café Mrs. Burridge gave a cry of surprise. "Why, how lovely to see you both! And so very hardy, sitting out of doors! Don't you find this wind rather cold?"

"We're all right in this corner," said Miles, getting half-heartedly to his feet. Tavy gave a scant smile and said nothing. Her hand, very plain and slender, was lying by the bunch of flowers.

"And flowers, too! Well, you *are* harbingers of spring!" She touched the flowers with her black glove and Tavy withdrew her hand. "You make quite a picture, my dear, with your white flowers. Quite charming and romantic!"

"The flowers are for Zohra," said Tavy coolly, "I just bought them in the market."

"Oh, I *know*, my dear—I was only teasing," and Mrs. Burridge moved off, looking pleasantly roguish.

Left to themselves they sat for a constrained interval in silence. Tavy was dying to communicate, but supposed she must not. Such an incalculable change, so undreamed-of in her eventless life and so imminent, was something she could hardly bear to think about alone. It was not something to keep to oneself but to confabulate over for hours with a bosom friend. She would do that of course with Zohra, as far as their Spanish allowed and as soon as she got home, but it would have been a comfort to know what Miles thought, too, in case she needed him. He was the only other person, apart from Panya, who gave her a feeling of trust and of whom she was not afraid.

Miles was silent for a different reason: the things he

longed to ask were precisely those it was impossible or
ridiculous to say. If he began, "Look—come back with me
to London," she would stare at him, quite rightly, and perhaps laugh. If he told her, "I can't bear to think of you with
that man," she would probably—again quite rightly—be
staggered by his impertinence. It could take months for
two people to get on such a footing together, and in a little
less than a week he would be gone. Yet it might be so
simply done, if he had the effrontery to do it. If he could
take the hand lying without guile so near his own, and say,
"*Please*, Tavy, *listen* . . ." But after that the image of Quattrell would rise between them, sardonically smiling—and
how could he possibly go on? Spoken in that mocking presence each word would sound more ludicrous than the
last.

"You didn't bring Joe with you," he said at last, breaking the silence. At this she turned her eyes on him, and for
the first time—or so it improbably seemed—they looked
full at one another. The look was so long and steady that he
found himself observing, as through a lens, the separate
lashes and flecks of green and grey in the blue pupil.

"He's too slow," she said, "and I can't carry him all the
way. He's got so heavy."

Miles felt there was a possible approach in this and
went on at random.

"Where will you send him to school, when the time
comes? Will you go back to England?"

"Oh God, I can't think that far ahead. It'll depend
what Rob wants to do. Anyway, he's only two and a half;
there are schools here if we want them."

"What sort of schools?"

"Oh, all sorts. You pass one every day, don't you, living
at Sam Hardback's? That's for the very little ones. They sit
on the floor and chant the Koran by rote at the tops of their
voices. You must have heard them."

"I've heard them, yes," said Miles, who had more than once passed the open doorway and seen the aged teacher and the clusters of dark eyes and shaven heads. "Would you really send him to one of those?"

"Why not?" She was at once defensive. "It's better than being on the streets, and he might as well learn decent Arabic. And after that there are French and Spanish schools. There's even a *lycée*."

"But do you intend to stay here indefinitely," Miles pursued, "even with Joe? I mean, mightn't it be a good plan for him to come back to England at some point, and have a normal education?" It struck him uneasily that he was using the same sort of arguments with Tavy that he had tried with Colin, with as little chance of success.

"I don't know," said Tavy, and sighed. The sigh was a deep one and ended in an involuntary shiver. "The thought of going back to England gives me the creeps." She smiled in extenuation, as though there were more to explain than could possibly be gone into. Miles let his eye dwell on her mouth and wondered whether, when they said good-bye, it would be possible to kiss her. It was a tender mouth, gentle and calm and not at all (if he could judge) voluptuous. He took his eyes away from it with an effort.

"But are you *happy* here?" he heard himself saying. "Because it seems to me that you're not, and I wish I could help you." He was astonished to hear himself say this, but Tavy seemed not particularly surprised. She was still, he could see, half absent in thought, deliberating something unspoken.

"Sometimes I am," she said, again meeting his eye fully. "Not always, but then who is? I'm miserable some of the time, but it'll be better presently."

"What makes you think so? *How* will it be better? It seems to me there's everything against it." Now that he had taken the plunge he went on recklessly. "You're alone half the time, away from your own people, living an extraordinary life—and what about Joe's future? Isn't there anyone in the world who cares a damn about you except . . ." He pulled himself up, on the verge of saying something outrageous that she might not forgive. "I'm sorry, I got carried away. You'll tell me it's none of my business."

"Listen," said Tavy, and put her hand on his. "You're kind, it's sweet of you, and there's something I want to tell you. Perhaps I shouldn't, but Rob's away in Rabat and I might need help. I'm not sure, but I might. Will you be at Sam's tomorrow? Where can I find you if I want to?"

"I can be anywhere you like." It came to him in a flash that she had made up her mind to leave Quattrell, and in another minute would ask him to help her escape. His mind leapt under the delicious shock, darting at once to ships, aeroplanes, passports.

"Rob and I are going to get married," said Tavy, looking down self-consciously at the table. She waited for the news to sink in, and at first was not surprised by Miles's silence. When he continued to say nothing she glanced at him curiously, and was shocked by his expression.

"When?"

"I don't know when. It depends. But at least there's going to be a divorce. That's what I wanted to tell you."

"I see." For a blank moment he could think of nothing to say. Tavy was looking at him enquiringly; he had hardly given the news a good reception. "I suppose I ought to congratulate you," he said at last. "Does that sound grudging? I'm sorry. The trouble is, I've spent the last two days building up something very different. I've been thinking about you in a ludicrously childish way, as if you were a character in a fairy-tale, or under a spell. I suppose I was going to bring you to life again, or set you free, or change you back from something. How I was going to do it I don't quite know. Rather a joke, don't you think?"

Tavy's hand was still in his; she moved it gently. "Let's not stay here any longer. Let's walk up to the house. I'd like to tell you about it, honestly; we can talk on the way."

On the descent to the *socco* and up through the Medina Miles forced himself to ask questions, trying, mostly against his better judgement, to arrive at some understanding of her state of mind. Common sense warned him not to probe, for almost every answer added to his discomfort and he knew he would do far better to leave the thing alone. If she were really on the point of marrying Quattrell, what business was it of his? He thought he detected a fugitive flavour about some of her replies, a hint of incongruity or evasion, as though she were concealing something. Yet her answers were candid enough, as far as they went. Panya, it appeared, had had news of the divorce, and judged it prudent to tell her. So much was clear; and she seemed to think it would happen soon, and that she might need help. "What sort of help?" he asked her. But the question made her uneasy: she could not formulate anything. "I don't know," she said. "I just feel it. I suppose what it is, I'm frightened, and would like to feel you were around."

Presently it all came out. They had threaded their way through a crowded quarter and now turned into a quieter street, where they could walk abreast. A person, said Tavy, would arrive tomorrow, who would ask her questions. She would have to see him alone, or with only Zohra; she made a great point of this, sounding both excited and afraid. What sort of a person, Miles asked her. She didn't know. Panya had called him a detective, but he wasn't the police. He was somebody the lawyer had decided to send from London, and she must tell him everything. She particularly stressed that Panya had told her to stay at home all day, so that there would be no fear of missing him. It became clear to Miles that she was hoping the interview would happen

as early as possible, while she and Zohra were alone. There
was a chance that by early evening Quattrell would return.

"But if he's being sent by the lawyer," said Miles, "he'll
want to see *him* as well." He knew nothing about divorce
procedure but was not simple enough to suppose that a
case could be constructed on Tavy's evidence alone.

"Yes, well, he might do that later, I imagine. Panya
said it was very important I should tell him the truth."

"He'll probably want to see you together, then, when
your friend gets home." He felt an extraordinary distaste
for Quattrell's name and a reluctance to utter it, as though
it had some sort of power, or were an omen.

"But I don't want him to," said Tavy. "Panya says
they're frightfully expensive, these people, so he won't
want to waste time. *I* shall have the whole day, you see,
and I want Zohra to be there."

From her sidelong glance, no more than a quiver of
the eye, he saw that she was not quite certain that he believed her. In that moment, too, it was plain that she did
not want Quattrell to be at the interview, and was confident there was not much danger that he would be. He
might react far from favourably to this news of the divorce:
that was the unspoken thing. She intended, poor silly child,
to manage it alone.

"And what will your friend . . . Rob's . . . reaction be?"
said Miles, bringing out the name with difficulty. "You
must have discussed it often."

"No, no, we never have," said Tavy hastily. "Not since
the beginning. There was no use discussing something that
couldn't happen."

"But now you say it will?"

"Well . . . yes. It rather looks like it."

"And he'll be delighted, naturally."

"Wouldn't you think? Isn't that what everyone would

want, in his position?" Again there was that sidelong look, the glance of a child who hopes its fibs are convincing.

They turned into a more than usually narrow passage, approaching a mosque. Miles had paused at this sombre doorway before, with Sam, and had seen the empty slippers lying on the floor and the trough where the faithful performed their ritual ablutions. All else was hidden by a curtain, through which a murmur of prayers was audible. As they passed the doorway a venerable figure emerged, feeling for the step with his stick. There were several children huddled together on the step, knotting some pieces of string into a plait of rushes. The old man sensed the obstruction and disturbed them with his foot. They moved without looking up, but only an inch or so, shifting perfunctorily on their bottoms. He stepped out in front of Tavy and Miles and turned in the same direction, with blind confidence. The face had a look of serene alertness, though the eyes were milky; blindness and age and sanctity had made it beautiful. As Tavy and Miles overtook him a small boy rose from a doorstep and silently touched him, and the two went on steadily together without speaking, the old man's authoritative hand on the boy's shoulder.

"But supposing he isn't pleased?" said Miles, when they were walking abreast once more. They were within sight of the steps leading up to Zohra's quarter.

"Don't worry, he'll be pleased all right. If not at first, then later. He'll come round to it."

"Then that's all right, since you're so sure. That's wonderful," said Miles bitterly. "And I suppose I shan't see you again, or know what happens."

"Of course you'll know. I shall tell you. I shall come over and find you as soon as I can. You've been a great comfort."

"I don't see how I can be a comfort, even if you

wanted me to. There are too many things I don't know. Why, damn it," he said violently, stopping at the foot of the steps, "you haven't told me a single thing that matters. You haven't even told me whether you love him."

"Haven't I?" said Tavy, again with that sidelong glance, turning to the steps. "But even if I hated him it wouldn't alter anything, would it?"—and went steadily up and away from him, no longer matching her pace to his or making allowances for his lameness.

★   ★   ★

In the middle of the next afternoon Sam came home, carrying a whisky bottle full of milk, a packet of tea and half a dozen coconut cakes wrapped in paper. Miles was lying on the brass bedstead in his shirt-sleeves, smoking. The windy brightness of the morning had vanished at midday and clouds of a threatening density had moved up from the west, making the house dark. In the mood of angry frustration in which he found himself he preferred to lie in this gloomiest corner of the room; the alcove was heavy with the sweetish-acrid smoke of Moroccan tobacco.

"Hey there," called Sam, putting down his parcel, "I met the Burridges in town, and they're dropping by to listen to some of my tapes. I've offered them tea—was that right? I thought maybe you could make it." He came to the foot of the bed and drummed lightly with his fingers on the brass rail. "What's up? You sick or something?"

"Nothing's up. I'm quite all right."

"Something upset you, then? You look kind of funny from here. I guess it's the light—it's going to rain like hell in a few minutes."

Miles roused himself with an effort and swung his legs off the bed, making the loose knobs rattle.

"I've got a bit of a headache, that's all. It'll be better presently."

"You're crazy to smoke, then. It's this change in the weather, I guess. I thought it was starting to thunder, but it's some ways off yet." He turned back to the table and gathered up the paper of cakes. "I kind of like it when it rains here; it's an interesting change, like living under water. Last time we had a storm there was a water-spout, just walking about on the sea like nobody's business. Lucky the recorder runs on batteries, the electricity usually conks out. I better check on the candle situation." He picked up the bottle of milk and the tea-packet and paused at the stair-foot. "Is it O.K. for you to make the tea, then? I might do something unspeakable by British standards."

"I'll come," said Miles, "you go ahead," and thrust his feet into his shoes. His heart sank at the prospect of an hour with the Burridges, still more at the thought of Sam's more esoteric recordings. Why the Burridges should be interested he could not imagine; no doubt they, or perhaps even Sam, had an ulterior motive. Nobody here, he reflected bitterly, seemed to do anything for the reasons they professed; himself least of all. He had told himself that he must stay in the house because Tavy might need him when the detective came, but it would be nearer the truth to admit that the last thing he wanted was to help her. If he could hinder the course she was so determined on he would do so, whatever the outcome. But what could he conceivably do, besides angrily wait? He was almost ill with disgust at his own impotence.

Sam was already pattering about in the kitchen, putting cups on a tray and arranging the cakes on a plate. They did not look very inviting, however he disposed them, but they were the least repellent objects the baker had offered; everything else had too obviously been fried in oil.

"Do we make it before they come," he asked Miles, "or wait till they arrive? I guess you can make it in the coffee-pot?"

"It won't taste very nice if I do."

"That's just too bad, then. There isn't anything else."

"Then there's no problem. I'll make it in the coffee-pot." Miles washed the pot cursorily at the sink while Sam lit the gas and put on the kettle. It was now so dark even in this upstairs room that the flaring gas-jet served as an illumination.

"Say, what d'you make of those two? Very British and all that, but a bit of a find, I'd say, as far as Morley's concerned. That bar of theirs was quite well done, if they hadn't had bad luck. It just occurred to me, if the new scheme goes well, some background music in the bar might be quite a feature."

So that's it, Miles thought, prising open the packet of tea. Drumming and prayer-rhythms in the cocktail hour. I might have guessed.

"It depends what you have to offer," he said, pouring some boiling water into the coffee-pot and dubiously smelling it, "some of your serious recordings might be above their heads."

"Yeah, but I've got lots of other stuff. You know, vocal, and some college harmony groups I recorded in the States. Nice easy nostalgic stuff, nothing like I do now. I'm not dumb enough to think they'd go for anything advanced."

"You can only try," said Miles, and stepped out on the narrow terrace to look at the sky. It was muffled in indigo cloud, each fold and billow hanging lower than the last, so that at the horizon, which was lead-coloured, it was impossible to distinguish sky from sea. Yet there were still a few remote figures on the darkening beach and the children playing in the street sounded unusually lively. As he leaned over the parapet to watch them he saw Dora Burridge, brilliant in mustard-yellow with black gloves and scarf, come cautiously round the corner at the foot of the steps. Almost at the same moment the first drops fell.

"Well!" she cried, when Sam had gone down to the door and she was halfway up the stairs, "if you hadn't been so prompt we'd both have been soaked! I said to Rex when we parked the car, I said, 'I hope you know the way, because in another minute, the heavens are going to open.' And now listen to it!" She paused at the head of the second flight, raising a gloved hand. Rain was coming over the roof like a wave breaking, with a rattle of drops like gun-shot as it splashed through the windows. Miles, upstairs in the kitchen, closed both window and door, but the floor was already wet and the whitewashed wall darkening with veins of water. He made the tea, but dared not risk carrying the tray down the ladder-like stair. He stood at the top and waited, pushing his hair from his brow, which was suddenly hot. In the few moments since he had closed the window the air had become oppressive.

"But it's like living in a lighthouse!" cried Dora Burridge on the ladder, her dark head and yellow shoulders rising out of the gloom of the lower level. "Nothing but stairs and stairs, and these fascinating little rooms! You must have the most fabulous view—is this the top?"

"I had to close the door," said Miles, "because of the rain." Sam and Burridge had followed from below, so that the kitchen was suddenly crowded.

"Well, that's the dilemma," said Sam. "You open the door, and it's like being at sea in a storm. Close it for half a minute and you start to sweat. It won't last long. In fact, it's less already." He opened the door gingerly and Mrs. Burridge looked out. "The damn thing's stuck again," he said, "the wood swells like hell when it rains." He pushed it with his knee and it opened further with a jerk, at an unnatural angle. "Oh *no!*" he cried, in accents of fury, "just

look at that, will you? The damn hinge's gone again." He
stepped outside, ignoring the rain, and went round to examine the damage. It was as he had feared: the hinge hung
loose from the rotten woodwork and the door leaned
drunkenly from the frame like a broken wing. He shifted it
into an upright position and set about fitting the loose
screws back into their holes. Mrs. Burridge tactfully took
no notice of this domestic accident. The view at this distance was hidden by the parapet, but a watery rent had
appeared in the cloud and in default of anything better she
was preparing to admire it when she found she had only
one glove, and turned back abruptly.

"I've dropped a glove! Oh dear, how unlucky! Rex, I
believe you're standing on it."

Miles and Burridge shifted obligingly in the small
space, but there was no glove.

"I had them both when I came in, I *know*, because I
was wearing them. I must have dropped it clambering up
that ladder."

"In that case it'll be there when you go down," said
Burridge, turning his seeing eye to the streaming window.
There was nothing that he could see to justify the climb.
"Funny thing, the mania people have for views: it's the
same in all these Medina houses. A lot of roofs and television aerials and the sea. Or just roofs," he emended, since
nothing else could be seen.

"Would you like me to go down and look?" Miles
offered doubtfully, but Dora was already half-way down
the ladder.

The glove was not on the floor below and she descended further, switching on a feeble light as she went
down. At the second landing she saw it, lying almost at the
bottom and barely visible even to her sharp eye on the
black and ochre pattern of the tiles.

"Success!" she cried, "I've found it!" and was stooping

to retrieve it when somebody rapped hesitantly on the knocker. "I'll go!" she called, and lifted the heavy latch. A woman was standing in the rain, pressed almost against the doorway, only the dark eyes visible under the hood of her *djellába*. A hand appeared from the folds of the sleeve with a scrap of paper which she offered diffidently.

"Oh, thanks," said Dora, briskly, nodding reassurance, and shut the door before Zohra could say anything.

She held the note up in the poor light and examined it. "Miles Ash," she read, printed carefully in pencil, "c/o S. Hardback. Urgent." It was not sealed, only folded in four with a pin across one corner. Upstairs there was a crescendo of voices and somebody laughed; evidently they were on their way down from the top storey. She withdrew the pin with care and opened the paper.

"Dear Miles," she read, her senses at pin-point sharpness for any sound above. "The detective is here and insists on seeing Rob. I have done what I can and while waiting he wants some kind of statement from Zohra. This means an interpreter—can you *please* help? Sam must know someone who speaks English and Arabic, who can be got quickly. *Please* will you ask him and bring them down as quickly as possible? After that he may want to see someone else so it's important to get them here before Rob returns. I'm counting on you as I said, so *please* help. Zohra will wait for reply. Love in haste. Tavy."

Pausing on the third stair to replace the pin through its original holes, Dora climbed to the first landing as Sam's feet pattered lightly down from the second. "I've found it!" she announced triumphantly as they came face to face. "I must have dropped it as soon as we got in." She held up the black glove.

"Oh, fine," said Sam, looking past her and down the stairs. "I thought that was someone at the door."

"It was. I answered it for you." She gave him the folded paper.

"Thanks a lot. Glad you found the glove all right." He stood aside to let her pass, glancing at the note. "For Miles," he said, following her up the stairs.

"Is it? I can't read without my glasses." She paused at the turn of the stair, a little short of breath.

"Sorry about these stairs. This landing, turn right. Miles has been making you some British tea. I didn't feel too confident about the cultural details."

"Lovely, lovely. What a tremendous treat." They came into the sitting-room, where Sam had lighted candles for effect. It was growing lighter outside; there was a pallid watery gleam on the rain-blurred windows. Even with these closed the air of the room was saturated with moisture.

"A message for you," said Sam, dropping the folded paper into Miles's hand. Mrs. Burridge was busy with the tea-cups, taking charge of the pouring out. She did not look up as Miles excused himself and moved abruptly to the window.

"Since you insist on the finer points," she was telling Sam, "it is considered vulgar to put the milk in first. Some people may not take milk; some may prefer lemon. So you pour it out neat, like this, and the milk and lemon are passed afterwards."

"But say everybody took milk," said Sam, "and you knew they did."

"It would still be exactly the same. To do otherwise is common. I'm not entirely clear why."

"And another thing," said Burridge, with sober interest, "it's considered bad form to stir the tea-pot. As bad, apparently, as for an American to eat with his knife and fork at the same time."

"I don't follow the connection," Sam objected. "There's a kind of logic in the knife and fork thing. Using the two together looks like you're too hungry to wait. Good manners being the furthest remove from the primitive, it's more civilized to suggest that eating's a leisurely activity, and there's plenty more where that came from."

"Exactly so," said Burridge. "The assumption of plenty is what counts, which is why it's letting the side down to stir the tea-pot. A pot needs stirring only if the tea's weak, and the tea's weak because you've been too careful with it. In polite circles one must always assume that there's always plenty of everything."

"I believe you've got a point there," said Sam. "British customs at the tea-table, the underlying laws of Arab hospitality—the same thing, surely? I believe one could construct quite a useful synthesis." He caught Miles's eye across the room and knew at once that there was an emergency. "Pardon me," he said, "I believe I forgot the lemon. Do try the cakes, they're fresh," and followed Miles up the stairs into the kitchen.

"Sam, I need help," Miles said at once. "There isn't time to explain. Just tell me how I can get hold of an interpreter for Tavy. Quattrell's being divorced, and there's someone come out from London, from the solicitor. He wants some evidence from Zohra, the woman Tavy lives with, and there's the language difficulty. Could you lay your hands on somebody right away, who speaks Arabic and English? I believe Zohra may be waiting outside for an answer."

Sam raised astonished eyebrows. "For heaven's sake, how did you get mixed up in this? When did it start, anyway?"

"I'll tell you later. Just help me over this interpreter. I mean now, Sam, not waiting for the end of the tea-party."

"Sure." Sam was mystified but co-operative. "Simplest thing is to go down to the bazaars. I know a couple of fellers who'd do, but you'd have to pay them."

"Of course. Could you get one of them right away?"

"Why not? It's nearly time for the gun, but they'll be open. I wouldn't be too sure they mightn't talk, though. Would it matter that much? So many of these guys have an arrangement on the side with the police."

"It wouldn't matter, probably, but get the best while you're about it. I'll look after the money."

"O.K.," said Sam. "An extra little fee might do the trick. You'll have to keep our British friends happy while I'm gone."

Dora Burridge waited to hear their tread on the floor above before turning to her husband. "I've got something important to tell you," she said in a low voice, barely moving her lips.

"M'm? What about?" He was feeling the coconut cakes between finger and thumb, testing them for freshness.

"I can't tell you here. It's a gift straight from heaven. About Q.," she added in a whisper. Aloud she said, "I think it's so clever, the way Sam's made a feature of that brass bed. Oh, I know they've always been a commonplace of Moroccan houses, but somehow *here*, in this very plain and masculine room, it looks almost *grand*." She enlarged on this without waiting for an answer, hearing Sam's slippered feet on the wooden stair.

★   ★   ★

After half an hour of such chatter Sam returned, bringing with him a young man whom he introduced as Larbi and whom Miles had seen before in one of the bazaars, inviting any likely looking passer-by to look round without obligation. He was waiting in the street when Miles came down and they set off at once for the Rue de l'Ecurie, leaving Sam to return to the Burridges.

"You speak good English, I think," said Miles as they went up the steps.

"That's right. I speak English, French, German, Spanish. In my business it is necessary."

"It's kind of you to help. A friend of mine is seeing her lawyer from England, and there's this language difficulty."

"I see. It's a pleasure. Your friend is Moroccan?"

"No, English, but there's a Moroccan woman concerned. The talk will be confidential."

"That's right. It will be good exercise for me." He seemed, indeed, delighted with the commission, and Miles could only hope that he would manage it discreetly. In his white shirt and flashing wrist-watch and with that prosperous gleam of gold in his front teeth he seemed well on the way to be a successful *commerçant*, and so presumably knew the advantages of discretion. "I have heard that fasting makes the brain clear," he said with a little laugh as they came into the courtyard. The cannon explosion was still reverberating, and Miles realized that the man would not have eaten since before sunrise and would be hungry. Most families were indoors by now, the hour of *harira*, but there was a group of children staring at Zohra's door.

When Tavy opened it there was a smell of food. Her cheeks were flushed and she seemed nervously excited. Perhaps in order to look as grown-up as possible she had put up her hair, but the upward sweep and coil and the knot of black ribbon, though they gave her a certain elegance, did not change her.

"Oh, you've *come*," she said with an eloquent glance, and shook hands with Larbi. "Mr. Stagg's been here for ages. You *will* stay, Miles, won't you? He's preparing a written statement."

She held back the door-curtain and they stepped in-side. Zohra was there in her brocaded best, looking palely handsome. The low table had been set in the alcove with a tray and glasses and the atmosphere was one of extreme formality, as though a ceremony were in progress on which much depended. Occupying the furthest corner of the divan, his bald crown catching the light, was a large fair unmistakable Englishman of imposing appearance, writing in a notebook. His hat and folded rain-coat were on the seat beside him, and it struck Miles that he must have made a sufficiently conspicuous figure on his way up through the Medina, treading behind a guide, as all strangers must who set foot in that blind labyrinth. But the professionalism of his manner was such that not even a beggar's apprentice could have taken him for a tourist.

"Pleased to meet you," he said to Miles and Larbi, and shook hands. "You'll excuse me if I finish this before we proceed to the lady's statement." He nodded in Zohra's di-rection. "I was just on the point of checking this over with Miss Williams."

They sat stiffly while Zohra brought bread and soup and poured buttermilk into the glasses. Nobody spoke. Larbi made a little smiling gesture of courtesy to the com-pany and began eating his soup, spooning up the thick broth and dipping his bread in it. Zohra ate hers at a little distance, sunk in an easy squat against the wall. The house was very quiet. Aminah and Khaimo were nowhere to be seen and there was no sign of Joe.

"When are you expecting Quattrell?" Miles asked Tavy in an undertone.

"Some time this evening, I hope. He didn't say."

"So it'll probably all be settled by tomorrow."

"Oh yes, I think so. Mr. Stagg's going to do Zohra next, and then we're going down to the hotel. He wants to see one of the chambermaids, for corroborative evidence."

The phrase sounded most improbable, coming from Tavy; her eyes kept returning anxiously to Mr. Stagg. Presently he glanced over what he had written, thoughtfully sipping his buttermilk. The flavour seemed to surprise him somewhat; he looked into his glass once or twice with an air of doubt and put it down unfinished.

"I want you to read this, Miss Williams, and confirm that it's correct, exactly as you told me. I must warn you that this statement, if you sign it, may quite likely be used in evidence in a court of law."

"Of course," said Tavy in a low voice, "that's what it's for."

"I ought to read it out to you, if we could go into another room."

"There isn't one, Mr. Stagg; only a landing and the roof. The others could go outside for a minute, if you think they should." She turned anxiously to Miles. "Would you mind terribly? He's only got to read it through, and then I sign."

Miles looked at her steadily for a moment and got slowly to his feet. He could feel himself suddenly sweating, as though a wave of anger were rising through him, or the room were insufferably hot. He could not for a moment think what he was doing there, in this gloomy and confined place among these alien people. Even Tavy as she met his eye had become a stranger.

"Of course we'll go," he said brusquely. "Larbi can wait outside. He knows where he can find me."

He moved with Larbi to the door and after a stupefied pause Tavy followed them.

"Miles," she said on the doorstep, touching his hand, "you aren't going, surely? Please, Miles. I'd rather you stayed."

"There's nothing more I can do, my dear Tavy. It's all going the way you want. You're in good hands."

"I know," she said, putting her hands to her cheeks and staring at him. "But I'm much less frightened when you're here. It makes a difference."

"Larbi will stay," said Miles. "He knows what to do. There's no point in having me around as a spectator."

"You aren't a spectator. I thought you were on my side, and were going to help. I'm dreading being left alone when this man's gone. Promise you'll come back later?"

"With Quattrell here? No, thanks. I'll probably be at Sam's tomorrow if you seriously want anything."

She was holding the edge of the door-curtain in both hands, but now dropped it despairingly and turned away. "Just as you like," she said, and went back into the house.

Larbi accompanied Miles to the end of the courtyard and then stopped. "I will stay," he said. "There is no need to worry. I will come and see you at the house tomorrow."

"Yes," said Miles. His heart was beating painfully, as though he had been running.

"That man," said Larbi, showing his gold tooth amiably, as though this were an afterthought, "he is from the British police, no?"

"No. He has been sent by the lawyer in London."

"He looks like an *agent de police*, you don't think? It is a type."

"He's certainly not in the police," said Miles; "goodbye," and raised his hand in a vague salute and left him.

★ ★ ★

He walked slowly, pulling off his jacket and throwing it over one shoulder. There had been a heavy shower while he was in Zohra's house and the street was clean and sparkling with running water. Already children were re-emerging like birds, hopping over wet door-sills and running to spatter barefoot in the puddles. Gutters and spouts dripped at every corner and the children darting in all directions kicked up a running spray. He paid little or no attention to any of them and presently found himself on a flight of steps which was not the accustomed one. It led down to a narrow gully ending in a *cul-de-sac,* and here there was an iron grating in the paving, swirling with water and all but choked with refuse. He stopped with a feeling of stupor and looked about him. He could go no further, that was evident; it occurred to him with indifference that he was lost. He was in a well between high walls, defaced with children's scrawlings at the lowest level and festooned above with a sprawl of electric wires. He was facing the only door, a forbidding one, studded with iron, its paint bleached and leprous with neglect. Someone had face-tiously hung a banana-skin on the heavy knocker, and Miles remembered the day when he had touched it. He had come there on one occasion with Tavy—ages ago it seemed, in a previous existence—and she had told him that she lived there once and that it was now empty. There was nothing to do but to retrace his steps. He turned and walked dully back the way he had come, passing the crevice in the wall where he and Tavy had seen a candle burning. There was no candle now, only a lava of sooty wax and a fragment of ancient crust as grey as pumice-stone.

It now seemed monstrous that he should have lost so many days in this delirium. It was over now. He had noth-ing to do with Tavy nor she with him; the thing was an illusion. It was incredible that he had allowed himself to be drawn into something so improbable, when the sole reason for his being there was to perform a specific task and return home. Nearly half of Mrs. Thewless's money was gone already, and he had accomplished nothing. He was oppressed by a sense of guilt like a physical ache, a dis-comfort about the heart which distressed his breathing. He paused at the top of the steps and laid his hand on the rail.

Only one course suggested itself: he would see Colin once more, tomorrow, and be explicit. At the worst he could only refuse, and if this happened he would write at once to Mrs. Thewless and go home. Her disappointment and his failure would be hard to bear, but she should not lose by it. From somewhere—from old Dowding, from his father, Purkess, anybody—he would borrow two hundred pounds and make good her loss. Whatever else he had on his conscience it should not be that. He would pay it back in six months, perhaps even less. He had only himself to fend for. He would manage.

He sighed profoundly and went on again, disregarding a child who had appeared from nowhere and was trotting beside him. He was a very small child, hardly bigger than Joe, with the same dark hair and pallid countenance; he touched Miles's hand and looked up at him confidingly. "Kasbah," he said in a piping voice, and pointed ahead. They were passing open doorways now and there was a diffused murmur of activity and a sound of voices. Whether the child knew what he was looking for Miles doubted; it was the final absurdity to be restored to the right street by this infant guide. He looked down at the boy and smiled, and the solemn creature gave him an answering look of enchanting sweetness, astonished and shy, delighted with his own achievement. He had done what older boys in his street did when they saw a tourist, though without any precise notion of why they did it. He stopped in his tracks at the limits of his small territory, and Miles came out into the narrow street that he knew. Here was the familiar *bacál*, the cavernous cell where the baker moved like a demon between fire and darkness, the place where Sam normally bought his bread and sugar and which now had a cluster of customers and was doing good trade. Even Miles could sense a change in the air this evening, a feeling of anticipation and excitement, as though spirits were rising at the end of the month-long fast and people already on the watch for the new moon.

Though his feelings were strangely numb a part of him dreaded the imminent encounter with Sam, and he let himself into the house stealthily. The silence of the stairs was reassuring; he mounted the first two flights without a sound. The living-room was full of nothing but twilight, all signs of the Burridges' tea had been cleared away and the table where Sam kept his tape-recorder was empty. Miles breathed a sigh of relief and stood for a moment at the foot of the ladder, listening. Everything was dark upstairs and the only sound from the kitchen was a tap dripping. He could bear anything, it seemed to him, if for once, for this last evening, he could be alone.

He had not eaten since midday but it did not occur to him that he might be hungry. After standing motionless in the room for a while, watching the falling dusk, he went up to the kitchen and poured himself a tumbler of wine. It was acrid and alien in his mouth, and he left it unfinished. Presently he went downstairs again, undressed in the half-dark without switching on the light, and got into the brass bed.

He forced himself to think of Colin and what he would say to him. He would perhaps try it this way—"Look, Colin, I've got something I must say to you . . ." but after that repeated beginning the words faded. Even Colin's face was difficult to remember, whether he closed his eyes or lay with them staring blankly at the darkness: only Tavy's face would materialize, always with a look of reproach and distress, as though she knew that he had failed her. At last he abandoned the struggle and turned over with his face and arms on the hard pillow. There's nothing I can do, my Tavy, he told her; nothing whatever to be done. But still the reproachful look was there, the look he had seen when she touched his hand and said, "But I'm much less frightened when you're here. It makes a difference." Well, she wouldn't be frightened now; it would all be over. Quattrell would be back from Rabat and would have made his statement. Everything would be going as Tavy planned, and he wished her joy of it.

When Sam returned a little after midnight Miles lay still in the dark, breathing regularly. He heard Sam's rubber sneakers on the treads of the ladder and the creak of the boards above as he prepared for bed. It was a long time after this that he fell asleep, long after the first quavering musical cry from the nearby mosque, a cry taken up by other and fainter voices, calling to prayer and praising Allah, for once (since the town was silent and most of the faithful presumably asleep) unmarred by the hideous electronic distortion. He listened to the rise and fall of the recitative and comforted himself at last with a resolve. He would say good-bye to Tavy and convince himself, if he could, that she was happy. He would go up to Zohra's house before he did anything; he would allow himself that last indulgence; they would part tenderly. He fell asleep on this, hugging the illusion of comfort, as though nothing were really irrevocable after all. But when morning came, and he left before Sam was stirring, he found Zohra alone in the house and Tavy gone.

★ II ★

Mᴵᴸᴱˢ stared blankly at Zohra and tried again. She was holding the curtain aside with an unwilling air, making no gesture to invite him in. She had not understood, apparently, and seemed not particularly pleased to see him. Her eyelids were a little inflamed, as though she had been crying.

"*C'est Mademoiselle Tavy que je voudrais voir,*" he said, keeping his foot on the doorstep. Zohra made a clicking sound with her tongue and wagged a forefinger. It was a gesture he had seen before, without knowing what it meant. She did this twice, with a discouraging look, and said something emphatic in either Arabic or Spanish.

Miles laid his hand on the curtain and looked at her attentively; the dark pupils of her eyes were without expression. Inside the house someone shifted a bucket across the tiles and he could hear the swish of a floor-cloth. "Aminah?" he said, remembering the daughter's name, "*elle est là?*" and lifted his other foot to the step, as though it were taken for granted he should come inside. Zohra drew back without protest and he passed under the curtain into the half-light of the interior.

An upheaval of cleaning appeared to be in progress.

Aminah, bent double from the hips like a croquet-hoop, was swinging a sodden floor-cloth to and fro over the tiles. The curtain which normally concealed the kitchen had been looped over its wire and in the corner a loose flagstone had been taken up, revealing a circular drain. Khaimo, barefoot like her daughter and granddaughter and with skirts pinned up over drawers exuberantly patterned with pink roses, was emptying a bowl of slops down this ancient hole. Miles had the feeling that Zohra's lack of welcome was perhaps no more than reluctance to admit him to these intimacies, and the brusqueness with which she covered the drain, pushing her mother aside and pulling down the reefed curtain, confirmed this impression. It came to him with surprise that this hole in the tiles was the answer to a question he had never liked to ask. Behind the curtain Zohra dragged matting over the loose tile.

"Mademoiselle Tavy?" he said to Aminah, pointing at the ceiling, as though he might suppose her to be upstairs. She straightened herself, wringing out her rag, and glanced away from him.

"*Elle est partie, monsieur. Hier soir.*"

"*Où est-elle?*" His French sounded awkward, even to himself. "*Je voudrais la voir.*"

"*Uh . . . sais pas.*" Aminah shrugged her shoulders. "*Elle est partie.*"

"*Madame votre mère sait où elle est?*" he persisted, his heart sinking with a sudden conviction of hopelessness. Try as he would, he could think of only the most elementary words, and in any case Zohra seemed unlikely to be communicative.

"*Non, monsieur, elle ne sait rien.*" She looked him in the eye and smirked, he thought, a trifle mockingly. "*Tavvi est partie; c'est tout.*"

"*Et le petit garçon?*" If Joe had been left with Zohra, Tavy would soon return.

"*Il est parti aussi, avec Tavvi et son père, tous les trois.*"

"*Mais où sont-ils, Aminah?*" He cast about anxiously for words, and found none to convey the urgency of his question.

Again Aminah shrugged, looking in every direction but at Miles. Zohra had reappeared from behind the curtain and they exchanged glances. Again there was that light click of the tongue against the palate, the discouraging lateral movement of the finger. "*Je m'excuse, monsieur,*" said Aminah, and glanced for approval at her mother.

"*Ils sont peut-être à l'hotel?*"

"*Peut-être. Elle n'a rien dit.*" It was clearly hopeless. Miles stood for a moment longer and then turned to the door.

"*Merci, madame, mademoiselle.*"

"*Pas de quoi, monsieur.*" The curtain dropped behind him and he knew they would say nothing more until he was out of hearing.

He had no idea of the name of Quattrell's hotel but remembered that it overlooked the port; Tavy had pointed it out on the night when they had walked on the beach and he had given her the gilt brooch. He set off in what seemed to him the right direction, following their route in reverse as far as he remembered it. Once he turned back from a street of shoemakers that he had never seen before and twice from a blind alley which led nowhere, but arguing that if he continued downhill he must come to it at last, he kept on. What he would say to Tavy when he found her he did not know. Simply good-bye, he supposed; she would be with Quattrell, of course, and there was nothing more to say. Even if he saw her alone it would be a painful meeting. And if she were not at the hotel, he asked himself, what then? Already he knew there was little hope of finding her. The suspicion that drove him on was that already she was out of reach, that she was gone for ever. Quattrell had returned from Rabat, and for reasons of his own, and without delay, removed her. If he had made his statement, as Tavy hoped, why were they not still here? He pressed on painfully, cursing his lame leg. If all else failed he would get Sam to take him to the street where the bazaars were; he would question Larbi. The tourist shops were already open, though there were not many people about; young men not unlike Larbi were hanging their doorways with sheepskin rugs, with striped and patterned blankets and tinselled brocades. Pedlars were busy setting their trays with cheap jewellery, with combs, scarves, plastic sandals, woollen caps, spurious-looking brassware and cheap drinking-glasses. This was not Larbi's street, which was in a different quarter, but it led, he was almost sure, in the right direction. Soon it widened out into a kind of square, where waiters were setting out chairs before the pavement cafés. In only one of them, the largest, were there any customers, young men with long and matted locks—English, American?—most of them muffled in anoraks and *djellábas*, who stared at him unwinkingly as he passed. The square ran down to a narrow street at each corner; he chose the one on the right, went down it a little way in shadow and came out into full sunlight. He was at the top of a flight of steps and knew exactly where he was. Below was the entrance to the port with its high wall, and beyond that the arid expanse of wharves and warehouses. A solitary ship was in dock; her decks were deserted and the cranes on the wharfside idle. It was possible to watch them unloading, he remembered, from Quattrell's balcony. Tavy had paused on these very steps, and pointed. Over there, she had said, on the other side, was where the cruise liners lay. They were lit up on summer nights with thousands of lights, so that the dullest vessel was changed into a fairy ship, sparkling and insubstantial, ethereally pretty.

At the bottom of the steps, where a woman crouched

with her head hidden in a shawl, holding out her hand, Miles turned to the left, and almost immediately caught sight of the hotel. As he approached, walking more slowly now that he was so near, a man in soft hat and rain-coat stepped out and stood for a moment on the pavement, taking his pipe from his mouth and looking at the sky. Miles recognized him immediately. No one in heaven could look so large, so solid, so British, so unconcerned, and not be Mr. Stagg.

"Morning," he said, when Miles was near enough, having identified him from a distance without appearing to do so. "Nice morning, after the rain. Pity to be leaving."

"You're going today, then? So soon?" This might augur well or ill, but whichever it was, and although he had scarcely exchanged three words with him, Miles was sorry to lose him. There was an air of reliability about Mr. Stagg, of judgement reserved and contingencies prepared for, which made one long to lean on him; nature had designed him with care as a father-figure. At the same time there was a touch of reserve and cynicism, as of a man too disillusioned to be deceived easily.

"Yes, it's a pity in a way," said Mr. Stagg. "I'd have liked to have seen more of the place if there'd been time. Quite interesting, by the looks of it."

"You saw Mr. Quattrell last night, then?"

"Well, no, as a matter of fact. The young lady thought he'd come to the hotel first, so after we'd seen the female employee—and by the way, that interpreter you brought was just the job; I'm much obliged to you. So after that was finished we waited here, and the young lady had dinner with me. But when it got late, about ten o'clock, she went back to the house to see what had happened, and I waited for Mr. Quattrell here." Mr. Stagg paused, giving Miles a sidelong look as he prodded the bowl of his pipe with a match.

"I see. And when did he arrive?"

"Ah, that's the question. Some time between nine and eleven o'clock, but not at the hotel. I went up to the house again at half-past eleven, and they'd both gone. Mr. Quattrell and Miss Williams and the child. *And* taken their luggage."

"I know," said Miles. "I've been there this morning. Apart from that I couldn't find out anything."

"Would you have any idea where they've gone? You're a friend of both, I take it."

"I'm a friend of hers, I suppose, but I've only seen Quattrell a few times. I was hoping you'd know where they were."

"I wish I could help you," said Mr. Stagg, "or that you could help me. Not that it's all that important. I've got everything I want." He gripped his pipe in his teeth and felt in an inside pocket.

"You've tried ringing Madame Lemaire, I suppose? She's quite likely to know something."

"She doesn't, unfortunately. I rang her last night, pretty late. She seemed rather upset by what I told her." He found what he was looking for in his pocket-book and handed it to Miles. It was a small head-and-shoulders photograph of Quattrell, of that blatantly unflattering type that appears in passports. It had been taken some years ago but was unmistakable—the grooves in the cheeks, the glint of amusement in the eye which Miles, when he had first met him, had found sympathetic.

"You recognize it, do you?" asked Mr. Stagg casually.

"Oh yes. It's a good likeness."

"M'm. I wasn't in any doubt myself, but I like to make sure. The young woman in the hotel, the chambermaid if that's what they call 'em, picked it out from half a dozen." He put the photograph away and returned the wallet to his pocket.

"So what's going to happen now?" said Miles, watching his movements as though he believed them to be symbolic. He had clung to a hope that at some point Mr. Stagg would at least produce a clue to where Tavy might be, or say something to lighten the foreboding that oppressed him.

"Well, that's not for me to say. I've got what I came for, and I'm off in a few minutes to the airport. Time's money in this business, as you're probably aware. The fact that the parties have blown doesn't matter, fortunately. It may make a difficulty later, of course, when it comes to serving papers. But as far as I'm concerned the job's finished."

"Well . . ." said Miles after a pause, "there's nothing more I can do, then." He looked at Stagg uncertainly, unwilling to let him go. "I might ring Madame Lemaire, perhaps."

"You do that," said Mr. Stagg in a fatherly tone. "It'll cheer her up. She sounded a bit down in the mouth at what I told her."

★   ★   ★

"Ah, Miles, my dear Miles, what has happened?" Panya's voice crackled woefully in the receiver. "Where are they gone, do you know it? Where is our poor Tavy?"

"That's just what I wanted to ask you," said Miles loudly, covering his other ear. The telephone booth had no door and a servant was shifting chairs on the tiled floor.

"I don't like it," said Panya, "I don't like it at all, Miles. Why did she not tell me she was going? She would know that I worry."

"I imagine there wasn't time. They seem to have left suddenly."

"That is what disturbs me. Why should they leave so

quickly? It can mean only one thing. You know what was happening, Miles? Did Tavy tell you?"

"I know about the divorce, yes. I took an interpreter to the house yesterday. Mr. Stagg was there, as you know; he wanted to talk to Zohra."

"Then Zohra will know where they are. You must go and ask her."

"I've been already. She either doesn't know, or she won't say. I've talked to the daughter too, but it's no good. They've taken Joe with them, apparently, and Tavy's luggage."

"She is such a fool, that Zohra, but it is possible she knows nothing. If he is running away from the lawyers he would not say where. He is not stupid. It is our poor Tavy who is stupid; she will not listen. I am trying all the time to telephone to London, so you must ring off now. Come round to the shop, dear Miles. We will talk later."

"You're ringing the lawyer, then?" The noise on the line had all but obliterated Panya's words, and he had to shout.

"No, I have put in a call to London, to advise with Constance. It is a complete *désastre*, because at last she has made up her mind, and now this happens. I am expecting this call, Miles, so I am going to cut. We will speak later." There was a sound like a distant explosion and the crackling ceased.

★　★　★

By the time Miles reached the *socco* his leg was hurting him, but in all the streets there had not been a single taxi. Here, to his relief, there were two on the rank and he stumbled into the nearest. He knew neither the name of the house nor the correct address, but he described it as well as he could and Crosier's name appeared to mean something

to the driver. He sank back on the seat and sighed deeply
when the taxi swung round and set off in the right direction.

Before he did anything—if indeed there was anything
he could do—he would take a last chance with Colin and rid
himself once and for all of that obligation. It was a matter of
indifference to him now whether Colin listened or not, but
at least he would tell him the truth and see what happened.
He searched in his pockets for a handkerchief and wiped
the sweat from his face, wondering what he would do when
the interview was over. It was possible that Colin might
know where Quattrell was heading for, but it seemed unlikely. If he had left like that, suddenly and at night, with
the obvious intention of eluding Stagg, it was hardly reasonable to suppose that he had told anybody. They might,
of course, he remembered with a start of hope, have gone
no further than the cottage. They were often there for days
at a time; it was the obvious hiding-place; but he saw at
once that this simple solution was futile. The sea-house
rose in his mind's eye with peculiar vividness. He tried to
imagine it as he had last seen it, with doors and windows
open and Tavy there; but it remained obstinately empty,
silent, shuttered. He would have been glad to think of her
there, even if it meant knowing she was there with Quattrell; but as the taxi ground up a slope that he remembered
and turned into a rough lane hedged with bamboo and
cactus he knew that nothing so simple and explicable could
have happened. He was sure of nothing but a growing con-
viction of disaster.

Mollie Brockhurst's Mercedes was in Crosier's drive,
neatly parked at the edge of the raked gravel. The door of
the house stood open; Miles touched the bell and went in.
Everything was perfectly quiet and orderly as usual, the
black marble floor impeccably polished, Morley's gloves
and a pot of orchids on the hall table. An elegant iron

umbrella-stand sprouted a bouquet of walking-sticks, some with ivory handles and one with amber. They looked too frail for Morley's weight but the stamp of his personal taste was on each one, as on everything in the house. It was easy to see, remembering Mrs. Thewless's drawing-room, why Colin found Crosier's habitat congenial.

No one was in the drawing-room; the french windows stood open and Colin's head could be seen in the jungle of plants that shaded the verandah. This verandah was one of the pleasantest features of the house, a glassed-in wooden structure running round three sides, full of exotic foliage and banana-trees in tubs, looking down on the lush garden. Colin was sprawled in a basket-chair, reading a motoring magazine in a haze of cigarette smoke. He turned a page at the sound of footsteps and looked up.

"Oh, hello. It's you, is it?" He returned to the magazine, frowning as though finishing a sentence, then put it down reluctantly. "Everyone seems on the move this morning. Did you want Morley? Ozzie's been here some time, they're doing a tour of the garden."

"I wanted to say good-bye to him," said Miles, "and to you as well. I shall be leaving very soon."

Colin hooked his foot round the leg of another chair and jerked it forward. "Well, sit down. They'll be up presently. Ozzie's cadging cuttings and things for Mollie's garden."

"Is she here too?"

"No, thank God. She doesn't get up before noon. This is Ozzie's time off." He made a grimace of boredom which was not without malice.

"I shall be seeing your mother very soon," said Miles, coming to the point without ceremony. "Would you like me to give her a message? That is, if you've anything to tell her."

"Oh, well, give her my love. Tell her not to worry." He

took hold of a leaf of creeper and examined it attentively.

"Am I to tell her you're coming home? Or not? Have you made up your mind?" He caught Colin's eye and held it. There was a wary silence.

"Look," said Colin, sitting suddenly upright and stubbing out his cigarette on the roots of the creeper. "She sent you out here, didn't she? Was it all arranged? I've had a feeling all along that's why you came here."

"Yes, since you ask. That was the only reason."

"How very extraordinary. I can't think why you should bother." Colin lay back in the chair again and stared at him.

"You find it extraordinary that she should be anxious, when you've gone off without a word, and transferred what money you've got to another country?"

Colin put on an expression of suffering patience. "So it's the money she's worrying about. I thought as much. I must say I don't find that particularly attractive."

"If she worries about the money it's on your account," said Miles, disliking him afresh. "She thinks you may lose it to people who're cleverer than you are, and then you'll be sorry. And if you want to know how I managed it, and why I bothered, it's because she paid all my expenses. She had two hundred pounds of her own, and she gave it to me for the purpose. It's about half gone already, and as far as I can see there's not the least point in wasting any more of it."

"Good lord," said Colin, rubbing his eyes and then staring at his knuckles, as though the possibility of such a thing had not occurred to him.

"Look," he said after a pause, meeting Miles's eye unwillingly, but with less hostility, "I wish you'd told me that at the beginning, because I could have made things clear. I thought I had, as a matter of fact. I hadn't planned any of this when I first came out, you know. I was just looking round. I'd more or less made up my mind to get out of

England, and then I met Morley and all that, and it seemed the answer. As it still does, if you really want to know. I wrote to the bank and had the money transferred to Gibraltar. I'd a perfect right to do that; she can't complain. I didn't want to write and tell her anything definite until it was all settled—there'd only have been a fuss. But I can write now, if you think I should. Actually I was just considering it."

"Good," said Miles, and went on looking at him steadily.

"I'd no idea she'd do anything so idiotic. Throwing away her money like that! She must be out of her mind."

"I don't think she is at all, but she's afraid you may be."

"Well, I'm not," said Colin crossly, rubbing his eyes again and staring incredulously at the ceiling. "Good lord, what a thing to do! She'll get hell all right if my father gets to hear about it."

"She's not very likely to tell him, and he won't hear it from me."

"No, well . . . I didn't imagine you'd do anything quite so dirty." Colin went on staring at his knuckles, bending and straightening the fingers. "I've had a lot of expenses one way and another," he said presently. "I'll get it all back in time, of course, but I've got to go a bit carefully." He waited for a word of encouragement but Miles said nothing. "What I mean is, I don't want her to be out of pocket. It wouldn't be my fault if she was, but still, I don't want to see it happen. I mean, I could probably send her something, so that if it ever came up she wouldn't have to explain to my father what she'd done."

"I think that's an excellent plan." Miles nodded approvingly. "She'd prefer to see you as well, but the money would be better than nothing, and I imagine it would make you feel more comfortable." And me too, he thought. Perhaps after all he had misjudged Colin? His selfishness, it seemed, was not impregnable.

"Well, I'll do that thing, then." He made a move as though to get out of his chair but changed his mind and picked up the *Autocar*. "I could probably manage fifty pounds without too much difficulty." He flipped through the second-hand advertisements. "Anyway, I'll talk to Morley."

"Oh, do you have to get his permission to send your mother anything?"

"No, of course not. It's just not as easy as you seem to think. Unless Mollie decides to come in with us I'm more or less committed. And the money's in Gibraltar, don't forget. I don't carry it around in my pocket."

"You told me you got five hundred over quite easily, the day we went out to the site. And anyway, why worry? You could send her the lot when you write, simply by making out a cheque."

"That's just where you're wrong. You can't send cheques from here to another country. There's a law about it."

"But the money isn't here," said Miles patiently, "it's in Gibraltar."

"Doesn't make any difference. I've been warned against sending cheques through the mails. Letters get opened, unfortunately."

"In that case you can make it out now and give it to me, and she'll have it in a few days. And at the same time write to Gibraltar and tell them to transfer two hundred back to London."

"I didn't say anything about two hundred. I might manage fifty." He dropped his paper with a sigh and peered through the glass of the verandah, as though hoping against hope that Morley and Ozzie would appear. The sun was bright on festoons of creeper and the bamboos were still. There was no sign of anybody.

"If you don't want her to be out of pocket," said Miles reasonably, "you'll have to manage rather more, I think. I don't like the idea that you might reproach yourself afterwards."

Colin gave him a suspicious look and there was a calculating pause.

"How much have you spent?" he said at last. "A minute ago you said only half of it was gone. You can't possibly have spent two hundred."

"No, I haven't. I can't tell you exactly how much, but a hundred ought to cover it so far. Luckily I've been staying with Sam, and I've kept a day-to-day account."

"Thank God for small mercies at least," said Colin feelingly. "Some of the hotels are murder. I stayed in one for three days when I first came out."

"So if you'll give me the cheque for a hundred today, I'll make it up when I get back. There'll be no difficulty."

"Oh, all *right*," said Colin sulkily, "that's exactly what I was going to do, only in two instalments."

"One cheque will save you trouble."

"Oh, very well. So that's settled. But I shall have to tell Morley."

"Just as you like, of course. But is that necessary?"

"Morley and I are partners, and curiously enough I'm not asking for your advice." He looked at Miles with hostility, his face flushing slightly. "And while we're on the subject, I don't like the tone you take about Morley; I don't like it at all. You're always hinting you think he's a crook or something."

"I know nothing about him. I'm just trying to suggest that you use a little common sense."

"Well, I do; and I've got sense enough to know when

I'm well off. Morley's a remarkable man, and also a very lonely person. He's been generous to me so far, and there's no reason why he should stop. He's a different person since I came; everybody says so. You don't seem to realize what it's like to be alone, and old, and not at all well, with nobody to care for. He's got nobody left in his family but an old sister, and everyone needs somebody. He's alone in this house with his garden and his collection, and nobody to give a damn or take an interest in them."

"Except you."

"Except me. Exactly. It might have been anyone else, I admit, but it just happens it isn't. It makes him feel young again, having me around. Even I can see the difference. Now he's got the camping scheme, and someone to take an interest in it and work with him, he's ten years younger. And since it suits me very nicely, what is there against it?"

"Nothing, except that it's perfectly possible you'll lose your money, and as it's all you've got that might be rather a pity."

"So what?" said Colin on a rising note, his face quite childish with annoyance. "Why keep on harping and harping about the money? It isn't the end of the world if I *do* lose it. I'm perfectly safe with Morley. He's got an income. And I'm bored with the way you assume that the scheme's going to fail. Even if Mollie doesn't come in he's going right ahead, and he's no fool, let me tell you. Rob Quattrell wouldn't be putting his finger in the pie if he didn't think it a good bet—and *he's* no fool, either. A bit too clever for my liking, if that counts for anything." Colin knocked a cigarette from his packet and put it in his mouth, taking out a small gold lighter that Miles had not seen before. He frowned as he stooped to the flame; his hand was not steady.

"So Quattrell's definitely in it," said Miles; "I wasn't sure."

"Of course. You knew that already. We only got back from Rabat last night; they had good reactions from everybody. Quattrell's coming up presently for a late lunch; we'll be doing the plans in detail."

"I rather think he may have gone away again," said Miles. He had caught sight of Crosier's bald crown among the grey-green mimosas and in a moment Ozzie emerged. They were coming gradually up the path towards the house.

"No, no, he's expected to lunch. Morley definitely said so. He's had ideas for a publicity scheme that we've got to discuss, and a target date for opening."

"In that case I mustn't stay. If you'll just make out that cheque for your mother I'll be moving." He waited until Colin was out of his chair and halfway into the drawing-room before adding, "But it's odd, because he wasn't at the hotel this morning, or at Tavy's house, and they told me up there he'd gone."

"Really? Who said so?" Colin had paused at a small writing-desk and was hunting vaguely among books and papers. From the far window, looking over the drive, there was a sound of a car on the gravel.

"Zohra and Aminah, the ones Tavy lives with."

"Oh, them." He appeared to have found his cheque-book and sat down at the desk. "I don't suppose you understood what they said."

"It seemed quite clear. I'm just about equal to Aminah's French."

Colin was writing laboriously and did not answer. Making out the cheque took him a long time; he filled in the counterfoil with care, checking and re-checking the subtraction. There was a sound of voices from the garden,

first Morley's and then a woman's, approaching the verandah. Miles moved away from the window. He was almost
sure that the voice was Dora Burridge's.

"There," said Colin, detaching the cheque from the
book and reading it for the last time, his lips moving. Still
holding it by one corner he addressed an envelope, put the
cheque inside, licked the flap and sealed it, moving his fist
backwards and forwards. He handed it to Miles with the
air of a child who expects to be justly praised; now that the
thing was done he looked rather pleased than otherwise.

"Thank you," said Miles. "I'll see that she gets it at
once. That's a very nice thing to do, Colin. She'll be
touched by your generosity."

"Oh . . . well," Colin was beginning, pleasantly embarrassed, for the first time reminding Miles of the schoolboy
he had rather liked, that summer at Headington, "I'm still
very fond of her, you know, and if she *will* be so hysterical
and silly . . ." but at this point Crosier and Ozzie and the
Burridges invaded the verandah.

"I *quite* agree," Dora Burridge was saying, "one's always so careful not to believe everything one's told, but
there's something very wrong, in my opinion."

"Well, sit down, Dora, do," said Crosier, "and let's get
this straight." There was a scraping and creaking of chairs.
Colin left his sentence unfinished and moved into the
doorway. "Who was it who told you this, in the first place?"

"I'd rather you didn't ask me," said Dora, "because it
was particularly confidential. But it comes from an impeccable source, you can rely on that."

"Well, I don't know, I don't know," said Crosier, and
broke off to wheeze and cough. The four of them were
sitting under the huge banana leaves, staring at one another.

"If I may make a suggestion," said Rex Burridge, clearing his throat, "I should have a word with the Commissaire.

You might learn something, y'know, and they're usually pleased if one tips them off about anyone."

"I don't like to do that," said Crosier. He looked gloomy. "Even if there's nothing in it it would leave a feeling of suspicion. Just when they're beginning to eat out of our hand, too. Couldn't be more unfortunate."

Colin strolled out on the verandah, his hands in his pockets. "What's happened?" he asked Morley.

"Why, my dear, it seems our friend Quattrell may be finding himself in a difficulty. To put it mildly. Rex and Dora have information—the source of which they haven't disclosed—that an inspector from Scotland Yard was here yesterday, asking questions about him."

"Here, in this house?"

"No, no, at his hotel, and that Arab house in the slum, where he keeps the girl. We don't know any more than that, but it's rather disturbing."

"Scotland Yard wasn't mentioned, not *specifically*," said Dora Burridge, in the tone of one who insists on being scrupulous. "In fact, putting two and two together, Rex thought it rather more likely to have been Interpol. Didn't you, Rex?"

"From one or two hints that were dropped," said Burridge, touching his moustache and looking military. His bearing, as ever, was impeccable; he might have been giving evidence at a court-martial.

"I wish you could say who your informant was," said Crosier, looking increasingly unhappy. "One could perhaps make a circumspect enquiry."

"Oh dear, how I wish we could!" Mrs. Burridge clasped her hands. "Unfortunately Rex had to give his word. Didn't you, darling?"

"Afraid so. Absolutely." Burridge stared at the table, stoically British.

"We oughtn't, in fact, to have said a word," said Dora,

"only in your case we felt it was our duty. The scheme depends so much on the probity of everyone—wouldn't you agree? As you say, it really couldn't be more unfortunate."

"Discretion can go too far," said Crosier. "I could see my friend in the police, perhaps, or put a fly over the consul, but I'd prefer to have a preliminary word with Quattrell."

"That might be a tactical error." Burridge shook his head. "Better not alert him at this stage, if you want to find out anything."

"But my dear man," said Crosier testily, "you seem to forget that we're in partnership. Not legally, perhaps, but morally. Your informant may have got it wrong, or there may be some perfectly reasonable explanation. He's coming here to lunch in any case. You can't expect me to talk to him as though nothing had happened."

Colin glanced over his shoulder. Miles was still there, standing in silence by the desk.

"Miles says he thinks Quattrell won't be coming. He says he's gone."

"Gone? What d'you mean, gone?" Crosier's lower lip hung open and one eye looked startled. The pale eye, as usual, was unconcerned, but it began to water.

"Ask him yourself. I'm only telling you what he said."

Miles hesitated for a moment and came out on the verandah.

"I think it's true," he said. "I was at the house this morning, and also the hotel. He and Tavy have gone away, and taken the child with them."

There was an incredulous pause, and then everybody spoke at once. "What did I tell you?" cried Dora Burridge. Crosier silenced her with a gesture and repeated, "I don't think that's very likely. They're probably spending the morning at the cottage."

"That I can't say," said Miles, "but I must tell you one thing, since I heard what you were saying. The man who came to see Quattrell isn't anything to do with the police. He may have been once, I don't know, but he isn't now. He's a private detective or enquiry agent employed by a solicitor. He wanted to see Quattrell in connection with a divorce."

"Good gracious, who told you that?" Mrs. Burridge smiled ironically.

"Tavy told me herself. It was all very confidential, I'm afraid, but it seems important to tell you. There's a divorce pending."

"In that case," said Crosier uncertainly, "why has he disappeared?"

"That I don't know. I can only suppose he had reasons for not wanting to give evidence."

"Quite. One doesn't disappear without reason," said Burridge, "and this story about the divorce is quite a clever one. It covers his tracks nicely. Only flaw in it is, it isn't what *we* were told." He gave Crosier a look which plainly said that men of experience were not to be gulled so easily.

"But Tavy told me about the divorce," said Miles, "and I saw the man myself. I even talked to him."

"And how does that prove it's true? Naturally she would tell the same story."

"Oh, rubbish," said Miles rudely. "I talked to him myself, this morning. He's nothing to do with the police, let alone Interpol. He's employed by a solicitor."

Burridge smiled in an aloof way and glanced at Crosier. "I've never heard that Interpol discuss their business or identify themselves to strangers. They're not half-witted."

Crosier creaked in his chair, frowning and feeling about in his coat pockets. Everyone watched while he produced a bottle of tablets and shook one into his palm.

There was an expectant hush while he swallowed it; his laborious breathing had become audible.

"We shall soon see," he said. "If he doesn't turn up for lunch I shall make enquiries. If he does, I shall frankly ask for an explanation. It's worrying from my point of view, in either case. Everything was going so well, and these things are tricky. A pity if we have to drop him, but we can't afford to be mixed up with anything suspicious. We'll have troubles enough of our own between now and the opening."

"What was it you told us, Ozzie," said Dora Burridge thoughtfully, "about Quattrell not being able to go with you to Ceuta? I distinctly remember something, but I've forgotten what. There might be some connection."

Everyone looked at Ozzie, who was sitting with his chin in his hand and had not yet spoken.

"There *was* that," he said, "and also something else that I'm trying to remember. It's all so enthralling, isn't it? I'm so riveted by what you've been saying I'm quite lost."

"Well?" said Crosier sternly. "Make an effort, my dear boy; we're all waiting."

"It was some time ago," said Ozzie with a spell-binding glance, "that first spring when Rob came out, and the Askew-Martins. They had an Italian boy with them—Enrico, do you remember?" Nobody did, though he looked all round the circle. "He was Gerald Askew-Martin's valet or something. Quite marvellous-looking in a way, but he didn't stay with them. He had quite a success for a time, and one used to see him around, and he told me that Gerald knew Rob, and was afraid of him. I never quite made out what the story was, but he *said* it was to do with blackmail."

Crosier made a sceptical face. "Did he give you any proof of what he said, or was it just gossip?"

"Well, everything's gossip, Morley, but occasionally it's true. I didn't ask to see the files."

"And what did you tell Dora about Ceuta? Was that from the same source?"

"Goodness, no. That happened with me and Mollie. We asked Rob to go with us to Ceuta one day, and he made quite a joke of it but said he couldn't cross the Spanish border. I know that's a fact because I asked Tavy later, and she said he'd been caught carrying a packet from Cairo to Barcelona, and had been put in prison."

"Prison!" cried Dora Burridge, staring at her husband. Colour rose slowly under the skin of her neck but her face stayed the colour of a biscuit.

"Oh, he didn't stay there," said Ozzie airily. "He jumped bail, Tavy said, which I dare say was very sensible of him. Judging by what one's heard about Spanish prisons."

"And what was in the packet," said Burridge, "if one may ask?"

"Oh heavens, I've no idea. Something deliciously illegal, wouldn't you think? He wouldn't be doing it for nothing."

"Drugs," said Burridge judicially, adjusting his eye-shade. "If that's true it fits very neatly into the picture."

"Well, that part's *certainly* true," said Ozzie, taking a peep at his wrist-watch and jumping to his feet, "but about the other thing, Enrico's bit, I wouldn't like to say. I *would* like to say, of course, because it's so obviously fascinating, but I feel I shouldn't. It's not impossible that Enrico was being just a tiny bit spiteful. And now if anybody wants a lift into town they must say so, because it's time I collected my plants and whizzed back to Mollie."

* * *

In the car, rocking smoothly over the ruts of the lane, Ozzie gave Miles a glance. "I *say*, what a drama! I'm not too surprised—are *you?* I don't know which went down best, your bombshell or the Burridges'."

"The Burridges are lying," said Miles. "All that rubbish about Scotland Yard and Interpol. There's not a word of truth in it."

"Well, I don't know. They must have heard *something.* I dare say they tarted it up a bit in the telling, but there's usually a grain of truth in these *canards.* But I don't believe the 'impeccable source' bit, do you? You could pick up stories about any one of us in any bar in town."

"I don't believe any of it because I know it's false. Do you know Madame Lemaire, who keeps that shop just off the boulevard? She knows all about the divorce. She's in touch with Quattrell's wife and she's also a friend of Tavy's. I've talked to her already this morning on the telephone."

"I know who you mean—that old Russian body. I dare say you're right, but if you want Ozzie's personal opinion I think the whole thing stinks from end to end. I'm so thankful I stumbled in on this morning's session; at least it'll convince Mollie."

"Of what?"

"Why, that the whole thing's dotty from start to finish and drawing in the wrong sort of people. Morley's been practically on his *knees* to get Mollie to put money in it. Imagine putting money into a scheme that was run by Quattrell!"

"I got the impression he wouldn't be running it much longer."

"No, wasn't it splendid! I could almost *see* poor old Morley's mind working. He's always been rather impressed with him for some reason, and now he's scared. He's always been so careful to suck up to the authorities, he's terrified of not being *bien vu* by the police."

"Why should he worry?"

"Well, most people do, you know, in a mild sort of

way. There's always this feeling that practically anything can happen, so you do the equivalent of putting out food to propitiate the spirits. Morley's been here a long time; in the past he's had occasion to be careful, I don't doubt."

"And still has, perhaps?"

"I wouldn't think so, would *you?* Morley must be over seventy, that makes him respectable. Not but what," he added reflectively, "seventy isn't *that* old, if you know what I mean, but Morley's in poor health and getting a bit grotesque. I fancy he likes having that booby Colin around because it makes him feel young again."

"Bad luck for Colin, though, if he loses his money while acting as a rejuvenator."

"My dear, he deserves it! Did you *ever* come across a more irritating boy? Wheedling away at Mollie when he thinks I'm not looking. I can't *bear* that insipid sort of good looks," said Ozzie resentfully. He swerved round a group of goats which had chosen that moment to wander on the main road. A boy sprang down from the bank, brandishing his stick.

"I'm bound to say," said Miles, "I think he's acting inadvisedly."

"Inadvisedly? My dear, the creature's a cretin! If he'd asked anybody who'd been out here more than five minutes —except silly old Morley, of course, but then he's besotted —they'd have told him that these schemes get started and then collapse practically every year. The beach would be clotted with wreckage if it weren't for the tide. All these fancy little beach-bars with coy names, up to the waist in sand as soon as the winds start, everybody cheating everybody and the local boys living on the refuse like a pack of jackals."

"You don't make it sound very attractive, certainly."

"Oh, the *idea*'s attractive enough, that's why they do it. It *ought* to work, but for some reason it never seems to.

It's as if there's a spirit in the place—one of those djinns or something—which just doesn't *want* Europeans to make a success of anything. There was this French company two or three years ago, which started exactly the same sort of thing Morley talks about, and on a much better beach. My dear, it was a shambles! You can still see the sordid remains if they're not already washed away. First of all there were gangs of tourists imported, females mostly, and for weeks they were under every bush, publicly coupling with Moroccans. *Inconceivably* disgusting. And then the local tradesmen didn't get paid, and there were complaints and scandals, and in the end the outfit went broke and the promoters disappeared to France in a hurry. I kept thinking of that, the day we went out with Morley to his frightful site. The place looked well enough to the naked eye —no shade or water, of course, but let that pass—but I could *see* the ruins of the silly chalets, and the poor old restaurant sunk in the sand and opening at the seams, and grass growing out of the cement where the bar had been and goats chewing the cud among the rubble. Their houses shall be full of doleful creatures, and dragons in their pleasant palaces and so on—as the prophet says somewhere or other."

"If that's what you saw I quite understand your not wanting Mrs. Brockhurst to put money in it."

"Well . . . *quite*," said Ozzie, and gave Miles a grateful look from under his eyelashes. "You see, Mollie's quite shrewd about some things, but about money—*not*. She gets frightened when people go on and on, and thinks she's got to do as they say. Which is where I come in, if I may say so. We're rather a good team, in our modest way. It works, surprisingly."

They were well into the town by this time, breasting the long hill which would presently bring them in sight of the walls of the Kasbah. Though the day was bright it seemed to Miles that the dazzle of sun on stone was hard and melancholy. He shrank from the idea—and each time he faced it it seemed more of a certainty—that he would not see Tavy again. If he had known how to propitiate the spirits of the place he would have done so. His ignorance was total and invincible; this was where he had failed her. He understood nothing. He had set out on a quest un-armed, without weapons or knowledge, and however much she might need him he would never reach her. The heavi-ness lodged in his breast had grown steadily more insistent since early morning. His nerves ached with the uneasy con-viction that Tavy was in trouble.

"I suppose you haven't an idea where Quattrell's gone?" he said at last, as the car rolled to a standstill in the square.

"Not an idea in the world. He might be anywhere. He'll show up sooner or later, when the coast's clear."

"I suppose so. I find it all rather depressing. I don't believe Tavy wanted to go. She didn't expect to."

"Well, that's her funeral," said Ozzie, with his delight-ful smile, "she must be used to it by now. I shouldn't fancy it myself, living with Quattrell, not *tremendously*, but then I'm rather set in my ways and a little bit old-fashioned."

★　★　★

Going slowly across the cobbles Miles found he was almost too tired to go any further. He stopped beside a heap of stones and lit a cigarette. Here, along the wall where cars were parked in the daytime, was a lorry with workmen unloading planks and metal tubing, preparing to erect a scaffolding. They moved with extraordinary slow-ness, as though the effort of lifting their arms to the tail-board were more than they could manage, dragging out the tubes languidly and dropping them with deafening clatter.

Miles stood and watched them, inhaling his cigarette. They already had an audience of a dozen children as well as a policeman in khaki tunic who observed them with idle interest, his thumbs in his belt. Of course, he remembered suddenly, the men would be fasting; they had neither eaten nor drunk since before sunrise, nor would they for many hours. It was hell, Sam said, trying to get anything done during Ramadan, even one's washing; what with fasting all day and sitting up half the night no one had any energy.

"*C'est très dur quand on jeune, ce travail,*" said a voice at his shoulder. He turned to find the policeman standing beside him.

"*Très dur,*" said Miles, trying to recall where he had seen this man before. He had a pleasant face, square and strongly moulded, with a small moustache.

"*Vous êtes en vacance içi?*" he asked Miles, planting his feet apart and settling down for an amiable conversation.

"*Oui, mais pour moi les vacances sont presque finies.*" The workmen released another length of tube and the smiling reply was lost in ringing clangour. "*Je vous connais, n'est-ce-pas?*" said Miles, when the din had subsided.

"*Oui, oui, nous nous sommes rencontrés là-bas, chez la fille de Zohra Azugag.*"

Of course. It was Aminah's policeman, whom he had failed to recognize with his cap on and his tunic properly buttoned.

"*La demoiselle anglaise,*" said Miles, choosing his words hesitantly, "*elle est partie, n'est-ce-pas?*"

"*Oui, oui, elle est partie hier soir, avec le p'tit gosse et son père.*" Miles considered this with an effort, sorting out the words from the strangeness of the man's accent. It was possible, after all, that Quattrell might be taken for Tavy's father, but he doubted whether this had been meant. If the man were on such terms with Aminah as he had seemed to be, he might know more.

"*Où sont-ils maintenant?*" he asked, raising his voice as a stack of planks prepared to fall from the lorry.

"*Je crois qu'ils sont à Fes. Oui, Aminah m'a dit qu'ils sont partis en auto pour Fes.*"

Fez! thought Miles, his mind darting instantly to Sam. The warren, the ant-heap, Sam had called it, the maze of a thousand wrong turnings, the marvellous place to hide.

"*Vous ne connaissez pas l'addresse?*" he asked quickly, knowing that nothing could be more unlikely, and added, catching the look of faint surprise, "*j'ai une lettre à les envoyer . . .*"

The policeman shook his head. "*Ah, non, m'sieu, je m'excuse. Aminah peut-être peut vous le dire.*" He looked puzzled, but anxious to be helpful.

"*Merci!*" cried Miles, his voice drowned by a fresh uproar, "*vous êtes bien aimable.*" They saluted one another through the dust and din.

"*Il fait beau temps,*" the policeman said as soon as he could be heard, offering a final civility, "*et en trois jours on verra la nouvelle lune.*"

Fez, thought Miles, turning away. How far? And how did one get there? All his plans for departure collapsed in a moment. If Tavy were there he must find her. He would get hold of Sam and go; they would go there together. "Not a year passes," said a voice from some crevice of memory, "without Fez, Mequinez, Morocco and Wazan in the interior being visited . . ." They might even start by nightfall if Sam were home.

"**N**OTHING MUCH CRAZIER than this ever happened," said Sam, when he could make himself heard. "You're plain crazy. I don't know what's gotten into you."

They were wedged together in a seat near the back of the bus, their feet pressed against their own and other people's luggage, at the beginning of what promised to be a long and singularly comfortless journey. The bus, a special, had arrived late and was late starting; they had stood for more than an hour on the wind-swept roundabout near the railway-station in a shifting confusion of baggage and passengers, nearly all country people with enormous bundles which had to be hoisted and lashed, a prodigious cargo, the whole length of the roof. Everyone was muffled against the cold, the women's heads swathed in wrappings under their huge hats, the men's faces shadowed by the hoods of their *djellábas*. The smell of sweat and wool was very strong.

"We're all crazy at times," said Miles, stuffing his raincoat between his leg and the edge of Sam's tape-recorder, "which doesn't mean I'm not grateful to you for coming. I couldn't possibly manage alone."

"Think nothing of it. I never need much of an excuse

for going to Fez." He looked at Miles speculatively. "What beats me is how you got into all this drama, and what you stand to gain by it."

"I got into it by accident, and I'll almost certainly gain nothing. I want to put my mind at rest, that's all."

"About what, exactly?"

Miles gazed at the vast straw hat of the woman in front of him, splendid in shape, the brim and crown decked and rigged with woollen ropes. Would another person ever understand his motives, when they were so difficult to interpret honestly, even to himself?

"I want to see Tavy before I go. I want to make sure she's all right. For various reasons I have a feeling she mayn't be."

"You're hooked on her," said Sam. "That fact I've grasped, astonishing though it is. I suppose it explains all the rest. Though why you think you're going to find her's another matter. You don't know what you're in for."

"I dare say I won't find her, but I can at least try. I'm just not prepared to leave without having made the effort."

"And if you do find her, what then? Won't our friend Quattrell be faintly surprised to see you in Fez, showing all this anxiety? I kind of assumed he regarded her as his property."

"Why should he be surprised? We've as much right to take a trip as he has."

"Oh, sure. So long as he doesn't suspect. I wouldn't care to tangle with that guy, not if there's any trouble."

"You won't. I'll see to that." Miles took out his cigarettes. His throat was dry and his hand for some reason unsteady. He felt in his pocket for matches.

"Say, must you really smoke? The air in this crate's pretty near unbreathable as it is. Chew on some gum instead, will you?"

Miles accepted a sliver from Sam's packet, and for a

while, in an aroma of mint, their jaws moved in silence. The bus was travelling fast through monotonous dusk on a straight and shining road across empty plain. There seemed to be neither villages nor trees, but it was difficult to see anything; the lights inside the bus made the landscape doubly dark and the stars and far-off mountains wholly invisible. Presently the diesel changed its note and they began to climb, swaying heavily against one another on the zigzag bends, double-horn sounding and lights signalling as they overtook and passed top-heavy lorries. The hubbub of conversation gradually died; the air was becoming cold. A baby wailed for a while and was presently silenced. Sounds of distress from the front of the bus, where someone was being sick, subsided abruptly; a conversation which sounded like fierce argument came grumblingly to an end. Sam folded a pull-over and wedged it under his neck to keep his head from rolling. He continued to chew peacefully for a while with his eyes closed, but presently his mouth fell open and he chewed no more. The bus ground its way upward into rocky country.

I must sleep too, thought Miles; but the muscles of his legs twitched and he was a long time awake. After a while he spat out the chewing-gum and detached the sticky nodule from his fingers. It fell to the floor after some difficulty and he closed his eyes. They seemed to have passed the highest point of the climb and were rocking from side to side in a long descent. He had lost count of time and knew only that his legs ached and that his hands were cold. Occasionally Tavy was beside him and he was trying through a roar of voices to explain something, but each time he jerked to the surface it was to find the bulb in the roof shining on his eyelids and Sam peacefully breathing against his shoulder.

Tavy, he said to himself, his lips moving. My poor lost Tavy. He could admit, at last, that he loved her, that the impetus which had set him off on this preposterous journey was not merely anxiety, as he had pretended to Sam, but an angry desire to take her away from Quattrell. His dislike of Quattrell, his resentment at the very thought of the life she led, was basically this: he wanted to take her away and transform the future. Miles's protective instinct had always been strong; it was something he had learned to recognize and make allowance for; there were even times when he regarded it with suspicion. The pain of his failure with Lucy had been chiefly pride, but there was this deeper element as well. He had been, quite simply, outraged by the callous frivolity of her independence. Tavy by contrast was dangerously vulnerable, and it was this aspect of her situation, the thought that she had no ally except Panya, which had tempted him into believing that she needed him. Now in his silent monologue he was trying to explain to Tavy that he needed her too. He had been a long time reaching this point, which should, he saw, have been clear from the beginning. From the first moment of seeing her from Sam's roof, when she had stopped at the turn of the steps and looked blindly up, something had stirred in him which he had been slow to recognize. When next he had seen her, with Quattrell, it had been a shock; and this, too, he had somehow, blindly, failed to interpret. He had fed himself on indignation and an obscure anger, which had been only the dark side of his own desire. Now, keeping his eyes closed and becoming a part of the bus's speed and vibration, he passed into a state of being in which he could see this clearly. He could explain it lucidly to Tavy and she appeared to listen, sitting with head bent, saying nothing. In imagination he felt for her hand and kissed it; this moved him profoundly. There was no difficulty, no resistance. Without perceptible movement she was suddenly, responsively, in his arms. It was like a home-coming. He held his breath, feeling the smoothness of her cheek as he sought her mouth. And then they were sighing peacefully in a long kiss, and everything was accepted. There was no need of explanation; there was nothing further to be said.

But supposing it was not like that? He stirred uneasily against Sam's shoulder. Supposing she really loved Quattrell, and refused to leave him? It was rational to suppose she did, but impossible to believe it. She had stumbled unsuspectingly into a trap, and now she had grown used to the thing, like a tamed bird. She was afraid to leave because it was all she knew. If she had once had courage on her own account she had lost it because of Joe.

Remembering the child with surprise, Miles considered him. He had never been afraid of responsibility, and the thought of Joe did not dismay him; he was surrounded with an aura of tenderness because he was Tavy's. He had a vision of the three of them going through the gate of the house at Richmond, a family established and acknowledged, visiting his father. It seemed not at all absurd, and he dwelt on it with pleasure. But Joe would not go to his father's school, or be subjected to Mrs. Mills. The smell of the cloakroom on wet days drifted into his consciousness, followed by the stupefying uproar in the dining-room when his father had said grace and the boys dragged their chairs from the long tables together.

When finally the bus halted in a dead town, a dusty emptiness staring with arc-lights, he had been asleep for an immeasurable time and the sound in his dream was the driver unroping and throwing down bundles from the roof. He shivered and looked at his watch. Still only ten o'clock; only Souk-el-Arba, desolate and ugly place, where the male passengers, their backs turned to the bus, were making water together at the side of the road.

Once when he awoke they were at Meknes, and the air was sharp and clean and smelt of trees. After that, under

the harsh street-lighting, they passed crumbling yellow
walls and pock-marked fortifications, and swept down ave-
nues bordered with orange trees, leaving the ancient town
and skirting the new, until once more they were out in a
country of rock and cactus, rolling and bare and veined
with dark ravines. And then again it was an endless plain,
where the road ran straight and the bus made reverberating speed, a lozenge of light in the darkness where nothing
existed but the tarmac and its telegraph poles racing to
meet the headlights in an endless stream. Later, when there
was a deluge of rain, even these were blotted out. Sam lay
with his head against the streaming window, and after a
time, listening to the skimming of the tyres, which became
the hiss of the sea along the sides of the ship, Miles lost
touch with his thoughts and again slept.

★　★　★

"First thing to do," said Sam, "is get breakfast inside us.
Then we can start operations."

They were sitting at a table looking out on the street,
with the dazed sensations of people who have slept either
too much or too little, and in the wrong place. No one
else had appeared in the dining-room and there was only
one waiter. He took a long time to produce two small pots
of coffee with rolls, and then leaned against a serving-
trolley at a distance, watching these early customers with a
look of envy.

"It's very different from what I imagined," said Miles,
lifting the muslin curtain to gaze out at a nondescript tri-
angle of street. It was a grey morning and the night's rain
still collected in the gutters. A man in straw hat and ragged
djellába was sweeping up mounds of mud and shovelling
them, very slowly, into a hand-barrow. Each time a bicycle

went by, or a horse and cart loaded with charcoal or vegetables, he ceased all activity and stood as one turned to
stone until it was out of sight.

"Whatever you imagined," said Sam, pouring milk into
his coffee, "it won't compare with the reality. Fez is two
cities—three, even—you knew that, I guess? This one we
came up to last night, the new town, might be anywhere.
The French built it at the start of the protectorate, so's not
to destroy the ancient city. Thank God they did. So the two
old towns, Fez el Bali and Fez Jdid, are inside their walls,
down there on the river"—he waved his hand vaguely—
"and haven't changed much since the days of Moulay
Idriss. It was the capital of the Idrissite dynasty and all
that. Just wait till you see it, that's all. Remember the walls
and gateway, where the bus stopped? Let's get the telephone business over quickly, so I can show you."

"You must stay and help me," said Miles. "My French
isn't equal to it."

"Sure I'll stay. Only don't let's waste time. We'll get a
list of hotels from the desk and ring them in descending
order. They're bound to be in one or another."

"You think so?"

"Of course. Quattrell's a man who considers his comfort, isn't he? If they're in Fez at all they're bound to be in
the new town."

But they were not. The ordeal by telephone was prolonged, endured by Sam with surprising patience and by
Miles with dismay which deepened at each new failure.
The reception clerk took pity on them at last and made the
calls himself, exchanging pleasantries in Arabic and spell-
ing out Quattrell's and Tavy's names in French, but always
with the same result. No such persons, he said, had
checked in anywhere, though there was a Mr. Dickinson at
the Palais Jamaï and a group of commercial gentlemen at
the Zalagh. Their friends, he suggested, would perhaps ar-

rive later in the morning? Miles and Sam looked doubtfully
at one another.

"I wonder if he's registered under a different name?
Mightn't that be the answer?"

"I don't see how," said Sam, "because they take the
passports. He wouldn't stay down in the Mellah, would he?
There are one or two doubtful little dumps down there,
probably not even on the telephone."

"Can we go and try?"

"Sure we can try," said Sam, "if you're really up to it.
You're not feeling too good, are you? You're a funny
colour."

"I dare say it's something I ate. It'll pass off."

"I'll give you something to take. One of my life-
savers."

They went up to the shuttered bedroom, one of a series
of cells on a passage like the corridor of a prison, and Miles
lay down on his bed in a sweat of nausea. It was only
fatigue, he told himself, and the wretched night; he would
be all right presently. He lay still with eyes closed, listening to the whisper of blood in his ears and his heart beating. Sam moved softly about the room, opening and closing
shutters, turning on taps in the bathroom, unstrapping the
tape-recorder. Feeling him near, Miles opened his eyes to
find him standing over the bed with a glass of water.

"Swallow these," he said, proffering two liquorice-
coloured pellets on the palm of his hand. "Guaranteed to
raise the dead, or cure anything whatever. Go on, knock
them back. I got up a bottle from the bar; it's not tap
water."

After a while Miles opened his eyes again, confused
and astonished to find he had been dozing. The sweat and
nausea had gone; he felt well, though not quite normal. His
limbs seemed to move of themselves, without intention or
effort, so that presently he found himself on the pavement

without any clear recollection of how he got there.

"What were those things you gave me?" he asked Sam when they were together in the taxi. He was not particularly curious, but it seemed necessary to say something. The open boulevard was streaming past in a way that was a little too smooth, and therefore interesting. He observed from a calm distance clay-coloured hills, a valley with trees, crenellated walls, an archway.

"They're really something, aren't they?" said Sam. "S. Hardback his recipe. Guaranteed, like I said," and Miles found this information sufficient and returned to his private and curiously fluid sensations.

They left the taxi in the Place Boujeloud and passed through an archway into a frowning corridor between high walls, the cobbles slippery with mud, sloping gently downhill. The passage turned to the left at a sharp angle and presently to the right, still without change or feature apart from a beggar crouching with outstretched claw against the wall. Miles slipped once or twice and steadied himself, putting an arm through Sam's. He was not sure whether he imagined it or whether in every part of this deep gully, beneath the paving perhaps or behind the walls, they were followed by a secret murmur of running water.

It was a persistent sound, and though he lost it when they turned into a more frequented channel there were fountains in the wall from time to time, stone basins brimming over and spilling the water like crystal over the cobbles. The strangeness in everything he saw was difficult to focus, still less identify; it pervaded everything, the confused but agreeable flavour of a dream. If it were indeed an illusion, and not real, he might understand it, for it was a dream he had had before, of being transposed in time. There was no one like himself or Sam in these thronged valleys, only people of a past age, living and moving in a world that had been long forgotten. The streets grew nar-

rower still and the crowd denser. There was a hum of
voices everywhere, broken by sudden cries; donkeys and
mules, inconceivably laden, thrust against his shoulder. At
one moment they were pressed against a booth filled with
glittering stuffs, at another threading with difficulty
through an alley smoky with incense, where the sole com-
modity on sale seemed to be candles. They were not candles as he understood them, but surrealist objects, hanging
in clusters from their wicks like sinister fruits, pink, choco-
late-coloured, green, mottled all over with brilliant and obsessive patterns. And then they had stopped at the open
doorway of a mosque, where women and children were
clustered and it seemed impossible to move further. The
interior was vast and brilliant, flickering with candles and
splendid with chandeliers. Peering between heads and
shoulders, uneasily wondering if they had strayed into a
forbidden precinct, he saw painted pillars, acres of matted
floor, the backs of a scattered congregation at their devo-
tions.

"Is it all right for us to be here?" he whispered to Sam,
and they edged circumspectly away.

Presently they came to a more open space where there
was a tiled fountain and a gateway closed with an ancient
door which might have withstood a siege. There was a
beggar on either side of this door, both blind, both crippled, one wrapped in a ragged *djellába*, the other a woman,
hideously old, nursing a deformed child. Sam stopped and
looked about him.

"I remember the route this far," he said, "but beyond
this I'm not sure." At the sound of his voice the beggars set
up their chant and he felt in his pockets and gave them
some small change, looking away from them as he did so.

"This is only the beginning," he told Miles, "but we
don't want to get lost. One of these days I'll find a plan of
this city and work it out properly. If we go back the way

we came there's a turning I remember; it leads to a lodging-house of sorts that I went into once. We can try there."

It seemed to Miles, as they moved on, that something was smoothly shifting inside his head, and that soon every-thing would be clear. This trance-like progress, which had all the portentous trappings of an allegory—a mediaeval poem, he imagined, bound in calf and tooled in faded gold —was worlds away from what he had hoped to find. What had this vision of the past to do with Tavy? And if she were really hidden in this seething maze, what hope could there possibly be that he would find her? Yet against all reason his mind was calm, as though time were of no account and the mere action of drifting through this teeming formicary would bring him at last to the very heart of the question. There was no need for struggle or anxiety; so long as he followed Sam he would arrive, and then, when his mind was clear, he would know what to do. Sam was the guide, showing him a vision of the world or perhaps of purgatory; all that was required of himself was to accept and follow.

Abruptly, at an intersection of passages, Sam in a burst of confidence took a new direction, and identification with the allegory became irresistible. He had been shown the glittering sanctuary and must now look on the pit, an in-ferno of noise and flame where blacksmiths beat red-hot metal and heaved at their sooty bellows in a shower of sparks. Cave after cave moved by in a reddish glow, each with its acrid flame and metallic din; and as though this parable were not enough there was a knot of people block-ing the street and two youths fighting like demons. A smith with tongs uproariously separated them and they fell apart to a chorus of shouts and laughter.

"This is like hell," Miles said, "a detail from Hierony-mus Bosch," but Sam only laughed and said the recipe wasn't supposed to work that way. It was supposed to calm him down, not distort perception.

By the time they had passed through the neighbourhood of the mosque again Miles was conscious of subtle change. The lingering miasma lifted and he saw clearly. The surprising thing was that there was so little difference; the ceaseless procession was still extravagant, like a sequence in a film. But the contents of the booths were different: they were less exotic than he had supposed. There were bunches of plastic sandals everywhere, cheap saucepans, pot-scourers, packets of Tide; the clothing shops were festooned with ready-made rubbish of a European character. There were innumerable barber-shops where turbans were laid aside and heads shaven; photographers' booths where grotesque enlargements were set out among plastic flowers; china shops crowded with every horror of meretricious table-ware stacked on the tops of gas-cookers and fancy radios. Miles noticed for the first time that the younger men and boys wore jeans and shirts and were not, after all, so very different from himself. But the main stream of the crowd was still ancient and strange and as continuous as ever. When there was a sound of music approaching he and Sam were swept bodily forward by the press of people.

"Oh God," sighed Sam, "why didn't I bring the recorder?"

It was a procession of men, all bearded and decent in white *djellábas*, preceded by musicians busily drumming and blowing a discordant rhythm. It was the last canto of the allegory, the final admonition, the wooden bier carried shoulder-high and on it the narrow corpse in its winding-sheet. The body was that of a man, if one could judge, with little flesh on his bones. Narrow, shrunken, dry, more than ready for the grave. The bandaged feet, solid as a pedestal, pointed to the sky; the arms were moulded to the sides and under the wrappings of the head the arch of a patriarchal nose was visible. It might have been a plaster effigy but for one detail: the linen over the mouth showed a spreading stain.

Miles had never seen a corpse before, and this one had been formalised to the last point of austerity. The figure on the bier was already remote from life; its stillness was absolute; it had an enviable dignity. Impossible to pity this unknown man going with such frank finality to the grave. It was natural and humble and fitting, and the friends accompanying him looked not at all dejected as they sang their hymn, but rather the reverse. Miles wished they could have concealed the death-stain over the mouth; that seemed to him the only breach of kindness. But even for this Sam had an explanation. It was a poor man's funeral, he said; he would pass by the mosque for a prayer and then straight to the cemetery. There was a practical briskness about a Muslim burying, and perhaps there was a blessing in dying now, at the end of Ramadan, when he would be full of sanctity. And the stain on the cere-cloth would not be blood or the flux of death, but perfume, poured by the women of the family as a last grace. He would go to the grave with his beard well combed and scented, an old man washed and decorous, offending no one.

★   ★   ★

When they were back at the hotel, eating under the eye of the same waiter, Miles said suddenly, "It's no good, Sam. I have a feeling they're not here."

"I see. And you think that's reason enough for not looking any further?" Sam's tone was sarcastic.

"Well . . . I'm not sure. It feels as though we're wasting time. In a city of this size—two cities—it seems hopeless to imagine we're going to run into them in the street."

"That's just where you're wrong, though. The street is

where people are. Maybe you hadn't noticed? People don't sit in their hotel rooms all day. It's too boring."

"I know, but the complexity! It's like you once said, an ant-heap. Even if they're here, if we walked the streets all day we wouldn't run into them."

"I'm not so sure. We wouldn't find a native Fassi maybe, but a European, yes. I don't know this town too well but I guess I know it better than Quattrell. He isn't in any of the hotels this side, so I guess he's down by Fez Jdid some place. He wasn't in the one we tried this morning, but there's some others. I don't know them, but we can ask. And if the one we tried's anything to judge by he'll only be in it to sleep. They'll stroll about, like we did this morning; it's irresistible. They'll sleep in the afternoon and do it again in the evening. They'll eat in the Ville Nouvelle, most likely, and sit about in the *cafés;* or go up at sunset to a place I'll show you, and have a mint tea. All Europeans do it, same as everybody else. It's too beautiful to miss. But they'll walk in the Medina again in the early evening. If they're not gone some place else it's only a matter of time till we run across them."

"I hope you're right," said Miles, and sighed. He also hoped, though he did not say so, that his leg would stand a repetition of the morning. It was not exactly painful, it was numb, but he suspected this was the effect of Sam's recipe and that another two hours on the cobbles might lead to trouble. When they went up to their dark bedroom he lay on his creaking mattress and tried to evolve a plan that would have some sense in it. Nowhere in the course of the morning had there been anything his imagination could connect with Tavy or with the possibility of finding her. He fell almost at once into a perplexed sleep.

At four o'clock they set out again, following a new route. The taxi covered what seemed an interminable distance, circling the sand-coloured walls of the town, passing tin-patched shanty settlements and groves of olive trees, then grotesque configurations of erosion that might have been carved by floods at the beginning of the world. Sam had a small tape-recorder slung from one shoulder on which he concentrated with intensity.

The taxi stopped at an archway and they went on foot into a rectangle of open ground between high walls, in which considerable crowds were congregated. A throng of strollers passed from one to the other, the groups perpetually melting and re-forming, so that the whole causeway was in motion.

"Keep your eyes open," said Sam, "they may well be here," and stopped on the edge of a story-teller's audience. He stayed there absorbed for some time, his tapes whispering. Miles studied the faces of the crowd and was puzzled to see that they were nearly all men; perhaps there was some reason why women were not supposed to listen to stories? The faces were rapt, entranced; the man in the circle moved round it with spellbinding gestures, delivering some ancient adventure in a powerful voice. When he cast up his eyes, as though for confirmation from heaven, he had the look of a blind man, but when the eyeballs slid down again he fixed his hearers with a look of frightening intensity. From time to time he tapped a leather-bound manuscript under his arm, as though to say, "It is all here in this writing, and therefore true." Once he stooped and touched the sole of his sandal, bringing up a pinch of dust and gravely scattering it. His eyes dilated and rolled, his gold teeth flashed. Intent on his tape-recorder Sam laughed silently.

"Can you follow the drift of the story?" said Miles. "What's it all about?"

"I think I've got some of it," said Sam in an undertone, switching off the tapes. "I've heard it before; it's romantic. A young man was in love with a beautiful girl and married her; and someone else, I'm not clear who, went to a witch in revenge and had a spell put on him. They took dust from the sole of his foot and mixed it with something else, and he became impotent, no different from a woman. He ran to doctors and hospitals, but nothing did any good. They said, 'Nothing will remove the spell but another, which is stronger.' "

"And then?" said Miles, seeing that the story-teller had stopped in the middle of his tale. A Negro crouching in the dust, whom he had not noticed until this moment, beat with the palm of his hand on a clay drum. This was evidently the climax of the performance; the story-teller was moving in their direction with a collecting-bag. Those who wanted the next instalment threw in a coin or two, while the rest—knowing the tale from infancy perhaps, or having empty pockets—moved on to the next attraction.

"He'll go on when he's had enough encouragement," said Sam, and moved away. "And when he's exhausted his repertoire he'll go on to some other town, where the stories are new." They began strolling slowly to the next circle.

Miles searched each crowd of heads, but there was no fair one. Tavy was not listening to stories or watching fire-eaters, or the performance of the wizard with a basket of dry and flaccid-looking snakes. It was all shabby, decrepit, dusty and somehow touching. Again, as in the morning, he had the feeling that a trick was being played with time, that he was back in an age when pleasures were childish and a man could keep alive by attending the fair with pipe and drum, or a boy by walking on his hands and turning back-somersaults.

"How the heck they do it fasting I don't know, though," said Sam, "they look hungry enough." And indeed, to judge by their looks, if most of them kept alive by their performance it was by a narrow margin.

In the busiest part of all, among pedlars and cheap-jacks, was one who appeared to be doing no business at all. He sat cross-legged on an ancient matting with the tools of his mystery laid out before him; some dusty packets, a bottle containing a tapeworm, a neatly arranged pyramid of human teeth. Sam lingered for a while near this dignified practitioner, hoping a patient would appear, but none came.

"Too bad," he said with feeling, fingering the button of his recorder. "An extraction with those pliers would have been worth having."

He tore himself away at last, seeing the light fade. The earth-coloured walls had taken a rosy tinge, and he was impatient to be gone. They drove back the way they had come and out on a winding road above the town, to a ramshackle open-air café among rocks and crags. There was nobody here but themselves; by the time their tea had been brought an erratic wind had sprung up and the air was cold. In the valley below, darkly contained within its walls, the city that in the morning had been white, grey, colourless, mottled from the winter rains, was turning from gold to crimson as the sun sank. The hills beyond were luminous; even the rising mist was silver and rose.

"I heard a car, I think," said Sam, tilting back his head. "They're pretty sure to come here some time; everyone does who knows it." But the car went on down the hill, making a sighing sound, and the waiter began to put up the shutters of the café.

The sky changed as they watched, losing warmth and colour. A flight of snowy egrets swept across, turning to the colour of flamingoes in the last rays. Lights were beginning to show in the Medina, and presently the standard arcs of the highway came on, orange at first and then greenish-white, a blinding fluorescent effulgence which hid the city.

★   ★   ★

Soon after ten o'clock next morning, waiting outside a *tabac* while Sam bought newspapers, Miles saw Tavy. She came out on the steps of the main post office, alone, and stood for a moment fastening her satchel.

She was a long way off, for the post office stood at the intersection of three thoroughfares, and Miles was on the corner of the further one. But even at that distance there could be no mistake; she was wearing the short grey skirt and jacket that Panya had given her, and as she bent her head her pale hair flashed like a signal.

The shock of recognition was so great that he stood for a second without moving. He had reached the point of knowing that the search was hopeless, yet there she was, not a hundred yards away, exactly as Sam had predicted. Without glancing in his direction she set off along the pavement.

Tingling with shock, Miles found himself missing a car, then causing a cyclist to brake suddenly. By the time he had negotiated the double crossing Tavy had paused for the lights at the next corner, and was still in sight. He began to run, not caring that he moved jerkily or that one or two aimless strollers turned to look at him. He was within calling distance when she stopped at the next crossing.

"Tavy!" he shouted, "Tavy!"

She paused in the act of stepping from the kerb and looked round with a furtive glance, as though she had half expected to be followed.

"Tavy," he said, "it *is* you!" and grasped her by the arm. They stared stupefied at one another.

Then Tavy whispered "I don't believe it. It's not possible," and put her hand to her mouth as though she were going to cry. Miles put his arm through hers and turned her gently back in the direction of the post office.

"I left Sam a block away," he said, "so I must go back and find him. He'll be worried; he'll think I'm lost." He was talking for the sake of talking so that she could pull herself together. She was holding him tightly by the arm; presently she brushed her cheeks with her fingers and stopped to look at him.

"What are you doing here, Miles? I can't believe it."

"I came to find you. I had a feeling something was wrong."

"I can't believe it," she said again, searching his face. "It's the one thing I've longed for. You can't imagine . . ." Her eyes filled again and he noticed she was very pale. "How did you know where we were? It seems like a miracle."

"There *is* something wrong, then?"

"Yes. Dreadfully."

"Don't tell me now. We'll find Sam first of all, then I'll go back with you."

They began to walk again, and there on the pavement opposite the post office was Sam with his folded newspaper, fixed to the spot but alert, like a well-trained dog.

"So Hardback's theory holds good," he said when they had crossed over. He noticed the tears on Tavy's face and made no comment. "What luck we ran across you," he said, "at least—not luck, it was predictable from calculation, and must be celebrated." They followed him docilely down a side-street towards a faded awning and a smell of roasting coffee.

"I won't sit down, I can't stay," said Tavy, realizing what was meant when they paused at a pavement table. "Rob's ill, I must hurry back. I only came out to send a telegram to Panya."

"Stay and have a quick coffee," Sam urged, "it'll do you good."

"No, no, I really can't. He's much too sick. He's been ill all night, and I don't know what's the matter." She rested her knuckles on the iron table and looked down at it, frowning. "If Panya will only come she'll know what to do. How long does a telegram take? She could be here by tomorrow."

"Have you seen a doctor?" Sam asked her.

"No. Panya's a doctor, or used to be. I told you, I've sent her a telegram."

"Why don't you see one here? It'd save time."

"I don't know any, that's why. And I'd rather have Panya."

"The hotel would put you on to a good one. Ask at the desk."

"It isn't that kind of hotel. We're not in the Ville Nouvelle. They're hopeless, they don't know anything."

"Well, for heaven's sake, I can ask at ours," said Sam, beginning to be exasperated. "You're crazy not to get one here. The place is full of them, even a few French ones, I guess. There's a hospital, for God's sake."

Tavy looked doubtfully at Miles.

"Do you think I ought?"

"Certainly you ought," he said, and caught a look of relief. For some reason she had not wanted to do it on her own, or had been afraid to. Perhaps it was Quattrell who had not wanted to see a doctor?

"Very well, if you think so," she said, but still stood by the iron table, staring down at it. Her lip trembled.

"Write down the name of your hotel," Miles told her, taking the ball-point from Sam's breast-pocket and the newspaper from under his arm, "and then Sam can go and look for a doctor while I walk back with you."

Tavy sat down at the table and laboriously printed something on the margin of the newspaper.

"I don't know the name of the street. We're not exactly in the Medina; I think we're sort of on the edge of the Jewish quarter, near the cemetery."

"The name's enough, I guess," said Sam. "The hotel clerk'll fix everything. It's on the phone?"

"There *is* a phone, but it's horrid, and very public. I didn't dare use it."

"O.K. I'll join you there as soon as I get hold of anybody."

When they had gone some way along the boulevard Miles took her arm and said, "Now you needn't worry any more. I'll look after everything. Darling Tavy," he added under his breath, and felt an absurd elation because at last he had said it.

She pressed his arm without answering. Again he had the feeling that silence was all she could manage, and that even that was precarious.

When they had crossed the wide intersection of streets again and were heading towards the next roundabout he said, "Take your time, but try and tell me what's happened." They were still walking arm in arm.

"I will, Miles. In a minute. I don't know what's the matter with me, I keep wanting to cry. I think it's the relief of seeing you." She said nothing more until they had crossed the roundabout, which like most things in the new town seemed to be in the process of either construction or demolition, and were passing the low wall of a public garden. The cloud of the morning was breaking under a clear sky and the pavement was chequered with patches of sun and shadow.

"If only you'd stayed," she said at length. "I know it was difficult, Miles. I'm not blaming you."

"What could I have done if I had? Be fair. I came down to the house next morning and you'd already gone."

"I know. We went that night, as soon as Rob got back from Rabat. I told him all about Mr. Stagg and everything, and he was just frightfully angry. He doesn't want the divorce, that's all. It's as simple as that." Her voice had a melancholy finality.

"So he came away to avoid him. I thought as much."

"He made me pack straight away and get Joe out of bed. He was upset when he found I'd told Zohra where we were going. He gave her some money and made her promise to keep quiet. Was it really Zohra who told you? It isn't like her."

"No. I couldn't get anything out of either of them. It was Aminah's policeman who told me. I met him in the street."

Tavy gave him a sidelong glance.

"So that was it. I believe she tells him everything. Some people say she's a whore—had you heard that? It's not true, really. It's only Youssef, that policeman."

"So you drove down here, at night; and then what?"

"We arrived about three in the morning, and had to find a hotel. There were lots of people in the Medina, it was quite noisy; but Rob had an idea about some place in the Mellah, where the Jews live, so we went there. It's a beastly place, but I don't think Europeans go there; so he felt safe."

"I see. He felt safe. And then?"

"He stayed in bed most of the next day, and we had food sent up. It was rather awful because Joe cried a lot, and I was afraid to take him out anywhere. Rob wouldn't let me, anyway; he said we had to stay put. So we spent the whole day in the room and Rob went on drinking. I didn't notice anything was wrong at first because I was worried about Joe. He'd been bitten in the night and had diarrhoea for some reason. And then that night, when I'd got him to sleep, I suddenly noticed Rob was a funny colour."

They had reached the crumbling wall of an older quarter, and passed under an archway. Here there was an open square full of people and buses. Cars, carts and hand-barrows were parked at random across the entrance of a garage; a knot of Berbers waited vacantly outside a cinema, which was plastered with posters of Indian films, princely heroes and ladies swooning with passion. They passed into a narrow street where the shops had a sordid look, dark booths set deep in the peeling wall, some of them closed with heavy shutters and padlocked. The whole place had a poverty-stricken and depressing air, but there was noise and activity everywhere, men and donkeys coming and going and cases of wine being unloaded among stacks of bicycles, nets full of charcoal, bales of wool, baskets of tomatoes and vegetables.

"We're nearly there," said Tavy, disengaging her arm. The pavement being crowded they walked for convenience in the road, among vegetable refuse and straw and trodden droppings. "Well . . . *then*," she said, taking a deep breath, "I thought it was only the whisky, and that he'd be better in the morning. He drinks quite a lot at times; it doesn't seem to affect him. But next morning he was sick after breakfast, and sent me to the French *pharmacie* to get a stomach mixture. I was afraid to go because of leaving Joe, but I asked the woman who cleans our room to look after him. Joe was all right by this time and had made friends with her, so I let her have him."

"And then?"

They parted to let a man with a donkey go by, the animal so hidden under a pyramid of timber that it seemed impossible the slender legs could carry it.

"Well . . . then in the evening he didn't seem any better, in fact rather the reverse. He would insist on drinking a lot of red wine, which he said was the thing for dysentery. But I think it was too strong or something, because he got very sick. He wouldn't let me get a doctor because he was sure it was only something he'd eaten; he didn't want to see anybody. He went on with this Jewish wine, being sick every time, and in the night he had cramps in his stomach, and I got frightened."

"My poor child, I don't wonder," said Miles. "But the doctor will be able to deal with it. You're not to worry."

"You think he'll know what it is? I mean, can they tell for certain, from the symptoms?"

"Oh yes, surely. It's unlikely to be serious. It's probably some kind of food-poisoning; they have things to deal with it."

"Oh, of course; I know," said Tavy, giving him an odd glance. "Europeans get upset so easily, don't they? And the food's beastly. He was perfectly all right until after the first meal in the hotel."

"In any case you've wired to Panya, and she'll probably come."

"Oh, yes! She *must*." Her voice had a note of hysteria, but she checked herself with an effort and went on more calmly. "She never minds shutting the shop for days at a time. She does that when she goes to Paris. She can leave everything with Concepción."

They were crossing a vine-shaded courtyard with a pump from which a group of women were drawing buckets of water. Women and girls alike had their faces uncovered and one or two were handsome. On the cobbles at their feet, in the splash of water and taking no notice of the women's clatter, a man in a yellow turban was scouring a cooking-pot.

"We're here," said Tavy, and stopped at a dark doorway. There was nothing to show that the place was an hotel except a broken electric bulb over the entrance and a panel fixed to the transom on which someone had painted a name in Hebrew characters.

The entrance was dark and smelled pungently of urine. Tavy led the way through a passage to a narrow stair and they went up to the first floor, avoiding a trickle of water which dropped from stair to stair as they ascended. At the top there was a fairly spacious landing lit by a skylight and protected by an iron railing from the well in the middle. One side of this was furnished with a plastic-covered table on which flies clustered. On the other were one or two cane-bottomed chairs and a bedstead with a naked mattress on which a young man lay with his knees up, staring at the ceiling. An extremely aged woman with bare feet, her skirt tucked up above her bloomers, was washing the floor and paddling about on the tiles.

"You'd better wait here," Tavy said in a whisper. "I'd better not say you're here, not at first. Do you mind? It'll be easier when Sam's here, especially with the doctor."

The man on the mattress put his feet to the floor and got up. From the apron he wore it seemed that he belonged to the hotel. He disappeared without speaking through a curtain and they heard his shoes dragging loosely along the corridor.

There were several doors to this landing, which seemed to serve a double function, and to be also, in spite of the constricted space, a dining-room. Crumbs on the plastic table-cover, where patterns of flies outlined the fresher stains, suggested that a meal had been served and eaten recently. Tavy crept to a door and turned the knob. She looked round it cautiously before going in and closing it behind her.

Miles drew a chair from the table and sat down to wait. The place was extraordinarily silent; the old woman had slopped away downstairs and he could hear nothing

but the sibilant whisper of a cistern. The life of the hotel,
such as it was, seemed to have deserted this level; presumably the work of the kitchen went on below. There was
a smell of oil and onions but no sound of anyone at work.
The walls had been lime-washed a long time ago and were
flaking badly; a calendar hung between naked patches and
a print of a religious character had been nailed to the
plaster.

Presently the door opened and Tavy beckoned. She
lifted a finger as Miles got up, and cautiously opened the
door a little further. Quattrell was asleep, lying with his
head thrown back on the pillow, his mouth slightly open.
His body, or as much as could be seen of it, was naked; the
hair of his chest was damp, the left breast patterned with
insect bites and the marks of scratching. The window-cur-
tain was drawn and the light poor, but it was obvious that
the skin of his face was an odd colour. It had the yellowish
tinge of parchment, and the same dead look. Even from
where they stood they could hear his breathing.

Miles gazed at him in silence, and at the wretched
room. It seemed even smaller than it was because the bed
filled it. It was jammed against the wall, as indeed it had to
be; there was no room for any other furniture. Between the
bed and the wash-basin there was scarcely standing room.
There was no table and no chair; his clothes hung from a
nail and their luggage was piled in a corner.

Miles softly moved back to the table and Tavy closed
the door.

"What am I going to do?" she whispered, and again
there was the shake of hysteria. "Don't you think he looks
frightful? Supposing he dies?" She gazed at Miles wide-
eyed, as though there were no possibility of horror that she
had not envisaged.

"Of course he isn't going to die. It's a good sign he's
sleeping."

"Sleeping? That isn't ordinary sleep. And look at the colour of his face! I don't like it."

"People can look much worse than that with food-poisoning," said Miles, "and be perfectly all right again in a day or two."

He knew nothing whatever about it, but remembered that several of his father's boys had sickened after one of Mrs. Mills's corned-beef economies, and had been rushed to hospital. There had been a lot of fuss from the parents but they had all recovered. He tried to think of reassuring circumstances.

Nothing very apposite occurred to him. Nothing, at least, that was likely to comfort Tavy. If Quattrell died he could bear it, himself, with fortitude. He would see him removed on a bier without compunction. He would behave adequately, he hoped; he would do all that was required; but it was useless to pretend that he would not be the most hypocritical of mourners. He could think of a thousand felicitous possibilities. Tavy's captivity would be over; she would go back with him to England. It would be strange at first, but she would be comforted in time. She would learn what it was to be loved. The nightmare would be over.

But supposing the nightmare, as he saw it, had its reverse side—was, in fact, mysteriously or perversely, what she wanted? Certain natures were happiest in captivity; it had its own excitement. And since life with Quattrell was all she knew it was possible, even probable, that she loved him. This thought was so grossly distasteful that he refused to consider it. It was not love that held her to Quattrell, but a kind of fear. She was fighting a hopeless battle and she knew it.

Miles sighed and looked despondently at Tavy. Quattrell was not going to die. He was tough, he was a born survivor. In a week he would be on his feet again, planning some fresh *démarche*. Tavy would be snatched away again and soon she would be back with Joe in the Rue de l'Ecurie, living her precarious life as though nothing had happened.

"Come into my room," she whispered, "we can sit in there." She opened the door next to Quattrell's and they went into an even smaller cell, furnished, like his, only with a strip of matting and an iron bed. But the window was open, reflecting a dazzling light, as though it were thrown upwards from a reflector. Miles moved in silence to the window and looked out. The light here was so strong, the scene below so incomprehensible, that he blinked in astonishment. He seemed to be looking down on a concrete desert, white as snow, set closely with blunt teeth. The teeth were arranged in symmetrical rows and extended to a great distance. There was not a tree, not a bush, not a blade of grass anywhere; only these extraordinary shapes of stone or concrete, painfully, blindingly white, dazzling, sterile.

"What on earth is it?" he said, mystified. Now that his eyes were no longer wincing at the glare he could see that there were whitewashed paths at regular intervals and that some of the teeth were carved with faint inscriptions. And they were not so much like teeth as petrified bolsters, sofa-backs carved in stone, preserved to parch for ever in this sun-bleached desert.

"It's the Jewish cemetery," said Tavy, leaning beside him on the sill. Something below caught her attention and she gripped the ledge with her hand and leaned further.

"Look," she said.

On the glaring concrete, perhaps forty feet below, there were three dabs of colour. They did not move, and at first it was difficult to distinguish what they were. Then one of them raised a triangular head and mewed silently, and Miles saw that they were kittens. They lay like rags on the hot stone, sharp-featured and hideously thin. They blinked in the strong light, aware of the voices above them and tilting their sharp-eared faces blindly upwards.

"I can't bear it," said Tavy in a defeated voice. "It's no use, there's nothing one can do," and drew back into the room. They sat together on the bed and held hands. There was nothing to look at in the room except one another. Miles let his gaze travel slowly over her hair and profile while Tavy stared at the floor. Once he lifted her hand and kissed the fingers, but it was quite different from the kiss in his dream. He felt only an ache of pity and foreboding; the sense of her nearness was like a physical pain. If I take her in my arms, he thought, it will all be different. But she continued to stare at the floor and the moment passed.

★　★　★

The time of waiting dragged on and Tavy became restless. Twice she wandered away in anxiety for Joe, who was in a courtyard in the bowels of the hotel, busy with a basket of pegs while the *fatima* washed sheets; but each time she was back within a minute, listening at Quattrell's door or sitting on the edge of the bed in an attitude of despondency. Miles tried to distract her by telling her about the dentist and the story-tellers, and she sat passively enough, her head on her hand, but without listening. She even smiled remotely from time to time, but the sense of what he was saying failed to reach her. She was so deeply sunk in her own woe that it was useless to reassure her.

She seemed obsessed with the nature of Quattrell's sleep, about which there was nothing to be done without the doctor. The idea of the doctor himself seemed also to disturb her. Would he discover the cause? Was it possible to tell? And when Miles assured her that it was, she shivered as though something cold had touched her. Presently she set Quattrell's door ajar, so that she would hear if he stirred. She was afraid he was going to die; she was afraid of the doctor; and there were even moments, or so it seemed to Miles, when her dread of Quattrell's anger was greater than either.

Once she said, tracing the pattern of the bedspread with her finger, "But you don't know the whole of it, Miles. There's so much you don't know," and reached for his hand again and held it, as though this steadied her. After that they sat for a long while without speaking, hearing only the susurration of the cistern and the strangely sepulchral sound of Quattrell's breathing.

★ 13 ★

AFTER THE DOCTOR CAME Quattrell's door was closed, and
Sam and Miles turned over the pages of the newspaper.
The aged woman reappeared on the landing. She unlocked
the door of another room, pushed open the shutters and
began slowly to strip the sheets from the bed and knot
them into a bundle. Her bare feet made no sound on the
tiles and she worked silently. They heard the squeak of a
tap being turned in Quattrell's room, then the sound of
water. Twice they heard Tavy's voice; it was sharp with
alarm, as though she were protesting about something. The
doctor's replies were brief and so nearly inaudible that it
was impossible to guess what he was saying. And then the
bed creaked heavily and Quattrell exclaimed in a hoarse
voice, and coughed.

"He's not dead, anyway," said Sam, turning to the
sporting pages.

Miles said nothing: he was trying to interpret the
voices. Once there was a retching groan, and the doctor
spoke sharply. Presently the door opened and he came out,
looking brisk and competent, leading Tavy by the hand. He
was small and quite young, perhaps something less than

forty, and disfigured by a birth-mark which spread from the base of his neck to the middle of one cheek. He had done what he could to conceal this with a small beard, but the growth, though dark, was sparse, and the stain showed through.

"*Messieurs, je m'excuse. Cette jeune personne vient d'avoir une crise de nerfs. Je vous conseille de l'éloigner pendant une demi-heure. Elle sera bientôt plus calme.*"

He looked enquiringly from one to the other and patted Tavy's arm. His manner gave no impression that he was dealing with an emergency, rather that he would like to be allowed, if possible, to get on with the job. Tavy was in tears again, and was obviously a nuisance.

"What would you like us to do?" said Sam in French.

"Take her for a walk, my friend, and assure her there is no danger. I have given her a mild sedative; she will soon recover. Entertain her for half an hour while I do what is necessary."

Out in the street with his arm in Tavy's, Miles walked her at a slow pace and at first said nothing. When they came to the pump she stopped, as though she had forgotten something.

"We could have brought Joe, couldn't we?" she said plaintively. "I've even forgotten to arrange about his dinner." This thought caused the tears, which had mercifully stopped, to flow again.

"We can go back for Joe very soon. Let's walk a little first. You left him with somebody, didn't you?"

"Yes, but supposing he starts to cry or something? His bites are rather bad, they make him miserable. I think there are bugs in the hotel." She sniffed and dried her eyes on Miles's handkerchief. "I wish to God we could sit down," she said. "I want to tell you something."

"There must be somewhere we can go. Can you think of anywhere quiet?" There was the usual clatter going on at the pump and there were inquisitive glances.

"There's the cemetery," said Tavy. "I know where the entrance is. Nobody seems to go there."

"We are certainly not going to the cemetery," said Miles. The thought of sitting with her in that wilderness of tombs was too appalling. "There must be somewhere else. There must be a café."

Tavy despondently considered.

"There's a place we went to our first evening. It's quite close, if I can only remember it."

They turned and went back the way they had come, passing the door of the hotel in its maladorous alley and emerging into the lane where the shops were. Almost opposite was a little booth selling dried fruit, nuts, herbs, bundles of steel wool, sieves and baskets. In the wall below the counter, almost at the level of the street, there was an arched grating, and this Tavy recognized.

"It's here," she said, and led Miles across the street.

It was, in fact, a cellar, and the entrance was very low. They bent their heads and went down steps into a place as gloomy as a cave. The room was small, under a ceiling of vaulted stone. There was a wooden counter near the steps with a smoky alcove behind it where a man in a woollen cap was preparing food. Beyond this, in the main part of the vault, there were half a dozen tables, each furnished with rusty and sagging tubular chairs. The only customers, two women in rather elegant *djellábas*, leaned with their backs to the wall in the furthest corner. They had pulled their veils down under their chins and sat in impassive silence behind empty glasses.

Tavy paused at the counter, looking with distaste at the row of bottles. "They have Coca-Cola here," she said. "I don't suppose you like it, but the wine's really nasty."

The man wiped two glasses with a rag and brought up

Coca-Cola from under the counter. They carried their
glasses to a table and sat down together. The grating was
high in the wall, a little above their heads; the feet of
passers-by made a rhythmic echo. Miles took her hand and
held it under the table.

"Rob likes this place," she said mournfully. "I don't
think it's interesting, do you? To me it's horrible. It's a
place where they come to drink Jewish wine where nobody
can see them. There was a party of men getting drunk the
night we came."

"It's the first time I've seen women alone in a café,"
said Miles. "I was told they never did."

Tavy glanced at the women and encountered their
stare.

"Those are whores," she said indifferently.

She sipped her drink, keeping her hand in his. From
time to time she caught her breath, like a child that has
been sobbing, but it seemed to Miles that she was soothed,
and was growing calmer.

"What was it you wanted to tell me?" he said, stroking
her hand.

She set down her glass with care and there was a curious silence.

"I want to," she said at length, "but I'm not sure I
can."

Miles felt his breath quicken with wild hope. "Try, my
darling," he said.

"The thing is . . ." Tavy frowned into her glass. "I don't
know whether the doctor knows what's wrong with Rob,
but I'm afraid I do." She drew a deep breath and gazed
painfully once or twice round the vaulted ceiling, as
though searching for words. "The thing is, you know, I
daren't tell him."

"Why not?" said Miles, his hope suddenly extin-

guished. Whatever mad possibility it had conjured up vanished abruptly. "You must, if you've got a clue. It may be
vital."

"I daren't, I daren't," she said. "I want you to tell me
what to do." Her hand was clenching inside his own. She
drew a difficult breath. "The thing that's made Rob so sick
is something I gave him."

Miles looked at her in surprise. It did not immediately
occur to him that this was a confession.

"Well, what was it, then? Something he ate? You must
tell the doctor at once, silly child. It'll probably help
him."

Tavy hung down her head and spoke very low.

"But I don't know what it was. It was something that
Zohra got me. I put it in his drink."

Miles looked at her again and his heart turned cold.

"Tavy," he said. "Tavy, listen. You must tell me about
this from the beginning." He saw again Quattrell's unconscious face and the dead colour of his skin. Patches of
darkness moved across his vision.

Tavy turned and looked him in the face, as though,
having said this thing, she could meet him fully. For the
first time he dimly knew why she was afraid, and the
knowledge shook him.

"Promise you won't be angry," she said pleadingly. "I
wouldn't tell you any of this if I didn't have to. It's just got
past that point. I don't know what to do. Oh Miles, I'm
frightened!"

"No need to be afraid," he said mechanically, "just tell
me from the beginning." A sudden calm invaded him.
Whatever Tavy had done, it could not be that. If she had
done some foolishness with Zohra it would not be beyond
remedy. Once she had told him everything he would know
what to do. At the same time there was an uneasy shadow
somewhere which he did not examine.

"Zohra's been very good to me," she said, "more than you could possibly imagine. And she knows a lot in a strange way. So many of them do." Her hand was calmer now, the fingers relaxed. He continued to hold it on his knee, absently stroking it. "I dare say you'll think it's all rubbish," she went on, "but that's because you don't know. They have ways of knowing things; it's extraordinary, really. And if they want a person to do something they can sometimes make them. Secretly," she added, glancing at Miles, "so that they don't suspect anything."

"You mean by magic?"

"I suppose you could call it that, though I dare say there's a much more sensible explanation. Herbs and things," she added vaguely. "Things other people have forgotten."

"Go on."

"Well. She knew that I wanted Rob to marry me, and for a long time she thought he was going to. Every time he went away she looked into the future, and at first it seemed all right, and I didn't worry. But recently, since he was in Paris, it began to go wrong. She looked in the ashes and the divorce was there all right, but nothing about marriage. So she said she could get me something that would increase his love. Something that would make him care for me and Joe above everything, and do what I wanted."

She paused and glanced at the women in the further corner. They were still fixing her with their black stare but there was no comprehension in it. The sight of these Nazarenes was sufficient entertainment.

"Then . . . do you remember that day when you lent me some money for something? Rob was away, and Zohra said she would take me to a *sahaara* in Larache."

"A what?"

"A *sahaara*. A sort of witch, I suppose. *You* know." She spoke as though the thing were a commonplace. "A kind of wise woman who knows about that sort of thing.

Zohra had been to her before, for various reasons."

"I see. So what you went to Larache for was to buy a spell."

"Exactly. It wasn't to do him any harm, and it was worth trying. At least, if it made him a little sick it wouldn't matter. No more than a headache, Zohra said, as if he'd drunk too much. The *sahaara* gave me a powder and I was to put it in his wine. But after I got back Panya told me about the divorce, and I decided not to use it. I felt, you know, the spell was working already. Which reminds me," she added with a start, "I haven't paid you back yet."

"My dear girl, do go on."

"And then, as you remember, Mr. Stagg turned up, and it looked as though *everything* was working. I made a statement, and so did Zohra, and the maid at the hotel. But you remember all that."

"Yes, yes; of course."

"I was terribly excited, and so was Zohra, because it seemed as if everything we wanted was coming true."

"If it's really what you want," said Miles, loosing her hand so that she turned to look at him. "You love him, then; is that it? You really won't be happy unless you marry him?"

"I don't know about being happy," said Tavy, looking scared again, "but what will happen to Joe and me if I don't? What can happen to us anyway? You know what I told you this morning. He doesn't want it."

"You can come back to England with me," said Miles, taking her hand again, "that's what can happen. *And* Joe. Please get it into your head that I want to marry you."

She stared at him blankly for a moment and then, her eyes softening, gave him a crooked smile.

"Dear Miles," she said, "you're frightfully sweet." The smile faded. It was as though he had paid her a charming but futile compliment.

"Well, then," she said, "Rob got home from Rabat, as you remember, and was very angry. I've told you all that before. So here we were, in Fez, and I was quite desperate. I thought what a fool I'd been not to use the powder. That it was all my fault, and everything was going wrong because I hadn't. So," she glanced at the women in the corner and spoke in a whisper, "so the first evening, when we came into this place for a drink, I decided to do it. I didn't see how I was going to, not at first; but when he'd drunk about half the bottle he went out for cigarettes, and I put about half the powder into the rest. I'm almost sure nobody saw me."

"Are you certain?"

"I think so. Only Joe, and he doesn't count. There was nobody here but the barman, and he was in the back. I didn't dare use it all, in case Rob noticed anything."

"And did he?"

"He didn't say so. Anyway he finished the bottle. It hasn't much flavour, really. I tasted it." She freed her hand to pick up her sachel from the floor, and cautiously opened it. "The rest of it's here," she said, pointing to a screw of newspaper in the pocket.

Miles took the packet and opened it under the table. It contained about half a teaspoonful of powder of a greenish-brown colour. He licked the tip of a finger and touched the stuff. It was very finely ground and looked innocuous. It might have been curry powder.

"You tasted it, you said?"

"Yes, just like that, on my finger."

"Without any ill effect?"

"None at all, but it was only a few grains. I gave Rob about half the whole thing, or a bit more."

Miles licked the greenish smear from the tip of his finger. It tasted of nothing very much, though there was a hint of the smell of cow-dung, as far as he could identify it.

It was unlikely to have been noticed in wine of a coarse flavour.

"My darling child," he said, "I believe this ridiculous powder is simply nothing. You've wasted your money, that's all, and done no harm. What he's suffering from is food-poisoning." He took the paper between finger and thumb and shook it under the table, then tightly screwed it up and put it in his pocket.

Tavy looked astonished.

"How can you possibly tell?" Her eyes widened. "These things *work*, I promise you. Zohra knows a woman whose husband died after one of them, which was exactly what the woman wanted."

"And you seriously believe, if that were true, that she'd give you something like that for Rob, when the idea was for you to marry him?"

"Not the same one, silly. Of course not. These things are all made up specially, to suit the purpose. It's possible she made a mistake, or that in Rob's case it worked badly. The effect could be different on Europeans. Don't you think so? And it's all very well to say food-poisoning, but we both had the same things to eat, and so did Joe. It would be wonderful if you were right, but I'm not convinced. If only you could talk to Zohra you'd think differently."

Miles was not convinced either, but he stuck to his point.

"I'm quite prepared," he said, "to take this paper back to London and have it analyzed. Would that satisfy you?"

There was a silence while Tavy fiddled with the buckle of her bag.

"You're awfully sweet," she said at length, "but I'd rather you didn't. Supposing they found out something?"

"They'd find out it was made of dust and dried leaves, with possibly a pinch of cow-dung and a hair of Rob's head. Not very lethal, in my opinion."

"All the same I'd rather you didn't."

"Good. So we don't bother. The paper shall be put down the lavatory."

They drank some of their Coca-Cola and Tavy seemed calmer. A little colour had crept into her cheeks. She looked, however, as though something were still worrying her.

"How much will the doctor know," she said, " by the time we get back?"

"That we can't tell until we see him. I thought he seemed fairly cheerful."

"I think we should go back now," said Tavy, "but I don't want to."

"I think we should, too, and get it over. You'll find it's all perfectly normal, and nothing to worry about."

"I worry about Rob as well. You seem to forget that."

"I don't forget anything," said Miles. "And while we're on the subject I want you to remember something else. As soon as he's better I want you to think about it very seriously. You must take in the fact that I love you, and want to marry you."

Tavy said nothing to this, but pressed his hand. Miles paid for the drinks and they went up the steps into the street. The two women in the corner, who all this time had exchanged not a single word, impassively watched them go, following their disappearing legs with the same unchanging stare of incomprehension.

As they turned into the alley which led to the hotel Tavy said, "But you realize I could never leave him, not after what I've done."

"My dear girl, you haven't done anything. I wish I could convince you. The whole thing's a lot of nonsense and superstition." Miles wished he could also convince himself, but that was less important.

"The fact remains," said Tavy, "that I know what I've done. It won't make any difference if he gets better, I must still make it up to him. I could never leave him now, even if I wanted to."

"And might you want to? Think carefully, Tavy. Think."

"What *I* want never enters into it," said Tavy, and went through the dark doorway into the hotel.

★ ★ ★

There was still a man lying on the landing mattress, but it proved to be Sam. He sat up at once, scratching himself through his shirt.

"I guess I'm not bitten yet," he said, "but I keep thinking I can feel them trampling. I should have stayed on a chair." He nodded towards Quattrell's door, which was half-way open. "The doctor's gone, by the way. He'll be back this evening."

"What did he say?" said Miles. He was conscious of Tavy lurking behind him, as though she wished to hide. Even though she knew the doctor was gone she lingered on the stairs. He turned to see her lean against the wall, her hands on the cold tiles.

"He's puzzled," said Sam. "He thinks it's ptomaine all right, but he can't figure out, if they all ate the same, why Tavy and the kid are O.K."

"Whatever it was, they had the luck to miss it," said Miles. "So how is he?"

"Well, not too famous, but a bit easier. The doc gave him one hell of an injection. He reckons it's too late for the stomach-pump. He should have had that earlier."

Tavy came up the last stair and leaned against the table. The last vestige of colour had drained from her face and she was breathing faintly.

"Tell me how he really is," she said to Sam. "Is it going to be all right?"

"Oh, sure. Take a few days, I guess. You can't rush it. He's to drink all the soda-water he can swallow, but he's asleep right now."

At the news that he was asleep Tavy breathed more easily. She would not have to meet his eye, or answer questions. She took care not to move the door as she looked into the room.

Quattrell was lying on his side, wearing his pyjama jacket, and his face looked strangely old. His mop of hair had fallen across his forehead and the grooves running down from his nostrils were very dark, creases of pain like furrows in the two-day beard. But he seemed more peaceful, somehow; the sleep looked real. The bed had been straightened and tidied and he lay more at ease. A chair had been wedged by the bedside and on it was a glass, some tablets and a bottle of soda-water. The curtain was still drawn but it stirred in a little breeze and the white light from the cemetery came and went fitfully.

Tavy drew a deep breath and leaned against the door-frame. Tears were running down her cheeks and she made no effort to check them; the strength had gone out of her completely.

"There's a telegram for you," said Sam, pointing to a folded square of paper on the table. "It came half an hour ago. I wondered should I open it."

"Shall I?" said Miles, seeing that she didn't move. He tore apart the gummed edges and handed it to her. She put out a hand very slowly and slowly opened it. It said, "On my way . . . love . . . Panya," followed by a cabalistic series of letters and figures.

"She's coming," said Tavy in a small voice.

She swayed as though she would fall and Miles put out a hand. She lurched against him with a sob and threw

her arms round him. They stood like that for a long moment while Sam considered them with interest, clasped in
each other's arms with her face hidden in his shoulder.

Presently she pulled herself together and sat down.

"Where's Joe?" she said, wiping away the tears with
the back of her hand.

"Right there in your room, fast asleep."

She gave Sam a grateful look and went quickly to the
door. There on the bed, sleeping his perfect sleep, Joe lay in
his underpants. His jersey and shorts were neatly arranged on
the bed-rail and his sandals were under the wash-basin.
One hand clutched a clothes-peg and the thumb of the
other was slipping gradually from his mouth. Tavy crept in
on tiptoe and sat down beside him. She rearranged his legs
more comfortably, knowing he would not wake, and then,
unable any longer to bear the effort of staying upright,
climbed over him very carefully and lay beside him.

"So what do we do now?" said Sam in an undertone.
"Quite apart from you and me she ought to eat something."
It was already past noon; to the smell of oil and onions a
powerful odour of frying fish had been added. Miles found
that he was hungry.

"I don't know. I'd rather stay here for the present. Do
you suppose we could have something sent up?"

Sam looked at him with genuine horror.

"You're not serious! With one case of ptomaine
snatched back from the grave, you're prepared to be another?"

"It smells all right," said Miles, and then remembered.
It was better that the food in this place should remain
suspect.

"Perhaps we could go out and buy something," he said.
"But I'd rather stay here."

"Sure. That's what I had in mind. You keep an eye on

the situation and I'll go buy something. I guess maybe she'd rather you stayed."

Miles followed him to the top of the stairs, aware that Sam was on the point of saying something further. He was feeling in his pockets for money, and looked up abruptly.

"So what's the programme?" he said in a low voice. "I'd just like to know what's cooking, before we go any further." He fixed Miles with his light-blue glance, very sober and penetrating. "And I don't mean the shopping," he said. "I just want to know where we're heading for, in this old-style drama."

"I wish I knew," said Miles, glancing over his shoulder. Tavy's door was still open and she had not stirred. Her arm was thrown across Joe and her face was hidden. She might have been asleep. "I shall stay until Panya comes," he said, "that's clear at least."

"She won't arrive before night. More probably tomorrow."

"Then I shall get a room in this place. There are several empty."

"You know about the bugs, I hope? You recognize the smell?"

"I didn't, but that's a detail. It's not important."

"Boy, are you hooked!" said Sam, counting his small change. "And when the Herr Gauleiter Quattrell wakes up, and feels better, what do you do then?"

"I'll decide that when it happens."

"*Et après?*"

"I don't know about *après,*" said Miles with a faint smile, "and until I do, I'm going to stay with Tavy."

"You're out of your mind."

"Very likely. It can't be helped."

"In that case," said Sam, considering, "it would look slightly better if we were here together. No?"

"Undoubtedly. But then there are the bugs."

"Oh, the hell with them," said Sam, "I'll buy a powder."

He pattered lightly downstairs, and Miles, startled into recollection, took the screw of paper from his pocket and began searching for a lavatory. There was none on the upper floor but he remembered the smell at the entrance and explored below. It was not difficult to find, for in a passage where the old woman was still washing, and where there was a wall-telephone, the odour of stale urine was over-powering. He pushed open a creaking door and saw a grooved basin in the tiles, with two places for the feet. Water was trickling down the hole between brown stains and there were several inches of chain hanging from the cistern. Here was the source of that whispering that he had heard for so long. He recognized it almost as a friend, and closed the door behind him. He aimed the pellet of paper down the hole, then stepped on the two plinths and urinated with satisfaction. The final flow of water was strong; it ran brimming over the basin and across the floor. The paper tossed and bobbed merrily in the vortex but was sucked down at last. Then the cistern groaned and clanked and resumed its whispering.

When Sam came back with a basket he had bought he produced from it a loaf of warm bread, tomatoes, onions, oranges, a paper full of skewers of meat still hot and smoky from the charcoal. Tavy and Joe were dozing, but they sat up quite eagerly when they smelt food, and helped to spread Sam's newspaper over the bed. Nobody enquired how Quattrell was; there was no sound from his room and everyone was prepared to assume that all was well. The occasion even became discreetly cheerful; they sat all together on the bed, picking the meat off the skewers and talking in whispers. Then Joe became thirsty, and Tavy, not trusting to the tap, kicked off her shoes and stole into

Quattrell's room for the soda-water. She was back almost at once and the report was encouraging. He had turned over. He was still asleep. His colour, she thought, was better. That matter satisfactorily disposed of they settled down in earnest, whispering to keep Joe quiet and nudging one another to pass the bread. Intermittently they had a hysterical desire to giggle, so that the whole thing developed a slightly crazy atmosphere, as though they were breaking the rules with a secret picnic.

★   ★   ★

That night Miles and Sam slept in the Mellah. They were given a room with a double-bed, and the proprietor, who now appeared for the first time and proved to be a stout young man in an openwork vest and remarkably dirty trousers, shook hands with them warmly and seemed both astonished and gratified to find himself entertaining such promising guests. He was normally full, he said; his having three rooms at liberty was a happy circumstance. It was true there was no wash-basin in the third room, but he pointed to a small trough in an angle of the landing which had a plug-hole and tap, and went through a pantomime of washing his hands and face and splashing water into his armpits, so that they need be in no sort of doubt concerning the amenities.

Quattrell was barely awake in the evening when the doctor came. Sam and Miles had gone out to eat, leaving Tavy on guard with a fresh supply of almond-cakes and oranges. She reported that he seemed fairly satisfied, and the patient, though weak and fretful, somewhat improved. He had been given tea without milk, and a piece of bread; it had been difficult to make him swallow but he had not vomited.

"I haven't told him you're here," she said, when they

had returned from their meal and the three of them were sitting in conference on the double-bed. "I'm awfully thankful you are, but it seemed best not to say anything. He's still got this thing about not seeing anyone, and I'm scared of upsetting him. I did tell him about Panya, though, and I think he was relieved. He doesn't mind her so much. He thinks she's reliable."

But this was not all. The rest she had kept to herself, and was bursting to communicate. Panya, it appeared, had telephoned; she was already established at the Jamaï, and was coming at an early hour the following morning.

"And she's got Mrs. Quattrell with her," said Tavy, looking ambiguously at Miles. "Do you think that's good or bad? She didn't say. She just said she'd phoned her in London, and she'd flown straight out. I said, 'What on earth for?' and Panya said it was obvious, and that everything would be all right. I imagine she's going to explain everything, as soon as he's well enough. He's got to understand it sooner or later, whatever he may think. So I suppose, on the whole, I'm glad she's coming." But she looked doubtful.

When Miles and Sam were in bed with the light out Sam said suddenly, "What's this about Mrs. Quattrell?"

"You know all about it. She's divorcing him."

"So what's the next move? They get married?"

"Tavy and him? Not if I can help it."

There was a pause while Sam moved his feet about under the bedclothes. The sheets had been powdered with D.D.T. and there was a curiously musty smell, reminiscent of cinnamon.

"You're crazy," said Sam at length, "but you know that. What makes you think you've got a chance, when that guy recovers?"

"Tavy says he doesn't want to marry again. He doesn't want to be divorced."

"Why not, for God's sake? The kid's his, surely?"

"It may be something to do with money; I don't know. Or he just prefers it the way it is."

"Well, I can see the point," said Sam, and sneezed. He had been particularly liberal with the powder on both pillows. "But what I don't see is why you're mixing yourself up in it. She's a nice enough kid, and all that; but not to marry."

Miles said nothing to this. He wished Sam would drop off to sleep, so that he could think. He was tired and painfully wide-awake, and there were a thousand possibilities to disentangle before morning.

"You're not mad at me, are you?" said Sam after a pause. He had at last stopped fidgeting with his feet, and sounded anxious.

"Not a bit. You're entitled to your opinion."

"It's none of my business, but I'd kind of hate to see you make a fool of yourself."

"You may have to, I'm afraid. And if there's a row, after all, you can put it on tape."

"O.K., I get it," said Sam, and sighed. "I haven't said anything."

After that they lay in a neutral silence, inhaling the odour of insecticide and following their own thoughts. It occurred to Miles that what Sam had said made Tavy seem even more vulnerable than before, and therefore, by a curious logic, more desirable.

*　　*　　*

The early hour which Panya had mentioned turned out to be ten o'clock. Sam had gone out for a morning walk with Joe, the doctor had come and gone and Quattrell was propped up on pillows and had even consumed some dry toast for breakfast. He was better, Tavy said, but very sorry for himself. He had made her bring him his shaving-mirror and the sight of his ravaged face, still an unwholesome tinge under the coarse stubble, had put him in a bad temper. He had scratched himself a good deal and the bites made him irritable.

"But he knows I'm doing the best I can," Tavy told Miles, "and the doctor said straight out he must think himself lucky. We can move to somewhere better as soon as he's able."

They were leaning on the window-sill in Tavy's room, which had become a refuge. The presence of Sam and Miles was still a secret, and here in this narrow cell, in the shadowless light thrown up from the tombs, they had a feeling of sanctuary. The old woman and her bucket had been kept out of Quattrell's way and the place was as quiet as ever. The door was ajar so that Tavy could come and go silently. She was mostly in Quattrell's room but she came in from time to time to report progress, and then they leaned on the sill and talked in whispers.

The quiet was suddenly shattered by Panya's arrival. There was the slam of a car door at the end of the alley, and then, after a pause, Panya's unmistakable voice on the stair and a woman's voice replying. Tavy flew out to the landing and into her arms. Miles followed more slowly, moved more than he would have thought possible by the sight of Panya's bulky form, solid and imperturbable, squarely planted at the stair-head with Tavy on her bosom. It seemed that everything must change through the mere fact of her being there; that she brought the specific touch to dissipate the nightmare.

"So, so," she said, patting Tavy on the back, "so now we are here, my child, and everything will be all right." She looked at Miles with surprise, lifting an amused eyebrow. "And you are not alone," she said, "and that is a good thing." It was at this point that Constance Quattrell appeared on the landing and stood and stared at the three of them through dark glasses.

"Well, for God's sake," she said, putting her hand to her pearls and drawing breath, "where's Rob?" She pronounced it Rahb, in a deep, slightly hoarse voice. She sounded unhurried and capable, but there was an edge of nervousness. Tavy was not the only one who had reason to dread the encounter.

Panya did the best she could with the introductions. "This is my young friend Tavy, about whom we were speaking. And this," she turned to Miles, "is another young friend, who fortunately is here also." She had forgotten his name but it was evident from her cheerful glance that she was glad to see him. Constance shook hands with them both, seeming quite at ease. She had a good smile, parting with expansive suddenness over large teeth, but the sunglasses made it impossible to guess what she was thinking.

"Well, *dear*," she said to Tavy, "take me to that ill-gotten husband of mine and let's see how he's doing." At the door of his room she paused and looked amazedly round. "But what a dump this is!" she cried, taking it in for the first time. "What in heaven's name made him bring you to a place like this?"

"It's cheap," said Tavy, "and he wanted to be quiet." She lowered her eyes, resisting the impulse to stare at Mrs. Quattrell's clothes. "He wanted to avoid people."

Certainly the place looked more than ever deplorable now that Constance was in it. She gave the impression that a great deal had deliberately been done for her appearance, and as deliberately forgotten. Her clothes were elegantly plain, her hair an expensive copper-colour with blonde streaks in it, her skin had a sumptuous tan and her pearls looked real. She moved and spoke, however, as though she had yet to learn the meaning of self-consciousness.

Tavy pushed open the door and stood back to let her pass. Quattrell was propped up on pillows with his eyes closed; silently the two of them regarded him. Then Constance removed her glasses and he opened his eyes. She was considerably less impressive without her spectacles: with them her face had the *chic* of a stylish mask, not beautiful, but striking; the charm of a *jolie-laide*. Without this disguise her eyes were small, and despite a large-boned leanness of feature one could see she was rather older than she wished to appear.

Quattrell gazed at her dully and struggled up.

"Con! What the hell are you doing here?"

"I might well ask the same of you," she said, and sat down on the bed. "You irresponsible goat, what are you doing in this hell-hole?"

"I've been very ill," he murmured, and closed his eyes. Tears of weakness crept from under his eyelids. He lifted a hand to his face, encountered the sturdy bristles and let it fall again. "Tavy's been very good," he said quietly, "but I'm glad you've come." The effort appeared to exhaust him, and he seemed thankful that it did so. He lay still with his eyes closed, holding her hand.

Constance considered him critically, then turned to Tavy.

"How long has he been like this?"

"He's been ill for three days. Ever since we came."

"You know what it is? Have you had a doctor?"

"Yes. He's been twice a day. He says it's ptomaine poisoning."

"Good God, and no wonder! Don't tell me you eat in this place?"

"We did, in the beginning; not since. He had tea for the first time this morning, and some dry toast."

Constance regarded her speculatively and resumed her

sun-glasses. "And you?" she said from behind them, "you've been all right? And the little boy?"

"Perfectly all right, so far. We seem to have missed it."

"You're lucky," said Constance. "The young are miraculously tough." She kept up her masked scrutiny, and suddenly smiled. "I'd like to see the little boy some time. Is he around?"

"He's been taken out for a walk; he'll be back presently." Tavy had kept her distance, but at this moved gently forward and laid her hand on the bed-rail.

"How old is he, dear?"

"He's two."

"Ah, that's the cutest age of all," said Constance, and turned back to Quattrell. He was watching them both with half-closed eyes, puzzled and wary.

"Con," he said, gripping her hand and opening his eyes accusingly, "tell me what you're doing here. I want to know what you're up to."

"I'm wandering around as usual, looking for trouble. And as usual you haven't failed to provide it."

"For heaven's sake, take off those hideous glasses."

"Not for the moment. The light's too strong."

"Nonsense. The curtain's drawn, and I can't see you properly." He lifted a hand towards the spectacles, but she eluded him.

"Listen, stupid. The first thing I'm going to do is get you out of this morgue. You're coming to my hotel, or if not that a hospital. You're going to get better first, and then we're going to talk. There's a lot of ground to cover."

Quattrell said nothing to this, but his eye glinted.

"Not a hospital," he said finally, moving his head to and fro on the pillow. "Not a hospital, Con. Have a heart." He closed his eyes again, adding after a pause and in his normal voice, "Where did you say you were staying?"

"Panya and I are at the Jamaï. You'll be really comfortable."

"The Jamaï," said Quattrell faintly, and this time a tear trickled slowly into the stubble.

"Listen, sweetie," said Constance, turning her black spectacles on Tavy, "I've got to have a talk with this man, and make him see reason. Just leave us alone for a while and close the door. You know what an obstinate bastard he is, as well as I do."

Tavy, who had been fingering the iron bed-rail, dropped it as though it were hot and went out abruptly, pulling the door behind her. Seeing no one on the landing but the old woman she went quickly into her bedroom and slammed the door.

★   ★   ★

"On that point," Panya was saying patiently to Miles, "there is no problem. He cannot stop the divorce; he can do nothing against such evidence. When he understands the strength of the case he will not defend himself. Useless defences cost money."

They were sitting on Miles's bed in a dazzle of sunlight. Panya was smoking a cigarette, holding it between finger and thumb in the curious way she had and directing the smoke with care towards the open window. From time to time she flicked ash on the window-sill, where it blew about giddily.

"I simply can't fathom his motive," said Miles. "They've been separated so long."

"Ah yes, but he knows his Constance. She is an emotional creature. She is formidable, yes, *mais c'est un cœur d'or*. He has behaved worse in this marriage than you, my dear young man, can imagine; yet whenever he has been in trouble she has helped him. This is important, you know, because he needs money. He has run through a great deal from time to time and it does not grow on bushes. In spite of all that has happened he relies on her."

"How very extraordinary."

"I agree, dear Miles, but you know women are strange creatures. They are not always rational unfortunately. Constance has been married three times, but this one is the only one that bit."

"That bit?" said Miles, looking startled.

"That took," said Panya, correcting herself. "She knows what he is like, quite well, but she has him in her hair. You understand that expression?"

"Yes. I see. So what will she do now?"

"She has made up her mind to divorce, but she is still concerned for him. I too, for the sake of Tavy. He is the father of little Joe and he should marry her. He will escape from the dilemma if he can, and for that reason I am anxious. When I heard from Stagg that he had disappeared I telephoned to Constance. She decided to come herself, to learn at first hand, and we were hardly back from the airport when came Tavy's telegram."

"Saying he was ill?"

"Saying he was very ill, and to come, to come. So we get out the Peugeot and do so, and here we are. I will have a look at him presently, when Constance has had her turn, but I think there is no longer any danger?"

"No danger that he'll die," said Miles, and sighed.

"Thank God for that! That would have been terrible for Tavy."

"I suppose so." He gave Panya a sharp glance, but her eye was innocent. "What I can't believe," he said gloomily, getting up to look out of the window, "is that Tavy will ever be happy with him. Even if they marry."

"Oh, probably not! I am too old to believe in guarantees of happiness. But it is what she has known for three years, after all, and what is the alternative?"

"She could marry me," said Miles, addressing the cemetery. "She knows that already, Panya. I've asked her, twice."

There was a pause, and then the bed creaked. Panya got up with an effort and threw her cigarette out of the window. It was caught by the wind and fell among the gravestones, sending up a wisp of smoke in the white wilderness.

"Miles, my dear boy." She put her arm through his and leaned on her bosom on the sill. "I am not sure if you are serious. It is possible to be too romantic, no? *D'être entrainé par ses émotions* in such a situation?"

"I'm perfectly serious," said Miles. "And I'm sure I love her. That's the only reason I'm here."

"You are a nice boy," said Panya musingly, after a calm pause in which she considered the tombstones, "and I confess it occurred to me once, when you came to the shop. But forgive me—I know nothing about you. And there is not only Tavy to consider. There is the child."

"Of course. I've considered all that. I've got quite a good job and somewhere to live, and my father's a schoolmaster. Tavy has relations in England, hasn't she? She would be with her own people."

"Ah," said Panya, "her own people. They are few and in between. A very old aunt called Miss Townsend, who lives in the country. An indifferent father who is not her father. The ones that Tavy is at home with are people like Zohra."

"And you think she should stay with them for ever?"

"Indeed, no. I think otherwise. But she will make her mind for herself, whatever you may do. Whether Quattrell marries her or not, the choice is Tavy's. She has had a *désenchantment* with life, you know, and it has formed her character. I love her like a child, but like a child she is often difficult to persuade. I am not very fond of that man —*je me méfie des individus de ce type*—but in the end she may choose that life, and there will be nothing we can say to her."

But for once, and somewhat to her surprise, Panya was wrong. Constance presently came out of Quattrell's room, shutting the door deliberately.

"The flies are bad in there," she said. "Can one get a drink in this place?"

"They have wine," said Miles, detaching himself from the sill and from Panya's arm. Constance was still enigmatic behind her spectacles.

"When I say a drink I mean Scotch. Is that possible?"

"I don't know, but I can ask. The proprietor's probably downstairs."

"That's very good of you. I need it." She moved to the bed and sat down. "By the way, where's the girl?"

"Tavy is in her bedroom," said Panya. "She must rest."

"So must we all, my God; but a drink first. My mind's in a whirl." She took off her glasses and pressed her fingers to her eyes.

Miles went downstairs and discovered the stout young man in an airless room which apparently served as the reception. He had no whisky, he said, but it could be obtained. He would send out a boy at once if Miles gave him the money. This Miles did, a little startled by the number of ten-dirham notes required, and strolled up and down the alley while the boy was gone. When presently he returned, bearing a bottle of the right shape but with a Spanish label, a tray and glasses were sent for across the courtyard and the old woman carried them slowly up to the bedroom.

Panya and Constance were sitting on the bed in a haze of tobacco smoke. Their voices had been heard in argument or protest from the stairs; Constance had removed her shoes and pulled out both the pillows to make herself comfortable.

"You are of course insane," Panya was telling her, "but I have known that a long time."

"Sure, so have I. So we needn't go into that." She took the bottle from the tray and examined it with amazement. "Jesus, where do they make this stuff? Will you look at that label?"

"It is Spanish, no doubt," said Panya, "and you will have drunk worse in your time."

Constance unscrewed the bottle and half-filled three glasses. "I don't trust the tap-water," she said, "but spirit from any quarter is mercifully sterile." She took a mouthful of whisky, waited a moment, then swallowed with a shudder. Since there was nothing but the bed to sit on Miles took his glass to his old position by the window.

"So all that remains to decide," said Constance, "are the practical details. I can manage for the moment with travellers' cheques, and the lawyer will look after the rest."

Panya caught Miles's eye and slowly smiled. Her face had flushed pink, perhaps from the shock of the whisky, but the smile had a look of conspiracy about it; it was almost roguish.

"Our friend Constance has changed her mind," she said. "Not, dare I say it, for the first time. Mr. Stagg has wasted his journey and there is to be no divorce. She is moving her husband to our hotel, and proposes that Tavy and Joe go home, and that you accompany them."

"Home?" said Miles in a croaking voice. Such a paroxysm had shaken him that he almost fell. He set down his glass in the window and laid his hand against the wall. "Home?" he repeated blankly.

"To Zohra's, of course," said Panya. "That will be best, yes. I will be there in a day or two, and we can decide what to do. She will need time, my poor Tavy."

"She can do everything the easy way," said Constance in a firm voice, pouring out another whisky. "She's in a hell of a fix, poor kid, but I'll take care of everything. A car to take them both home, for instance. That's easy. Or does she drive Rob's old thing? I'll be surprised if it can still move."

"She does not drive," said Panya, "so you can provide a car, certainly. We will not ask her to do a bus journey."

"Sure. Of course. Everything will be taken care of." She got off the bed and began looking short-sightedly for her shoes.

"Has Tavy been told?" said Miles. The joyous ringing in his ears subsided slowly at the thought of Tavy in her room; Tavy face-downwards on the pillow; not knowing anything.

"She has not been told," said Panya, "but I shall go to her now. She has a certain courage, poor child, or she would not be where she is. She has Joe, and if she is not bewitched out of her senses she will have you. She will accept the inevitable."

★ 14 ★

THE FIRST SIGN, if such it was, that even in her woe Tavy had briefly glanced in a new direction was her sudden protest against the extravagance of a car. Constance and Panya had returned to their hotel to arrange for transport, and she was alternately packing and weeping into her suitcase.

"But it's out of the question," she said, straightening herself abruptly. "Of course we must go by bus, and save the money."

"My darling girl, it's being paid for. Mrs. Quattrell's doing all that, and a lot more. There's not the least problem."

Tavy's face was swollen with crying but at the thought of this brilliant economy her tears vanished. She looked at Miles seriously.

"But she could give us the money instead, don't you see? We'd have something in hand."

That "we," so casually spoken, made his heart leap.

"In hand for what?" He met her look directly, but was still uncertain.

"Why, for all sorts of things. It'll cost more than fifty dollars. I heard them say so."

"And you also heard Panya say that Constance is generous, and means to do something for you and Joe, and that you're not to worry."

"Yes, yes," said Tavy impatiently, snatching up a ribbon from the bed and tying back her hair, "but the bus is cheap, and fifty dollars is a fortune. It's something like twenty-five thousand francs."

"Listen," said Miles, taking her by the shoulder and gently shaking her, "I've got quite enough money to get us back to England, and if I haven't I shall borrow from Panya or Mrs. Quattrell. Or from Sam or Ozzie or Crosier for that matter. So the bus is out."

"Who said I'm going back to England with you?" said Tavy, sniffing. She did, however, give him the beginnings of a smile. "All I said was, it's ridiculous to waste that amount of money." She went back rather fiercely to her packing, stuffing Joe's shoes into the bag.

"And *I* say," said Miles, "that we're going by car. Think how much nicer for Joe, to say nothing of ourselves. So let's hear no more about it."

She took this with surprising meekness, and no more was said.

Joe could be heard from the courtyard, shrieking excitedly to Sam and beating on something which sounded ominously like a drum. Sam had been so rash as to buy him this very article during their walk. It was a vase-shaped object of clay, the open end neatly covered with a taut membrane. There had not been much choice, certainly, since all the toys on sale (and there were many, because of the imminence of the feast) were designed with a single object in mind, to make as much noise as possible. There were whistles and plastic trumpets and things which squeaked, to say nothing of explosive caps which detonated beyond belief when thrown to the ground. Joe had naturally wanted all of them, but Sam for aesthetic reasons had chosen the drum. It was, after all, of native manufacture, it belonged to the rhythms which interested him, it was made of clay, not plastic, and it had not been imported from Japan.

Tavy went on with her packing, which was soon done. The hired car arrived in the Place de Commerce, a stone's throw from the hotel, and at last the moment arrived for taking leave of Quattrell. She had not been near him since Panya had talked to her in her room. Miles had expected her to rush to him in a passion, but she had not done so. He guessed, with a pang of pity, that her courage had finally failed at this last treachery. But when presently she went to his room it was with an impassive face. She had washed and made herself tidy for the journey, her hair pinned up in a knot with a black ribbon. In her unbecoming skirt and jacket she had the air of a schoolgirl prepared for some intimidating end-of-term ceremony.

Panya and Constance had tactfully withdrawn and were studying the Jewish cemetery from Sam's window. Sam still had Joe in charge; little rolls and obbligatos on the drum could be heard, now near, now far, reverberating in the alley. Miles lingered uneasily on the landing, dreading the outcome on his own account as much as on Tavy's, but unable to persuade himself to go out of hearing.

"Well?" she said, standing at the half-opened door and going no further.

"My dear girl!" Quattrell's voice was surprised, a little injured. "Where have you been all this time? Why didn't you come to see me?"

"I've been packing," said Tavy. "I'm going home. Didn't you know? I thought the two of you had arranged it all between you."

"That's what I wanted to talk to you about, darling, only you never came. I've been lying here, waiting. Wondering why you didn't come, and feeling lonely."

"So I see." There was a pause. "Did you want anything?"

"Of course. Come here and sit down, my poppet. I want to talk to you."

At this she went slowly in and the door closed behind her.

Miles walked irritably up and down, trying not to listen. He felt in his pockets for cigarettes, found none, and went in search of Panya.

"How did she take it, Panya?"

The two of them turned from the window, looking almost merry. Constance had a glass in her hand and there was a fine smell of whisky.

"She is calm," said Panya, "but that, I am sure, is shock. The bad time will come later."

"Don't let her stay in there long. He's bound to upset her."

"Poor kid, poor kid," said Constance, and drained her glass. "I'm glad she's got you to travel with. And the young are miraculously resilient."

Sooner than Miles dared to hope Quattrell's door opened. Tavy lingered with her hand on the knob, listening to some final injunction.

"Very well, if I'm still there," she said. "But I may be gone."

Quattrell said something in a coaxing, teasing tone, but Tavy did not smile.

"I don't think I will," she said. "You don't really want to see him. You needn't pretend any more, not at this stage. And he'll never miss you."

She shut the door quickly on this and went back to her bedroom. Miles waited for the outburst of tears, but all he heard was the click as she fastened her suitcase. She came out with her bag and knapsack, holding herself very upright, and looked meaningly at Panya.

"I'm ready," she said, "darling Panya. Let me know when you get back."

"My child, I shall come very soon. Most probably tomorrow." And then Miles had taken her luggage and she was in Panya's arms. She said good-bye and shook hands with Constance and was suddenly gone, going smoothly downstairs and out of the hotel as though this were the end of a visit and nothing was the matter.

Sam was waiting by the car with Joe, who had been in and out of it a dozen times and was looking pleased and solemn.

"I won't come with you," said Sam with a touch of embarrassment, as though this had been in question. "I guess I'll stay on for a day or two and pick up some more stuff. It ought to be terrific in the Medina tonight. Have a good trip." And then the doors were slammed and the car was moving.

Presently, as they moved through the crowd and threaded a narrow gateway Miles took her hand and pressed it, but there was no response. She sat very upright with Joe in her lap, her face averted. One would have said she was wholly absorbed in the stream of life and movement that she saw from the window.

★　　★　　★

The bad time, as Panya had predicted, came a little later. She wept with abandon into the collar of Joe's jersey, hiding her face with her hand. Miles let her cry for a while and then lifted Joe from her lap and took him on his knee, pointing to goats on the roadside, to a donkey braying in a cactus compound, to a man on horseback. Joe was in good spirits, even keenly conversational after his fashion. He exclaimed and pointed, pressing his fingers to the glass, so that presently it was covered with smears, and these deeply interested him. After a time he became sleepy and Tavy took him back again. He kicked about for a while, his thumb in his mouth, regarding Miles with interest, but presently the legs subsided and his gaze became dreamy. Tavy settled him comfortably and touched Miles's hand.

"I'm better now," she said. "It won't happen again." They sat for a while in silence, their fingers interlaced. Presently she said, "I haven't thanked you for all you've done, but you know I'm grateful."

"Darling Tavy, you don't have to be grateful." If it had not been for the driver's eye in the mirror he would have kissed her. "I just want you to recover from everything, and try to be calm. As soon as you can, we've got to talk to one another."

"I know, but you must give me time. I'm not used to deciding things, and now I've got to."

"And time's not unlimited," said Miles. "I've got to get back to London. I want you to come with me, you know, and then we can decide everything."

Joe was asleep by now, his head on her breast. She drew the thumb from his mouth, taking care not to wake him.

"I don't want to talk about it yet. You mustn't do something you'll regret, just because you're sorry for me."

Miles laughed, and this time, ignoring the driver, he kissed her cheek.

"You seem to have forgotten that I love you. Do try and remember."

"How can you, though? It's absurd. You hardly know me."

"Or you me," said Miles. They turned and looked at one another in wonder.

Presently she said, "When did you first begin to feel like this? It seems so extraordinary."

"The first time I saw you, I think, only I didn't realize it. You came along the street, near Sam's, and I was on the roof. You stopped at the steps when the lights came on, and you looked up. I believe it all started then."

"It seemed so extraordinary," she said again. "I didn't see you, did I? Not till you came to Zohra's that time, with Morley Crosier."

"And you weren't aware of me at all."

"Oh yes, I was. I thought you looked rather nice. I noticed your hair," said Tavy, doing her best, "it's so thick, and such a nice colour." She touched it with her fingers and they smiled at one another. "And then, the next time, I noticed how good your teeth were. They hadn't struck me before because you don't smile much."

"I shall smile a great deal from now on," said Miles.

"And another funny thing," Tavy went on, "I was never afraid of you. I'm usually afraid of everybody, but with you I wasn't. I think it was because . . . because . . ." She broke off awkwardly. She had started to say, "I think it was because you were lame," but caught herself in time. "I don't know, it's so hard to explain. I suppose there's a reason for everything."

"Of course," said Miles. "The trouble's usually choosing the best one afterwards." A buoyant sensation of happiness invaded him. The car was climbing smoothly into hilly country and he noticed for the first time how rich the earth was, and that the flanks of the hills were green where the new corn was growing.

"Well, don't let's talk any more," said Tavy. "I shall have to think." She gently withdrew her hand and gazed ahead.

The thing that her mind refused to grasp was that in four hours or less she would be home again, and everything

would be different. Zohra's image rose before her like a
vision; she thought of her with longing. Her house was a
haven, a refuge; a place she had shared for so long she
could imagine no other. There was no corner of it, no beam
of the roof or break in the pattern of the tiles, that was not
intimately known to her, and the roof, among flapping
garments flying from the line like flags, had been Joe's territory from the first. It was a house besieged by noise and life
but it had the security of a cave. One stepped from the din
of the street and the shrieking children and immediately
there was peace. Inside those walls, with the curtain
dropped and the door shut, the world outside fell away and
could be forgotten. Everything was cool and clean and
nothing out of place, the cushions against the wall and the
bedding rolled tightly away in a wooden chest and Zohra
pattering about barefoot at her bread-making.

Of course it was not always like that. That was how
it appeared to her now, as a vision of peace, but there were
times when it was full of bustle and voices and this, too,
was comforting. Old Khaimo would be crouched in a
corner, cutting up tomatoes and onions and scraping the
seeds out of green peppers, and Aminah would be pounding clothes in the washing-vessel on the roof or beating
blankets and holding a long-distance conversation with a
neighbour. And then, when Zohra's dough was ready and
patted into flat rounds she would open the door and beat a
deafening tattoo on the iron baking-sheet, so that the boy
from the nearby oven would hear it and come running. She
would cover the loaves with a cloth and he would settle the
tray on his head and go off to the bakehouse, which was so
near one could smell the burning wood and the delicious
bread-fragrance. It would come home hot within an hour
and Zohra would prop it on the kitchen shelf and it would
still be warm when they ate it. Zohra, she knew, would be
baking today, in preparation for the feast. Not only the

common loaves but thin pancakes of dough made with milk which would be cooked on a charcoal fire in a crock on the roof. Embers would be glowing in the blackened pot and Aminah would be feeding the fire with twigs and fanning it with a scrap of matting. There would be savoury smells of cooking everywhere and children would be darting about like bats in the smoke. Joe would stay up tonight; it was good that he slept now, on this long journey. He would be dressed in his best, in his finery, and be treated like a little prince by the whole family. It was a blessing to have a child in the house; he was their greatest treasure. But how would it be when she took him away from this loving place, and everything was different?

She stroked his legs with her hand, keeping her eyes closed. Whatever else he had missed in his short life Joe had never lacked love. It was women's love entirely, and he had managed to thrive on it. She could not bring herself, yet, to think of Quattrell. Her thoughts clung sadly, fondly, to the image of Zohra. How had she acquired such strength, in a life without men? Tavy had no idea precisely how old she was, but she could hardly be more than forty and was probably much less. She had been married twice, once widowed, once divorced, and if to live without men in this man's world was counted a misfortune then Zohra certainly seemed to have come to terms with it. She was poor, but so were her neighbours; she had an easier life than most of the women in her vicinity. Her uncle, the Hadj, saw to it that she had enough to live, and for three years there had been the money for Tavy's keep and the little that Aminah earned, which was something of a mystery. She worked fairly hard, of course, but not as hard as her neighbours, who had broods of children to work for and feed, sons and husbands to be waited on. She had sometimes said, in those long fragmentary conversations when they leaned on the parapet in the summer and listened to the drumming and music of a nearby wedding, that she would not marry again if she had the chance. And naturally there was no chance, since time was against her. Aminah was the one who must marry, if God willed it. If she married Youssef that was well enough, but otherwise—Zohra would smile and shrug—there were certain freedoms and benefits which made life tolerable. Her house was her own and she did as she pleased. Neighbours she gossiped with had husbands who were never satisfied, who gave them a baby a year and brought their friends home at unreasonable hours and sometimes even beat their wives when they had been drinking and the idea occurred to them. Zohra turned a sardonic eye on these excitements. Life was not dull, for all that. Hardly a week passed without a tea-drinking in her own or a neighbour's house, a name-giving or a visit to relatives, and there were endless diversions in the summer, the season of marriages. Then she would put on her brightest brocade and her finest muslin, paint the palms of her hands and her feet with henna and get out her high-heeled shoes and her patent-leather handbag. Veiled, in their dark *djellábas*, she and Aminah would walk through the streets to the reception, elegantly indistinguishable from their neighbours. The Hadj's family was large, and they were not forgotten. In all the festivities—in the gatherings of women, that is, the noisiest and most amusing—they had their place. Except for the Hadj, who had authority, men had no place in Zohra's life, and there was sometimes a glint in her eye when Quattrell came which made Tavy suspect she hated them. Quattrell was important for many reasons and she treated him with deference; but there was no disguising the fact that she thought it a blessing he went away so often. Men, she would indicate with a gesture, were difficult to control; so demanding and unpredictable that it was hardly worth the trouble. The only defences were secret ones, and the power

of spirits, unfortunately, was incalculable. It was only because she had proved her over the years that she had
chosen the *sahaara* at Larache to look after Tavy.

"Tavy," said Miles gently, "I want to talk to you." He
knew she was not asleep because she had sighed deeply.
"Don't sigh like that, my darling. You mustn't be sad."

"I know," she said, rubbing her eyes. "It's just that I
can't stop myself thinking."

"Then think aloud, to me. There's so much you haven't
told me."

"I don't think there's much to tell. You know everything."

"I've never known whether you loved him," said Miles,
bringing it out at last. "It's something I need to know, so
that I can understand. You must have been in love in the
beginning, or it wouldn't have happened. And he with you,
my darling, surely? Was that how it was?" He glanced in
the mirror at the driver, suddenly and painfully afraid of
the coming answer.

"No," said Tavy, and fetched an even deeper sigh. "It
wasn't like that; not in the beginning. I never think about it
if I can help it. It's better forgotten."

"But you must have been happy, at first?" He concentrated on the road, straight and flat and striped with the
shadows of eucalyptus-trees. They were crossing the plain
he remembered as a rain-swept darkness and which now
was a tender green, chequered with sunlight and the shadows of moving clouds.

"I was a little misery in those days," said Tavy, "and he
didn't love me at all. He was in love with somebody else,
somebody I liked a lot, who wouldn't have him. I happened
to be there, that's all. He did it as a sort of revenge, I
suppose, and afterwards made the best of a bad job. I was
much too stupid at that age to realize what was happening."

"And what did happen?"

"Oh Miles, dear Miles, do we have to go into it?"

"Please, if you can. It'll be easier if I know."

"Well . . ." she said, and put her hand to her cheek, so that her face was partly hidden. "There was this house next door, where I used to go. It was empty, and we used to explore it, because it was secret. There was this boy I knew, quite a kid, and we used to go there together, and I had a little cat I kept there, and used to feed. I wasn't allowed to have it, you see, so I kept it in the empty house. And one day when I went to feed it Rob came and found me. It was a horrid house, nobody lived there. I think a begger slept in it at night, so there was this old mattress. We sat on it for a bit, I remember, and talked, and then . . ." She slid her hand over her mouth and shook her head hopelessly. "It's no use, Miles. I can't tell you. But that was the beginning of it all. That was how it happened."

"I see," said Miles. There was a painful silence. "And then," he said, "you went away with him."

"He took me away," said Tavy. "I was in an awful mess, and so frightened I couldn't think about anything. He took me to his hotel and packed a bag, and we went away in the car. I never saw any of them again. Aunt Phoebe, I mean, or Uncle Lytton, or any of them. I don't even know what happened to the kitten; I've often wondered. I was so worried about it at first I didn't think about the others. A long time after I heard that Uncle Lytton had died, but so much had happened by then it didn't seem to matter. Panya made me write to Aunt Phoebe after Joe was born."

"And she's still alive, your aunt? You could get in touch with her?"

"I suppose so. As far as I know. If we go to England I imagine I shall have to write to her."

"We're going to England all right," said Miles. "But by

'we' did you mean only you and Joe, or the three of us?"

Tavy considered. She turned and looked at him thoughtfully, then smiled.

"I'm not sure, but I think I meant the three of us. Do you mind if I don't say, until I've talked to Panya?"

"Good. You talk to Panya. Have you got a passport?" The knot in his solar plexus began to unclench itself and he took her hand with a feeling of joy and certainty.

"I've got a passport, yes, but Joe hasn't. Do you suppose that can be arranged?"

"Easily. Give it to me in the morning and we'll go to the consulate."

Tavy looked doubtful at this, as though she were unwilling, but it proved to be nothing serious that was worrying her.

"I'll take it myself, if you don't mind. I'd rather you didn't see the photograph."

"My dear child, why ever not?"

"Oh, it's *awful*," said Tavy, looking woebegone. "I was only fifteen when it was taken. It makes me sick to look at it."

Miles laughed. "If that's all you're worrying about, my darling, I promise not to look." He was touched by this little evidence of vanity.

After a while, choosing her words with care, she said, "I don't want you to think it was all agony, because it wasn't. Rob was very kind at times, and he can be marvellous company when he feels like it. Most people like him, you know, and he's frightfully clever. It's just that he's rather a bastard, and a bit difficult."

"He's a bastard all right," said Miles. "Don't let's talk about him any more."

"All right, but you did ask. It was always this question of money, you see. He was always expecting advances and things, and they never came. He had a lot of worries."

"Including some with the Spanish police, I hear. What was that really about?"

Tavy thought for a moment and frowned slightly. "Oh, that," she said. "That was ages ago, before I knew him. Why is everyone always so interested in it? I know what it was, it could have happened to anybody. He was asked to take this package with him, on the plane from Cairo, and I suppose somebody tipped off the police or the customs, because he got caught. They let him out on bail, and he got away. It was bad luck, really; most of the money he was paid for doing it had to go on a faked passport, to get out of Spain. And he was very hard up to begin with, or obviously he wouldn't have done it," she concluded reasonably. "He was always thinking up schemes for making money. Sometimes they worked and sometimes they didn't, and occasionally there was a little trouble."

"So he left you alone in Zohra's house while he went off to Paris and London and God knows where."

"Oh, I didn't mind *that*," said Tavy earnestly. "Not at all, in fact. I was happier with Zohra, after Joe was born, than almost anywhere. It's extraordinary, really, and I can't explain, but I felt *safe*."

"And so you shall again," said Miles, "I promise." He lifted her hand to his lips and kissed the fingers.

"And she'll be frightfully glad to see us, in time for the feast. You'll eat with us tonight, won't you? She'll have gone to so much trouble; it'll please her."

"Where else would I eat," said Miles, "if not with you? Did you expect me to boil an egg at Sam's, or go out to a restaurant?" He put an arm round her shoulders and drew her to him and they kissed across sleeping Joe while the driver observed them with sympathy in his mirror.

★   ★   ★

The homecoming, a little before four o'clock, had all the effect on Tavy that Miles could have desired. She had slept a little in the last hour but Joe had wakened her, and at this, as though sleep had blotted out her woe and she now saw it in the light of day for the first time, her calm deserted her. She wept afresh, silently, sitting with Joe in her lap and her face turned to the window. As they approached the outskirts of the town, however, the evidences of excitement caught her eye and the quiet sniffs grew fewer and the tears stopped. Children ran recklessly in front of the car as they threaded the poorer suburbs, sheep and goats were being led or driven to the town and crocks of charcoal smoked in innumerable doorways. The town itself, gleaming white and gold on its hill in the last sunlight, shone as complex as a broken honeycomb pricked out with minarets and television aerials. It had a clarity and a beauty that Miles had not seen before. The sky was without a cloud and the air so bright it seemed, though one could not see it, to reflect the sea.

When they came to their own quarter there was such coming and going in the streets it was impossible to believe anyone was still indoors; yet there were few women about; the crowds were all men and boys and delirious children, and Tavy knew that Zohra, like her female neighbours, would be intent on her preparations and out of sight. All must be ready when the gun fired, for then the streets would empty as though by magic and lights would shine behind shutters and everywhere one would smell the savour of roasted meat and the warm bread-fragrance.

They walked slowly from the square because of Joe, carrying their luggage. At the bottom of the long steps, near the Rue de l'Ecurie, Tavy stopped. The street was less noisy than usual and some of the *bacáls* were closed, but there was an almost palpable vibration in the air, as though everyone, even the children, expected the world to change and were waiting for a sign.

"Don't bother to come any further," she said. "You'll want to take your things home, won't you? And I can manage."

"Of course I'll come with you. What next! Do you expect me to leave you like this, in the middle of the street?"

"Just as you like." She gave him a shy look, with the beginnings of a smile. "I just didn't want to be a bother."

"Oh, naturally it's a great bother," said Miles, and they went on. She kept her head down, giving a finger to Joe, and he saw that she looked pleased, and was still smiling.

At Zohra's door, which was open, they stopped and looked at one another.

"Shall I come in? Or not? Tell me what you'd like best."

"I'd better see Zohra first, but come back in an hour. Or sooner," she said, helping Joe up the step, "come as soon as you can," and touched her lips with a slight gesture and went in through the curtain.

★   ★   ★

In the open space near the steps leading down to Sam's house a taxi appeared, and Miles glanced at it in passing, too absorbed in his own happiness to wonder who was in it. For once it was not besieged by children; although the gun had not sounded the hour was near, and he supposed that most of them were indoors. Nobody appeared to get out of the car when the driver held the door open, and Miles was already joyously descending the steps when he heard his name called. He stopped and turned doubtfully back, not sure that he had really heard it. A foot and a creased trouser-leg protruded from the taxi, then a walking-stick, and he saw without enthusiasm that it was Crosier.

"My dear boy," said Crosier wheezily, when Miles stood before him and had taken his extended hand, "where are you off to, at that extraordinary pace? I've ventured into this rookery partly, but not, I admit, entirely, in the hope of finding you."

"Well, here I am," said Miles. "What can I do for you?"

Crosier heaved ineffectually for a moment and gave up the struggle. "These things are too difficult to get out of," he complained. "No, thank you, you needn't pull. I shall stay where I am."

"Would you care to come down to the house for a drink?" Miles's tone was not pressing, but he felt that some such offer was expected. Before Crosier could draw breath to reply the cannon boomed, and a sound like a great sigh went up from the town.

"Most kind of you," said Crosier, "extremely kind, but I think not. I gather, from the duffle-bag on your shoulder, that you're just off somewhere?"

"I've just got back from Fez. I did a trip with Sam Hardback."

"Ah, it's really Sam I wanted to see. Quattrell too, if he's back. Colin picked up a rumour that he'd gone to Paris. Do you know if there's any truth in it?"

"He's in Fez," said Miles guardedly, "staying at the Palais Jamaï."

"No!" Crosier was evidently thunderstruck. "But that's a most expensive hotel! Has he come into money or something?"

"I don't know. I think there's some new scheme on foot that he's interested in."

"You don't say so! Well, I'm glad to hear it." Crosier looked anything but pleased. "That relieves my mind of a most embarrassing problem. I've been really worried."

"Yes?" said Miles, dropping the bag from his shoulder and resting it on the ground. The gun would sound again any second, and time was passing.

"My dear . . . er, Miles, the whole situation has been

most worrying. One has been given some very disturbing information. You know, of course, that the police have been making enquiries about our friend Quattrell."

"No, I didn't. I told you before, there's no truth in that."

"But things have been happening since. I am sorry to say I am convinced. The Burridges have spared no efforts to get at the truth, they've been quite splendid. Rex Burridge had a long conversation with London yesterday, in a most confidential quarter. Forgive me if I don't mention names, but you can take it from me our suspicions are confirmed beyond a doubt. They are really invaluable, those two. I don't know what Colin and I would have done without them."

"I'm not suite sure what you mean."

"Why, my dear, it's obvious. Whatever you may say, Quattrell is *not* a man to be involved with financially. Or in any other way, to speak plainly. I was hoping and dreading to find him this evening, to clear up the situation. But if, as you say, he's now occupied elsewhere I am relieved of a disagreeable obligation. The scheme can now go ahead without any of these worries. Colin and I will be on our own, and the Burridges will look after everything."

"Including themselves," said Miles, who was longing to be gone.

"Well, naturally. They're taking on the contracting for us, and coping with the builders. Colin and I will supervise, but the Burridges, thank God, will do the dirty work. Such a comfort."

"I'm sure they will." Miles permitted himself a smile at the picture this conjured up. He could almost hear Ozzie's voice, describing the crumbling concrete and the driving sand when the autumn winds started blowing. He was not going to get involved. It was the moment for shedding his responsibility for Colin.

"So Colin's decided to stay, has he? In spite of the difficulties?"

"But the difficulties, as you call them, have evaporated. We can go straight ahead. Oh, I know what you mean, I suppose, but it would be the greatest folly for that boy to go back to his parents. Utterly impossible people, and what a future! Whereas *here* he can live in comfort, and with a little help from some other quarter, which we shall raise in time, he'll have a thriving business in hand and can increase his capital."

"I take it you mean Mrs. Brockhurst. Have you convinced Ozzie?"

A look of disgust crossed Crosier's face. He coughed irritably.

"My dear Miles, that boy is a monster of selfishness. Don't tell me you haven't heard the news? Everybody's talking about it."

"I've heard nothing. I've been away."

"Why, three days ago, if you'll believe me, those two sneaked over to Gibraltar and got married. Not a word to anybody, if you please! Applied for a special licence, apparently, and did it just like that. Everyone's disgusted."

"I don't see why," said Miles, receiving this news with more sympathy than surprise. "It strikes me as rather sensible."

"Well, if that's your view I'm astonished. It strikes *me* as disgracefully cynical. She's twice his age and he's done it entirely for the money. What else has she to offer, poor creature? No, no, the whole thing's obscene."

"I dare say she'd rather offer it to Ozzie than anyone. He's earned it, wouldn't you say? Though I quite see it's disappointing for you and Colin." Miles picked up his bag by the string and put it over his shoulder.

"My dear young man," said Crosier, fixing him with his dark eye while the pale one helplessly watered, "that was a very uncalled-for remark, and I shan't answer it. I thought you were a friend of Colin's, but I see I was mistaken. And since this seems to be the moment for plain speaking, don't imagine I'm unaware that you touched him for a hundred pounds when I wasn't looking. Much against his will, poor boy, he had the sense to tell me."

"Colin said that?" Miles stared at Crosier for a moment in amazement, and then laughed. "If that's what he told you, and you believed it, I can wash my hands of both of you. It's marvellous: you're cut out for one another. Just tell him you told me, will you? That's all. Good-bye."

He paused half-way down the steps for a final glance and saw Crosier's leg slowly withdrawing into the taxi.

★   ★   ★

When presently he returned by the same route, washed and brushed and in clean shirt and trousers, the light was failing and the streets were practically empty. The gun had fired repeatedly, so somewhere, he supposed, the new moon must be visible, though he could not see it. The *bacáls* had put up their shutters and there were lights in most of the windows; in several houses a raucous transistor was playing.

He was short of breath when he reached the Rue de l'Ecurie; he had come up the steps at an absurd pace, his heart beating happily. He heard Joe's voice as he reached the house and paused on the doorstep to recover. Everyone, it seemed, was talking at once: the women's voices were shrill and there was a burst of laughter. Beside the step was a gallon-tin which might, in some earlier phase of its existence, have contained frying-oil: it was filled to the brim with vegetable peelings and crowned with a grey mess of skin and entrails. He knocked on the door and the voices ceased abruptly.

"Miles, what an age you've been!" Tavy held back the curtain and made only a murmur of protest when he kissed her. She was dressed exactly as he had first seen her, in pale shirt and jeans, with the gilt brooch pinned to her breast and her hair coiled neatly in a knot with a black ribbon.

"I came as quickly as I could; forgive me. What a wonderful smell, and how splendid you all look!"

Under the naked electric light, reinforced in the alcove by candles, the room was so full of splendour as to be overpowering. Khaimo and Zohra and Aminah were in their best *kaftans*, of the gaudiest brocades to be found anywhere in the *souks*, the transparent overdresses held in tightly with tinsel belts and the high necks loaded with necklaces of every description. Each had a gauzy scarf on her head and wore gold earrings. Even Joe was in a tiny *kaftan* of glittering pattern and trotted from one to the other, holding up two objects like outsized thimbles, which were the budding horns of the goat and his special perquisite.

Miles shook hands with them all and was conducted to the alcove, where Aminah arranged the cushions and Khaimo placed a strip of matting under his feet. Zohra regarded him with amusement, patted his arm several times and then his cheek, said something incomprehensible to Tavy and burst out laughing. Her usually pallid face was flushed and she looked quite beautiful.

"Zohra's pleased," said Tavy, looking rather sheepish, "because she thinks it's all her doing."

"What is? What does she mean by that?"

"It's extraordinary, really. I'll tell you later."

They sat together on the cushions beside Khaimo, and when the ritual hand-washing was over, Aminah holding the vessel and towel and pouring the water, Zohra brought bowls of soup. A loaf was divided into six portions and placed on the plastic cloth. The soup was hot and thick and the colour of coral; it had beans and tomatoes in it and scraps of chicken and something that might have been spaghetti. They supped it with metal spoons and dipped their bread in it and it was very good. Tavy tied a handkerchief round Joe's neck to protect his finery.

"There's been a terrible drama with the goat," she said, when for a while there had been no sound but the drinking of soup.

"I hope Joe didn't see it killed."

"Oh no, that was all over. He missed it when he got home, of course; he was looking forward to it. I've told him it's gone away to a place in the country. But really, you know, it was rather awful. *They* think it's funny, mind you. It committed suicide."

This was an accident, apparently, which had occasionally to be reckoned with. The little goat had broken its tether, and being nimble and resourceful had leapt on a ledge of the parapet and was wandering on a neighbour's roof before it was discovered. Aminah had climbed across to catch it, without success. Trailing its string and bleating it had eluded her at every turn, and when Zohra arrived to help her it had leapt across to a further parapet, overlooking the street, so that they were afraid to approach it.

"But of course they couldn't leave it there," said Tavy, "so the man next door came up and gave them a hand. He nearly had it once, but it took fright and jumped over. Luckily there was nobody passing, because it might have killed somebody."

"Were they upset?"

"Oh no. It happened two days ago, so they haven't had to pay the butcher. Zohra's quite good at the cutting up and all that, so it was all finished by the time we came home."

"And Joe has the horns now."

"Joe has the pathetic little horns. I don't think he

knows what they are, so it doesn't matter."

After the soup a *tajine* was brought to the table and Zohra uncovered the great crock with a flourish. Inside was an unidentifiable joint of meat, glazed with the slow cooking and its own succulence, lying on a bed of *cous-cous* surrounded with vegetables. There were raisins and olives among the yellow grains, and almonds swimming in the oil among shreds of lemon. It was almost too hot to touch, but Zohra detached a fragment of flesh with three fingers of her right hand and laid it on Miles's bread, smiling at him as she did so; there was something both flattering and intimate about the gesture. Then she did the same for Tavy and Tavy divided hers with Joe, popping the food into his mouth as though he were a young bird. Khaimo and Aminah helped themselves bashfully, with little murmurs and whispered exclamations, and the meal went on peacefully and more or less in silence, which was very comfortable. Zohra watched Miles's progress with amusement and explored the meat to find him the tenderest morsels. Somewhere in a nearby house, like a gentle accompaniment, someone began to pluck at a stringed instrument; it might have been a lute. Miles stopped eating and listened. From near and far, felt rather than heard through the walls of these habitations like cells in the rock, there was a tapping and rhythm of children's drums and a hum of voices. It was not loud yet, but persistent; sounds that a child might fancy it heard in the wainscots of an old house. Miles took Tavy's hand but she drew it away and helped Joe search in the dish for a fat raisin.

"Tell me what Zohra was so amused about. What does she think she's done?"

"She thinks she's done everything," said Tavy, "and perhaps she has." She gave Joe his raisin and another to Miles, putting it between his lips. He caught her hand again and held it firmly.

"Meaning what, exactly?"

"Well, it worked after all, you see. The spell, I mean."
Tavy was suppressing laughter, her eyes shining. She
reached to the dish and pulled off a crisp gobbet and put it
into his mouth. Khaimo and Aminah giggled and Zohra
nodded approvingly.

Miles chewed and swallowed with an effort and his
eyes watered. The meat was considerably spiced and still
hot.

"Stop filling my mouth with food, silly girl, and explain yourself. What is all this nonsense?"

"It isn't nonsense, my dear, and you'd better admit it.
It just worked for *us*, that's all. The stuff that I got from the
sahaara. We both tasted it."

"Good God, and you really think . . ." He had a feeling
of helpless astonishment at her credulity.

"Oh yes, you superior creature, I can think as well as
you. Why didn't it work for Rob, you'll say next? But it did,
it did!—only in the other direction! We only had a taste, I
know, but it worked just the same. If it didn't, will you
kindly explain why I'm feeling so different?"

At this Miles gave up in despair and put his arms
round her. "You hopeless, hopeless child," he said, and
kissed her.

Khaimo clapped her hands and Aminah covered her
face and laughed at them through her fingers. Zohra removed the *tajine* and the remains of the bread and carried
them to the kitchen. Presently she looked round the curtain
to see how they were getting on. The feast was only half-
way over; there was a lot more food. Tavy had an arm
round Joe and Miles had her other hand and her head was
on his shoulder. Smiling, Zohra beckoned to Aminah, and
they brought in the tray with the cakes and the glasses of
buttermilk.

Margaret Lane was born in Cheshire, England. After taking an Honours Degree (M.A.) at St. Hugh's College, Oxford, she worked for several London newspapers and a wire service in New York, Washington, and Chicago. When her first novel, *Faith, Hope, No Charity*, appeared in England in 1935, she gave up journalism; the novel was followed by three more works of fiction, three biographies, and two books of personal adventures in Africa. *A Night at Sea*, published here in 1965, was her first novel in many years. Margaret Lane is married to the Earl of Huntingdon and they make their home in London.

A NOTE ON THE TYPE

★ ★ ★

THE TEXT of this book was set on the Linotype in Janson, a recutting made direct from type cast from matrices long thought to have been made by the Dutchman Anton Janson, who was a practicing type founder in Leipzig during the years 1668-87. However, it has been conclusively demonstrated that these types are actually the work of Nicholas Kis (1650-1702), a Hungarian, who most probably learned his trade from the master Dutch type founder Kirk Voskens. The type is an excellent example of the influential and sturdy Dutch types that prevailed in England up to the time William Caslon developed his own incomparable designs from these Dutch faces.

Composed, printed, and bound by
The Haddon Craftsmen, Inc., Scranton, Pennsylvania.
Typography and binding based on designs by
GUY FLEMING